A Hermit's Secret

George C. Kyros

ISBN: 978-1-4269-4106-1 (soft)
ISBN: 978-1-4269-4123-8 (ebook)

*Our mission is to efficiently provide the world's finest, most comprehensive
book publishing service, enabling every author to experience success.
To find out how to publish your book, your way, and have it available
worldwide, visit us online at www.trafford.com*

Trafford rev. 9/7/2010

 www.trafford.com

North America & international
toll-free: 1 888 232 4444 (USA & Canada)
phone: 250 383 6864 ♦ fax: 812 355 4082

Contents

Dedicated to the memory of some 48,000 Greek, citizens of Thessaloniki, Greece, who perished during World War II because they were Jews.

Preface

The idea to write my first novel is not recent. It was conceived sometime in the summer of 1959, gestated until now and was born as *A Hermit's Secret*.

I first arrived in the USA in 1959, took employment in my uncle's restaurant, and met a Jewish store keeper who spoke the Greek language without an accent. Later on, I was surprised to learn that this fellow was one of the few World War II holocaust survivors who was born and raised in Thesssaloniki. The memory of this casual acquaintance stayed with me all this time and finally prompted me to write this book.

A Hermit's secret is the product of an untold number of hours collecting, organizing, and verbalizing thoughts in a clear and concise way for the reader to draw enjoyment and pleasure while turning its pages. Narrating the story in a concise and simple language, I will attempt to bring to your attention the historical fact that innocent people are still prosecuted and exterminated simply because they believe in some deity different from the one the ruling class believes in. Human history is rich with instances where entire populations vanished to oblivion because they are classified as heretics. *A Hermit's Secret* pays tribute to the 48,000 citizens of Salonika who perished during World War II, not because they were enemies of Germany, but because they were Greek Jews.

The story revolves around a secretive stranger and a local high school boy.

The stranger, who appeared in a rural community of southern Greece with nothing else but a guitar in his hands, is a total enigma to the local inhabitants. No one knows who he is, or where he came from. Even his name is shrouded in mystery. He appears to be well educated, behaves as if he is of noble birth, and because he is always instrumental in resolving disputes among local people, he acquires the name *Nestor*. He wanders around the territory for a while playing his guitar with a local music band and finally, he settles on top of a mountain where he builds a lavish mansion. In this oversized dwelling, he lives alone until his death.

The high school boy, *Theovulos,* Theo for short, wants to know the real truth about the world around him. He is not satisfied receiving status-quo answers from his high school teachers, and the answers he gets from his parents and the local clergy do not completely quench his thirst for the truth. This void in the young Theo's mind makes him restless and forces him to seek the explanations to his perplexing inquiries elsewhere. Serendipitously, he visits Nestor in the mountain one day and he realizes, there and then, that the hermit holds true answers to questions that gnawed his mind. He is also convinced that the hermit could not only be his real teacher and mentor but his truest friend to whom he can confess his inner self. This casual acquaintance between them precipitates into a life long admiration for each other's brilliant mind. Nestor awes at the boy's intelligence and draws pleasure enlightening the young man's mind. Theo is grateful receiving satisfactory answers to his questions and at the same time, he cannot help admiring the hermit's wisdom. This sort of admiration for each other's intellect and astuteness blossomed into a unique friendship. Their relation must not be misunderstood however. It is not a friendship based on some biological need for each other's company nor is it based on satisfying some social or political gratification. Their friendship is a spiritual communion between a teacher and his pupil. It is a virtue far and above what we commonly call friendship between two people, and, although they end up living across the ocean from each other, their admiration and respect for each other continuous until the hermit becomes aware that the end of his life is near. At this point, he summons Theo to his death bed and entrusts him with the distribution of his sizable wealth. Unfortunately, he dies before he completely divulges to Theo all the secrets he kept to himself until now. Theo lives up to the promise he made to his dying friend and at the same time, he launches a search in the hermit's past life. At the end, when Theo is completely satisfied that he knows all that should be known about Nestor's hidden past, he returns home to his wife.

Aside of the undisputed fact that we should not judge a person on the basis of his appearance or by his way of living, *A Hermit's Secret* teaches us to be aware that the world around us is a small place, indeed. People we meet daily have an interesting story to tell. Sometimes, their story is directly or indirectly interwoven with our lives. Infrequently, if we listen attentively enough, we find that their story contains elements which are directly connected, in some way or other, to our own past experience.

Whatever your taste in reading is, rest assured that you will find an unusual plethora of puzzles, cliff-hangers, and unexpected twists in the story. Attention-grabbing historical truths, a bird's eye view of rural living in today's Greece, and philosophic contemplations are skillfully interwoven in the fabric of *A Hermit's Secret*.

Acknowledgements

I wish to express my deepest appreciation to Dr. Michael G. Davros who took time from his busy schedule of teaching and writing to read my original manuscript. His comments and constructive criticisms of the story solidified the framework of *A Hermit's Secret*.

The encouragement I received from my daughter Jackie Hertz and her husband Marc, who read *A Hermit's Secret*, fortified my strength and desire to go on with this project.

Finally, my gratitude goes to my dear wife Adrienne, who spent many hours without my company, during the time I was composing *A Hermit's Secret*. An additional "thanks" belongs to her, for reading the final manuscript and pointing out errors that skipped my attention. This work would have been impossible without her help and understanding.

A Hermit's Secret

A novel by
George C. Kyros

Chapter one:
"A Summons"

Theovulos (Theo) returned home from a pleasant golf game with his three long time friends, kicked his shoes off, and took a cool shower. It was hot and very humid on the golf course today, and his clothes, soaked with perspiration, were stuck to his skin like plastic bags. He did not even check his mailbox as was his habit upon returning home in the early afternoon. He took his shower, put on clean and comfortable clothes, inserted his bare feet in the sandals his son gave him for Father's Day a month ago, and settled on his patio under the ornate umbrella to sip his lemonade and watch the summer sunset. His wife was visiting her Aunt Katerina today and a perfect silence prevailed inside the house. Across from his patio, colorful birds of all sizes raised havoc as they came and went to the Mulberry tree at the other end of the property to pick at the ripped, dark- red berries. Theo enjoyed spreading himself on the heavy quilt his wife had placed on the lounge chair that he built with his own hands using hard wood from broken wood pallets he brought from work during the time he was still working. He experienced a sort of tranquility watching the birds feeding on the berries, looking at the sun disappearing behind the trees that lined the west horizon, and seeing dwindling colors turning day into night.

He felt good today. He had received a clean bill of health from Dr. Stein the week before, had a good golf game today, and had enjoyed the company of his long time friends uninterrupted for six hours on the golf course. He had known his three golf partners, Jim, Chris and Gus for several years now. All four of them and their wives socialized often. The men and the ladies had a lot of things in common and enjoyed each other's company. Jim had turned his law business over to a group of young lawyers several years back and had officially retired from practicing law. Chris had just given up his life-long dream to make a difference as a high school teacher. And two years ago, Gus turned his restaurant business over to his two sons. To his disappointment, neither son had the ambition or inclination to go on for further education.

The four couples became acquainted in their church during Sunday school hours and at the time that their children were small. A casual acquaintance flourished into a warm friendship over the years, and now that they all had retired from their life-long jobs, husbands and wives lunched together on Sundays after the liturgy and attended social gatherings together. Two to three times a week, weather permitting, the men met at the golf course for a round of golf while the women went shopping, or congregated in one of the homes for a cup of coffee and a friendly chat. During cold winter days, or when the weather was not fit for a round of golf, the four friends congregated in one of their homes for a friendly game of poker, or just to talk. All four of them were not dedicated as Greek orthodox. They were open-minded on the subject of religion. They enjoyed exploring the validity of the Christian teachings. They had long conversations unsuccessfully exploring the nature of the Begotten and the Unbigoted. Fruitless were their long sessions on the subject of weather or not "the Father is greater and the son is inferior". You may say, they were Neo-Platonists in their personal philosophy, for they spent a great deal of time trying to figure out whether "wisdom" precedes "knowledge" on the ladder leading to understanding the meaning of God. "Faith" or "believing" was not enough to answer their questions. They never discussed politics and certainly never dwelt on social issues. They considered them to be subjects of gossip, nothing more.

Spread out on his lounge chair with his lemonade glass firmly secured in the holder located on the arm rest, Theo dozed. In deep slumber, he had the same dream that he dreamed before, but in a different setting. He dreamed that he was going somewhere and got lost on the way. In his dream, he was walking on a goat path along the top edge of a long, deep cliff. He wanted to cross the ravine but could not find a bridge or another path to get to the opposite side. The chirping of the birds on the mulberry tree was interpreted in his brain, as chatting coming from a large crowd of people speaking a foreign language that he could not understand. After an arduous walk along the edge of that endless cliff and through thick brush and sharp stones on which he kept stubbing his bare feet, he finally came upon railroad tracks that he attempted to cross. As he tried to cross the track, the wind blew in his face and hindered his advance. He was stuck in the middle of the tracks, and no matter how hard he tried to get across them, it seemed impossible to move fast enough to avoid the locomotive barreling toward him with a loud roar.

Suddenly, he jerked in his sleep as if a high voltage electric current ran through his body. As soon as he opened his eyes, he became aware that he was dreaming and laughed at the trick his mind played on him. Copious perspiration flowed from his forehead and his hands were still shaking. He felt the blood pounding in his temples, and his heart thumped at a higher rate. When he came to full consciousness, he realized that the roaring of the train in his dream was not a locomotive at all. It was loud thunder from the celestial vault above, still reverberating in the dark sky. He rubbed his eyes with his hands and when he opened them again, he saw dark clouds rolling from the west toward him. He noticed that these clouds were unusually dark, and it looked as if soot from a gargantuan locomotive was mixed with the white clouds he saw wandering across the sky before he fell asleep. The birds had flown away to find shelter elsewhere and the color of the mulberry tree was several shades greener due to the darkness that had penetrated the entire creation. A cool wind was blowing from the west and violently shook the branches of the tree, forcing them to sway in all directions. Arcs of electric discharges crossed the sky, and the thunder became louder with time. Gradually the crackling of the thunder intensified; the lightning that preceded the thunder became more frequent, and the clouds grew bigger and darker as they rolled toward him from the west. It looked as if a heavy rain was about to hit the area.

Although he did not want to abandon the comfort of his chair and relinquish the tranquility of the late afternoon, he picked up his glass in one hand with some of the lemonade still in it, and with the quilt tucked under his other arm he went inside to protect himself from the storm brewing overhead. When secure inside the house, he finished the rest of his lemonade, stored the quilt in the closet, picked up one of his favorite books from his well stocked book case, and began reading from where he left off on the morning before the golf match.

Theo was not reading chemistry books any more. Being a chemist all his professional life, he was tired memorizing complicated chemical formulas. He did not want to dedicate anymore of his life reasoning through the various potential reactions one substance could undergo when in contact with another. He had enough of that thinking while working as a chemist until his retirement. He wanted to read the books he desired and not those he was forced to read. He had lost interest in the chemistry that had consumed his thoughts in the past. He wanted to do something else now that he had retired.

Lately, Theo enjoyed reading philosophy, astronomy, and history. The book he was reading nowadays was written by the celebrated astrophysicist, Stephen Hawking. It was a very short book titled *A Brief History of Time,* yet it was packed with a great deal of new astronomical information that Theo was not aware of. He opened to the page he had left off this morning and read: "We now know that our galaxy is only one of some hundred thousand billion that can be seen using modern telescopes, each galaxy itself containing some hundred thousand million stars…" Further down he read, "We live in a galaxy that is about one hundred thousand light-years" (approximately, 943.5 quadrillion miles) "across and is slowly rotating. The stars in its spiral arms orbit around its center about once every several hundred million years. Our sun is just an ordinary, average-sized yellow star, near the inner edge of one of the spiral arms." The statements, "one hundred thousand billion", "one hundred thousand million" as well as "one hundred thousand light-years", made Theo pause for a few seconds to understand the magnitude of those numbers and to comprehend their vastness and their meaning. In the midst of his mental exercise to grasp the enormity of those numbers and under the pounding of the rain that was coming down in successive waves, he heard the garage door opening and the familiar voice of his wife Anastasia calling him. After she had visited her *Thea* (Aunt) Katerina, Anastasia did some grocery shopping and had just returned home. She called Theo to assist her in bringing in the parcels of groceries that she had stuffed in the trunk of her Cadillac.

"Theo, are you home?" He heard his wife's voice calling him.

"Yes dear, I am here." He answered in a moderate voice, still absorbed in his contemplation of the passages he had just read.

"Do you mind helping me bring the groceries in the house? Some of them are heavy and I can't lift them," she said in a pleasant tone of voice and opened the door to the house.

Theo placed his feet back in his sandals, walked to the garage where Anastasia had parked her Cadillac next to his Toyota, placed a warm kiss on her cheek, picked up some of the heavy parcels and brought them in the house. Anastasia wiped away a few drops of rain off her face and began unpacking the groceries to store them away. He returned twice to the car, brought more parcels in and finally, lifting the last bag with one hand, he closed the trunk with the other and entered the house. He closed the garage door, placed the last parcel on the kitchen table, and initiated a routine conversation with Anastasia.

"How was your visit with Thea Katerina today? How is she?" he asked. He was very careful to intone his words properly so that he would not be ambiguous in the meaning of his question. Certainly, he did not want to rub salt on the wound he created when he chose to play golf with his buddies this morning, instead of joining Anastasia to visit her aunt.

"She's doing quite well for her age. You know she is 92, no, 93 and she can go any day", she responded and continued placing the groceries in the refrigerator.

From the corner of his eyes, Theo noticed an unusual expression on his wife's face and at the same time, he received a strange look through her constricted eye lids. He understood at once that she was disappointed with him for not joining her this morning. He wisely dropped the conversation, and a dead silence rained in the room for a while. Then she said, in a rather pleasant tone of voice.

"Did you have good time at the golf course today?"

Theo heard a sarcastic note in the pleasantry and replied.

"Yes, I did."

His laconic answer let Anastasia know that he did not wish to talk about the subject any more and she complied. He feared that he might inflame Anastasia's anger for not going with her to visit her aunt. She, likewise, felt that she had said more than enough to make her feelings known.

Katerina Ivanovna Anastachevich was a widow. She had lost her husband several years ago and had no children of her own. She was living alone in the two-flat frame house she inherited from her husband's family, and she met her expenses on money she was collecting from renting the second flat and on her monthly income from Social Security. Anastasia was her closest relative, and old Katerina depended on her to visit places and conduct her personal business. Anastasia drove Katerina to the bank, to the doctor's office, to the supermarket for groceries, and assisted her meeting all her obligations and needs in her daily life. Anastasia even drove Katerina to the cemetery to pay her respects to the memory of her late husband. Every time the two women visited the place, Katerina kneeled in front of her husband's tombstone, deposited a bouquet of freshly cut flowers, told him that her life was meaningless without him, and wept quietly.

Anastasia had just finished putting the groceries away and turning to Theo, she said.

"I assume you haven't eaten anything yet". When Theo's answer confirmed that, she returned to the refrigerator and pulled out slices of the roast leg of lamb, the cooked string beans, the fried potatoes, and the home-made bread that were left over from the last night's dinner. She warmed them up in the microwave oven and placed a generous portion for each of them on the table. She also brought out of the refrigerator the bowl of rice pudding that Theo made on Sunday for his grandchildren and placed it in front of them for dessert.

They were frugal nowadays, for they were living on a fixed income; left-over food was not wasted. Either of them did not mind eating left over food from the day before. Tonight, they sat at the table, one across the other, and ate in silence. For some reason, different thoughts occupied their minds, and their stereotype conversation, which was followed by their silence during dinner, revealed the diversion in their thinking. They even neglected to say their usual prayer before dinner to thank the Lord for the abundance of things they had received from above. They only crossed themselves by touching four spots on their body with the three first fingers of their right hand bunched together. They first touched their forehead, then their stomach, then the front part of their right shoulder and finally, the front part of their left shoulder. At last they positioned themselves comfortably in front of their dishes at the dinner table and ate supper in peace with God and with each other. As soon

as they had finished their dinner, Anastasia washed the
dishes and Theo dried them and put them away.

It was past eight o'clock when they settled on the
couch to mark the end of the day when the telephone rang.
Anastasia picked up the receiver and in her customary polite
voice, asked,

"Hello, who is this?"

The man at the other end spoke Greek, and Anastasia,
being born in the USA from non-Greek parents, did not
understand a word the man said to her. She motioned Theo
to come to the phone and whispered in his ear that one of
his Greek friends was on the phone. Theo placed the receiver
to his ear and said in his standard way of answering the
phone in Greek,

"Go ahead, who is there, please?"

"This is your cousin *Fotis,* from the village, a voice came
back in Greek. I am calling to relate to you a message from
your old friend and teacher, the hermit. You remember him,
don't you? I was there to see him several days ago, and he
told me that he is gravely ill. Do you know that Theovule?
He asked me to tell you that his life is at its end and wishes
to see you once again before he dies. I am sure you have
received my letter by now in which I told you all the news
from the village and specifically, about the condition of your
old friend *Nestor.* Did you receive my letter?"

Theo did not directly answer the questions his cousin
had thrown at him. Instead, he said,

"Oh yes, old Nestor. Is he still living as a hermit up on
the mountain by himself? He must be in his 90s now. I
remember him being in his middle or late 30s when I met
him at the time I was a high school boy." Theo paused for
a few seconds, placed his right eye brow between his right
thumb and index finger and stroked it from left to right,
something he was accustomed to doing when he was in deep

thought. He then ruffled his hair with the same hand and continued the conversation.

"Tell me Fotis, did he mention what he wants to see me for?"

"No he did not. But, it sounded extremely important to him that you get his message. I don't have the slightest idea what he wants you for. I suspect he has a big secret to tell you. I have a hunch that he does not want to take his big secret with him to the world beyond. You know him! He does not believe in confessions, does not trust priests, and for that matter, he trusts no one else but you. What do you think? Are you coming? What shall I tell him?"

"Tell Nestor I will consider the matter and that in a few days, I will call the public telephone in the coffee shop of the village, and I would leave a message with whoever answers the phone. Check for messages daily; will you, Fotis?" He then went on with the conversation and asked for clarification about some of the gossip he read in the local newspaper Theo was receiving from Fotis monthly. At the end, he said goodbye to his cousin and hung up the phone.

Anastasia was accustomed to hearing her husband conversing in his native language, which she did not understand. Normally she did not care to know the substance of those conversations her husband conducted with his Greek-speaking relatives and friends. But Theo was always considerate to his wife and gave her a brief synopsis of who the caller was and the reason of the calling. Tonight's call however, needed a detailed explanation for two reasons. First, the call came from Greece and second, the word "hermit" and other bits and pieces she gathered from the conversation fueled her curiosity. She wanted to know more about the man who made the call and about her husband's connection to this "hermit". The word "hermit" is *erimitis* or *ermitis* in Greek and phonetically, it sounds similar in either English or Greek. During the conversation, she heard and understood the word "hermit" as it was spoken by her husband, and that alone made her curious to know who the hermit was.

Theo paced the kitchen floor a few times to consider the news he received from his cousin and to organize his thoughts for a meaningful and concise explanation for Anastasia about the phone call. He felt that he owed his wife a detailed explanation about the conversation he conducted in Greek on the phone. Anastasia sat on the couch pretending that she was not interested in knowing the substance of the strange call from Greece, and she acted as if she was absorbed in reading her newspaper. In reality, she was dying to know what was going on. She was very interested in who the caller was and what he said that had such a profound effect on her husband's mood. Theo paused for a second in the middle of the kitchen floor, took a deep breath, and said in a voice drawn from thought and contemplation:

"The last thing I expected tonight was to hear from my cousin Fotis who still lives in the village," he said, and, stroking backward his gray hair with both his hands, he added. "He told me that a man I met when I was a high school boy is about to die and wants to see me before he is gone. This person lives as a hermit and his name is Nestor. He has a past shrouded in mystery but he has a terrific brain. He seems to be well-educated and very rich. I haven't met another human being who matches Nestor's wisdom and wealth."

Theo fixed his gaze directly at his wife's eyes and with emphasis and conviction in his voice, said. "I learned more things from him than from both of my parents and all the teachers at the schools I attended. This man did not teach book material, mind you! Rather, he guided me to open my heart and my mind to truly love and respect people. He showed me the way to look for the answer to my question of who I am. He taught to be fair in my deeds, be a dreamer in my life, and venture into things that look impossible at the beginning. He showed me the way to distinguish right from wrong and above all, he helped me perceive a truer understanding of who God is."

"These things belong in the past," Anastasia said. "They should not concern you any more. We all go through those kinds of experiences during our adolescence".

"Dear," Theo interrupted, "It is a matter of respect for the man who offered things from his heart, freely and generously. He gave me things that money cannot buy. He gave me constructive advice at the time I needed someone's guidance. You see, dear, I was a poor farm boy thirsty for knowledge and for the answer to questions my parents could not provide. I am sure you understand that, don't you Anastasia?"

"Are you telling me that you have an obligation to go and see him?" Anastasia said in a tone of voice that betrayed her disapproval for Theo to make such a long trip for that reason only.

"I am not sure. Let me sleep on it. I will decide tomorrow," he mumbled.

"Oh, by the way," he added. "I forgot to take the mail out of the mail box this afternoon," and he slowly walked to the front door to fetch the mail. He returned with a bunch of envelopes containing bills, a few loose pages of local advertising flyers, periodicals, and other junk mail. He piled the mail on the kitchen table and asked Anastasia to look at it later. In his hands, he was holding a letter from Greece addressed to him. This was the letter Fotis had mentioned earlier. Theo carefully opened the envelope and read the one page letter which was written in Greek.

Dear cousin Theovule,

By way of this letter, let me first inquire about your well-being and that of your lovely wife and the rest of your family. Things are well in our village, and I send my love to you and to Anastasia.

I visited your old friend Nestor a few days ago, and I learned directly from him that his life is at its end. He told me to write to you and tell you that he would like very much to see you and talk with you again before he departs from this earth. It seems to me that he hides something deep inside his heart, and he wishes to share it only with you. I don't know how long he will last, and it will be a shame to take his secret with him to the other world. Please respond to this letter as soon as possible. I promised him an answer even if the answer is no.

I am sure you saw on television or read in the newspapers the destruction the brush fire caused on our area. Most of the olive trees are charred and it looks as if a number of them are destroyed for good. Fortunately, the government sent the army with their fire fighting equipment and they saved the houses from the conflagration. The fire moved so quickly that several people died from smoke inhalation in the surrounding villages. The authorities arrested the son of a gypsy in a village west of ours and charged him with arson. Like they say, "the son of the gypsy is the grandson of the devil".

There is nothing else happening here that may be worth mentioning to you.

Awaiting your decision as to whether you are coming or not, I remain,

Sincerely, Fotis

Theo read the letter one more time. Then, he sat next to his wife on the couch and took the time to translate the letter into English. In the past, he was courteous to his wife in this regard. The day he married Anastasia, he promised her that she would be an inseparable part of his life, and in this instance, he felt a rush of that promise sweeping through him. He unfolded that piece of paper again and carefully and methodically went through it, word-by-word, translating its contents in English. He tried to convey to her the exact meaning of Fotis's words without paraphrasing anything. When he had finished the translation, he went through it one more time upon Anastasia's request; after that, they headed for bed and nothing else was said.

Lying in bed next to his wife, Theo wondered why Anastasia asked him to translate the letter a second time. He chose not to ask her for an explanation, however. He probably knew her reason. They both fell asleep a few minutes after they had lain in bed.

In his sleep, Theo had that same dream of insecurity again in yet a different setting. He dreamed that he was going somewhere with Anastasia, and on the way there, they were overtaken by a big crowd of people. In his dream, he somehow lost sight of Anastasia. Desperately, he was pushing himself through the mass of people to find his wife, but the crowd hindered his forward movement. He called her name but received no response. He kept pushing people as hard as he could to move them out of his way, but he couldn't advance. He was still at the same place, regardless of his effort to move forward. He kept calling her name in a louder voice, to no avail. He was stuck in the same spot and he had no sight of her. He heard no response to his calls. In the agony of his dream, he apparently awoke Anastasia with his jerking body and the incoherent sounds he was making, calling her name.

"What's the matter dear?" he heard her alarmed voice. At the same time, he felt a soft elbow to his side. When he came to his senses, he was still shaking but very pleased that this experience was only a dream. He re-positioned his head on his pillow and said,

"Oh, it was one of those dreams that come once in a great while to remind us that nothing is absolutely certain in life. Let's try to go back to sleep," he added, and with that comment, he took Anastasia in his arms and went to sleep until the next day came and woke him up.

Theo woke up early as he always had his entire life. He felt well-rested and as he usually did, he made breakfast for himself and his wife. He brewed fresh coffee, the smell of which woke Anastasia; then, he called her to join him on the patio for her egg and cheese omelet with toast, butter, and orange peel marmalade, he himself had made during the winter.

Theo loved cooking. He worked as a cook in several restaurants for five years while a college student, and that experience made him proficient in cooking. To him cooking was not a chore, it was a pleasing experience. He loved to prepare the family's meals in their kitchen or barbeque in the back yard of the house. When he had the opportunity to talk about his college life, he drew pleasure and satisfaction narrating his experiences in the restaurants he worked at the time. He talked with pride about the hardships he went through to make the money he needed to finance his college education and meet his living expenses. No one believed that he taught himself the English language, and that he self-financed his college education at the same time. "Those years were tough," Theo used to say. "Imagine yourself living in a country where you cannot understand or verbalize the language the people use. I was a stranger among strangers, without material or spiritual support, trying to earn enough money to meet my personal needs and to continue my college education. Try to understand that feeling of isolation. I felt I was an island in the middle of the ocean, and that no one gave a damn about me. I had the feeling that no one cared to know if I was alive or dead, just like a stray dog in an alley. That lonely feeling kept chewing me inside, day and night. Perseverance and hard work prevailed, my boy! Everything is possible", was his final answer when people asked him to tell them how he did it.

Theo was proud being an American citizen and thankful to his adopted country that gave him the opportunity to get the things he wanted in life. He wanted a college education, but that higher education was the privilege of the wealthy in the country of his birth.

The sun was about to pop up from behind the branches of the trees that lined the street east of Theo's house. The sky was cerulean today, and not even a speck of clouds marred the blue dome over his head. From what he could see, another perfect day was in store for him and his friends to play a round of golf. Blue jays, cardinals, robins, and other colorful birds had returned to the mulberry tree early this morning and were jumping from branch to branch again. They were picking the berries that had ripened overnight and were chasing one another during the feeding process. It was July now and the sour cherries, which had laden the branches of the cherry tree Theo planted years ago in the middle of his back yard, were gone. The cherries were the bird's first treat before the mulberries became ripe.

The steaming coffee, the two cheese omelets, and the hot toast were perfectly arranged on the patio table when Anastasia walked through the door. She placed an affectionate kiss on Theo's unshaven cheek and greeted him good morning. They exchanged a few love-expressing words and sat at the patio table to enjoy the morning and to eat their breakfast. Before they picked up their utensils or took their first sip of coffee, they clasped their hands together, placed them against their chests, and Anastasia recited one of the short prayers they used to say before their meals. She took a deep breath, closed her eyes, and said in a solemn, low tone of voice,

Dear Lord. Grant us the serenity and wisdom to choose and do all the things You want us to do in our lives.
Bless us with Your infinite love and guide us to be worthy of Your kingdom for ever and ever. Amen.

They crossed themselves three times, picked up their utensils, and began to eat their breakfast in perfect harmony with one another and with the peaceful surroundings.

Breakfast on the patio in summer time, especially under the clear sky of the countryside, was more than an eating experience. They talked to each other with a clear mind after a good night's rest, listened to the chirping of the birds and satisfied their hunger at the same time. This was the time they thumbed through the newspaper and planned their daily activities without being interrupted by the ringing of the telephone.

Sitting across the table from Anastasia, Theo's mind drifted into the past. Looking at himself in the mirror this morning, he realized that his whiskers and his hair were mostly white and his face was generously decorated with age lines and little brown spots. Planting his garden several days earlier, he became conscious that his stamina and endurance to do things had substantially diminished. As he was eating his breakfast and sipping his coffee today, his attention was focused on the appearance of his wife who was sitting across from him at the patio table, under the big umbrella that the gentle morning breeze moved from side to side. For the first time in his life he noticed wrinkles on her face, drooping eyebrows without makeup, bagging skin under her chin, veins visible under the spotted skin of her hands, and white hair covering part of her forehead. Unnoticed by his wife who was pre-occupied enjoying her breakfast, he realized that they had become older and the spark of youth was gone from their faces. He then paused for a moment and wondered where the years went.

In his heart however, he saw the Anastasia he met 45 years ago. He met her in a picnic the church had organized for adults of all denominations. There stood that girl, the princess of the occasion, shining brighter than all other girls in the crowd. There was that vivacious brunette with the enigmatic eyes and the glowing personality that attracted like a magnet the attention of all the bachelors in the gathering. A remarkable, melodious and quavering voice was coming out of that mouth that went well with the well-defined features of her face. There stood God's perfect creation with that perpetual smile and the two pomegranates hidden under her thin blouse. She was the lovely Anastasia whom Theo approached and introduced himself to, for the first time.

This morning, she was still as beautiful as ever. Her aging did not matter at all, and her voice changing from quavering to a trilling sound amused him. The things he noticed on her face, her hands, and her voice were only there to remind him that she was blessed to live long enough to develop a different kind of beauty.

When they finished their breakfast and before they picked up the dishes, Anastasia said.

"I guess, from what I see on the expression in your face, you are determined to go and see that hermit in the old country. Aren't you Theo?"

"I am seriously thinking about it, but besides my wish to see him again, I find no other justification for such a long and expensive trip," he responded. He was surprised that his wife read his thoughts on his face like the headline on the newspaper she was folding at the time she made her comment. Then, he continued. "What do you think about the idea of both of us taking this little trip? You can do whatever pleases you there, or even better off, you can spend time with my sister who still lives in Athens while I go to see my friend Nestor for a few days."

"It is out of the question for me to join you on this trip. I had enough of Greece and of the village the last time we were there. Besides, my aunt needs me here. Thea Katerina does not have anyone in this world but us, and it would be irresponsible for both of us to be horsing around in Greece during these critical moments of her life. Don't you agree?" she said in a convincing tone of voice, and added, "You do what your conscience tells you to do, and I will obey mine. Please don't misunderstand what I say. I am not telling you what to do. I am only telling you that I will stay home."

Theo did not detect any dismay in her voice. She knew that he was stern in his resolutions. She knew that she couldn't make him change his mind once he decided to do something, and that quality had earned him the nick name "Theo, the bull head".

"Since you don't mind me going without you," he added, "I will call the travel agent and procure an open return ticket. I want to be able to return to you quickly in case something happens to Katerina," and with that statement, they focused their conversation on how they would finance his trip to Greece.

The rest of the day went by undisturbed in Theo's home. After he had finished his breakfast with his wife, he called the public telephone number in the village and left a message for Fotis.

"*Zacharias,* this is Theovulos from America. I am sure you remember me, don't you," Theo said to the man who answered the phone at the other end. Zacharia was the man who owned the only *taverna* (coffee shop) in the village where people stopped at night for a glass of wine and to exchange news on events that took place in the surrounding villages. This was the place where the postman from another village delivered the mail, and where the only phone in the village was located.

"Hey, Mr. Theovule, how are you," Zacharia said in a surprised voice.

"Zacharias, tell my cousin Fotis that I am coming from America to see him in two days. You will not forget, will you? It's very important that Fotis will get this message," he emphasized.

"Consider it done, Mr. Theo," Zacharias said, and a "click" from the receiver put an end to their brief conversation. Later on, that morning Theo called his travel agency and requested and economy class, open-return, round-trip ticket to Athens for the next day. He checked his international passport to ensure that it was still valid and later on in the day, he took his passport to the travel agency and received his ticket and his permit (visa) to re-enter Greece. Finally, he went to his bank and withdrew enough money for his trip. He estimated that he needed money to rent a car and to buy food for the duration of his stay in the village. He did not need any money for a hotel. The paternal house in the village was still in habitable condition and was available to him. It had been well kept through the years and was equipped with all necessities for comfortable living. Electricity had been installed a few years back and recently, it was equipped with comfortable beds. It had hot and cold, running water in the bathroom and the kitchen, a modest refrigerator, and an electric cooking stove. A television and an ample supply of cooking and eating utensils were also to be found in the kitchen.

Theo did not play golf today. He had to get ready for his long trip. Besides, he felt obliged to keep his wife company who was already packing a large suitcase with clothes and other necessities for the duration of his stay in the village.

In the evening, he phoned his son and told him about the impending trip. He also asked him to watch over his mother and to attend to the house. Lastly, he called the airline and confirmed his reservation for his departure the next day. Finally, he dined with his wife and went to sleep early.

He was in bed at 10:30 hoping to get a good night's rest, for he knew well that he would not sleep the following night during his overseas flight. Anastasia joined him thirty minutes later and found him quite awake. His mind was racing in all directions, from the deep past to tomorrow and beyond, contemplating the events of the future. He was mentally preparing himself to press the hermit to tell him who he really was, provided he found him alive. What would he do if he found him dead? What if he was already deceased and interred before his arrival? He was not troubled about the money he was spending for the trip, or for the inconvenience he was putting his wife and himself in making this trip. Grant it, he was not a wealthy man, but he felt that he was spending his money for a good cause. The possibility that he might face Nestor's customary silence about his past, kept Theo stirred up. Will Nestor open up and tell his true identity and the source of his income, or will he ramble along on subjects of lesser importance?

All of his life, Theo wanted to know the true identity of the man who appeared in the territory in his thirties and would be seen with nothing in his hand but a guitar. He played local music for a while with a band from another village and sang songs that people never heard before. All of a sudden, one day, he announced to the band leader that he wished to quit the band and become a hermit. He only said that he desired to live alone and as far away from the world as he could possibly withdraw. No matter how hard he was pressed to re-consider his decision, he refused to change his mind or to explain the reason in making such a drastic change in his life.

At first, he chose to erect his temporary dwelling on the ruin of the monastery of Saint Elias the Prophet. The ground where the monastery stood years ago is on a plateau atop the summit of a mountain north from Theo's place of birth. There were no roads leading to the summit, and for this reason, the spot was accessible only to shepherds and hunters. The area immediate to the summit was deforested, years ago, by the builders of the monastery, and because of its elevation and the removal of the big oak trees from the summit, this spot offered an unobstructed view of the territory for miles in all directions.

When the monastery was built, a healthy oak forest covered the mountain in its entirety, and lush vegetation grew everywhere. According to folklore, the monks, who built the monastery and lived there for centuries, cleared the trees, chiseled the rock away, and filled the void with fertile soil that they found in precipices and crevices close by. According to the legend that persists to this day, the monks sifted the soil and discarded the stones, before carrying the good soil in baskets to the plateau. In this way, they created a sizable lot of arable land for their gardens. Years later, the monastery, and its surrounding quarters where the monks lived, was destroyed by fire. That accident forced the monks to leave the area and the land was vacated. At the time that Nestor came to live there, the foundation of the monastery and its peripheral walls that enclosed the edifice were still discernible. The cistern, in which the monks stored rain water for irrigation and personal use, was filled with soil and stones. The ground where the gardens were cultivated in the past was now either overgrown with weeds or littered with stones and pieces of broken, ceramic roof tiles. The apple and cherry trees that the monks had strategically planted in several places within the gardens were dried out. Only two stubs of their trunks protruded between the weeds and the construction debris. The rest were not even visible. The wooden crosses, that marked the burial grounds of the dedicated monks who lived and served the Prophet and who died there, were gone too. Shepherds used the wood to feed fires for either roasting a stolen goat, or to keep warm at night. Other than that, there were no other noticeable signs to testify that human beings ever lived in this place. This was the place where Nestor built his impressive mansion and spent the rest of his life in total seclusion.

Even Nestor's name was a mystery. The tradition was that men before they became monks or hermits must relinquish and forget everything that belonged in their pasts, including their names. They were to change their lives completely and dedicate themselves serving their patron saint. That tradition became part of the folk's religion and was respected by both the authorities of the land and its curious inhabitants. Following this tradition, the stranger settled at the plateau and adopted the name Nestor. This name fitted perfectly to the hermit, for he was skillful negotiating disputes among the people living in the surrounding villages. Like old king Nestor from Pilos, who consoled the Greek chieftains in the camp during the war of Troy, this man found equitable solutions to problems that occasionally arose between simple-minded villagers.

His place of birth, his family history, and even his nationality were as unknown as his true date of birth and education. No person knew where Nestor came from, and nothing was known of his parents or his siblings. It appeared that his education was diverse and extensive, for he was knowledgeable about a lot of things; yet, nobody knew anything about his schooling. When he was confronted with personal questions regarding his lineage and his background, he skillfully avoided answering them. "It seems, it will rain today," he used to respond, although the sky was as blue as it could be and no clouds were to be seen above.

Pondering all these things in his mind, Theo was unable to fall asleep tonight. In his desperation, he decided to take the medicine he knew alleviated insomnia. Careful not to wake Anastasia up, who was sleeping next to him, he crept off the bed, tip-toed to the kitchen, poured some Southern Comfort into a glass, and gulped it down. He felt much better and more relaxed when he sent down the second shot. Returning to bed, he found Anastasia still purring like a kitten. Cautious not to disturb her, he sneaked under the bed covers and went to sleep too.

The next morning, Theo woke up at his usual time. Today was the "big" day. He was to fly on a domestic airline flight to New York; then, he was to embark on an international flight to Athens. His wife joined him to make breakfast and the couple sat on the patio and ate as usual. After breakfast, Anastasia broke the deafening silence and said to her husband,

"No matter how busy you are during the day, I will expect to hear from you before you go to sleep. I don't want to worry about you and your safety anymore than I have to. Use your cell phone and call me before you go to sleep."

"Rest assured that you will hear from me every day without fail," Theo promised her while holding her hands affectionately. "Besides, you can call me at any time, if there is an emergency."

His flight was taking off at noon and it was time for him to get to the airport. He stuffed his suitcase into the trunk of his wife's Cadillac and drove to the airport with Anastasia sitting next to him. He stopped in front of the departure area and there, they hugged each other and exchanged kisses in their tender, loving fashion. Anastasia moved behind the steering wheel to return home, and Theo with his suitcase hanging from his hand, walked into the airport. He stopped at the counter of his airline, surrendered the suitcase to the clerk, received his boarding ticket, and entered the line to go through security. A few minutes later, he was at the boarding gate with his book in his hands and a million questions and thoughts congested in his mind.

Anastasia entered the expressway entertaining a strange question regarding the sincerity of her husband. Did he tell her the real truth about the trip, or was there something else other than a hermit that called him back? Through the years of being Theo's wife, Anastasia had gathered a few bits-and-pieces of information to conclude that he was faithful. Yet, his life in Greece was virtually unknown. Did he have another family in his native country? Was it possible that he had another woman and children there? It did not make much sense to assume that her husband was spending money they did not have to just visit a lonely, old friend. Granted, the hermit and her husband had exchanged letters in the past, but they had not seen each other for a long time.

Chapter Two:
"The Trip to the Village"

Theo sat in the waiting area at the boarding entrance for a while watching people walking busily about the corridors and gateways of the airport. His mind was still occupied with thoughts concerning the potential outcome of his trip. He did not open his book, for he knew that he couldn't concentrate on reading it. He just sat there and casually studied the faces of the people sitting around him or those who happened to go by. He wondered what thoughts occupied their minds and what were their individual destinations or the purpose of their travel. Were they going somewhere on business, for a happy occasion, perhaps, or were they to participate in some sad, social or family gathering?

There was that mother with her teenage son sitting across from him. She was constantly flipping through the pages of her fashion magazine, while her son was rhythmically rocking his body back-and-forth listening to some kind of music that was coming from a tiny electronic device connected to his ears with a fine wire ending to a pair of ear plugs. Next to them sat, what appeared to be, a business man. He was starring out of the window while fiddling constantly with a pencil he held in his hands. He, most likely, tried to organize his thoughts in his mind for some business proposition. Occasionally, his mannerism was interrupted, and he scribbled notes on a yellow pad he had just retrieved from his leather briefcase. with the logo of a firm engraved on one of its sides. Next to him sat a dozing middle-aged man who rested his head on the back of his seat and had his mouth half-open. A young man in his 20s was resting next to the sleeping man. He was snugly resting his head on a young woman's lap. The woman kept stroking his uncut and uncombed hair with one hand holding a book in the other. The book had a colorful cover depicting a half-naked girl in a rose garden; its title was *LOVE IS ETERNAL*.

To Theo's right, a man in his expensive suit told him in an arrogant and rude tone of voice that he was "going back home to New York". The tone of his voice indicated that he was not interested making conversation.

To his left, an overweight gentleman with a short grey beard and a moustache that extended vertically along both sides of his mouth to meet his beard , pointed at the book in Theo's hands and asked him if he understood "the stuff'" he was reading in *A Brief History of Time*.

"It's not easy reading," Theo responded in a casual manner trying not to embarrass the other man who apparently knew nothing about astronomy, or was confident that probing in God's creation was a sin. Then, Theo continued,

"Do you read books on astronomy?"

"I am of the firm conviction that reading these books is like questioning the wisdom of the All Mighty and 'Lord have mercy on me', I made a point in my life not to read them," he said to Theo with emphasis on the phrase, "All Mighty". At this moment, the cell phone of the bearded man rang and interrupted their conversation. The bearded man politely excused himself, took the phone out of his pocket, and walked away to answer his call.

A woman's voice that was heard through the paging system finally announced that the passengers of Theo's flight were to board shortly. The little crowd in the waiting area stirred at the announcement, picked up their belongings, and formed a line to board the airplane that had taxied to the gate minutes earlier. Theo followed the person in front of him, entered the airplane, found his assigned seat which was by the window, and sat comfortably for the first leg of his trip.

Next to him sat a sweet, old lady and from her appearance, Theo concluded that she was not an American. She wore a black kerchief over her head, just like the kerchief some women in his village wore when he was a child. The rest of her attire consisted of a long sleeve black sweater that loosely draped over the upper part of her black dress. Her dress covered her from neck to calves. Her swollen feet, covered in dark stockings, were stuffed inside a pair of dark, brown shoes with low heels. She wore no makeup on her face, and her nails, trimmed short, were neither colored nor glazed.

Theo smiled at her when they exchanged glances but she did not reciprocate his gesture of good will and friendship. She was preoccupied with the rosary she held in her hands. Her size and her appearance kept Theo's attention, nevertheless. She resembled his grandmother, as he remembered her years ago. She had the same wrinkled face and the hands he knew so well. She had hands like those of his grandmother that deloused his hair and applied butter on the sores of his bare feet at the time he was a little boy. Those were the same identical hands that fed him, gave him water, and left their marks on his rear end when the need arose for discipline. Theo couldn't get away from comparing his new neighbor to his late grandmother while the strange lady kept manipulating her rosary in her hands. Unmistakably, she was afraid of traveling in an airplane.

At last, the engines of the airplane roared and the big bird with its human cargo started to taxi toward the runway for takeoff. The final thrust of the engines shook everything and accelerated for its ascent into the sky. At that moment, the little old lady reached over and grasped Theo's left hand with her free hand while placing her other hand, still holding her rosary, over her mouth. Theo turned his head toward her and noticed that she was praying with her eyes closed. He tried to comfort her with words and with a firm squeeze of her hand, but she couldn't understand him; she spoke some other language, not English or Greek. She did not understand his words, but the human contact was plenty to assure her that she was safe and everything was fine. The hand grasping and praying repeated itself each time the airplane hit atmospheric disturbance and vibrated.

In between hand holding with his neighbor, Theo's mind drifted from the unknown of the future to the reality of his past. Under his feet, he saw the sprawling city where he lives. Beneath him was that city where he arrived penniless years ago, unable to speak the language of the land and where he attended college as a stranger among strangers. This place was the city where he worked all his life, established his social life, met Anastasia, built his home, and raised his children. This was the only promontory in the entire universe where he was granted the opportunity to live and fulfill his life's dreams. While he kept his eyes closed, his mind flew back and re-visited places and people he had forgotten. He harked back to the faces of his supervisors, those of his subordinates and remembered events, places, and faces. He mentally returned to some of the places he visited during his professional career and retrieved the memories these places held for him. Lucid were the memories of temptation he experienced meeting peers, subordinates, and inviting girls he met in the work place. He felt good that not even once had he been unfaithful to Anastasia, although the opportunities presented themselves several times at work and during his travels. He was gifted with a strong will to resist temptations and return home pure in heart in the eyes of God, a proud man, and a devoted husband.

When the airplane landed in New York, the old lady made a gesture that stirred a great deal of emotion in Theo's heart. She took his left hand in both her hands and as she did with her rosary on the plane, she kissed it several times. She apparently wanted to express her gratitude and her appreciation for his help and his understanding during their flight. She couldn't express her feelings in words, but she expressed them in her own little way. In turn, Theo gave her a gentle hug and they parted company without saying a word to each other. They were strangers when they met and parted company as strangers. They were people from two different worlds and other than being desirous to live and to love, they had nothing else in common.

New York's international terminal was at the other end of the airport and after going through the customary inspections, Theo found the gate where he was to catch his overseas flight to Athens. He found an empty seat, sat down and opened his book. Many people around him were conversing in his native tongue, while others spoke English with a heavy accent. He knew that he could converse with them in either language but he chose to be silent. He had plenty of time to speak his native vernacular with Nestor, with his relatives, and with the public at large during his stay in Greece. For now, he did not feel like talking to anyone. He wanted to be alone with his book.

He opened his *A Brief History of Time* to the page where he had left off during the rainstorm and began to read. To his astonishment and disappointment, he couldn't concentrate on his reading amid the noise and the commotion. In the midst of all the din and hubbub that the people were making, his attempt to read was useless. Besides, his mind entertained a thousand other ideas that cluttered his thoughts. The substance of those astronomical theories he was reading about in the book needed his total attention to be understood. The demand on his faculties to have a handle on the theory of cosmic creation overloaded the circuitry of his reasoning and his comprehension. He finally realized that it was a waste of time to continue reading. He put the book on his lap, closed his eyes and mentally shifted through the things he had to do on his arrival at the village. In his mind he assigned priority to each of the things he had to do and considered other options available to accomplish his task. When he finished the mental exercise of prioritizing things, he stretched his legs forward and his arms in opposite directions to relieve the cramping sensations from being confined in a chair for such a long time. Then, he decided the course of action. As soon as the plane landed, he was to go directly to the village without notifying any of his relatives and friends. For now, it was imperative that his arrival be unnoticed. He knew that his old friends and relatives living in Athens would expect him to spend time with them before going to the village, and that was something he could not afford to do at this time. Socializing must be postponed for some other time, he said to himself. It was of extreme importance to go to the mountain as soon as possible to see

Nestor who was breathing his last breaths. Without delay, he must arrive at Nestor's mansion in time to see what he wanted to tell him and, hopefully, learn something about his secret existence.

It was past 8:00 P.M. when the announcement came through the intercom informing everyone that it was time to board the plane. The announcement stirred everyone out of their sprawling spots as if a sharp needle pierced the butt of everyone. Those who were dosing in their chairs or were resting on the floor rose to their feet, stretched themselves, and gathered their belongings to enter the plane. Mothers lifted their children in their arms and everyone formed the customary line to enter the plane. Two passengers in wheel chairs, followed by parents with small children, led the way toward the inspection station and one-by-one, disappeared into the tunnel that led into the plane. Theo stayed in his chair until most of the people had gone inside the jet way; then he leisurely unfolded himself from his chair and walked to the inspection counter. He politely greeted the flight attendant who was inspecting the boarding passes, and, he too, walked into the boarding tunnel.

He stopped by the cockpit for a minute and exchanged a few words with the co-pilot who stood by the entrance to the cockpit, greeting the incoming passengers. When most of the passengers ahead of him had found their seats and the aisle became less congested, Theo walked down the corridor and found his assigned seat. This time he had a seat facing the aisle and he was pleased for that convenience. It was easier to get out of an aisle seat to walk around and stretch your legs during the long flight that traversed the distance over both the Atlantic Ocean and the west-to-east length of the continent of Europe.

He was even more fortunate tonight; the plane was not full and the seat next to him was not occupied. To claim the empty space next to him, he placed his wind breaker on it and laid his *A Brief History of Time* over it. This flight was a non-stop eight hour trip from New York to Athens, and it was sheer torture to be strapped in a small seat for all that time.

The other two seats toward the window were occupied by a couple in their 40s. A bald-headed, double-chin, well-dressed man, at least forty pounds over-weight, perspiring profusely, sat by the window. He was clean shaven and wore a long sleeve white shirt with two oversized gold cuff links. The red tie around his neck exaggerated his double chin, and he seemed uncomfortable being stuffed in his seat. He wore a pair of new shoes made from crocodile skin, and on his right pinky, he wore a huge diamond ring that you would expect to see on the finger of some billionaire. His overall appearance, especially the way he directed his demands to the flight attendants, indicated that he was rich, arrogant, and rude.

The woman next to him was something else. She was thin and shapely with a tightly fitted pair of dress slacks that allowed one to see the laced outline of her mini underwear. A low cut pink blouse emphasized the size of her firm bust. Her long hair was tinted blond, and a generous dose of makeup covered any imperfections she may have had on her oval face with its distinctly protruding cheek bones. Most noticeable however, were her artificial eye lashes and her lips. Her eye lashes extended at least one inch away from her light-blue eye lids and her fleshy lips that protruded away from her white teeth, were painted dark red. She looked as if she were thirsty for attention, for she smiled at every person who went by. Her perfume, a mixture of lavender and jasmine, overwhelmed Theo's olfactory senses.

Across the aisle sat a man about Theo's age. He had a laptop on his knees and kept busy typing something in

Greek. Next to him sat two noisy boys who traveled with their mother and who, apparently, were not related to the man. The man with the laptop was so absorbed in his writing that the mischief of the little boys did not bother him at all. His face was familiar to Theo, and Theo had the impression that he knew him from somewhere. Other people were buzzing in front and behind him but they did not attract his attention. He did not have a clear view of their faces and he was not interested in their chatter either.

"Hey, pal! Do you visit the old country often?" the fat man said to Theo, mopping his face with an oversized, white handkerchief.

"Once in a while," Theo retorted and to be polite, extended his hand over the blond lady's lap to shake the man's plump hand with the huge diamond. "My name is Theovulos, Theo for short," he announced to the other man.

"Friend, they call me *Giorgo Fataulas,*" the other man said and began to tell Theo about his business, still holding Theo's hand in a tight grip. "If you ever come to Boston, don't forget to look me up. I'll treat you to an unforgettable dinner at one of my finest lobster restaurants in town."

"Where were you born, landsman? Your face looks familiar," he continued, and he released Theo's hand from his grip.

"I was born in a small village up in the mountains of the southern part of Greece. I am sure you haven't heard the name of it. It is a tiny village in the middle of nowhere and has no history to speak of," Theo said, hoping that the other man's inquires would abate.

"I am a man of the world and I travel extensively the southern part of our country. There is no village I haven't seen in this part of our land, friend. You may also be interested to know that I was born there too," he responded with an air of confidence that he knew all the towns and villages in southern Greece.

When Theo told him the name and the approximate location of his village, Giorgo shook his head from side to side and said with a sarcastic laugh.

"It must be a collection of goat dens hidden away from the world!"

"Not exactly," Theo said with a tone in his voice and with a facial expression that sent a clear message to his listener that his sarcasm was in bad taste.

The blond lady turned her face toward Theo and made a gesture with her eyes that she disapproved her husband's laughter and perception of Theo's village. She then smiled to reassure Theo that she was sorry about her husband's arrogant and belligerent behavior. Theo, perturbed with the chatting, turned his face toward the aisle and initiated a conversation with the familiar man who was taking a break from his writing. He had finished rubbing his eyes with his hands and was stretching his hands outwards when Theo said to him.

"I hope you'll excuse me for intruding into your personal life, but I think I know you from somewhere."

"You are Theo, aren't you?" the other man said with a friendly voice and a snap of his fingers that instantly stirred Theo's memory.

"Now that I hear your voice, I remember your name too. You are *Kosmas Tsaruhoprokas,* my college friend, aren't you?" Theo said in an exuberant voice and reached across the alley and shook the other man's hand.

"Lord! It was like yesterday that you and I competed for the attention of the same girl. What was her name?" Kosmas said.

"Yes, I remember her. Her name was *Erato*. She was a student here from Cyprus," Theo retorted.

At this moment, a voice came over the intercom interrupting the conversation and requesting that all passengers fasten their seat belts in preparation for departure. A few minutes later, the plane taxied down the runway and finally, its big engines, with a piercing hiss and a deafening roar, lifted the plane up into a cloudy sky. Seconds later, they were over the Atlantic Ocean heading toward their final destination.

Theo sat quietly in his seat for a while. There were so many thoughts in his mind associated with his arrival in New York some forty years ago. He came to the USA on a passenger ship that made the trip from Greece to New York in twelve days, with several stops in Italy and Canada along the way. Ellis Island was closed by now and immigrants were processed on the boat after the boat docked in the harbor. It was here that Theo received his official permit to enter the USA as a student to fulfill his lifelong dream of getting a higher education. He first set foot on American soil in New York with a small suitcase in his hands, twenty three dollars in his pocket, great hopes for his future, and unable to say even one word in English. New York was the starting point for his American life.

As the plane flew eastward from New York toward Europe, Theo saw the Atlantic Ocean spread far and wide beneath his feet. On the surface of this vast pond of turbulent water, Theo had spent ten days of his voyage from the time the boat left the straits of Gibraltar to the time it entered the harbor of New York. The blue sky above his head and the vastness of the blue water on which the boat bounced like a coconut shell, were his constant sights for ten consecutive days and nights. The friendships he developed during this time did not last long. In contrast to his memories, the friends and acquaintances he made during the ten days disappeared like fog after sunrise. The people he met in that boat just walked away and became a component part in "the melting pot" of American society. Disembarked passengers just vanished in the crowds and their existence, but not their memories, were lost for ever.

With his eyes closed, and in the midst of the noise coming from the six jet engines of the plane, he re-lived some of the most wonderful moments he had with a lady passenger in the boat. Theo was a friendly, young man, thirsty for adventure in life. He was gifted making friends from complete strangers or ordinary acquaintances. She was at least ten years older but the age difference did not matter. She was vivacious, presentable, polite, and above all, she had the same desires and expectations from life as he did. She spoke the Greek language with difficulty, and Theo spoke none of her English. During their brief relationship that followed their initial introduction to each other, he never asked her who she was, and she never volunteered any information pertinent to her place in society, her marital status, or her national origin. The only thing that was important to both of them was the torrent of feelings that gushed out of them as a result of their need for each other. Theo remembered the first moment he seized her and kissed her first on her lips, then all over her face. Finally, he kissed her on her neck, on her throat, and as he was doing that, he became aware that she was enjoying his advancements. As their relationship continued during the ensuing days, he became involved more emotional and hinted that he may be in love with her.

"Kid," she said, looking directly in his eyes. "If you cannot handle our friendship as a simple relation between two mature adults, let me know. I don't want you to get hurt. Get rid of that Romeo and Juliet stuff. I like you the way you are. Don't try to be someone else."

Theo never heard such straight talk from a woman before and changed his tune quickly to save and keep a good thing going. Their limitation in verbal communication was offset by the need for each other's company and the mutual desire to be together. He thought that he knew all about the emotions associated with relations with women, but as he snuggled close to her in the small movie theater, he experienced feelings and emotions he never felt before. His inner self was shaken to its foundations and his sleep became restless at night.

He danced endlessly with her to the Greek music and still remembered his reaction to the warmth that radiated from her bosom and from her face that was glued to his face during their dances. Unforgettable were the experiences of his intimacies with her. The memories of before, during and after their dances were still lucid in the repository of his memory. But like the rest of his new friends, she said goodbye to him with a passionate kiss when the boat reached its final destination and, she disappeared from his life for ever. The rest of his experiences during the twelve day trip from Greece to the USA were routine events and he had either forgotten them, or they blurred in his mind. In the mist of recollecting his experience of his trip to America from Greece, he imagined himself sleeping next to Anastasia in their bed and felt the need for a snooze.

Theo was not sure whether he took a nap in his seat or had closed his eyes for just a while to rest. When he opened his eyes, he felt like Rip Van Winkle who slept for twenty years in the wilderness. People around him looked different now. Their hair was messed up and their clothes wrinkled. Most of the people had taken their shoes off and either snoozed in their seats or walked in the aisles to restore the circulation in their feet. Kosmas Tsaruhoprokas was not in his seat, and his laptop was resting on the empty seat. The blond lady was sleeping and had re-positioned herself in such a way that her rear end was crushing Theo's choice book. The eyes of poor Stephen Hawking in his picture that decorated the cover of his famous book were looking directly at the outline of the lady's underwear. Theo reached over and very carefully pulled the book away from its precarious position and placed it elsewhere in a safer place. He slowly took his shoes off and walked toward the toilet where Kosmas and several other men were engaged in a conversation. Theo handed a five dollar bill to the flight attendant and received a double shot of Southern Comfort with ice in a plastic glass. He then approached the little crowd to listen and to, hopefully, participate in the discussion. Kosmas was doing all the talking and the rest of the crowd was listening.

"The male goat doubles its body weight every year," Kosmas said to his listeners. "For example, if a two month old male goat weighs fifteen pounds, it becomes thirty pounds when it becomes one year old. At the age of two, it will be sixty pounds, one hundred and twenty at the age of three, and a whopping two hundred and forty pounds at the age of four, when it reaches maturity. Of course you have to castrate the goat in order to make it manageable during its mating season and to stimulate its body to accumulate fat. After that, you only need a goatherd to keep the herd together during the day. If a man buys fifty yearling, male goats every year and keeps them in his herd for four years, he will be able to sell the first fifty at the end of the forth year. His original investment is the purchase of a fifteen pound animal, but after the forth year, he will sell a two hundred and forty pound goat, realizing a net profit of two hundred and twenty five pounds goat. Translating this to dollars (assuming that the price of the goat meat is two dollars/lb.) our goat owner pockets four hundred and fifty dollars/goat." Kosmas continued his lecture on goat raising secrets and about the financial aid and the tax incentives that will be available through the Greek government.

Theo had enough listening about raising goats. He walked away from the gathering at the time that Kosmas started to explain the procedure of castrating them, maintaining their health, shearing them, and rendering their hides. Theo turned to the flight attendant who made his drink and said to him in a whisper.

"What is this talk about raising goats? Were you here from the beginning of the discussion?"

"Friend, the brain of this Kosmas character has 'taken in air' and has gone bad as good wine becomes vinegar when the bottle is not corked tight. You know what I mean," the flight attendant responded in an equally hushed voice. Then he continued, "He was telling us before you came that he is writing a book about raising male goats for profit. He even had a theory to use their horns for making glue to laminate plywood together. I am telling you, the guy is gone."

Theo did not know what to think about the flight attendant's assessment regarding the sanity of Kosmas. He just stood there, starring at him for a second and making no comments to support or refute the other man's opinion about the sanity of Kosmas Tsaruhoprokas.

"Another drink?" the flight attendant asked and pointed at Theo's plastic glass with several half-melted ice cubes dancing around inside it.

"No thanks, I had enough," Theo responded with an expression of gratitude in his face and with that comment, he returned to his seat.

The fat man and the blond woman had lifted the arm rests of their seats to make more room for the long flight. They had even lifted the arm rest that separated her from the empty seat between Theo and her. When Theo returned to his seat, he found the couple sound asleep occupying the three seats between him and the window. All was quiet in front and behind, and he thought that it was an excellent opportunity to spend time with his book. He took it out of the pocket in front of him and began to read about the duality of matter as defined in the Quantum Theory. "….. Although light is made out of waves, Planck's quantum hypothesis tells us that in some ways it behaves as if it were composed of particles: it can be emitted or absorbed only in packets, or quanta…." and further down he read. "…There is thus a duality between waves and particles in quantum mechanics: for some purposes it is helpful to think of particles as waves and for other purposes it is better to think of waves as particles…." Theo paused at this point hoping that he would be able to understand this point in its fullest meaning. If light is a particle at a given moment, he argued with himself, it cannot be a wave at some other instance. Theo cannot be Theo now and someone else later. He closed the book, shut his eyes tight and recalled his simpler analogy of duality in his mind. Is it possible that Theo is Theo and someone else, or is he two Theo's that manifest themselves differently in accordance with some convenient way and at different circumstances? No, it cannot be. I am either Theo or not Theo, he said to himself. Perhaps, my being does not obey the Quantum Theory and I am or I am not what I believe I am, and all I know and perceive are questionable in the strict scientific sense, he thought again.

I hope I will find Nestor in a clear state of mind, he replied to himself. He will have an opinion about the duality of things in general, and with that thought, he made a mental note to ask his old mentor the question.

The blond next to him shifted her body in her seat to make room for her snoring husband and as a result, she squeezed Theo in his own seat with the lower part of her body, crushing his windbreaker between them. He got up again and to no avail tried to free his windbreaker from its perilous position. To get her attention that he was trying to retrieve his garment, he gently tapped with his finger on the part of her body that held his wind breaker in place. She opened her eyes, delivered her customary smile, excused herself, and re-positioned herself between her seat and the empty seat between her and Theo. Half of her seat and the seat by the window were occupied by her sprawling husband who was still asleep.

After a while, Theo decided to take another walk and he tottered toward the tail of the plane to help improve the circulation in his swollen feet. Most of the people had positioned themselves in their seats in any way they could be more comfortable. Some were sleeping, others were reading their books, and still others were listening to their music through a set of ear plugs attached to their recorders. When he reached the emergency exit of the plane, he noticed through the tiny window that the sky ahead was lit by the morning sun. He automatically surmised that they were flying over Europe and that they were close to their destination. He immediately returned to his seat, took out of his coat pocket the small pouch that contained his toothbrush, his toothpaste, and his shaver, and walked to one of the bathrooms to brush his teeth and shave. The "early birds" were already lined up in front of the lavatories to do likewise before the final descent for landing. In his turn, Theo entered one of the lavatories, brushed his teeth, shaved his beard, and washed his face with cold water to wake up; then, he returned to his seat and sat down again. Both his neighbors had vacated the three seats they occupied all night long. Kosmas had sunk his face to his laptop, reading the material he typed all night. The big man and his wife returned after a while and took their places by the window again. A half an hour had elapsed and the flight attendants served breakfast with coffee and orange juice. Theo drank the juice and the coffee and pushed away the rest of the food, for it was not prepared to his liking. The lady next to him ate half of the food and drank the orange juice without making any comments about its quality. The fat man kept complaining about the quality of his breakfast, yet, he devoured everything that was placed in front of him, plus the portion that his wife left on her plate.

Several minutes after the attendants picked up the empty plates, the bilingual attendant announced in English and Greek that the plane was about to land at the international airport in Athens. The announcer requested that all passengers return to their seats, place them in the upright position, and fasten their seat belts. He also said that the local time was 10:17 A.M. After a while, the plane approached the airport from the sea coast and glided toward the landing strip. At last, its wheels made contact with the ground and with a soft jerking motion, it continued to roll toward the designated gate where it parked and shut off its engines. The passengers released themselves from their seat belts and filled the aisles in preparation to exit and to continue the final leg of their trips. Theo, like the rest of the passengers, was anxious to walk out of the plane's confinement to relieve the soreness he felt throughout his body from being stuffed in a tiny seat for eight hours. He lifted himself from the seat, picked up his windbreaker and his book, and following Kosmas in front of him, he inched forward toward the exit. On his way out, he exchanged a few words with Kosmas who was walking in front of him and with Giorgo Fataoulas who was behind him. He learned that Kosmas was going to Thessaloniki and Mr. and Mrs. Fataulas were staying with relatives in Athens for a while before they were to tour other villages around Giorgo Fataulas' birth place. At last, Theo walked to the baggage claim station, retrieved his suite case, and followed the line to the customs inspection station.

The customs inspector examined Theo's passport, stamped it with his rubber stamp, took a look at his suitcase, and without asking any questions, waved him to exit the airport. Theo walked into the parking lot, stretched his aching back and his sore legs, took several deep breaths, and approached the line where taxis were lined up. He approached one of them and asked the driver in Greek if he was available to take him to the train station.

"Hey friend, do I look Albanian? Name the place and you'll be there in a flash," the taxi driver said in his slanted tone of voice, characteristic of the dialect of the Athenian taxi drivers. "This machine and this sport behind its driving wheel can take you even to Ankara. Hop in and don't waste breath asking silly questions, patriot." Although Theo was offended by the way the taxi driver addressed his inquiry, he entered the taxi and slammed the door shut. The driver placed the suitcase in the trunk, sat behind the wheel, slammed his door close, and stepped on the accelerator. The wheels of the taxi made a squeaky sound on the hot pavement, and the vehicle sped away toward the train station which was located several kilometers away in the center of the city of Athens.

"You are an American, aren't you?" the driver said to Theo as soon as they entered the freeway toward their destination. "I can tell from your haircut and from the clothes and the shoes you have on."

"Yes, I am," Theo answered modestly.

"Why don't you stay in our town for a spell? I can show you luxurious hotels, world famous restaurants, and I can provide you with a pretty woman to keep you company at night," he said with a broad smile. "Stay in town tonight and live the meaning of *kefi* (party mood), *kapsoura* (burning desire for someone), and *filotimo* (helping someone because it is the right thing to do)." As he was making his comments, he kept glancing at Theo in his rear view mirror to measure the impact his sales pitch had on his listener.

"No thanks. I have important business elsewhere tonight," Theo said, and to get out of the taxi driver's inquisitive conversation, he took out his cell phone and called Anastasia to tell her that he was in Athens, and that he was on his way to the train station for his final destination.

The taxi driver, without making any additional comments about the conveniences and pleasures the city had for travelers, pulled up at the entrance to the station, and receiving his fare with a generous tip, he disappeared into the crowded street. Theo walked to the train station, purchased his ticket, and inquired about the time the train departs for *Turcohori* (Turkish Village). The person behind the ticket window told him that the train will leave at 1:45 P.M. Theo was hungry and had plenty of time in his hands to have a good lunch before the train departed. Turkohori was the town where Theo was planning to rent a car and drive it to the village of his birth.

The restaurant was not air conditioned and although the doors were wide open, the air inside the place was stale and stifling hot. Scores of house flies crawled on the tables and the fly papers that were hanging from the ceiling were saturated with dead insects. Yet, the food was fresh and flavorful, and the chilled wine had a characteristic aroma unique to the wines produced in the area of Attica. He ordered a second glass of wine and ignored the swarming insects that insisted on sharing his lunch with him. Theo ate his lunch, rested in his comfortable, wreath chair for a few minutes, and struck an interesting conversation with the waiter about the recent Turkish atrocities in north Cyprus. Finally, he paid his bill, lifted his suitcase in one hand, and walked across the floor to where his train was standing idle. He boarded one of its two cars, found an empty seat, and made himself comfortable until the conductor's piercing whistle signaled the departure. His hunger was gone now, and he felt lethargic and content from all the food and the wine he had in his stomach.

Being in a state of a perfect tranquility, Theo thought about some of the nearly forgotten events he had lived through in this city years ago. There were memories from the time he was living with relatives when he was just thirteen years old, to the days that he was a soldier and later on, when he lived there as a private citizen. He wondered if any of the people he knew then, those whom he dearly loved and those who loved him with passion, were still alive. Wouldn't that be a nice gesture, if I could look each one of them up and surprise them with a personal visit? I wonder how some of them will react seeing me again after all these years, he cogitated.

Most vivid was a memory held by a special rocky corner of the seashore he saw by the road in route to the city from the airport. There was that remote sandy spot between big rocks where he spent an unforgettable afternoon and half of the night with the most beautiful girl he knew up to that moment in his life. That little nook was still untouched by construction that was going on in the area. It still looked the same as he remembered it forty five years ago. It was in that little outcrop of that land that his tears and the tears of his girlfriend uncontrollably dripped on the white sand underneath them. The unbearable sadness they both felt in knowing that they were to be separated for ever was too much for their tender hearts. At this isolated corner of the earth, they spent their last evening together, holding each other in their arms. It was here that they promised to each other to keep the memories of their love alive forever, regardless of the big ocean that would stand between them. He was going away to another country, across the ocean, and she was to stay behind. He was going to start a new life elsewhere and she was to stay in that status quo society where poverty and hard work were inevitable for poor girls like her.

His mind visited other people and places too. For example, he remembered his dancing excursions during weekends or after work, and he mentally re-lived the fun he had with friends and acquaintances during those days. The food and the wine he consumed amidst the havoc of live music were still clear and bright in his nostalgia of the past. He even remembered names of wonderful young men and women he met during those social engagements, and scenes of some of the unforgettable experiences he had with some of these people came back to stir his emotions. Unfortunately, all these events belonged in the distant past, and that reality saddened him. He would like to know what happened to all the people he knew and met during that brief and care-free part of his youth. Did his girlfriend find another man worthy of her love and if so, did she have a family of her own, or did she stay single, as she said she would before they said their last goodbye? He was hoping that she would be as happy and still as beautiful as she was that unforgettable night.

He knew that his two employers were deceased now, and their children had inherited their business. He also knew that his friend Luke with whom he had soldiered was still alive and married with children. He felt the impulse to phone him, but he knew Luke well. He would expect Theo to stay where he was until he arrived to pick him up, bring him to his home to meet his family, entertain him overnight, and renew their friendship. But, spending time in Athens was the thing Theo could not do. He had to get to the mountain as soon as he could to find and talk to Nestor.

The train conductor blew his whistle several times and interrupted Theo's contemplations. He walked from the front to the rear of the train calling everyone in a loud voice that the train was about to depart. People of all ages and shapes filled the cars and sat on the empty seats. Moments later, the two-car train moved forward; first, it moved on a snail speed, but as time went on, it accelerated and moved faster and faster. Its noisy wheels ground on the rails below and its engine belched a big, black cloud of diesel smoke that filled the air above. A few minutes later, it picked up the speed and traversing through the olive orchards of Attica, it barreled toward Turkohori. The man who sat across from him was about his age and as he rolled up the sleeves of his shirt, Theo noticed an ugly scar on one of his arms. This scar was really noticeable, for it was located above his right wrist. This feature in that man's arm connected him with an almost forgotten story Theo's mother had told him years after the civil war was over.

"Excuse me patriot," Theo said to the stranger. "Your appearance stirs unexplained emotions in me. Do you mind telling me if we ever met somewhere?" The other man looked at Theo bewildered and responded,

"I don't think I ever had the pleasure of knowing you, friend," he said with an inquisitive look in his face.

"My name is Theovulos. People call me Theo for short," Theo said, and extended his hand to shake the hand of the other man, and as the other man stretched his hand for the customary hand shake, Theo had a closer look at the big scar.

"My name is *Koutos, Petros Koutos*. I see you are from another country, probably America. Are you not?" the stranger said to Theo. "Call me Peter," he continued with a broad smile that expressed his confidence that his assessment of Theo's nationality was on target.

"You are correct. I am from Chicago," Theo said in a pleasant voice.

"Ah, boom, boom, boom, Italian mafia," the other man said and pointed the finger of his right hand at Theo every time he said the word "boom".

Theo smiled broadly and went on to describe to Peter the setting of his village.

"Hey, the devil takes it, I spent a few dreadful days hiding away from the security police in a cave east from your village with a devastating, bullet wound on my arm," he said, and pointed with the index finger of his left hand, to the bullet scar he had on the other arm. "At that time, I was a partisan with the communists," he added. "There was an angel shepherd who brought me food and water, dressed my wound every day and applied her own salves on my infected injury. Fearing that I may implicate her for hiding a fugitive, she never told me her name and I was not about to ask her either. I just called her 'mama'. After a few days of nurturing my wound, I found my way elsewhere and eventually survived the upheaval of our civil unrest," he said with astonishment and content.

"You are right, I never met you but I heard of you," Theo said to Peter. "That angel with the dark complexion, the long black hair, the long nose, and the caring hands was the same angel that brought me into this world and took care of me during my childhood. Peter, this angel you called 'mama' was my mother," he answered, feeling proud that his mother had saved a human being from sure execution. Peter Koutos's eyes became twice as big as he was listening to Theo's description of his mother's characteristics, and his chin dropped several inches to form a wide gap between his lips. "She told us how our shepherd dog found you in that cave and the grave condition you were in at the time. Tell me Peter; is it true that your wound was infested with maggots when my mother found you?" Theo said to convince Peter that he was indeed the person he claimed to be.

"Is she still alive? I would like very much to go and see her again and thank her in person for what she did," Peter inquired with the uneasiness of a potential negative answer from Theo.

"I am sorry to tell you that she passed away years ago in Florida where my older sister lives. According to her wishes, we brought her back to the village and buried her in the local cemetery, next to my father. My sister and I had brought her to America after my father had passed away, and mother never returned to the old country alive," Theo said with a discernable sadness in the tone of his voice. "She is sleeping next to my father in the cemetery of the old village. We all missed her very much," he added with a deep sigh.

Peter cleared his throat several times to get rid of the obstruction he felt in his wind pipe and said. "I don't want to appear that I am sticking my nose in your business, and I will not ask you to tell me your final destination, or the purpose of visiting your village. Nevertheless, in the memory of your mother, I would like to invite you to spend time with us in my home before you go back to America. I want you to meet my family," he said and told Theo the name of his own village and a few things about his family.

"It would be an honor for me to take you up on your kind offer, but my business does not allow me to socialize at this time. Still, I will keep you in mind. If I finish my business earlier than anticipated, I'll stop by for a few moments," Theo continued, keeping in mind that Nestor might be gone by the time he arrives at his village, and if this happened to be the case, Theo will have free time to visit Peter.

The two, not strangers to each other anymore, continued their lively conversation until the train pulled into the station where Theo disembarked and Peter continued on with his trip. With his suitcase hanging from one of his arms and his windbreaker in the other, he summoned a taxi and went directly to the place where he was to rent a car for the duration of his stay in the area. The clerk behind the desk filled several forms and handed them over to Theo for his signature. Theo made a partial payment as a deposit and received the ignition key to a little Fiat with 100,000 kilometers on its odometer. He placed his luggage in the trunk and readied himself for the final leg of his trip to his village of birth.

It was late in the afternoon, and the sun was throwing its setting rays on the valley, tinting the tops of the citrus and olive trees with gold. It was about to disappear behind the mountains that lined the west horizon of the plateau where Turkohori was located. The streets were busy with cars and pedestrians going about their business. Theo got in the car and started driving along the main boulevard that he had walked every day when he was a high school boy. Some of the shops he remembered were still the way they were then. Other stores were renovated to meet the demands of the new society. A few of them were completely gone to make room for the multi-level condominiums and apartment buildings that lined a portion of the boulevard on both sides. He made a left turn at the main square of the town and went several blocks east to see his old high school. Like most of the other old sections of the town, this area had also succumbed to progress. The two buildings that housed the classrooms were replaced by a cluster of modern homes, and the area he used to practice throwing the javelin was now a play ground for children with slides, teeter-totters, and merry-go-rounds.

The mud brick-wall house where Theo rented a room the first year he was in high school was not there any longer. In its place, there stood a three-level apartment building with ornate verandas and modern, glass paneled windows. A wrought-iron fence with a massive iron gate on one of its sides enclosed the building with its well combed garden. A fountain occupied the spot where the big chestnut tree was growing years ago.

The bakery was still standing at the opposite end of the block. The new owner had completely renovated the place, and he had converted the hat shop, next to it, into a pastry shop. Theo made a quick stop at the pastry shop and bought an assortment of sweets to bring to his cousin Fotis at the village.

The new high school, a new building that now housed both male and female students from the territory, was located on the southern outskirts of the city. It was built on the same grounds where the Armenian refugee camp was standing at the time Theo was a high school student. The structure of the new school looked to be a roomy building from the distance. An outdoor stadium was erected on one side of the main building and an indoor, Olympic-size swimming pool occupied the other side. Theo yearned to visit, but time was of essence to him.

On the way out of the city, Theo stopped at a small grocery store and bought a few edible things he thought he might need for the days to come. Finally, he re-entered the Fiat and drove passing between the same hills he had walked so many times when he was a boy. At long last, he reached the village of his birth. Before he went to the parental house, he stopped at his cousin's home to procure the door keys that Fotis kept. Fotis was not home, and Theo learned from an old neighbor that Fotis was already at Theo's old house cleaning the place and making it comfortable for a guest.

Theo entered his car again and drove directly to his parental home. He pulled in front of his old home and parked the Fiat in front of the outside gate. He entered the area that used to be the coral for the farm animals and, unnoticed he walked up the cobble stone stairs to the second floor. Fotis was dusting the dinner table at the time Theo entered the room, and he did not notice his cousin tip-toeing behind him.

Chapter Three: "Nestor"

Fotis turned to re-arrange the chairs by the table, and he suddenly found himself looking at the face of his cousin. He dropped the dust cloth he was holding in his hands and with a cry of surprise embraced Theo. Both men held this posture for a few seconds until the initial burst of emotions subsided, and when they had recovered enough composure to speak to each other, Fotis said to Theo,

"I was expecting you to be here later. How was your trip and how are Anastasia and the kids?"

"Theo had not recovered from his initial shock yet. He could not believe that he was at the place he was born and raised. When the barrage of initial emotions subsided, he gained his composure and said, "Oh, everything was fine with the trip, and Anastasia sends you a ton of love. How are things with you and your kids, Fotis? I see you put on a little weight since the last time I saw you!"

"Well Theo, since I lost my wife, life has become less and less interesting. The only thing I still enjoy nowadays is food," Fotis said with a depressing chuckle in his voice. It was only two years ago that his wife died suddenly in the arms of their daughter who was living in a nearby city, and that event had changed Fotis's outlook on life. He was not living anymore; he was just tolerating life from day-to-day, waiting his turn for the inevitable. Theo walked around the room and noticed that the pictures of both his grandparents and his parents were still hanging at the same place on the east wall of the room. Later on, Theo, being followed by his cousin, returned to the car and brought in the suitcase and the few groceries that he bought in the city. Theo handed Fotis the parcel with the sweets and stored the perishable food in the refrigerator that stood in one of the corners of the kitchen. In return, Fotis thanked his cousin for bringing goodies to him and took out of the refrigerator a full flask of golden *retsina*.

"Let's have a glass of wine to celebrate our re-union," Fotis said, and filled two glasses to the brim.

The two men sat at the newly dusted table, munched at pieces of roasted lamb that Fotis took out from the refrigerator, and they drank the wine at leisure. Fotis suggested that they should prepare something for dinner, but Theo declined the offer. He said that he was not hungry, for he had a big dinner before he left Athens. In reality, he was tired from the long trip and was overwhelmed with everything that happened in the last two days. He wanted to go to bed early tonight. Their conversation went on for an hour inquiring about each others family, relatives, and friends. Finally, Theo felt that it was time to ask his cousin about Nestor. He did not ask that question earlier because he feared that he may offend his cousin if he inquired about a stranger before he asked about the members of their family. Fotis did not bring the subject up either, probably for the same reason. Theo thought that the same thoughts were probably prevailing in the mind of his cousin.

"Oh, by the way, how is Nestor doing," Theo asked.

"I was there yesterday and when I told him that you were on your way to see him, he became very excited. He is in bad shape, you know! It looks to me that he has reached the end of his life. Yet, he looks forward to seeing you again."

In a voice that expressed a great deal of bewilderment and anticipation, Theo said to his cousin. "Do you know what the hell he wants to see me for?"

"Theo, what shall I tell you? The devil takes him, I know as much as you know," Fotis retorted with frustration and threw his hands upward as if he were to say a prayer.

"It really does not matter. We will know the answer to this question tomorrow, when I go up there to see him," Theo said in a contemplative tone of voice.

"I will come with you to keep you company. There isn't anything that cannot wait for another day," Fotis said.

It was past 10:00 P.M. and Theo felt tired and sleepy. His eyelids felt heavy and he had difficulty keeping them open. Regardless of how hard he tried to keep up with the conversation that Fotis had initiated about the conflicts in the Middle East, he was unable to do so. Finally, Fotis noticed that his cousin was sleeping with his eyes open and suggested that it was time for them to go to bed. He got up from his chair, said good night to Theo, and holding the parcel with the sweets in his hands, he descended the cobble stone stairs and went home. As soon as Fotis was gone, Theo undressed down to his underwear, turned off the lights and threw himself on the bed to sleep. He did not even take a shower, as he usually did before going to bed. He was spent of energy and hoped that he would get a good eight-hour sleep. He would rather take his shower in the morning. He knew that a cool shower in the morning would rejuvenate his mental and physical stamina, something he needed to help him drive the treacherous road up the mountaintop and meet Nestor.

His wish for a restful sleep was not granted however. At exactly 12:10 A.M. a terrible dream woke him up. He turned on the lights and looked around to see if there was another person in the room besides him. He saw nobody else there. Only a dead silence rained in his room and he did not hear a "beep" throughout the rest of the house. Sweat was pouring from his forehead, and his hands were still shaking from the emotional state he was in at the moment. He got off the bed, wiped his face with a wet towel, ran the events of his dream through his mind again, and sat on a chair to re-gain his composure and make sense of what had happened. In a few seconds, he found himself sobbing, and he felt tears filling his tired eyes. He sat for a minute longer with his head between the palms of his hands. When his despondency subsided, he got dressed and proceeded to do what he had to do to put himself at peace with his subconscious, which had manufactured the sorrowful and disturbing dream.

In his dream, he saw his departed mother standing over his head, just the way she stood over him when he suffered from malaria at the time he was a child.

"My dear son," she said to him in the dream. "You came all that way to see your friend and forgot your own mother who is still waiting for you to return." In his dream, he felt his mother's hand gently stroking his head and heard her voice saying in a chanting, sad tone. "You see, my child, the love that a mother harbors in her heart for her child is endless. I came to visit you tonight to tell you that I only wanted you to remember me. A small candle in front of the icon of all mothers and a prayer to our Lord to forgive my earthly sins was all that I wanted from you. Is that too much for a mother to expect from her son?"

Shaken with deep emotions, Theo put on his clothes and shoes, descended the cable steps of the farmhouse to ground level, and took the dark path leading to the village burial ground. The cemetery was adjacent to the church and was located a few yards away from the last houses of the village. This was the graveyard where departed village folks, including Theo's parents and grandmother, were interned.

The full moon was directly over his head; the sky was void of clouds and other than the flickering sound of bats swooping over his head to catch insects that he attracted, the creation was sunk in perfect silence. The moon lit his way and his memory navigated his steps to the place he knew so well. He found the unlocked door leading into the church and entered. Walking as a blind man would, he found the matches in the same place the priest kept them for late comers. In total darkness, he struck one of them and lit a stub candle to find his way around inside this house of God. With the stub candle in his left hand, he approached the holy icon stand, made the sign of the cross with the other hand, kissed the icon in front of him, and deposited his offering in the receptacle below it. He picked up three big white candles (one for his mother, one for his father, and one for his grand mother) and stepped in front of the icon of the Virgin Mary. He silently said his prayer, lit one candle at a time and placed each one of them on the stand in front of the icon; then, he walked out to visit the actual grounds where his parents and grandma were buried. Under the bright moonlight, he wandered in the cemetery for a few minutes reading the names on the grave markers until he found the two white marble crosses, one next to the other with the names of his parents on them. He threw himself prostrate between them, placed one hand on one cross and the other hand on the other, and talked to both his parents through his heart in perfect silence. No one heard what he said except the three of them. He felt the cold marble on both hands and his emotions ascended farther and farther to the level of perfect serenity and peace of mind. He was certain that he made contact with the other world and that his parents heard him talking to them.

After an hour of sobbing and silently talking to his mother and father, he rose to his feet and searched for the grounds where his grandmother was interred. It was not difficult at all finding the spot; he was there a few years ago. He stood there for a few minutes, said another prayer for her and with a heavy heart and a light conscience, he slowly walked back home and threw himself on the bed again. This time the sleep came fast. He slept undisturbed until Fotis pounded on the door in the morning.

"It's already eight o'clock," he said to Theo. "I see you slept well all night long."

"I had a wonderful night," Theo told his cousin. "Give me a few minutes to clean up and we will be on our way to see Nestor."

Moments later, the two cousins entered the Fiat and after several attempts to start its engine, they finally succeeded to do so. They drove north on the paved road for a few minutes until they arrived at an intersection where the paved road crossed a dirt road. This crudely constructed path was winding upward like a giant snake from the base of the mountain to its highest summit where Nestor had his mansion. The fame of the mansion had traveled far and wide throughout the land, and interesting articles about him and the mansion were written in respected magazines and newspapers in several European countries. The Greek army had built this road on the north-east slope of the mountain to transport materials for the erection of a communication tower. Winding as a ribbon from the base of the mountain to its top, this road was the shortest yet the most treacherous way to the summit. The ride was perilous and uncomfortable, for the road was narrow and not properly maintained. Furthermore, it traversed through two tunnels that were cut in the perpendicular cliffs that rose from the base of the mountain to the summit. To compound matters a bit more, the ride was even more uncomfortable because one rode over potholes and loose gravel. Additionally, Theo had to navigate between falling rocks and through tight turns that brought them only feet away from the edge of cliffs. It would have been a more comfortable road if the engineers had built it on the south slope where the terrain was not as steep. It appeared, nevertheless, that the construction engineers had sacrificed comfort and safety for the shortest distance to the summit.

The predominant flora and the fauna at the base of the mountain were different from those found at higher elevation. Blackthorn and tall holly trees dominated the base, while mountain sage and bush holly grew on higher elevations. Thistle and nettle were common on lower elevations while fennel, wild onion, and mountain sage were more common toward the summit.

The magpie was the king of the lower land, but the summit was patrolled by kestrels that hovered in the air, like helicopters, scouting the terrain below for lizards, small rodents, and snakes. Partridge, owl, hare, and fox made their homes on the slopes from the flatland to the highest elevation.

The Fiat with its two passengers had to make two stops on the way up to allow the engine to cool and to add fresh water to the radiator. At last, Theo and Fotis reached their final destination.

The grounds where the monastery of Profit Elias stood years ago did not look anything like the grounds Theo saw as a teenager. The very first time he saw this place was when his father took him there to see remains of the Orthodox faith. At the spot where he saw the rubbles of the monastery scattered around, he now saw Nestor's enigmatic mansion with its surrounding garden. The plateau was cleared of all construction debris and the area had a new look. A green garden and a massive building, enclosed inside a four foot stone wall topped with a six foot ornate wrought iron fence, stood in front of him and his cousin. A heavy iron gate that closes and opens electronically was built on the south end of the wall. That gate was the only entrance to the property. The surrounding wall was shaped into an ellipse with a north to south orientation to fit the shape of the plateau. Construction-wise, the wall was durable and unique in appearance. It was built with two rows of stone held together with cement mortar. The builders had taken their time to shape the stones that faced the exterior of the wall. One inch of each stone's outer periphery was finely honed to form a smooth area. The rest of the stone's face was natural. Looking at the wall from a distance, you had the impression that the outer periphery of each stone was covered with a one inch tape. The masons who hammered and placed these stones in place were aware that beauty, durability, and appeal were essential elements of architecture.

Enclosed within the peripheral wall, were the garden and the mansion itself. The soil was bark, rich, and fertile, for it was enriched with goat and sheep manure for many years. The original soil was the red earth that the monks carried in their baskets to fill the plateau that had created when they removed the rocks to make room for the church of Profit Elias. The area that was not covered by the mansion itself was now cultivated and meticulously cared for to provide fruit and fresh vegetables for the new occupant. Fruit trees grew in straight lines, and rows of vegetables were cultivated in the spaces between them. Cobblestone walking paths, lined with flowering shrubs on both sides, dressed the trees and the vegetable patches. Where there was tillable ground outside the walls, Nestor had planted cypress trees that grew tall and beautiful. They provided protection from the gales of winter and offered shelter and nesting grounds to a variety of local and migratory birds. The ground, where monks were buried in the past, was still wasteland. The immediate grounds around the mansion were planted with a variety of rose bushes that often flowered from March until November. A most powerful aroma that filled the air in summer and early fall had emanated from the flowering of the two jasmine shrubs that grew on each side of the main entrance to the mansion.

When Nestor settled on the summit, he discovered that the monks had built a small, underground cistern to store rain water for both their personal need and for watering the garden. He realized at once that this tiny underground water storage cavity was not sufficient for him and he decided to make it bigger. He hired local labor and experts in using dynamite to clear the hole and make it bigger. The laborers removed the rubbish, enlarged the hole, and coated the inside surface with a water impervious substance. The upper part of the new cistern wall was gradually narrowed to a dome, beehive form ending to a small opening on ground level. This opening was big enough to allow a person to lower himself into the cistern for cleaning and repairing leaks. In order to avoid any accidental fall in the cistern, Nestor placed a hinged heavy metal plate over the opening as an additional precaution. The plate was secured in place with a padlock. It was estimated that the cistern's capacity was 25,000 gallons when filled to the top. Nowadays, an electric pump brought up the water, but the rope grooves that were cut on the stones, forming the lip of the old cistern, testified that the monks used goat-skin baskets to bring it up.

The northern grounds of the enclosure, where the church of the prophet stood years ago, were now occupied by the mansion itself. In front of Theo and Fotis rose Nestor's unusually massive and elegantly constructed mansion. Its appearance reminded the viewer that a complex and rich man of grand descent must be its architect and occupant. The three-level structure was designed in such a way that each floor graciously supported the structure above it, just like Nestor's reasoning did to support his arguments. Each floor, made from a slab of reinforced cement, was extended outward to form spacious balconies. Reinforced, perpendicular, concrete columns supported the horizontal concrete floors. The entire architectural marvel rose 35 feet above the tip of the summit and was visible for miles. Honed stone walls, large glass windows, and a massive main entrance filled the spaces between the floors and the supporting columns. An elaborate gutter system piped the rain water through a filtering system into the cistern.

The floors throughout the mansion were covered with marble tiles of various sizes, shapes and colors. Some areas were tiled in the traditional way with numerous of rectangular or square tiles that harmonized into artistic designs of flowers, trees, and animals. Other floor areas were covered at random with tiny, irregular chips of marble which were embedded in the cement when it was still soft. After the concrete was cured, these floors were polished several times to make the surface flat and to bring up the color of the marble chips. This floor preparation technique produced an aesthetically unusual multi-colored effect, like that of Jackson Pollock's art which he created by randomly splashing colors on canvas.

At the beginning, kerosene lamps were used to light up the place, but when electricity was brought to the summit to power the military communication antenna, Nestor was allowed to connect the mansion to an electric line and converted kerosene lighting to electric.

Each floor of the mansion was a perfectly formed, circular, concrete plate. The plates that formed the ground and the second floor were exactly 99 feet across, but the diameter of the third floor was only 33 feet.

The entrance to the mansion was a massive, two leaf door constructed from solid oak wood and trimmed with copper sheet metal. Its knocker was a two-headed falcon cast in solid brass. When one walked through this door and entered the mansion, he faced an oversized fire place in the center and four rooms lining the periphery of the circular floor. The architect had allowed several feet of space between the rooms and the fireplace to be used as a waiting area for guests and as a corridor to access the rooms. Two bathrooms and an oversized coat closet were located close to the entrance.

The first room to the immediate right from the entrance was the kitchen. This room was equipped with an assortment of cooking and eating utensils, a modern refrigerator, an electric cooking stove, and a small table with four chairs around it. The sink and the spacious countertops were pastel-colored marble. From this room, one had a wonderful view of part of the garden through a large window that faced the south-easterly direction.

Next to the kitchen was the dining room. Most of the floor space was covered by an ornate, oval-shaped, black walnut, dinner table with twelve mahogany chairs around it. Three china cabinets and two abstract paintings occupied the wall space on both sides of a large window that offered a spectacular, north-easterly view of the garden and the sprawling valley in the distance below the mountain.

A game room was next to the dinning room. Two card-game tables with carved wooden legs and a green velvet top occupied the space close to the entrance. Most of the floor space, however, was dedicated to a massive billiard table. A collection of billiard sticks with ivory handles was neatly mounted on racks that were fixed against the two opposite walls next to the billiard table. Two couches and several chairs were placed on the floor in such a way that they did not hinder the activity around the billiard or the card tables. A large window offered a north-westerly view of part of the garden and of the mountain ridges in the far distance.

To the left from the game room, was a meeting room with a long, rectangular table on the center of the floor and several chairs around it. A number of portraits of Greek heroes from the 1821 revolution against the Ottoman Empire were hanging on the walls on both sides of the only window in the room. This window was facing south-west and offered a splendid view of the forested valley in the far distance where Theo's village was located.

Marble pedestals, on which marble busts of Plato, Alexander the Great, Darwin, and Newton rested, stood next to each door that led into the four rooms. Couches and more chairs were cleverly planted on available space around the fire place for guests to sit and relax there, especially in the winter time when the ground was covered with snow and cold wind blew from the north.

A spiral staircase was wrapped around the exterior wall of the fireplace's exhausting chimney, and it extended from the first floor all the way to the third floor.

Climbing the spiral case to the second floor, one found himself walking on a balcony that protruded over the space between the fireplace and the rooms on the first floor below.

Three spacious bedrooms, built 120 degrees apart from each other, occupied the outside periphery of this floor. Wide breezeways separated one room from the next, and several potted, flowering plants were hanging from the ceiling above your head. A sliding glass door led from the breezeway to the exterior veranda.

Each bedroom had a main entrance facing the spiral case and a large window facing the garden. This window allowed ample natural light to enter the room and offered a breathtaking view of the immediate valley and the mountains in the far distance. A king-size bed, two night tables with an electric lamp on top, and two chairs occupied the floor space. A closet and a bathroom were built in each bedroom.

The spiral case extended upward through the second floor, all the way through the floor of the top room in the mansion. The encased venting pipes extended all the way to the roof where the smoke generated in the fireplace below was vented out of the building. This room, which was locked all the time, was a perfect circle and was squarely rested over the three bedrooms below. The only opening was a door next to the chimney. Three large windows were positioned at equal distances from one another, with a tinny window up high, facing north. The large windows offered an unobstructed view of the valley as far as the human eyes can reach. The petite little window appeared to be out of place and frankly, it was a sore eye to look at. This was the room where Nestor retired at night to catch up with his correspondence, or play his guitar and sing his bucolic, wailing songs. His rustic songs were as mysterious as the singer's life, for nobody had heard them before nor understood the meaning of their lyrics.

Engineers who had examined the building had diverse opinions about its architectural stability. Some thought that the massive reinforced concrete plates with their supporting beams and columns kept the structure together. Others saw a marvelous balance of intersecting walls that were positioned brilliantly between concrete beams and concrete plates. Unmistakably, the mansion stood there without a crack or a fissure, exactly the way it was constructed.

Theo and Fotis found the outside gate open and with their hearts beating as fast as if they were entering the church of *Agia Sofia* in Constantinople, they entered the garden area and proceeded to the main gate with the two-headed falcon knocker hanging on one of its panels. Before they had the chance to lift the knocker and announce their arrival, the hinges of the massive door squeaked and Magdalene greeted them and invited them in. Magdalene was the mother of two boys and the widow of a poor farmer from a neighboring village, who had taken employment at the mansion after Nestor became ill. Her world was limited, for she was illiterate, but she was a hard worker and a great cook.

"My master is up early this morning and feels better knowing that you, Mr. Theovule, are coming to see him," she said in a shy mannerism and with a voice that stuttered at the intonation point of each word she used.

"Where is he now? Where is he?" Fotis interrupted her faltering talk.

"He is resting in his favorite bedroom. As you know, he can't get up anymore and cannot use his meditation room either," she said, and pointed with her finger toward the room on the third floor. "The meditation room," she continued, "has been locked since the time Mr. Nestor was confined in bed. He is expecting you. He…Please, follow me," she said, and started ascending the spiral case to the second floor with Theo and Fotis behind her. The door to Nestor's bedroom was closed, so Magdalene knocked softly. A grouchy, barely discernable, voice was heard after Magdalene's third knocking.

"Come in Theovule! You do not need permission to enter my bedroom. Please come in and let me take a good look at my favorite friend and pupil," Nestor said, and without much success, he made an effort to lift himself up on his bed.

Theo had not in the least expected to see what he saw on the bed or what he felt when he entered his mentor's room. He was aware that Nestor was ill, but in his imagination he had expected to find Nestor in a state of self control. He had expected to find the physical signs of the approach of death but never expected to find only the living skeleton of the robust man he remembered.

In a clean and orderly bedroom with the freshly painted panels of its walls, in a well aerated atmosphere and on an immaculately clean bed, a body laid covered with a light blanket. Both arms were resting over the blanket with wrists distorted and appearing to be connected to long spindles that were straight from the end to the middle. The head lay comfortably on a pile of pillows, but the hair seemed to be wet at the temples with sweat, and the drawn forehead looked transparent.

This cannot be the body of my teacher, thought Theo, but as he went closer and saw the face, his doubt vanished. Theo had only to take a closer look at those eager eyes that were raised as he approached and at those sticky lips, to realize that this almost-lifeless body was his living friend and teacher, Nestor. The glittering eyes looked directly at him as he came closer, and immediately Theo established a living connection with the man under the blanket.

When Theo grasped Nestor's hands, the sick man delivered a faint smile, but the stern expression of his eyes did not change. He kept staring at Theo without lowering his eyes, and a second smile with a deep breath was delivered with a greater effort.

"I see that you did not expect to find me in this condition," Nestor whispered with difficulty.

"It was wishful thinking to hope that I would find you the way I remember you," Theo said, hesitating over his words. These were the only words that came to his lips at this moment, and he uttered them so as not to be silent, but silence followed.

"Magdalene, bring me a glass of cold water and fetch refreshments for my guests," the dying man said with a struggle. "Oh and when you have done that, leave us alone," he continued, looking at Theo with a lively brightness in his glare.

Magdalene did as she was asked to do and minutes later, she returned with a tray on which stood three glasses of water, a bottle of ouzo, and two glasses with a single cube of ice in each one of them. She placed the tray on one of the night tables next to the bed and walked out of the room. Theo sat on a chair close to the sick man's bed and Fotis occupied the other chair on the other side of the bed.

"Three days ago, I received the sad news that you are ill, uncle Nestor, and that you wished to see me," Theo said breaking the unbearable silence and at the same time, he lifting the bottle with the ouzo, and poured some of its contents into the glasses with ice. "I left everything to be done at a later date and came to see you as soon as I could," he continued with hesitation, fearing that he had overemphasized the urgency he had placed upon his trip.

"Dear Theovule," the sick man uttered. "It was a distinct pleasure meeting you when you were a high school boy, and a burst of hope filled my heart when I heard that you went away to another world to pursue your dreams in life. Now, I am honored that you made the sacrifice to be with

me during the last days of my life. I knew I was correct in
my assessment about your potentials, and now I feel proud
and rewarded to see that my expectations of you were not
in vain.

"Do you remember the first time you came to ask my
advice?" he said, and made another effort to re-position
himself on his bed. He took a deep breath and continued
with bitterness,

"Death is cruel to me like the fox who tortures her prey
before killing it. Don't misunderstand me; I am ready to face
the inevitable. I only wished it to be a little less painful, or
a bit quicker."

Theo sat in his chair motionless and overwhelmed with
emotion listening to Nestor's compliments. His emotions
boiled over however, when Nestor uttered the word "death"
and felt as if a piercing dagger traversed his heart, especially
when he saw the uncovered chest of the sick man, at the time
he tried again to re-positioned himself in his bed. It looked
like a hairy thin linen material draped over a cage that
moved up-and-down, and that inside this cage was a living
thing desperately trying to free itself from its imprisonment.
The cartilage of his larynx moved in concert with his voice
as he spoke; his collar bones protruded like the antennas of
an overstretched umbrella under its thin fabric, and his ribs
looked as if they had lost all the muscle between them. Fotis
was moved by the sight of the sick man and felt his stomach
churning. He gulped down the last drops of the ouzo in his
glass and walked out of the room on the pretext that he had
to go to the bathroom. The sight of the dying man was too
much for the simple-minded villager.

Theo thought that this was the opportunity he was
waiting for, and he mastered the courage to ask Nestor
about his true identity. They were alone and Nestor was in
a talkative mood. Using all the diplomatic talent he could

muster, he took Nestor's boney hands in his and with a voice full of feeling, he said, "Uncle Nestor, you summoned me here for something more than just to see me," he articulated, looking directly at the other man's eyes that flickered like oil laps running out of fuel.

"Do you remember the first time you asked me for my advice?" Nestor repeated, as if he never heard the question Theo had asked him. "It was about the love you felt for a girl in your high school. Do you remember that instant, Theovule?"

"I certainly do," Theo added, disappointed that his listener had avoided answering the question he had rehearsed so many times in his mind. Was it possible that Nestor lived in the past and that he was incapable of comprehending current events?

"I remember I advised you to ignore your emotions and concentrate on your academic achievements, for love at that age is a passive experience that all young people go through in one form or another. Do you feel that this advice is in harmony with what you know now about love?" Nestor inquired.

"At the time, I had doubts about the validity of your advice. My mind was cluttered with emotions that were associated with that new experience to the point that I 'could not see the forest through the trees', as the saying goes. Only later, I understood the validity of your advice," Theo responded with a smile that expressed a sort of shame for being so naive at the age of eighteen. "You said that 'love is unconquered in battles,' and 'love dwells on the cheeks of young maids,' quoting the play *Antigone* from the drama of Sophocles, to distinguish brotherly love from the erotic love.

"What I remember more distinctly however," Theo continued, "is the time when you spoke to me about organized religions. You said that 'religion is an adherence to a set of beliefs or teachings that concern the deepest and most elusive mysteries of human life. Its members," you said, "are on the quest to understand where the origin of life on earth is, and what it means to be a human being. Is there a force that is greater than the human force which is responsible for things, how a person of good will should behave, and finally," you said, "its adherents ask themselves if life as we know it is all there is, or are we destined for an adventure that goes beyond the earthly life?"

"Nothing has changed my mind since then," Nestor responded. "All religions, large or small, old or new, primitive or contemporary attempt to answer the same question of where we came from and why things are the way they are; nothing else. All of them probe to answer the same questions from a different point of view, thus different forms of religion have been created throughout the ages of human history. I personally believe that there is a force that is responsible for all the things that exist, but our ability to comprehend it is limited. This force does not have to be in the form we call and understand as God, or Prophet, etc. It could exist in some other form that we humans are not aware of or are unable to quantify and therefore, we can not express it in mathematical units like we do with magnetism, gravity and electricity, for example."

He opened his eyes a little wider, cleared his throat with a weak cough and reached for Theo's hand. Theo extended his hand toward the sick man and asked if there was anything he could do for him. It never entered his head that he could make those gaunt legs and spine that were lying huddled up under the blanket more comfortable. His blood ran cold when he thought of the emaciated skeleton draped over with a thin layer of skin. He knew that there was nothing he could do to prolong his friend's life or to ease his suffering, and this thought made Nestor's condition more painful for Theo. It was agonizing to be in the room of his dying friend and to be there unable to help him was intolerable.

"The doctor is here to see you, Mr. Nestor," Magdalene said, standing at the door, wiping her hands with the corner of her apron.

A dignified man stood next to her with a medical case hanging in his left hand and a walking cane in the other. Theo concluded that he was Nestor's attending physician and he was there to examine the ill man. He was well dressed, wore prescription glasses, and his hair from the top of his head was gone completely. He wore a thin moustache that lined the lower part of his upper lip from one end of the mouth to the other. He produced a stethoscope from his bag, connected the forked part to his ears, and placed the button-looking part on several spots in Nestor's chest to listen to the thumping of his heart. He placed it on Nestor's back and listened again to the hissing sound that was coming from his lungs. He pulled down to the blanket to the waist, placed one hand over his liver area, and tapped at it with the fingers of the other hand. He returned the instrument to his medical bag, took a look at the uncovered torso of his patient, and shook his head from side to side wearing a sad look on his face. Finally, he stuck a slow releasing medical patch on the sick man's chest, and covered the exposed part of Nestor's body with the blanket. Noticing Theo standing there, he said to him inquisitively,

"Are you a member of his family? Oh, I am Dr. *Gliadis,*" and before Theo had a chance to answer his question, the doctor said, "This man is very sick Mr....", and started to walk toward the door.

Theo followed him and with a few quick steps, he stepped in front of the doctor's way forcing him to stop at the door before he exited the room.

"Theovulos, Theo for short," said Theo, and shook the doctor's hand.

"Mr. Theovule," the doctor said. "Nestor has only days left. I give him not more than a week. Realistically speaking, he will not be with us two days from now. If I were you, I would make all necessary preparations for the inevitable. I suggest you have a priest come up here to give him communion; in the meantime, you should make arrangements for his burial," and with that comment, he passed Theo who stood in his way. He hurriedly descended the spiral case to the main floor, walked through the garden urgently to probably see another patient, and disappeared down the road toward the place where he had parked his car. Theo returned to the sick man and sat on the chair to keep him company a little longer. He was determined to stay as long as Nestor was able to continue talking.

"What did the doctor tell you at the door," Nestor inquired with a voice that started to fade away.

"Oh, he did not say anything new. He told me that you are not well and that someone should take care of you, day and night."

Nestor looked around the room and noticed that Fotis was not in his chair. He also noticed the sadness in Theo's face and said, "Do not sadden because of me reaching the end of my life. Remember that all of us are pre-destined to die as soon as we take our first breath. Even before we open our eyes to see the light of the day and utter our first cry, we are destined to die. Remember what I told you sometime ago. Everything that exists now follows a path in the span of time. All living and non- living things look as if they appear from nowhere, stay in one form or another for a while and gradually fade away. They disappear to make room for something else to take their place. Nothing is permanent. For example, the monks that were here years ago are gone.

The fruit trees they planted are gone and the Church of Profit Elias they built is also gone, to be replaced by the things I put in their place. Even the mountain itself will be gone some day. Erosion or some other geological upheaval will work in reverse to undo what was done eons ago, when continental drifts pressed this part of the earth to push itself upward from the bottom of the sea and form the very mountain we sit on, at this moment."

"I accepted this proposition when I was a boy and have no reason to question its validity now," Theo retorted. "Yet, I have a problem explaining the non-material aspect of our existence. What can we say about what we call 'feelings' and 'emotions' that we experience at times? Is there a soul inside each one of us which escapes our body after we die? Does this soul go somewhere to stay, or will it return to earth and reincarnate itself to something else?

"Some of these things, my dear Theo, are functions of the matter that makes us all. Other things that you are speaking of are the result of genetic adaptation, and still others are learned during our lives, like 'hate,' for example. As far as the existence of a soul, do not waste your time searching for something that does not exist. When man advances to the point that he will be able to understand himself, then and only then, will he be able to answer your question. We attach a mystical value to things that are beyond our comprehension simply because we want to satisfy our curiosity, and because we want to ease our fear that we vanish after death. We do not vanish at all. We just return to the form we were before. Remember dear friend, 'nothing starts from nothing and nothing goes to nothing.' The dot of infinite density and infinite smallness from which everything came to being was there. If you ask me to tell you where this dot came from, I have to confess that I don't have an answer for you. I can only tell you what happened after the Big Bang, at the time that the "dot" exploded. From the moment this monumental explosion took place to this instant, things only change from the forms in which we perceive them."

Theo was glued to his chair as if he were spellbound, listening to Nestor who spoke with effort, stopping at times to draw a deep breath, and finding the energy he needed to make his next statement.

Theo's visit with Nestor was not like the old times when they sat across from each other on the big limestone seat next to the temporary shelter Nestor had built. In total concentration, they asked each other questions and listened to reasoning for explanation. Nestor was a young man then, and Theo was an adolescent just finishing high school. The former was a mature, educated, and a wise man; the latter was a very young lad who had a lot of questions about the world around him. Nestor's personality was as commanding as it was now and Theo's inquisitive mind to know was receptive. There were other young men who spent time with Nestor seeking his advice, but their connection to him was not like that of Theo who had established a rapport with his teacher. There was a magnetic force that held the pupil's attention to the teacher's words. Theo was fascinated with the answers he received from his mentor to the point that he memorized them like a computer copies and stores in its memory the commands of its programmer.

The teachers at his high school had recently noticed changes in Theo's personality. His attitude toward the status quo in the high school educational system was very obvious. His religion teacher expressed his concern to the principal that Theo would turn out to be another revolutionary when he grew up, and the gym teacher gave up hoping that Theo would get the championship in throwing the javelin, during the interstate competitions. The concerns the teachers expressed to the principal prompted him to review Theo's academic record and the principal concluded that "the lad will graduate the school with high honors" in two months. Still, he summoned Theo to his office and in the presence of five of his seven teachers, he said in a fatherly tone of voice; "Son, we have noticed that you are different from the student you were before. Your teachers worry about you. For example, you don't attend church anymore, you are gone during most of the weekends, and your gym teacher tells me that you gave up practicing javelin throwing that you were so good at it. Is there anything that I, or your teachers, can do to help you return to your normal self, anything at all? You have a great potential to be someone, and we are here to help you achieve it."

Theo, regained his composure, looked at the principal and at his teachers who stood around the principal's office, and addressed the principal's concerns. He fixed his gaze at the principal and said with conviction, "No sir, there isn't anything that anyone can do to answer the questions that have occupied my thinking at present. I have to sort things out on my own. I have to find the answers to my questions on my own. I hope you are finding my grades in good order, aren't you, sir?"

"As I said earlier, this lad looks like he will graduate from my school with high honors which is a rare achievement," the principal said to the teachers and excused Theo to go.

On his way out of the room, Theo heard the voice of his math teacher demanding his attention.

"Wait a minute young man," he heard the voice of his math teacher calling him at the time he was opening the door to escape the stifling atmosphere of the crowded office. "We want you to know that we called you here to offer our help, and it looks like you walk out of here disenchanted with our offer. You did not even express your gratitude for our good intention."

"Oh, I am so very sorry sir. The emotions that your presence stirred in me overwhelmed my composure and I forgot my good manners. Please forgive me for not thanking you for all the things you are doing for the entire student body. I hope I am not too late to beg your pardon," Theo said, and with that statement he exited the office that felt as if it was an interrogation chamber.

The moment Theo walked out of the principal's office he took the road toward the summit of the mountain for another session with Nestor. On his way there, he thought and re-thought about the event of the interrogation he was subjected to. He considered it to be a trivial incident and found no value worth discussing it with Nestor. The issue of "cosmos" occupied his mind lately. His math teacher (he was the same math teacher who taught an introductory course in astronomy twice-a-week and trigonometry three times-a- week) told the class that there is a countless number of stars and planets in the sky. Theo distinctly remembered hearing that these celestial objects obey a set of laws to move constantly in the vastness of space without crashing into one another. The teacher also said that life exists only on an insignificant planet we call "Earth". These two statements stuck in Theo's mind and he was on his way to talk to Nestor about them.

Theo, sitting in his chair next to Nestor, noticed that the voice of the ill man begun to fade away. It looked as if he wanted to take a nap and Theo thought for a moment that it was best to leave the sick man alone. Yet, the memory of Nestor's teachings and his present condition made him re-consider his mental debate of leaving or staying a little longer. As Nestor continued his irregular breathing on his bed, Theo reminisced the sessions he had with him in the past. Looking at Nestor's bald head and his gray hair on his bony chest, he remembered the day when he explained to him the principles of heredity. "It's all simple to understand, if you accept the fact that God had nothing to do with your hair being straight and mine being curly," Nestor had said to the high school boy. "The genes that determine the shape of my hair are different from the genes that regulate the shape of your hair, my dear young man! This is true for all other characteristics, like height, color of eyes, facial characteristics, and bodily dimensions, for example. It's a different 'color of a horse', if you ask me who put these genes there. As life evolved on earth, adaptation through natural selection enabled some animals to survive while others became extinct. But, we will get to the subject of evolution some other time," Nestor had said to young Theo. Presently, he felt that he should let Nestor rest. He slowly lifted himself from his chair with the intention to leave the ill man alone without having the answer he was hoping to extract from him. As Theo turned his eyes toward the door, he felt Nestor's bonny fingers grasping Theo's hand and heard his whispering voice say,

"I hope I'll see you tomorrow early. You know, we have a lot of things to talk about and we are limited in time. Oh by the way, I heard what you asked me earlier. When Fotis left the room, you said that I must have another reason summoning you here. Yes I do. However, we will leave this subject last. In the event that the dear doctor has miscalculated the time I have left to be with the living, start your quest by examining the only ring I wear on one of my fingers," he added, and wiggled one of the fingers in his left hand to show Theo the worn ring that fit loosely on it. Go now and rest well," an exhausted voice said, and the bony fingers released their grip. That was Nestor's voice coming out of his emaciated body that was hidden under the blanket in the bed in front of him.

Without undo delay and with a heavy heart that was loaded with all kinds of feelings and emotions, Theo walked out of the sick man's room, descended the spiral case, and seeing Magdalene in the kitchen occupied with her chores, he asked her where Fotis was.

"Mr. Fotis is resting under the grape vines in the garden," she observed. "He had a little something to eat, a glass of ouzo with ice, and several fresh figs from one of our fig trees. Would you Mr. Theo like something to eat? I'll be glad to prepare it for you."

"No thanks Magdalene," Theo answered politely. "The day is practically gone and you should devote your attention to the sick man upstairs."

"How is Mr. Nestor," she inquired in her naïve country girl's voice. "Christ and Virgin Mary, I hope there is nothing serious with him, is there? I pray day and night for him and hope God will listen to me. You may want to know, I keep burning the flame that I brought from the resurrection liturgy in front of the icon of Profit Elias. The saint will make Mr. Nestor well again. I know it. Would you like to see the flame and the icon?"

"Not now dear. I will be back tomorrow morning, and you can show it to me at that time. For now, I must be on my way."

Magdalene escorted him to the door and with a slight bowing, she closed the door behind him.

Theo walked to the shaded area under the grape vine canopy and found his cousin sitting on one of the wooden benches with a frightened grimace on his face. Fotis was mentally preoccupied with the sight and the condition of the old, dying man, and the thought that he would be in the same predicament some day, sent chills up his spine and convulsions in his stomach. He did not have the strength to return to the sick man's room neither could he forget what he saw there. Instead, he kept company to Magdalene in the kitchen sipping the contents of the bottle of ouzo that was resting almost empty on the end of the counter. Theo sat next to Fotis who apologized for not having the stomach to face the reality of the wasted body. Theo, in turn, explained to Fotis that it was only natural for him to get depressed looking at Nestor. "There is no need to feel guilty or ashamed for expressing your emotions and displaying your human weakness," Theo said to Fotis, and patted him on his back with brotherly love. "Come on, cheer up old pal!" he added, and they walked to the Fiat that was waiting for them in the small parking area.

Before they entered the vehicle to roll toward the village, Theo stopped for a moment and fixed his eyes at the mansion with its gardens hidden behind its impressive stone walls with its wrought iron fence mounted on top of it. He paused there several minutes and admired the mansion that stood supreme with the rows of cypress trees projecting against the blue horizon in the background. Was there any symbolic meaning to the fact that the mansion consisted of four rooms and a foyer on the first floor (five spaces all together), three rooms on the second, and a single room on the top? Did the ground level, with its five spaces represent the "Five Pillars of Islam" or, perhaps, the five points of the Star of David? Did the three rooms above it stand for the trinity of Christian faith? Finally, did the single room at the top symbolize monotheism from which the other two religions stem from?

His eyes searched the verandas of the second and third level for his living and dear Nestor, but he saw no one there. What he was looking for was lying in bed drawing his last breath. The verandas were deserted. He fixed his gaze on each window hoping to see Nestor waving goodbye, but he saw no one there. His eyes finally rested on the top room of the mansion with the tiny window and wondered what secrets were held inside this dimly lit tower that was kept under lock and key. Are there things hidden inside this room that will help him find the answer to the question he came for? Or an old guitar and a few books resting on a table would all that Theo would find? But again, if there was nothing of interest in there, why was this room off limits to all, except to Nestor himself?

The day was still hot and the wind coming from the west was not blowing strong yet to cool off nature. The sun was still unobstructed from any clouds, and it shone brightly halfway down toward the west quadrant of the sky.

The two men entered the Fiat and took the down hill road toward the village in complete silence. They had so much excitement all day, and they needed time to absorb the things they had seen and heard during their visit with the hermit.

Chapter Four:
"A Hermit's Death"

The little worn out Fiat rolled down the steep dirt road with ease now. It occasionally bumped upon stones and potholes and jerked left-and-right as it went but, in general, the ride was comfortable. The sun was blazing on the other side of the mountain at this hour, and the eastern side, where the road was built, was shaded. For that reason, the air was cool and it made the ride more comfortable. When the two cousins reached the valley where the dirt road intersected the paved road, Theo spoke and asked Fotis if he had any ideas for dinner.

"We can go home and cook something or drive a few kilometers south to the next village," Fotis said. "There is a little outdoor *taverna* there; its owner is my *coumbaros*. I'm sure that he will make something good for us."

Theo found the second suggestion more attractive than the first one and took the paved road toward the next village.

He was not in the mood for cooking dinner and cleaning dishes tonight. Besides, he wanted to look up some of his old friends and see if any of them were still living. When he was a young man, he was a frequent visitor to that village, and he had developed close friendships with several of the young lads who were living there at the time.

"Your idea sounds good, Fotis. Let's dine out tonight," he said, and continued driving toward the village Fotis suggested.

The road was paved and made the drive comfortable in the cramped vehicle, and the immediate landscape around them was flat and dotted with small, white houses. Rows of olive and citrus trees could be seen from one end of the valley to the opposite end. In between the tree rows that stretched in front of them for several kilometers ahead of them, the people cultivated gardens where they grew all kinds of fruits and vegetables. Theo's olfactory sense was overwhelmed by the fragrance that came from the orange tree blossoms and from the ripe, honeydew melons that were in season. He was tempted to stop and pick a few melons for later, but Fotis told him that there was a stand by the road two kilometers down the road where they could get their supply. The village of their destination was built on the top of a flat hill at the far end of the valley, and because of its elevated position, it could be seen from a long distance.

After a few minutes driving, the two men reached the stand. Theo stopped the car on the shoulder of the road, turned off the engine and walked out of the car to take a closer look at the beauty of the surrounding landscape. Fotis approached the stand, greeted the lady attendant, gave her some money, and returned with two big shopping bags with several ripe honeydew melons. They placed the bags with the fruit in the trunk of the car and drove until they reached the outskirts of the village. From here on, Fotis had to direct Theo through the streets to the taverna, for things had changed so much since Theo last visited the place. He could not recognize the streets or the houses any more. The streets were widened to allow for cars to go through, not only for donkeys, and the buildings Theo remembered looked different. Almost all of them were renovated and had taken on the appearance of homes for modern living. Only a few of them looked the way Theo remembered them. The taverna was located in the center of the village, next to a gigantic plane tree that Theo remembered very well. The circular dancing area, still paved with flat stones, was still intact, just the way he remembered it. It was here where the youth of the surrounding villages gathered and danced to live music on April 23rd after the liturgy in the church of Saint George. Yes this was the place he remembered so vividly. It was here where he met his friends, ate roast lamb, drank local wine with them, and eyed the young maidens dancing with finesse and poise to the tune of their traditional songs.

The taverna was nothing more than a little hut built next to the proprietor's home. The roof had no ceiling and cured ham, garlic braids, and strings of sun dried figs hung from nails hammered into the rafters above. The floor was one half covered with wood planks, and the other half was still dirt floor. Several wooden benches surrounded by rush chairs occupied the unfinished, dirt floor. It was summer now, and the wood burning stove stood idle in the center of this area waiting to blaze hot during the cold days of the winter. The portion of the floor that was covered with wood planks extended from north to south and served as the working area for the proprietor. Half of this area was covered by a wooden bench on which the owner stored things like drinking glasses, made coffee over an alcohol burner, and kept a cigar box with his money in it. Against the wall that faced east from the bench, he had mounted two sets of wooden shelves. On these shelves, he displayed non-perishable merchandise like cigarettes, canned food, notepads, pencils, matches, writing paper, envelopes, and a jar filled with colorful, hard candies. Between the counter and the east wall, a set of steps led downstairs to a tiny basement. Here, in this small basement, he kept several barrels with wine. This below ground level, storage area, kept the wine cool in the summer and protected it from becoming too cold in the winter. Common wisdom had taught the taverna owner that he should store the wine in a place where the temperature does not fluctuate; for otherwise, it spoils and becomes vinegar.

Theo parked the car in front of the place and followed Fotis inside. Two benches were occupied by customers who were munching on hunks of boiled goat meat and drinking retsina. One of the groups was engaged in a heated conversation about the alleged mismanagement of foreign aid on the national level. The other group was absorbed watching a card game between two crafty old villagers. The owner heard the sound of the Fiat parking in front of his place, wiped his wet hands on his apron, and hurried to the door to greet the new customers.

"Hey coumbare, how the heck are you," he said to Fotis. "I haven't seen you since I came to the memorial for your wife, God bless her soul."

"Things have changed considerably for me nowadays, *Stavros*! I don't get around as often as I want to see my friends," Fotis said, and gave the other man a bear hug.

"Who is your companion?" the taverna owner said, in a bewildered voice and extended his hand to shake Theo's.

"Oh I am sorry. This is my cousin Theovulos from America," Fotis said and pointing at the taverna owner, he said to Theo. "This man is my coumbaros Stavros. I was his best man on his wedding day, and I became the godfather of his first born, according to our custom." Stavros and Theo shook hands and all three men walked into the room. They pulled up chairs, sat at one of the empty benches, and continued their introductory conversation. Some of the customers made inquisitive looks at the new comers while they continued eating, drinking, and gesturing with their hands and conversing with one another. A few seconds later, Stavros got up, walked behind his counter, and returned, holding in his left hand three glasses of wine. He handed one glass to Theo, the second to Fotis and kept the third for himself. Standing up with his glass in his hand, he announced in a loud voice to everyone in the place that he had something very important to say. Every patron in the place stopped doing whatever they were doing at the time and turned their faces toward Stavros to hear his announcement.

"Hey men, we have a distinguished friend with us tonight. I call on all of you to drink to the health of Mr. Theovulos from America," he said, and with the hand that held the glass with the wine, he pointed toward Theo. Everyone in the establishment lifted their glasses and said in the same tone of voice, "*Yiasu xene!*" (to your health traveler). Theo, overwhelmed from the cheer and the spotlighting, asked Stavros to fill the glasses of all the customers, and to bring more goat meat and bread to their tables. When the food and the wine arrived, each one thanked Theo for his generosity and wished him good health and a long life. Stavros sat at the table with Theo and Fotis, and in a low voice, he whispered, "Hey friends, I hope you are hungry tonight! Something was telling me all day that I will have special company for dinner. I kept the best part of the goat meat for the three of us." When he received an affirmative answer from Fotis that they were starving, he went behind the counter and came back with three big plates of steaming, succulent goat meat seasoned with local spices, carrots, potatoes, onions and garlic, that had been simmering all day in a pot. He also sliced a round loaf of home made bread in thick slices and placed some of it at the center of the table for the three of them to share. Two liters of wine, compliments of the occupants from the other tables came to their table also.

The three men sat around their table and ate all the meat and vegetables with bread, they cared to eat, and drank plenty of the home-made wine. As a desert, a bowl of fresh yogurt topped with local honey was brought to their table. Finally, slices of delicious honeydew melon sprinkled with cinnamon and lemon juice completed their dinner. Theo and Fotis, lethargic from all the food and the wine they consumed, got off their table and began to mingle with the rest of the men in the restaurant. Theo in particular, struck a friendly conversation with one of the men who seemed to be respected by the others and inquired if any of his old friends were still living in the village. He learned from the "old chap" that each one of his friends had migrated either to foreign countries or moved to Athens years ago. Only one stayed in the village, but he had died a long time ago. Theo found this simple villager friendly and rather talkative, and he ventured to ask him if he knew the hermit who lived on the summit of the mountain.

"Yes, I heard people talking about him, but I never had the pleasure of meeting the gentleman," the sun-burned farmer responded; and reached under the visor of his cap and retrieved a cigarette he kept there. Holding the cigarette between two of his fingers, he lit it, drew several smoke puffs and said, "People tell me that he is an unusual character. I hear that he has a lot of money yet, nobody knows anything about him. He does not bother us living alone up there, and as long as he minds his own business, it is ok with the rest of us and with the authorities. There are several rumors flying around about him," he continued and blew a ring of smoke from his mouth. "Some people say that he is not a Greek, and that he inherited his money from his family. Other people claim that he is a converted Christian and earned his fortune in Europe in the stock market. Still another rumor persists that he made his money in a fraudulent way. He became a hermit up there to conceal himself from the authorities and of the place where he committed the wrong doing. Who knows the truth, friend! I myself believe that he inherited his fortune. I also believe that he had a traumatic experience of sort and decided to give up normal living and to become what he is now, just a hermit. As I said, as long as he does not bother us, let the authorities ask those questions." When he finished talking, he extinguished his cigarette, placed the unburned part under the visor again, re-arranged his cap on his head, and said nothing more. Theo asked Stavros to fill everyone's glasses one more time and re-positioned himself on the wooden bench to re-consider what he heard from the mouth of the other man.

Three of the customers paid their bills, thanked Theo for the food and the wine and walked out of the establishment. The rest of patrons including Theo, Fotis and Stavros, congregated around a table and began to offer their opinions regarding Nestor's mysterious living.

"I think the man made his money moving opium from Turkey to Europe, and when he made his bundle, he came to live among us," one of the villagers said, in a voice that expressed self-confidence.

"Nonsense," retorted the man who chatted with Theo earlier. "The man has character, wisdom and class. He does not fit your characterization and on second thought, I don't believe he gave up normal living just for a woman either, as some people claim. Sacrifices of that magnitude belong in fairy tails. They do not exist in real life."

Stavros had just finished cleaning the tables and served his patrons two more liters of wine with fresh glasses.

"This drink is on me," he proudly declared, and joined the crowd in the conversation about the enigma on Nestor's life.

"In my business fellows, I have come to know many people and have heard all kinds of stories about this chap. I heard many rumors and stories about him in the course of the forty years I ran my business, and I have formed my own opinion about the man. He is honest, well educated and abundantly wealthy. His character does not fit to be a criminal or a devious person. The question of his wealth can easily be answered by assuming that he inherited his money or came across a hidden or lost treasure serendipitously. Remember that this country was the center of civilization years ago, and every one knows; fame is connected with wealth. During the wars that followed the decline of Greek glory, one has to assume that immense treasures were found in places that were stashed away during those turbulent days, or are still buried awaiting lucky men to dig them out. Furthermore, a lot of money exchanged hands during and after the Second Word War between the conquering Germans, our western alliances, and citizens of our country. He might have been in the position to pocket some of that loot. His age fits this scenario. To me, his personal information is more puzzling than his money. Who am I to ask questions about a fellow citizen of good standing? The man is a lawful citizen and there isn't any warrant out there for his arrest, is there?" Stavros said, and he lifted his glass to wish good health to everyone in his company.

"Let's drink to everyone's health before flies fall into our glasses and spoil my good wine that I worked so hard to make, and place it in front of you," he said, with a comical chortle in his voice.

Every one in the company rose to their feet; some of them cleared their throats from the cigarette smoke that filled the air, and all of them lifted their glasses one more time, gently tinkled one against another, and wished good health and prosperity to all.

It was past eight o'clock in the evening now, and the wine made their heads heavy and their hearts content. The speculative conversation of who Nestor really was wound down, and the noise they made talking about him had subsided. Suddenly, the door opened and a priest from another village entered. He lifted his right hand, and with his thumb crossing over his finger next to the index finger, he made the symbol of the cross in the air, to bless the crowd. Every person jumped off their chairs, took off their hats, and one-by-one respectfully took the hand of the priest in theirs and kissed it with a moderate bow of their heads to express their obedience and respect to the representative of God.

"My dear Christians," the priest said, "sit down, please sit down. I hope that I haven't interrupted anything important. I am summoned to your village to bless Mr. *Giannis Kavouras* who is ill and wants to receive his last communion."

Stavros got off his chair and in a low voice with a tone of hypocrisy said,

"May we offer you a glass of wine to ease your pain for walking all the distance from your village to ours to do God's work?"

"That's a wonderful idea, my son," the priest retorted and took his place at the head of the long bench where the other men had already taken their places. "Tell me the news of your village. Is there anything of interest happening in your town that I should know?" the priest added.

One of the men in the group answered the priest's inquiry, and he said that the only new thing in town was the visit of Fotis and Mr. Theovulos from America, pointing to the two cousins sitting at the far end of the bench.

"Ah, from America," the priest said and alternated his glances from Theo to Fotis and back to Theo, trying to figure out who was the American. Theo lifted himself up from his seat to identify who the American was, and to express his respect for the priest; then, he sat down again.

"What brings you back to 'our neck of the woods,'" the priest queried.

"Oh, visiting friends and relatives for a few days," Theo responded in a casual manner.

Stavros appeared with a glass filled to the brim with wine and with a small plate containing the last pieces of the goat meat that was still in his pot. He placed them in front of the priest and took his seat next to him.

"Blessed son, was it necessary to bring food too? The wine would have been plenty; but since you put it in front of me, I'll eat it not to offend your kindness," the priest said, and he began to eat with delight. The food and the wine disappeared quickly, and Theo asked Stavros to bring one more glass of wine for the respected father, and said to the priest,

"Father, you came in here walking on two legs, therefore, you should have two glasses of wine, as they say in my village." His comment caused a freshness to spread in the faces of the men at the bench, while Theo delivered a pleasant laugh.

"We were talking about the hermit on the mountain before you walked in father," Stavros said, and he placed the second glass of wine in front of him. The priest re-positioned himself on his chair, stroked his long beard with one hand, breathed deeply several times as if he were a fighting bull, re-positioned his hat on his head with the long hair, wiped off the perspiration from his forehead with his handkerchief, and responded to Stavros.

"He is a big sinner, my son. That's what he is! He desecrated the land that belongs to our Saint Elias the Prophet. Several years ago, I tried my best to convince him to come to my church and save his soul, but I could not make him listen. The man does not believe in God and I don't believe he belongs to any religion at all. His soul is possessed by the devil, I tell you! He had the guts to tell me to my face that our religion is not any different from any other religion, and that all religions on earth are creations of men trying to give substance and form to things they do not understand or cannot explain to their satisfaction. What a distorted mind he has! He ignores all the miracles Jesus Christ performed. He had the audacity to call them 'trickery' or things that were fabricated by the evangelists after the lord ascended to heaven. I hear that he is very ill lately, and I wonder to whom he will surrender his sinful soul. It will not be our Lord Jesus Christ who will accept him in his kingdom if he redeems himself. If he does not repent and does not confess his sins, he will be condemned to dwell in the burning hell for eternity. I wish I could reach inside him and wake him up, to make his confession and to ask our Lord for his forgiveness. Our Lord has an abundance of love for all of us. You just ask for His forgiveness and you will receive it. He forgave the sins of the two thieves who were nailed on their crosses next to Him, and He opened the gates of paradise for them. This Nestor can do the same," he said, and he made the symbol of the cross with his right hand saying at the same time, "in the name of the father and the son and the holy spirit, amen," to indicate that he was through eating, drinking and talking. He lifted himself from his chair, straightened his long black garment that drooped over his body from his neck to his ankles, thanked Stavros for the food and the wine, greeted everyone good night, and walked out of the taverna.

"They are all the same," Stavros said after the priest had gone, "They talk shit and free-load when the opportunity presents itself. Did you see him? He sat down, ate our food, drank our wine, criticized an innocent hermit, and the 'he-goat' did not even offer to buy a glass of wine for us. He only came in to free-load, the pig!" Stavros' language and sarcasm brought a roaring laughter to the company. When the laughter from the humor subsided, Theo asked Stavros for everyone's bill. He felt good in their company, and he wanted to express his feelings by paying for everyone. At the end, he thanked Stavros for the special consideration he and Fotis received and got up to leave. The rest of the customers got up, shook hands with Theo and Fotis and one-by-one, walked out of the place to go home. At last, the two cousins said good night to Stavros, got in the Fiat, and took the road toward their own village.

It was late at night and the road was dark. The sky was free of clouds and everything was quiet and still. Theo had forgotten how many stars one can see in a sky that is unobstructed by artificial lighting. The only source of light was the full moon, which had just risen above the eastern horizon to tint the olive trees a different green color. The Milky Way stretched from northwest to southeast, and the mountain ahead looked twice as big against the starry sky. A hare, blinded by the beams of light coming from the headlights of the car, jumped in front of them and stopped in their path. Theo slammed on the brakes to avoid hitting the animal and heard his cousin cursing at the same time.

"Devil, get out of our way before you become ground meat!" The animal leaped forward from where it stood and with one bounce disappeared into the brush that covered both sides of the road. When they recovered their composure from the close encounter, Fotis turned to Theo and said,

"Did you learn anything new about Nestor tonight?" He fixed his eyes on Theo to read his reaction.

"Not a thing," Theo said with a negative tone in his voice. "Everything I heard is either a rumor or a conjecture. None of the things I heard in the taverna can be substantiated, Fotis! I am inclined to believe that parts of these theories will turn out to be the truth about Nestor but until then, they must be treated as tittle-tattle. Only time will reveal the truth. I might be lucky and get an answer directly from him when I see him tomorrow again. I hope I find him alive and talkative when I get there," he said. Turning to Fotis he added, "Fotis, you don't have to come with me tomorrow. I assume you have things to do around your house. Besides, I may have to stay longer with him, and I hate seeing you sitting in the shade of the grape vines all the time waiting for me. Stay home, and if I have any news to share with you, I will stop over when I return from my visit with him tomorrow evening."

Fotis sat silent in his seat and made no comments to Theo's suggestion. He could have things to do, as Theo said, or he may have felt that his cousin did not want him to be with him for some unexplained reason. Whatever the case, he sat in the car in silence until they reached his home. Theo drove the car to the front of his cousin's door and Fotis exited the car. They said good night to each other, Fotis thanked his cousin for treating him to dinner, opened the entrance to his house, and went inside. Theo continued his drive until he reached his parental house. He parked in front of it and entered. The first thing he had to do before he retired for the night was to call Anastasia as he promised before he left. They talked on the phone for a while, and he assured her that he would be with her soon. She in turn, told him that she missed him very much and that she was anxious to be with him as soon as possible. He did not forget to inquire about Katerina and their children. Hearing that they were doing fine, he said good night to her, and sat in one of the chairs to re-consider the events of the day. All the rumors he heard in the taverna were spinning around in his head like dry leaves and pieces of straw caught in a whirling wind. None of the theories he heard tonight offered a true picture of Nestor's identity. The only piece of solid information he had collected today was Nestor's statement that he made before Theo left his room. "If I am not with the living tomorrow, start your quest with the only ring I wear on one of my fingers," he said. Did that worn-out ring hold the truth he was after? Theo knew that Nestor was an honest man and his statement could not have been fictitious or a ploy to keep him at his bedside as long as possible. Nestor had no reason to do that. He was a loner all his life and having company for a long stretch of time, was not that important to him. Probably, he had inscribed the information Theo needed on the inside face of the ring. Theo was convinced that the key to Nestor's secret was inside that old ring. On second thought however, Theo deduced that the space inside the ring was not adequate to fit all the words needed to explain who Nestor really was. The old man will not make things easy, Theo said to himself. He probably will have just enough information on that ring to send me elsewhere, where he keeps the answer to his secrets, he muttered under his breath. Whatever it is, at least I have a starting point, he added, and kicked his shoes off his feet to shower and to get to bed.

Again, the sweet sleep did not come as he was expecting, after the shower. His mind was flying in all directions and the memory of the events of the day came and went like migratory birds. The house was quiet, and a breath of air wafted through the two open windows. All he could hear was the blood pounding in his ears.

Stretched on his bed motionless with his eyes closed, he tried to impose his will on his mind, as he had done so many times when he was a college student. He held his breath for a whole minute at a time to deprive his brain of needed oxygen and slow down his mental activity, thus forcing himself to fall asleep. He tried to take his mind out of thoughts that kept him awake and ventured to think about things of less importance, but this approach did not work either. No matter what technique he tried to use to slow down his mental activity and go to sleep, he stayed perfectly alert as if he had slept for ten uninterrupted hours.

Good and bad memories from the distant past kept coming and going through his mind. Like army troops in review, these recollections marched in front of him one behind the other. He felt as if he was a king standing on a platform reviewing his armies after the end of a long campaign. Good memories paraded like the victorious troops with their standards up high, while his bad memories dragged themselves, like a battered army with missing or torn standards on low posts.

He lay there with his eyes shut and mentally shifted through some of the events from his life in the village that had happy or pleasant ending. He tried to ignore those memories that had unpleasant consequences, but they kept coming back again and again. At one moment, he thought he heard the laughter of friends that he knew were dead years ago, and with his eyes still closed, he saw their silhouettes dancing in the empty room like ghosts. He felt the presence of his grand parents and parents and heard their voices greeting visitors. He saw pitchers filled with red wine standing on banquet tables, and he noticed plenty of carved, roast lamb piled on platters for some important occasion. It was true that such gatherings had taken place inside this room many times before. The events he saw in the dark room tonight were real; only the timing was not. They belonged in the past like everything else in the village.

The houses that buzzed with life during his childhood were either deserted or occupied by a single senior citizen now. Glass panels were missing from the windows of the school he knew as a boy, and to which he had generously contributed for its renovation after he came to America. There were no children in the village anymore, and the school was abandoned to bats that roosted on its ceiling during the day. There was no priest, either, to preside over a liturgy, for there were no people to be in attendance. Zacharias kept the taverna going, but he was an old man too. His customers were a few old people like Fotis, for example, who lingered around, waiting to die. They occasionally dropped in for a package of cigarettes, a cup of coffee, a glass of wine, and a friendly chitchat with Zacharias. They existed on money their children were sending them on a regular basis from far away lands where they had migrated to find better living.

The land had sunk into antiquity too. It was not cultivated any longer, and those olive trees that were located away from the immediate vicinity of the village were not pruned or maintained any more. Indigenous wild growth occupied the spaces between them, and the stone terraces that kept the soil in place were broken. The fertile soil was either washed away by the rain, or it was overgrown with parasitic vegetation that sapped nutrients away from the olive trees. Only a few hills around the village itself were attended by men who lived in nearby cities. These far-sighted, "good doers", planted additional olive trees on some of the slopes, repaired the stone terraces, and used small tractors to till and fertilize the soil around them. During the harvest season, homeless Albanians harvested the olives, pressed out the oil, and retained 50% of the product. The other 50% went to the owner of the olive trees.

Theo's odd experiences belonged in the past too. All the aberrations he saw, heard and felt in his dark bed room, were his recollections from the past. Nothing triggered thoughts regarding the present and certainly nothing, but nothing, could be connected with the future. He mentally kept company with people who were not living any more. He either had traveled back in the past to re-live some of the events that happened years ago, or his memory dug things out of its archives and brought them back to life. He couldn't tell which was what. He could only tell that the wine he was drinking had nothing to do with his insomnia. He only could tell for sure that he was in a desperate need to get some sleep. He was just tired and wanted to chase away the silly thoughts and oddities he was experiencing tonight. He wanted to go to sleep, but the depravation of sleep continued to annoy him. He knew that he had a long day tomorrow. He must have a clear mind when he meets with Nestor again.

Theo heard the church bell tolling twelve times and knew that it was midnight now. He dragged himself out of bed, stretched his arms and his legs to improve his circulation, poured a tall glass of cold water and with the glass in his hands, walked on the veranda outside his bedroom. He threw himself into one of the two wooden chairs, downed the water in one continuous gulp, and resting his head on the back of his chair, he stared at the sky above. The moon above looked as bright as ever, and the stars glittered like big diamonds in the cloudless, deep blue dome above his head.

A barn owl kept hooting on the big oak tree across the way, and bats zipped constantly around him. A gentle northerly breeze barely moved the leaves of the pear tree that grew in the yard in front of his veranda. During moments that the bats were away from his ears and the owl was taking its breath for his next hooting, a dead silence prevailed. It was so quiet at those moments, to the point that Theo could hear the thump-thump of his heart. He also took notice of the noise his eye lids made when he closed or opened his eyes. Above his head, the Pleiades, the cluster of the seven daughters of Atlas with the lonely nymph, were still pursued by Orion. The Big Dipper appeared much bigger and brighter against the cloudless azure sky. The North Star was distinctly obvious, standing still on the north quadrant of the dome above. Falling stars zipped across the dotted wonder above his head, and a countless number of stars decorated the celestial ceiling above his head, like sparkling diamonds.

Theo stared at the stellar marvel for a while and gradually realized that his mind became disengaged from the thoughts and fantasies that kept him awake. His vision started to wander aimlessly in the beauty of the universe, and his brain did not care to ask questions about the things his eyes were seeing. He appeared to be deeply engaged in contemplating the moon as it waded through the heavens and minutes later, he knew that he was ready to get off his chair and retire. His neck felt a little stiff from resting his head on the back of the chair. He returned to his bed, wrapped himself with his soft blanket, and fell asleep in an instant. No ghosts of dead people, or their voices, interrupted his peaceful slumber for the rest of the night.

The new day arrived, and the hot rays of the morning sun came into his room through the east window and woke him up. The sky of Peloponnesus was really filled with light, and the sun was beginning to bear down on the earth, getting hotter and hotter by the minute. Theo got out of bed, stretched his extremities, lightly rubbed his eyes with the knuckles of his index fingers, and readied himself for the drive to the mountaintop to visit Nestor again. He showered, shaved, brushed his teeth, dressed, drank his coffee, and ate two slices of toasted village bread. The sky was still blue and no clouds or fog distracted the beauty of the surroundings. Apollo had chased away all the stars and the moon, and regained his domain once again. He reigned supreme one more time in his silver chariot above the eastern horizon, while a cool breeze swept across the land and forced the fruit laden branches of olive trees to sway back-and-forth in harmony with the waves of the gentle wind.

"Good morning Mr. Theovule," Zacharias greeted Theo from the street below. "I see, you are an early bird," he continued without giving Theo the chance to reciprocate the wish for a good morning.

"Good morning Mr. Zacharias. How are you this beautiful morning?" Theo managed to say, before the other man fired another question, just at the instance he was re-positioning his hat over his partially hairless head.

"Is there anything I can do for you to make your stay in our village a little more comfortable? I am in my caffenio all the time, and I would be delighted to offer whatever I can to make your stay more pleasant."

Theo felt good hearing that besides his cousin Fotis, there was another man in the village willing to assist him. With a thankful tone in his voice, he assured Zacharias that he would knock at his door if the need for help arose.

"I will stop at your caffenio soon to have a glass of wine with you," Theo said, and with that comment, the two men went on attending their own affairs. Zacharias said good day to Theo and led his stray donkey back toward its confinement. Theo, likewise, reciprocated the wish for a good day and entered his rented Fiat to visit Nestor.

Before he reached the point where he had to start climbing the slope of the mountain, Theo stopped to take a look at his father's best, olive tree plantation. He remembered his father telling him that there were 106 trees on this slope, and father proudly said that this prize property was his personal creation. He felt good saying that he had cleared this slope with his own hands and had planted and grafted all these trees without help. He could tell from what remote, rocky cranny his dad uprooted each one of them and had transferred, transplanted, and grafted each one of them.

As Theo remembered it, the soil was always meticulously tilled. Each tree was expertly pruned and fertilized, with the manure his father collected from the den, where he kept the goats in the winter. He even had a dozen beehives at the far end of the property, from which he collected the honey for mother to make sweets, and to sweeten the *tsucalocafto,* (a potion of hot wine with cloves, cinnamon, and honey) to treat cold congestion in the winter.

What he saw now was nothing like the plantation he remembered. The land was a continuous field of burdock dotted with tall thistle that touched the lower branches of the olive trees. The trees had not been pruned for years, and the beehives were gone. Most of the topsoil was washed away by the rain, and the well that his father dug to irrigate the garden was filled with soil that drifted downward from the slope above it. The only things that thrived and grew bigger on each side of the well were two fig trees. These were the two fig trees that Theo planted when he was a grammar school boy. Both of them had grown so big that they had shaded the entire garden area. Big black figs were hanging from their branches, and blue Jays came and went to gorge on them. Theo, risking potential stinging from the thistle that stood in his way, walked to the fig trees, and collected enough ripened figs to fill the cavity of the baseball hat he wore.

This site was a special place, not for Theo's father only. It held a special memory for Theo, but not for the same reason that was so important to his father. No, the fig trees he planted were not the reason either. The figs, almost as big as billiard balls, looked like the "figs" she was hiding under her thin blouse. It was here that Theo met that shepherd girl, from the other side of the valley, and it was here that he and her experienced a new kind of human relation for the first time. An unending need to see and be close to each other ensued, until she went to South Africa to become the wife of someone else. Theo moved out of the village to pursue his own destiny. The pleasant memory rendered Theo's mind melancholic. With his hat filled with ripened figs, he walked to his Fiat and sat there for a few minutes. Captivated by old memories, he peeled two of the figs, drew in his mouth the honey-sweet contents and gulped it down with contentment. After a few minutes of contemplation, he placed his cap with the rest of the figs in the passenger's seat and drove away to visit Nestor. This site held potent memories of his youth that did not last as long as he wished. This spot together with the memories it held, belonged in Theo's past too, like everything else in the village.

The steep incline to the summit was not that strenuous today, for Theo was familiar with the turns and the potential hazards ahead. The Fiat moved swiftly as if it had a mind of its own and as if it knew where it was going. In no time, Theo reached the parking area by the mansion, parked the car there, turned the engine off, and walked the rest of the way to the outside gate. He found it wide open and entered the garden area. Ahead of him, he saw Magdalene running toward him on the cobblestone path that connected the outside gate with the main entrance of the mansion. She appeared to be very disturbed, and Theo thought the worst took place the night before. When she came closer, she articulated,

"Come quickly, Mr. Theovule. Something very terrible will happen today," she pronounced in her stuttering voice and grabbing Theo's hand, she led him into the kitchen as if he were a little boy.

"Look, the Easter flame I kept alive above the icon stand is gone. That means that St. Elias refuses my request to make Mr. Nestor well again." Pointing at the extinguished flame with her finger, she sobbed and wailed in a tone of voice that made Theo feel sorry and ludicrous at the same time. He placed the figs on the kitchen table and tried to quiet down the wailing woman.

"Calm down Magdalene, calm down and compose yourself," he said. He looked away from her to conceal the sorrow he felt for her believing in sainthood and miracles. He didn't want to tell her that the flame she kept alive all this time could not reverse Nestor's deteriorating health. Instead, he allowed her to vent her sorrow for a few seconds, and when she was in a condition to speak and listen, Theo asked her.

"How is Mr. Nestor today? Did you go upstairs to see him?"

"Oh, he looks the same to me! I made his favorite breakfast and put it on his night table as he instructed me. Seconds later, he told me to leave him alone," she said still sobbing a little. She composed herself, wiped her tears and her runny nose with the same handkerchief she pulled out of her apron pocket, re-arranged the black kerchief she always wore on her head to indicate that she was a widow, and asked

Theo if he wished to have a cup of coffee before visiting the ill man in his bedroom.

"Do you mind bringing my coffee to his room? I will go upstairs and keep him company." Without saying anything else to her, he climbed the spiral staircase and un-announced, walked into the dying man's bedroom. Theo greeted Nestor good morning and without any hesitation, he sat in one of the two chairs next to Nestor's bed.

Nestor opened his eyes and in a barely discernable voice expressed his pleasure in seeing Theo back by his bedside. Nestor's breakfast was still standing untouched on the table, just the way Magdalene had placed it there earlier.

The sick man looked worse today. The color of his skin had changed from pale white to faint purple. His eyes were sunk deeper in the sockets of that voluminous skull, and his lips looked dehydrated. The entire head seemed draped over with a thin layer of skin and his cheeks, covered with a hefty growth of beard, pulsated in-and-out like bellows, as he was breathing. His hands appeared bonier than yesterday and felt cold when Theo touched them, to express his warm friendship toward the man he respected and admired all his life.

"How are you feeling today?" Theo articulated to initiate a conversation.

"I feel that I have reached the end of the road, friend," Nestor managed to say in a gurgling voice and continued. "Soon, I will not be with the living, and that saddens me, Theo! It saddens me because I did not have enough time to learn all I want to learn about life, myself, and about the world around us. It also saddens me because I did not have enough time to do all the things I wanted to do, friend! I have only scratched the surface of knowledge," he added, and continued. "Like all mortals, I made mistakes in my life and caused suffering to myself and to others. I wish I could live this life one more time to find those I hurt with my deeds, apologize to them, and ask for their forgiveness. Unfortunately, I will take these desires with me to where I am going shortly." He paused for a few seconds, and as if an angel came down from heaven, became invigorated and continued his monologue in a clearer voice.

"Theo. Do you remember the time we discussed Plato's idea concerning the duality of things? I remember that you disagreed with Plato's statement that the 'object' and the 'form' are two different things of the same being. What is your opinion on this subject today?" he said, and he paused to hear Theo's comment.

"Funny, you brought this subject up, Mr. Nestor," Theo said. "I was reading a book on cosmology in the airplane yesterday and a passage in this book prompted me to ask you the question you just asked me just now. I still don't have an answer to it; I only have an explanation of why I am incapable of answering the question. I believe that human beings haven't advanced to the point that they can fully understand the wonder around them. I confess that I am one of those imperfect beings, I guess."

"Your reply is too simple to answer my question satisfactorily," Nestor managed to say with a great effort. "We should not attempt to understand the issue of 'duality' in terms of human experience. We must elevate our thinking above our experience, but that's where the problem is. Man cannot understand things that are beyond his experience! It is like we expect a blind man from his birth to understand what the red color looks like. Look deeper into this limitation of our knowledge. We know some of the things we can do with electricity and magnetism for instance, but we know little of what those things are in the strict scientific sense. We call electricity 'energy' and magnetism 'force', but we have constructed theories only to understand their true nature."

At this point, Nestor stopped talking, took several deep breaths and without success attempted to clear his throat. Instead, he clenched his fists and stared toward the ceiling as if in pain.

Magdalene appeared at the door with Theo's steaming coffee on a tray. Theo signaled her with his hand to enter the sick man's room without asking permission to do so. She tip-toed toward them and placed the cup on the night table next to Theo. The sick man opened his eyes, took a look at her, closed them again, and said,

"You can take my breakfast back to the kitchen, dear. I am not hungry today."

In her stuttering voice, she managed to ask the sick man if he needed anything else, and when she saw him shaking his head back-and-forth twice, she understood what he meant with this gesture. She picked up the tray with his breakfast, and slowly, she disappeared in the corridor with an audible sobbing mixed with a faint whining.

The sick man, exhausted from talking, kept his eyes closed. He relaxed the clenching of his fists, reached over to where Theo was sitting, touched his left hand, and attempted to say something. Theo felt the cold hand of his friend, but he said nothing, for a chill ran from his feet to his head. Instead, he picked up his cup, took a noisy sip and wondered if it would be wiser to leave Nestor alone for a while. During his deliberation to stay or to leave, he kept looking at his most dear friend and wondered how much longer he would stay alive. He felt that he accomplished nothing sitting there, looking at the dead body of his living friend. On the other hand, his common sense told him that it would not be wise to stimulate another conversation or to walk out of the room and leave him alone.

Minutes later, he finished his coffee and decided to get up and look out of the window to change the depressing scene. He slowly lifted himself off his chair, and before he had taken two steps toward the window, he heard the wheezy voice of his friend calling him back.

"Theo, don't leave me alone now. I breathe my last breaths. Stay with me and hold my hand. I want to die in the attendance of the man I trusted and whose opinion I respected," he muttered.

Theo, shocked by what he heard, returned quickly to his chair, grasped the cold hands of the sick man and said to him with definite emotion in his voice,

"I am here friend! Stay calm and get some rest. Everything will be fine."

A faint smile blossomed on the dying man's lips, and Theo heard him saying in a voice that sounded as if it came from another world.

"Everything will be fi…ne."

Theo heard steps in the corridor, and before he knew it, Dr. Gliadis entered the room. He took a look at the sick man, shook his head up-and-down and asked him how he was feeling today. At the same time, he turned his face toward Theo who stood by his chair, nodded his head and waved the palm of his hand to acknowledge that he had noticed him too. He lifted part of the blanket that covered the chest of the sick man and listened to his heart with his stethoscope. The ill man had not said a word yet and kept his eyes closed, probably to avoid reading the doctor's facial expression. He most likely had predicted the doctor's diagnosis for his future, and he did not wish to hear his voice delivering the bad news about his deteriorating condition. Dr. Gliadis placed another time release patch on Nestor's chest and motioned Theo to follow him into the corridor. There, the doctor stopped and explained the future of the sick man, as if Nestor was Theo's father.

"Nestor will be gone by the end of the day. His liver, his kidneys, and his pancreas are shutting down. Make all necessary arrangements for his burial. I will see that you will have a death certificate as soon as you call me and let me know that he is gone. You should know that you cannot inter a person without a death certificate issued by a licensed doctor." Before Theo had the time to respond, the doctor added,

"Is there anything else I can do for you Mr. ….Theo," he said and paused for a second to receive the reply from his listener.

"Thank you doctor," Theo said, "Thank you. I will manage the rest. Oh, by the way, how are you compensated for your services?"

"Do not let this issue bother your mind. Your friend took care if it," Dr. Gliadis said, and he hurried down the stairs to his car. The weather looked unsettled and he wanted to return to his office before a summer storm breaks out and makes the driving difficult.

Theo returned to his friend's bed and stood speechless and motionless over Nestor's head, looking at his face for a long time. Finally, he sat in the chair, and being unable to do anything else for his dying friend, he took Nestor's cold hand in his. He wanted to provide assurance that he was by his friend's bedside. His breathing was irregular now, and an occasional twitching of his lips disturbed the tranquility in his face. Theo interpreted the involuntary distortion of the lips as a desperate effort the dying man was making to say something, but the words he tried to articulate were locked deep inside his chest. Theo bent over him and bringing his ear as close as possible to Nestor's mouth, he softly asked the dying man if he wanted to say something.

"Look for the north star," Theo heard Nestor saying distinctly, and he felt the grip of the cold hand relaxing. A convulsive and jerking movement shook his body, and a guttural and groaning sound escaped his mouth mixed with his breath. That was the last manifestation of Nestor's life. The hermit became motionless, stopped breathing, and fell silent for ever.

Theo had seen dead and dying people before in his life, but Nestor's death shook his being from its foundations. This man had played an important role in Theo's life. He was spellbound to him for life. Nestor meant to Theo more than his father! He was a guide and a teacher during his volatile years of adolescence. He felt free and comfortable talking to Nestor about all kinds of things and was completely satisfied with the explanations and answers he received. "The lonely man on the mountain", as he used to call Nestor, answered all his questions. He never told Theo that it was improper to talk about a subject of morality or about subjects that questioned God's wisdom, as his father used to say, to avoid talking about sensitive issues regarding religion and sexuality, for example.

Theo's wise teacher and mentor lay motionless on his bed in front of him now, and he had to take the initiative to see that he was interred with dignity and respect. He tore two strips of linen from the dead man's pillowcase, and with one of them, he tied the dead man's chin against his upper jaw to keep his mouth closed until the body became stiff. With the other strip he tied his hands together over his chest. At last, he straightened the legs of the motionless body and straitened up his wrinkled pajamas. He, then, gently removed the dead man's ring from the bonny finger, and put it in his pocket. While re-arranging the dead man's hands over his chest, he noticed that Nestor wore a leather charm around his neck, and he thought that the charm might contain something connected to his past. He carefully removed the object from around Nestor's neck and secured it in the same pocket with the ring. Finally, he covered the corpse from head to toe with the blanket and hurried down the stairs to talk to Magdalene. On his way to the kitchen, he stopped at the top of the staircase, pulled out his cell phone, and phoned Dr. Gliadis to tell him that the hermit was dead. The doctor said that he would try to be there in person, in the morning, and hand Theo the death certificate he needed to bury his friend.

"If something urgent happens and I cannot come, I will have it in your hands as soon as possible by special messenger," the doctor said, and expressed his sadness for the demise of their mutual friend. Theo returned the phone to its holder and walked into the kitchen to bring the unpleasant news to Magdalene.

Magdalene was seated in one of the chairs in her kitchen and was sobbing uncontrollably. Her head was resting on her knees and the palms of her hands were resting over her head when Theo entered. As soon as he walked into the room, she got off her chair, wiped her eyes with the palm of her hands and in her stuttering voice, she asked. "How is Mr. Nestor? Is he ok?"

Theo shook his head back-and-forth, and she understood the meaning of his motion. She broke into a constant wailing that reverberated throughout the mansion and started to hit her head with her hands. Theo reached over, took her hands in his like a father would do to comfort his unhappy child, and with a compassionate voice, he tried to calm her down and explain that Nestor's death was inevitable. Finally, he asked the question he had in mind to ask her.

"Magdalene, your cries and tears will not bring him back to us. He is gone, and he is gone for ever. Try to understand that. He is with the angels above. You and I have things to do now, and I need your help and cooperation. Tell me, did he mention anything about his burial?"

Magdalene thought for a second, took a few deep breaths, blew her nose into a handkerchief that she took out of her apron's pocket, and responded in a voice that was constantly being interrupted by her sobbing and the sniffing of her nose. "His clothes and his casket are in the other bedroom upstairs. He also has some envelopes under his mattress with people's names on them. He told me to give them to the people he indicated on the envelopes, after he dies," she added. She burst again in a continuing wailing, which was interrupted by periodic sniffing of her nose and by hitting her head with the palms of her hands. Theo took her in his arms with fatherly compassion and allowed her to vent her sorrow for a minute. When her sobbing subsided, he continued,

"Splendid. Now that you feel better, let's go upstairs and see what is available and what other things we need for tomorrow. There is so much to be done and we are running out of time."

Theo, leading the way with Magdalene behind him, climbed the staircase and entered the bedroom next to the one in which the remains of Nestor were located. In front of them, a walnut coffin stood open. A new black suit, a white shirt, a black tie, and a pair of black shoes were meticulously placed inside the empty casket. Theo took a quick look at the articles, and taking Magdalene by the hand, they walked in the other room where the dead man lay on his bed, under his blanket.

"Magdalene, be courageous and control your emotions," he said to her. "All you have to do is, slip your hands under his back and retrieve the envelopes. You don't have to look at him. Do you understand me?"

"I understand," she muttered and both approached the bed where Nestor was laying under the blanket. She closed her eyes, slipped her hand under the upper part of the dead man's body, and came up with three brown envelopes. With her eyes still closed, she extended her trembling hand with the envelopes toward Theo, and another burst of sobbing escaped her lips. Theo took the envelopes in one hand, and assisting her with the other, they both walked out of the room. On their way out, he glanced quickly at the three envelopes and led Magdalene down the spiral case into the kitchen. There, he sat on a chair by the table and took his time to examine the sealed envelopes. One of them had Magdalene's name on it. The second envelope was addressed to the philosophy department of a university in Thessaloniki, and the last one was addressed "to whoever will bury me." Both Theo and Magdalene sat speechless, at the kitchen table for a few minutes, alternating glances at the envelopes and at each other. At long last, Theo handed Magdalene the envelope that had her name written on its front panel and said to her,

"Magdalene, this is for you. It looks like it has money in it, a lot of money. I advise you to take it to your bank or to some person you absolutely trust and ask them to invest it in something that will bring you monthly income. I'll be glad to help you, if you trust my sincerity."

Magdalene did not answer. She stuffed the envelope in her bosom and went over to the stove to make fresh coffee. Theo placed the other two envelopes in his pocket and mentally made plans for the burial of his friend. He only needed four men to dig the grave and carry the coffin from the second floor to the grounds of his interment. Nestor never believed in organized religion with its formalities, therefore, calling a priest was not necessary. "Priests are sinners like the rest of us. They do not have any special relation with God, to negotiate with Him our fate after death," Nestor used to say.

Theo took time to sip his coffee and suggested to Magdalene that she was free to go home now. He even offered to drive her home. On his way he would find laborers or volunteers for tomorrow's digging. Magdalene thought for a while and decided to take Theo's offer. She also offered to call on people in her village who may be willing to do the digging.

On their way out of the mansion, they locked both the entrance and the outside gate, and Magdalene handed the keys over to Theo, with a sad expression on her face. She probably resented relinquishing the privilege of being the key holder for the place, but in this instance, she felt that she had no other choice but to hand the keys over to Theo.

The ride down the slope of the mountain and toward Magdalene's village was easy and effortless. She sat in her seat as if she was petrified and said nothing. Theo kept his mind occupied with thoughts associated with the things he had to do tomorrow and during the days that will follow the burial. Unconsciously, one of his hands kept returning to the pocket where he kept the ring, the charm, and the two envelopes, while the other hand was clenched on the steering wheel.

Inserting his hand in the pocket with mysterious contents, Theo felt the shape of the ring, but the contents of the leather charm were not discernable. One of the envelopes definitely contained money, but the other, the one that was addressed to the university, seemed to contain only a few sheets of paper, nothing else.

Magdalene directed Theo through the narrow streets of her village, and when they arrived in front of her house, she turned to Theo and offered him a bed for the night. Theo politely declined the offer. Instead, he drove to the caffenio of the village where people gathered in the evening. He parked the car in front of the establishment and walked into the place looking for the owner, or for someone who could help him find workers to dig the grave. He introduced himself to an elderly man who greeted him at the door and sat in one of the empty chairs.

"I stopped here to have a glass of wine and ask you to help me," he said to the aged store keeper. "The hermit who lived up there died today, and I need people to help me bury him tomorrow."

"Don't say! Is the hermit dead?" the keeper exclaimed. "Are you his son, or one of his relatives?"

"No," Theo retorted I am only one of his friends. "My name is Theovulos, Theo for short."

"It seems that nobody around here knew anything about him," the tavern keeper commented and continued. "He was a mystery man all the years he lived up there. People who knew him had the best things to say about him. They said that he was a wise man and had an impeccable character. Personally, I never met the man and I know nothing about him."

"I know nothing about him too," Theo said, "but I am here not to explore his aloofness and his secretive past. I am looking for four or five men to help me bury him tomorrow. Do you know anyone who will be willing to come up there tomorrow morning to dig the grave and to lower the coffin into the ground?"

"Of course I do," the caffenio keeper said. "I'll get you the four Albanians who live here in our village. They offer their labor to whoever needs their help and for a reasonable price, mind you! I am sure they will do the job for a small fee, probably for five hundred Euros," he added, and fixed his gaze on Theo's face to judge his reaction to the price.

"That's fine," Theo said, and he asked him for a glass of wine to wash down the dryness he felt in his mouth. The caffenio keeper brought the wine to the table and said that the first one is always on him. He, then called his grandson and ordered the lad to go and fetch the Albanians, who had their tent on an abandoned patch of land across from the village's cemetery. Before the young man left to do his errands, Theo interrupted the grandfather and asked the young lad to stop by Magdalene's house, after he had secured the commitment from the Albanians, and tell her not to look for laborers. Now that Theo had solved the most pressing problem of finding help for tomorrow, he relaxed his mind and felt as if a heavy burden was removed from his back. Holding his glass in his right hand, he raised it up high above his head and delivered the customary salute to the store keeper.

"To your health, friend," he said, and he brought the red liquid to his mouth. The store keeper did likewise and before they knew it, each one of them had downed three glasses talking about each other's family. After a while, the grandson escorted by the senior of the four Albanians entered the room and introduced his companion to Theo.

"Is five hundred ok with you?" Theo asked the Albanian.

"No sir. Make it six hundred. I have a wife and six small children back home, and they need food and clothes for the winter," he said with a pleading tone in his voice.

Theo tried to figure out whether the man was sincere in his statement, or he was a good actor. The begging expression on the Albanian's eyes prevailed over Theo's suspicion about the honesty of the other man, and a deep emotion of sympathy for the Albanian surfaced in Theo's inner self.

Theo knew all about hunger and poverty and understood the other man's concern for the well being of his family.

"Ok, I will give you the six hundred to dig the grave two meters deep, lower the casket in it, cover it with soil, and place a line of rocks around it," Theo said.

"My three brothers and I will be there early tomorrow morning and we will do what you said. We will also help you with whatever else you need to make the deceased man's trip to eternity as pleasant as possible, God bless his soul," the Albanian said. At last, he picked up a glass of wine that the keeper had placed in front of him, and sent it down with one gulp. "God bless his soul and let his memory be eternal," he said. He gave a great audible out-breath of "A-a-ah" and smacked his lips. Before he left, he re-assured Theo that he and his three brothers would be at the mansion early the following morning. Theo felt that there was no need to hang around this place any longer, for he had accomplished his objective. Besides, he had enough excitement all day, today. His mind was spinning like the windmill visible on top of a hill across the valley. He paid the bill for the wine, thanked the keeper for his help, entered the Fiat again, and started to drive toward his village. On his way out, he stopped at Magdalene's home and told her not to worry about finding help for the digging. Finally, he continued on toward his own village, having the intention of briefly stopping at his cousin's home and going to sleep early tonight.

It was getting dark now and the road to his village was unlit. I must go to bed before ten and wake up early to be at the summit before the sun is up, he said to himself. I will have a very busy day and I need all the rest I can get. But, when he reached the intersection that led to the summit, he thought that it would be best if he slept at the mansion tonight. It would be best if he was there when the grave diggers arrived, for he realized that the gate was locked up.

Besides, he had to select the spot where the grave would be dug. He decided there and then to go back to the mansion instead of driving to his village. He took the road to the summit again and in no time, he found himself in front of the mansion. He parked the car in front of the gate, opened it with the keys Magdalene had given him earlier, entered the garden area, and locked the gate behind him. The mansion in front of him was not lit tonight, and it appeared ghostly in front of the line of the cypress trees that lined the other side of the property. The blue and twinkling sky in the distance was unobstructed by any man-made lighting, thus it looked brighter tonight. He approached the massive front door with the double-headed falcon, door knocker, unlocked it, turned on the entrance light, and locked the door again behind him. He had not eaten anything yet, and the wine he had at Magdalene's village was raising havoc in his empty stomach. His head was aching and he realized that he must eat something. He found home-made bread, cured olives, goat cheese, and Greek salami in the refrigerator and satisfied his hunger with a fat sandwich. He also helped himself to the fresh figs he brought earlier and to some of the pears that Magdalene had collected earlier from Nestor's trees. Finally, he quenched his thirst with a glass of cold water. He ignored the tray of other fresh fruit that were piled in a wreath basket resting on the kitchen counter. He was not sleepy yet, and he decided to go upstairs and take one more look at the corpse of his mentor. He also wanted to re-examine the clothes and the shoes that Nestor would wear in the morning. He entered the dead man's room with a strange feeling of sadness, not with fear of facing a dead man alone, in this remote place. He pulled away the portion of the blanket that covered Nestor's face and took a close look at his facial expression, as if he was expecting Nestor to say something. The dead man looked peaceful with his eyes and mouth closed. Nothing had changed since Theo wrapped the linen cloth around his lower jaw. He covered the face again and walked over to the other room where the casket and the clothes were located. He took another close look at the articles and found them suitable for tomorrow's events. Finally, he walked to the bedroom that was directly opposite and entered. Instead of going to bed, he opened the door that led to the veranda and took his place in a chair, facing the garden and the gate below. He turned the light on and thought that this was the perfect moment to examine the things he kept in his pocket. He wanted to know what was in the envelope that was awarded to the person who will burry the deceased hermit, was hopeful to discern any writing engraved on the inside face of the ring, and finally, he was dying to find out what was inside the leather charm he removed from Nestor's neck earlier.

He, first, tore open the brown envelope and found a stack of Euros with a note written in Nestor's own handwriting. "*I hope this money is enough for my burial,*" the note said. Theo did not bother counting the money at this time, but for the feel of the money he was holding in his hands, he estimated that he had more than enough to pay the laborers and to install a marble marker on Nestor's grave.

He returned the money to his pocket and took out the ring. He brought it close to the light and read a professionally engraved inscription on the inside surface of the golden object. *"Start your quest at the north star window,"* the inscription read. Nothing else was written on it, and nothing else was interesting about the ring. It was not a graduation ring or a wedding band. It was just an ordinary, worn out, gold ring. Was it a memorabilia given to him by a special person in his life? Theo could not say.

He returned the ring to his pocket and took out the leather charm that looked more like a talisman or an amulet than a charm. He drew the tiny zipper toward the opposite direction, and the small pouch revealed its contents. Inside it, there was a small key and a piece of paper that appeared to be blank on both sides. When he unfolded the paper and took a closer look at it against the light, he could see that something was written on it. It looked, though, that the ink had faded away and caused the writing to be indecipherable. He could only make out the letter *"I"* on the far left of the paper, which meant that the writing started with the capital letter "I". Theo placed the paper back in the little pouch, zipped it closed again and returned it to his pocket. He kept the key in his hands to examine it for a while longer. It was a small, flat, common key like keys we use to open our house door. It, definitely, did not look like keys belonging to a P.O. box, or a key to open a safe deposit box in a bank; there were no numbers stamped on it.

All the things that happened today were too much for Theo. He was mentally and physically exhausted; he did not have the energy to do anything else tonight. He did not even care to think about the meaning of "the north star window," the illegibility of the writing on the seemingly plain paper, or the lock that could be opened by the key he still held in his hands. Frankly, he had second thoughts of sleeping alone in this place tonight. There were too many memories attached to these rooms and to the motionless inhabitant of the place. He never forgot the things he learned from the man who lay dead across the hall. Nestor could not talk anymore, but he still commanded Theo's attention, his respect and his admiration. For the time being, Theo did not care to know who Nestor was and what he had done in his past. He only valued the things he learned from him.

When still in high school, Theo asked Nestor to explain the true meaning of Genesis. Nestor, with his calm voice and his broad smile said, "Evolution and natural selection explain everything, my dear young man! Darwin postulated that a gradual change of things brought life to its present form. Besides, recent scientific excavations conducted by paleontologists in several parts of the world verify Darwin's theory." Theo remembers Nestor halting briefly in his explanation. Finally, he added,

"My son, it will take us several sessions like this one to fully answer your question. You said earlier that you have your final examinations starting tomorrow and obviously, you cannot keep coming up here on a regular schedule to hear the explanation in its entirety. Let me then give you a brief synopsis of how the world was created and how life evolved on earth. Remember, though, my explanation will be simple and as you know, one runs the risk of being misunderstood in trying to simplify complicated issues.

"In some distant past, billion of years ago, the vast space we see around us was 'empty'. It was void of the things we see or detect with our sophisticated instruments. There was no light anywhere and no matter or any other form of energy as we know it. Science agrees with Genesis up to this point. Theocracy and science disagree about the creation from this point on. Contrary to the explanation that Genesis offers about creation, science says that 'everything that is' was packed into a tiny 'dot'. This dot of everything was of infinite density and infinite smallness.

"At some point in time, the contents in the dot became so hot that they converted into several forms of energy. Finally, our dot of everything reached a critical temperature and exploded to cause 'The Big Bang', as the astronomers call this event. This explosion of unthinkable magnitude filled the universe with several forms of energy. At this point in time, the sky was hellish-hot and everything existed only in several forms of energy. The instant the explosion took place is also the beginning of time, for time has no meaning before the explosion. As time passed, some energy escaped in the vastness of the universe as heat and the sky began to cool down. Finally, a little bit of the remaining energy condensed and began to form sub-atomic particles and eventually matter. Some of this matter agglomerated together and formed the nucleus of our celestial bodies. Gradually, the newly formed nucleus attracted more matter that kept forming from the rest of the energy that floated everywhere. Huge masses of matter swirled around centers of gravity and either condensed to form bigger bodies of matter or exploded and became material for stars that were in the process of being born. Eventually this upheaval settled down and became the harmony you see when you look up into the celestial dome."

"Mr. Nestor," interrupted Theo. "Your explanation sounds wonderful to me. However, it contradicts everything I was taught in both my grammar school and my high school."

"My dear young fellow," Nestor added, "Your ancestors believed that there were a bunch of gods living on top of Olympus; they spent untold sums of wealth and a great deal of energy to please them. Are we to continue making the same mistake believing that some higher power was there before cosmogony, and that God snapped his fingers six times to create the wonder of everything? If that's the case, tell me Theo, what God was doing before that, since there was nothing there, according to Genesis? How can we explain the undisputed facts that our galaxies keep drifting apart from each other, and that living things mutate, to survive in an environment that changes continuously? What are we to say to science that has proved that man has evolved from an ape-like creature? Genesis says that God created man 'in His own image'. Does God look like an ape?

"Since our conversation brought us to the subject of evolution that I mentioned earlier, let us investigate it a bit further," Nestor said, with a degree of satisfaction in his voice.

"From the instant the Big Bang took place up to this very moment, things evolve from one form to another. Energy changes into matter and matter forms celestial bodies. Some of these celestial bodies convert to energy continuously, and they adopt the prevailing conditions in which they happen to be at a given time. For example, stars burn up their nuclear fuel and implode; ultimately, they explode and scatter their remaining matter and energy into their surroundings. These remains are then absorbed by other nuclei and become part of other stars again. Our earth was formed that way. A ball of hot metal mix settled around our sun and attracted interstellar matter which formed the outside cover of its hot core. With the passage of time, the outside shell cooled down and the water settled in the lower valleys to form the seas and the oceans. At the earthly biological level, one can observe the evolutionary pattern more clearly than cosmic evolution. Some matter and energy combined together and formed myriads of life forms. Those forms of life that did not fit in the prevailing conditions at the time became extinct, and only those that happen to fit into their environment survived and propagated. Still, as conditions changed, some of the survivors mutated and adapted to the new environment while others failed to do so and became extinct.

This process goes on today. Just a few million years ago, the dinosaurs failed to adapt to their new environment and became extinct. The little shrew, from which we descended, adapted to the new conditions, changed its shape and became a primate, then changed again to become a primitive man and finally, evolved to a modern man like you and me. Many other life forms did not mutate to adapt to the prevailing conditions and became extinct. We see their remains on certain rock formations. Only the fittest survived and continued to propagate its specie. The fittest became fit simply because it mutated and adapted to the new environment. The body of an Eskimo for example, mutated to survive in extreme temperatures. He lived on a diet of seal blubber. On the other extreme, the body of the African man mutated to produce melanin, to withstand the harmful effect of the ultraviolet rays of the sun.

Adaptation can also be seen in the world of insects and microbes. Insects mutate constantly, to tolerate insecticides; microbes mutate and become immune to antibiotics. In short, things did not happen the way Genesis describes the events. They happened gradually and evolved into the things we see today, my boy."

Lessons like this overwhelmed Theo and fortified his admiration for Nestor's wisdom and knowledge of things. He remembers returning to his high school feeling gratified, obtaining true knowledge of the world's creation. He could no longer accept anymore the teachings that the universe was created the way the Old Testament describes it. What other false beliefs did he have that needed to be clarified, he wondered, as he was walking back to school from the summit?

When the session ended, Theo took the path back to his school with the feeling that he possessed a unique and truer knowledge about the world around him. He had a kind of knowledge that was not in his books, and no other student in the entire school was privileged to have this information.

Well, those were the wonderful days of youth, Theo said to himself, and he rose from his chair to go to bed. Yes, that was the time when my mind was thirsty for knowledge and sucked it up like a dry sponge sucks water, he muttered under his breath.

He took the cell phone out of his pocket and called Anastasia to tell her that he was fine and to give her the news that Nestor was dead. He did not overlook asking her about her aunt Katerina, about their children, and before they said good night, they both expressed their burning desire to be together. "I love you dearly," he said to her, and she responded with the same passion. They finally turned their phones off. He took off his shoes, undressed, and went to bed. It was morning in Chicago, and Anastasia went to see Aunt Katerina for breakfast, as she had promised her the night before.

From the corner of his eyes, Theo caught sight of a light on the road approaching the mansion from the distance, and as the light source came closer, he determined that the roaring sound was coming from a motorcycle that was speeding toward the gate of the mansion.

I wonder who would be this maniac who dares to come up here at this hour, Theo said to himself, and he went downstairs to meet the late visitor. The motorcycle stopped on the other side of the gate, and Theo saw that the driver was Zacharias, the coffee shop keeper. His passenger was no one else but his cousin Fotis.

"Thank the Lord, you are ok," Fotis exclaimed as he dismounted the motorcycle and approached the gate that was lit by the head light of the noisy motorcycle. "I thought something terrible happened to you. I expected to see you back in the village tonight, and I became concerned for your safety when I did not see you back," he said to Theo. "What's happening? What is going on?"

"The inevitable happened," Theo said, as he turned the key to unlock the gate. "The hermit is dead. He expired this afternoon, and I became involved with arrangements for his burial. I am sorry I caused all this trouble, Fotis! I'll stay here tonight. You are welcome to keep me company."

"I think I will do just that," Fotis replied without thinking through his spontaneous response to Theo's statement. "I hate to see you being alone up here all night."

"Do you think I'll be of any help if I join you too?" Zacharias asked the two cousins.

"You are welcome to stay Zacharias," Theo said. "However, you will waste your time staying with us. There is nothing to be done until tomorrow."

"In that case, I'll be heading back home. I'll see you tomorrow," Zacharias said. Mounting his motorcycle again, he said good night to the two cousins standing by the gate, and he disappeared into the darkness of the night. Then, Theo and Fotis closed the gate and went inside the mansion in complete silence. They stopped by the kitchen, and Theo located an unopened bottle with ouzo. He opened it and poured some of its contents into two glasses, handing one to Fotis and keeping the other. Theo raised his glass eye-high and said in a solemn voice. "May the Lord forgive his sins and place him with the legions of His angels where he belongs," and he brought the rim of his glass to his lips. Fotis acknowledged Theo's exclamation with an "amen", and he took a sip from his glass too. The two cousins sat there for a while longer, and Theo briefed Fotis on the events of the day sipping on a second glass of ouzo.

"Did he mention anything about his real reason for wanting to see you?" Fotis said.

"He wanted to reveal his true identity to me, but he ran out of time. He only gave me a few hints that might help us answer the question you are asking," Theo replied. "We should go to bed, pal! I see your eyes flickering like an oil lamp running out of fuel. We need rest. Let's pick this subject up after we fulfill our obligation to the dead man and bury him in a dignified manner," Theo continued, and padding Fotis on the shoulder with the palm of his hand, they broke the conversation, and they went to bed. Theo slept in the bedroom that contained the empty casket and Fotis slept in the room next to it.

Chapter Five:
"Last Clues"

Before the sun was up, a loud pounding on the gate woke Theo up. He looked out of his window and saw the four Albanians standing by the gate holding picks and shovels in their hands. He quickly put on his clothes, walked to the gate, opened it, greeted the four men good morning, and let them in. Leading the way with the four men behind him, Theo walked to the burial grounds, where the monks had been buried in the past, and selected a flat spot in the center. "Dig the grave here," he ordered the four men and stood there for a moment to be sure that they understood his instructions. The oldest of the four men ordered the other three, in their native language, to start digging and turning to Theo, he said in Greek,

"I was a mortician back home, and I am willing to clean and dress Nestor's remains for his trip to 'eternity.'" Theo welcomed the suggestion and accepted the man's kind offer unquestionably. The senior Albanian turned to his three brothers and gave them specific instructions on how deep, how wide, and how long the hole should be dug. At last, he followed Theo to the room where Nestor lay in his bed, still covered with his blanket. The Albanian took a look at the dead man and after inspecting the casket, the clothes, and the disposable shaver he found in Nestor's bathroom, he said to Theo,

"Sir, you can go now. I'll handle the rest myself. Everything I need is here."

Theo went to his room where he washed and shaved, straightened the collar of his shirt, tied his shoes, combed his hair, woke Fotis, and went to the kitchen to make fresh coffee. While the coffee was brewing, he went back to the gate and moved the Fiat to the parking area. He was expecting visitors today who wished to come to say their last goodbyes to the hermit, and his Fiat was blocking the entrance. Returning to the kitchen, Theo found his cousin having a cup of coffee with toasted sweet bread that Magdalene had stored under a glass, cake cover on the kitchen table. Theo helped himself to the coffee and to the toasted bread too. The two men hadn't quite finished drinking their coffee when they heard a motorized vehicle approaching the gate. From the kitchen window, they saw a well dressed police officer coming out of the car and walking toward the main entrance. Theo hurried to the gate, opened it, politely greeted the officer good morning and invited him in.

"I am the Assistant Commander of the police force responsible for this territory," he said in an authoritative voice. He pulled the ends of his official jacket down with both of his hands, and continued, "May I inquire to whom I am talking?"

Theo looked at the visitor from head to foot and said, "My name is Theovulos and I am the departed man's best friend. Please come in Mr. Assistant, and tell me what prompted you to visit us at this early hour." He guided the distinguished visitor into the kitchen, introduced him to Fotis, and asked him if he cared to have a cup of coffee with them.

"No sir, thank you. I am here on official business. The purpose of my visit is to verify the cause of the man's death before you bury him. This country is governed by laws, and there are people like me who see that the laws are obeyed and enforced. Do I make myself clear, Mr. Theovule?"

"You are perfectly clear Mr. Assistant," Theo retorted. "I assume you want to see the corpse, don't you sir?"

"That and the official death certificate," the officer sneered. "Before interment, the authorities must be certain that the man is indeed dead and that his death is not caused by some act of violence."

"You can see the remains now, sir. However his death certificate is not here, yet. It is on its way from the doctor's office," Theo said. He led the assistant to the room where the Albanian had just finished dressing and placing the remains of the deceased man inside his walnut casket. The assistant took a cursory look inside the casket and walked out of the room with Theo on his heels. They both walked back to the kitchen, and the assistant pulled out of his pocket a short questioner. He proceeded asking Theo a number of questions about Nestor, filled in the empty spaces and signed it.

"We can settle this affair quickly, if you are willing to cooperate, or we can make things complicated and difficult for both of us," the assistant said. "The death certificate is not here, and I have the authority to stop everything and wait for it, or give you this permit in advance to proceed with your obligation to bury your friend."

Theo understood the assistant's threat. He reached in his pocket, folded a one hundred Euros bill and with it in the palm of his hands, shook the assistant's hand and said,

"Mr. Assistant, it was a pleasure meeting you." The assistant felt the folded bill in the palm of his hand and quickly inspected it from the corner of his eyes.

"The pleasure was mine, sir," he said to Theo, and handed over to him the burial permit. Without saying anything else to them, he exited the kitchen and walked toward his car whistling a tune of a country song in a low pitch. He finally entered his car and drove away, feeling good that he had executed his duty as a law enforcing agent of the government and a good Christian. Theo felt equally good for buying his way out of a sticky predicament.

Nestor looked wonderful in his new clothes and shining shoes. The senior Albanian washed his hands with soap and water and hurried over to his three brothers to oversee the digging process that was halfway completed. Everything looked fine up to this point. Theo was satisfied with the digging progress, was pleased with the preparation of his teacher for his last journey, and relieved with the outcome of getting the interment permit from the assistant. Even the weather was cooperating today. The sky was blue, and a gentle breeze shook the cypress that lined the outside periphery of the wall that enclosed the mansion. The temperature was comfortable at this hour, and Theo was thinking about his next quest. He was planning to immerse himself in the task of understanding the meaning of the writing inside the ring and the seemingly plain paper he found inside the charm. As far as the key was concerned, he found out last night that it opened the secret room on the third floor. He thought of it in the middle of the night when Fotis was sleeping. He put his clothes on, sneaked out of his room, walked upstairs to the secret room, and tried to unlock the door. To his pleasure the door opened when he turned the key, but when he attempted to push the door open, the hinges made a squeaking noise. Instead of entering the room, Theo slowly closed the door again. He quietly locked it and returned to his bed. He did not want to make noise and risk the chance of waking Fotis up at that hour.

At about the time the digging of the grave was completed, Theo noticed that several vehicles were approaching the mansion. Most of the people in that small crowd were friends who came to pay their last respects to the departed hermit. A few of them were reporters. Some of the reporters held cameras in their hands and others held voice recorders. A lady reporter held a writing pad in one hand and a pencil in the other. Zacharias and Magdalene were among them, but Dr. Gliadis was not in the crowd. Everyone parked their vehicles in the parking area and slowly congregated in front of the outside gate. The reporters started snapping pictures of the place, and a general havoc dominated the small crowd. At the head of that assembly stood a priest dressed in black from head to toe. Presently, he climbed on an elevated spot, removed his tall hat, mopped his forehead with a white handkerchief, and addressed the crowd in his loud voice.

"Ladies and gentlemen, I expect to get your full cooperation for the next hour or so. We must make this occasion solemn and the burial of our beloved brother respectful. Everyone stays here until I return with the person who is in charge of the place now. Shortly, I will go inside to bless the remains, and deliver the *trisagion* (thrice holy) to our beloved brother. It does not matter if he is dead or alive. Our Lord forgives, for He knows that all of us are sinners." He repositioned his black hat on his head, stroked his long beard with one hand and holding the incense burner in the other, he proceeded to the entrance of the mansion. Fotis, not Theo, greeted him at the door, kissed the hand that held the incense burner, and invited him in. When the priest was informed that the dead man was on the second floor, he climbed the stairs and met Theo at the door leading inside the deceased man's room. He greeted the priest in a respectful manner and showed him the casket with Nestor's remains.

"Father, it is very generous of you to come and bless my friend before we lower him into the ground," Theo said, as he led the priest to the casket.

"Son," the priest retorted, "This is my duty. Before I was ordained a priest, I committed my life to God. I am here to bless the soul of your departed friend and to ask our merciful God to forgive his sins and place him among the saints and the legions of His angels," he replied, and at the same time, he pulled out of his big pocket a book with a black cover, and he began reading in a solemn tone of voice. While he was reading the book, he kept swinging the already lit incense burner back-and-forth like a pendulum with a rhythmic motion. The humming of his voice echoed throughout the mansion; the white smoke coming from the smothering incense penetrated every crevice in the room. He paused at times, handed Theo the incense burner, turned to another page in his book, and took out of his other pocket a small vial with olive oil. He dipped his finger in the oil, traced the symbol of the cross with his oiled finger on Nestor's forehead and hands and without interruption, he continued reading more passages from his book.

"Let the memory of our beloved brother be eternal," he finally intoned, three times. In conclusion, he ended his chanting in a loud voice that was even heard outside the building, "In the name of the Father and the Son and the Holy Spirit, amen," he voiced, and made the symbol of the cross three times. For the last time, he took the incense burner from Theo's hands, and swinging it over the remains several times, he walked around the casket three times. He placed the vial with the oil back into his pocket, closed the casket, and motioned to the four Albanians, who stood there with their hands crossed, to carry the casket to the grave.

The priest, at the head of the funeral procession, walked solemnly behind the casket toward the cemetery chanting the same phrase over and over again, "The blessing of the Lord and His forgiveness come to us all." When they arrived at Nestor's final rest place, he read more prayers from his book, and asked the Albanians to lower the hermit into the grave. At long last, the casket was lowered in its place, and the priest declared in a loud voice, "From ashes to ashes and from dust to dust…" He took a handful of dirt, gently sprinkled it over the casket, and asked Theo, who stood next to him, to say a few words about the "departed brother."

Theo was not prepared for this surprise, and he hesitated to speak for a moment. He knew that he was capable of delivering a speech without rehearsing the presentation, but he was caught unprepared at this moment. He had spoken impromptu many times during his professional life, but this speech was different. In the space of the moment, he organized a few ideas in his mind, stepped forward, and said in a clear voice that was appropriate for the occasion.

"Respectful father and friends of our beloved brother: We are gathered here today to say our last goodbye to a man of whom we know nothing about, the place of his birth, his family, his nationality and his religious affiliation. Even his true name is shrouded in mystery. However, all of these unknowns should not be of importance to us. Their answer will only satisfy our curiosity to know his past, not the man himself. Let us therefore, not ask who Nestor was. Instead, let us inquire what he did for others. Nestor extended his help to any person who asked his advice. He did what his heart told him to do without reservation and without expectation for any material gain. Every man who knew him, spoke well of him and admired his wisdom and his kindness. No man ever spoke ill of him. For me, Nestor was the man who taught me to love and respect others. He coached me to understand the true nature of the world around me. He guided my thinking and my actions during my troublesome years of adolescence. The principles of his teachings became part of my life, and I never regret spending time with such a wise and kind human being. He was my second father, and the best teacher one could have. I owe a lot to the man whom we just lowered into his grave." Theo lifted a shovelful of dirt and sprinkled the soil over the casket. "May your memory stay with us forever, dear friend," he said in a trembling voice. He stepped back to wipe a tear from his eyes and to return to the mansion. He had taken only a few steps away from the burial grounds, when he heard the screeching voice of Magdalene wailing loudly. He turned around and saw her standing alone on the other side of the open grave, beating her head with her hands and pulling her long hair frantically. He hurried to her, took her in his arms and with a fatherly touch and a voice that betrayed his own hidden emotions, he tried to calm her down. "Let's go inside Magdalene," he said to her. "You and I will miss him very much, but there is nothing we can do to bring him back," he added, and he began to walk toward the mansion with her next to him. No other cries came from the crowd that listened to Theo's brief eulogy. There were no parents, a wife, children, grand children, uncles, aunts, or other first degree relatives in the congregation, to cry for the death of their loved one. People who came to participate in the occasion were merely motivated by either curiosity to know something about the hermit, or they were there to fulfill their social obligation toward their neighbor.

Theo and the sobbing Magdalene had made only a few steps toward the mansion, when a group of reporters fired questions at him.

"What do you know about his family, Mr. Theo?" one of them said.

"Nothing," Theo retorted laconically.

"Is it true that the man was a war criminal?" another said.

"You answer that question, sir!" Theo said, with a discernable irritation in his voice.

"People say that Mr. Nestor was a wealthy man. Is it true, sir?" another reporter said.

"You should ask the people who gave you that information to support their claim. I don't have an answer for you," Theo responded and resumed his walking toward the mansion, holding Magdalene by the arm.

The "barking" of other reporters followed him to the door, but he was determined to avoid them, for he was shaken by the incident with Magdalene. Besides, they were asking questions that he had answered in the opening statement of his brief eulogy. Repetition was like gossiping to him, and he avoided it as much as he could. "You say it more than once to a donkey, for the beast to register your command. You are supposed to say it once to a man," his father used to say, to emphasize the art of communication and attentive listening.

The four Albanians finished covering the grave, lined its outside periphery with large stones, and when they had finished the work, they washed their hands and face with water from the cistern. Some of the reporters walked around the ground, snapping more pictures and engaged in conversations among themselves. Others, including most of the casual visitors, walked to their vehicles and drove away. The senior of the four Albanian brothers lifted the end of his shirt, wiped his hands and his face with it, and walked to the mansion to be compensated for their labor. It seemed that the weather was deteriorating, and people wanted to leave as soon as possible to avoid the impending summer storm that was brewing on the western horizon. Theo met the Albanian at the kitchen door, handed him a wad of Euros, and the recipient counted them.

"Thank you boss," the Albanian said to Theo, and stuffing the money in his pocket, he waved to the other three to follow him. Only the priest, Zacharias, Magdalene and two reporters lingered behind to say goodbye one more time, and to extend their condolences to Theo and his cousin. One of the reporters mustered the courage and asked the question that no one asked earlier.

"What will happen to the mansion now that its owner is gone?" she said, to Theo.

"That's a question that entered my mind too, young lady," Theo responded. "Unless Nestor has a will, this place will become the property of the state. However, the issue becomes complicated. I don't think the deceased had a title of ownership to the land. On the other hand, he lived up here for many years, and the rule of eminent domain may apply in this case. It would be nice if this place could be converted to a tourist center. In this way, Nestor's memory will be kept alive for sometime to come."

The two reporters looked toward the western horizon and seeing dark clouds rolling over the valley across the way, they said goodbye to Theo and Fotis, walked to their car, and drove away. Magdalene accepted a ride from the lady reporter and left with her. Zacharias mounted his motorcycle and followed the reporters. The priest stayed behind and behaved as if he had something important on his mind for Theo, but he did not have the fortitude to speak up his mind. Instead, he kept rolling the end of his belt in his hands, and continuously paced the kitchen floor expressing disjoined thoughts and burbling constantly.

Fotis was fumbling through a drawer to make a fresh cup of coffee for the priest before his departure, but his attention was fixed on the priest and at the bewildering expression on Theo's face. At a particular moment when the priest was walking toward Theo, Fotis from behind him, lifted his right hand above his head, and rubbing his fingers against each other, motioned to Theo that the priest wanted money for his service. Theo understood the meaning of Fotis' signal and turning to the priest, he said in a direct manner, with consternation in his voice, "How much do I owe you, father?"

"Son, ask your own conscience that question. Give whatever you can give to the humble servant of God. Remember, God is everywhere and witnesses our doings in life. Whatever you will give, it will go toward spreading the words of Christ, our Lord," he said, without even looking at the man he was talking to.

Irritated by the priest's hypocritical talk, Theo handed him a handful of Euros and thanked him for his service. The recipient stuffed the money in his pocket, and without saying anything else, he walked down the garden path and disappeared into the dusky clouds that had rolled over the summit. The two cousins heard the roaring of the priest's car and saw him drive away in the rain that started to fall over the thirsty land. "All are the same," Theo retorted, and he continued verbatim Stavros' expression. "They talk shit and free-load when the opportunity presents itself."

Dark clouds kept rolling from the west, and lightning was followed by loud thunder which shook the mountain. A strong wind brought a mixture of rain and hail from the west that hit the earth with fury. Bursts of rain, wind, and hail pounded the earth as if God was venting His wrath on someone who had committed an unforgivable sin. As the clouds were pouring their contents on the thirsty ground, the two cousins sat calmly by the kitchen table, sipped their coffee , and talked about dinner. Neither of them had eaten all day. They were in desperate need to get away from there and find a place that will offer wholesome food to satisfy their hunger. Theo in particular felt stifled in the mansion's ghostly atmosphere and was anxious to get away as soon as the rain subsided.

"What do we do now Fotis? If we don't find a place to have a good dinner, I will die from starvation," Theo said, and he chuckled at his own humorous exaggeration about his hunger.

Fotis smiled too and scratched his head. He shrugged his shoulders, and with his hands motioned that he did not have any suggestions. "All the little coffee shops in the villages around the valley do not stock their refrigerators with an ample supply of food," he said. "Occasionally, they boil a hunk of goat meat with vegetables and spices, or they make chicken soup, which they either serve fresh or offer it for sale the next day."

"I have an idea that will take us out of our predicament," Theo said. "Turkohori is only a short distance from here. We can be there well before the restaurants close. We can have our dinner and return in time to go to bed. As soon as the rain subsides, let us get in the Fiat, drive to the city, find a good place to eat, and rest our minds. We had plenty of activity today. What do you think about that Fotis?"

Fotis was at first hesitant to go along with Theo's suggestion. He was not accustomed to riding a long distance at night, especially in this weather. He felt leery and insecure in a car after dark. Besides, he had trusted his nanny goat and his chickens to his neighbor all day. But, finally, he gave in to his cousin's insistence and as soon as the weather cleared, they locked the place up, entered the Fiat, and drove toward Turkohori.

Before they reached the base of the mountain where the dirt road met the paved road, they noticed human activity on one of the tight turns. When they came there, Theo pulled the car on the side of the road, and both cousins came out to see what was going on and, hopefully, offer their help. To their surprise, they discovered that the priest had lost control of his car, skidded off the road, and landed in a muddy ditch. The car's two front wheels were buried in the muddy depression; the priest was unable to extricate himself from there. A farmer from the nearby village came by with his two mules attempting to pull the car away from its impediment, while the priest stood on the side of the road soaked in rain and mud. With a voice denoting frustration and distress, the priest told Theo that he had to walk in the downpour all the way to the village to get help. His cylinder-shaped, black hat was resting on the passenger's seat in the up-side-down position. Inside it, he had placed his incense burner and the prayer book he used earlier during Nestor's burial. The farmer with his two animals had the situation under control and it was apparent that they did not need additional help to pool the priest's car out from the ditch. The two cousins expressed their sympathy to the priest for his misfortune, and without any additional delay, they entered their fiat and drove away.

"Did you do all the things you came here to do on such, short notice?" Fotis said to Theo, hoping that his cousin would open up and tell him something new about the hermit's secrets. He could see that his cousin was falling into deep thought quite often, as if he were struggling with something that needed his total concentration. There was no doubt about it. Fotis also knew that Theo was an honest man; therefore, he expected to hear from him everything he knew about Nestor. So, he risked their good relation and put Theo in the thorny position to either lie, or tell him anything he had kept from him so far.

"I still don't know anything about him or his past," Theo said. "I know that you do not believe me but that's the God's truth."

"Yesterday before he expired, he gave me clues that may lead us to answering the questions we all ask about him. He gave me a ring that he wore on one of his fingers. This ring has a message engraved inside. I also have the key to his private room, on the top floor of the mansion."

He did not mention to Fotis the plain paper or the brown envelopes. These items were not materials associated with the question Fotis was asking.

"Fotis, let's not talk about these things now. Let's eat first, and we will continue our conversation during or after dinner. In the meantime, try to figure out what the statement 'Start your quest at the North Star window,' means, for he clearly articulated these words to me before he died. The complete answer about his identity, or part of it, is hidden in this clue," Theo said, and kept driving. While engaged in the demanding task of driving a small vehicle on a road whose perils he was unfamiliar with, he kept mulling the abstract statement over-and-over in his mind. He was hoping that he would extract some sensible meaning from it. Fotis was sunk in deep thought too.

"Ah ha, this statement has something to do with one of the mansion's windows that face the North Star," Theo said exuberantly.

"Precisely," Fotis said with alacrity. "There should be a spot somewhere on the floor of the mansion from where we can see the North Star through a window, and that spot or view, is linked to Nestor's secrets. When we return, let us examine all the windows through which we can see the North Star and see if we connect your hunch with something meaningful."

The lights of Turkohori became visible ahead of them, and before too long, they were driving through the main boulevard of the town. It was still early in the evening, and the streets were packed with pedestrians, bikes, motorcycles, cars, and trucks of all sizes and makes. The neon sign, "Famous Dinning", caught Theo's attention and made him slow down to take a good look at the place. On first sight, the outside of the establishment looked orderly. The two hungry cousins looked at each other and speechless, agreed to give the place a try. Theo parked the car in front of the place and they entered the restaurant. A well-mannered and impeccably dressed young man cordially greeted his new customers at the door and escorted them to their table. He offered them a table that faced the well-waxed dancing area, with floodlights fixed on the beams overhead. Across the dancing area was a small stage where a four piece band was tuning their instruments at the time Theo and Fotis entered the place. The violin, the guitar, and the accordion harmonized nicely with each other, but the *bouzouki* sounded like an old guitar out of tune.

The place was not crowded yet, and the waiter came promptly and took their order. Theo and Fotis asked the waiter to bring them a cup of soup, a village salad with plenty of home made bread, and a full order of lamb with spaghetti, cooked in the oven. They also requested a liter of local retsina. The soup and the salad came first, and the main dinner followed on time. While the two cousins were enjoying their dinner, the music began to play tunes that brought sweet memories to Theo. These were the songs he sang when he was a young man, and he had memorized both the lyrics and their words. At first, the loudness of the music and the melancholic voice of the bouzouki player bothered Theo's ears, but as time went on, he became accustomed to the noisy environment and found himself enjoying it. After a few minutes, the place was swinging to Greek music, and the smell of the food, mixed with that of the wine, made the air in the restaurant smell aromatic and delicious.

A man in his late twenties, escorted by two beautiful and well-shaped ladies of his age, entered the dance floor. The man loosened his tie, rolled his sleeves halfway up his hairy arms, and interlocked elbow-to-elbow one of his arms with the arm of the lady to his right and the other, with the arm of the lady to his left. Then, the fun began. Locked together arm-to-arm, the trio began dancing to the tune that was dominated by the bouzouki notes. All three made several steps back-and-forth and from side-to-side in a coordinated motion as if they were one person. The rest of the customers started to clap to the rhythm of the music with an occasional "*opa!*" exclamation. Before too long, other young people entered the dance floor; the music became louder, and the overhead lights lit up in several iridescent colors. Pitchers filled with wine kept coming to the tables, only to be emptied and returned for re-filling. Theo, enthused by the lively dancing, caught himself singing along with the bouzouki player in a low voice that barely escaped his lips.

It was past nine o'clock when the musicians took a break, and everyone returned to their tables for another sip of wine. The two cousins, who were the only senior citizens in the crowd, realized that it was time for them to get out of there and return home. Theo paid the bill and before the music started to play again, they walked to the car, and with a full stomach, they started their trip back to their village.

"Wow! What a place and what a wonderful dinner we had tonight. The bouzouki made me feel young again," Theo said to Fotis, as they drove away from the restaurant.

"I never had the opportunity to dine in this place before," Fotis added. "I have to admit that the food and the wine were outstanding." Fotis said nothing about the music and the dancing, and Theo understood the reason for his apathy. He was still grieving over the death of his wife.

"While the music was playing and the people were dancing," Fotis said, "my mind was turning over the thing you said about the North Star window. What is so significant about the North Star, why not another star, or the moon for that matter? The moon is more obvious in the sky than any of the stars, isn't it?"

"Oh, that's simple," Theo said. "The North Star is the only star in the sky that does not change its position when the earth rotates. It lays on the imaginary axis around which the earth turns," Theo added, and paused for a second. "Does Nestor try to tell us that there is a spot on the floor that lines up with the North Star, through the opening in one of the windows, in the mansion?" he asked. "Maybe, that's the break we need, Fotis," he exclaimed, and he immediately added. "We have to locate the window that faces the North Star! Thinking ahead, we need chalk or masking tape to mark the area on the floor from where we can see the North Star through that window. The marking must be done at night when the stars are visible. I am sure that the spot we are looking for is not so obvious. It must be an inconspicuous place that is not noticeable to a casual observer. I only hope that there is only one window that lines up with the North Star," he said, concluding his thoughts.

"Looking for the coffee in Nestor's kitchen this morning, I distinctly remember seeing a large role of masking tape in one of the drawers", Fotis exclaimed. "We can use it to mark the floor, as you suggest."

"You don't propose that we go back to the mansion tonight and do the marking, do you?" Theo asked Fotis, and he looked at him to receive his answer.

"Someone in America said; 'Do not leave for tomorrow, what you can do today,'" Fotis said. "I'll help you do the marking tonight; afterwards, you can take me home. I have things to do around the house that must be done tomorrow. Besides, my poor chickens and my nanny goat will die without food and water," he commented.

"Are you sure that doing all that tonight will not be too much for you? We can let the marking wait for another day," Theo responded.

"No, I feel good. Besides, I will be busy with chores around the house for the rest of the week, and it will become difficult for me to get away to help you. Tonight is the perfect time for it.

Chapter Six: "The Mansion"

Without any additional deliberation on the subject of marking the floor, Theo took the road back to the mansion. It was almost ten o'clock at night when they arrived there. A dense field of stars above their head, stood out like diamonds of all sizes glued on black velvet.. The North Star, hiding the hermit's secrets, was easily identifiable high above the north horizon. Theo unlocked the outer gate and one behind the other they entered the garden area. Walking silently, they reached the entrance to the mansion; unlocked it, and Theo asked his cousin to go into the kitchen and find the tape. He stayed behind and called his wife to tell her that everything was well. He made his conversation with his wife brief, secured the phone back into his pocket, entered the mansion, and found Fotis standing by the kitchen door, holding in his hands a large roll of masking tape. Walking one behind the other again, they entered the game room and pulled open the drapes of the north window. Regardless of where Theo stood on the floor of this room, he couldn't see the North Star that glittered in the cloudless sky. The other rooms on the first floor did not have a northerly view at all. They were facing either east, west, or south.

"I don't think the first floor is the place we should spend time looking for a window with a northerly view," Theo said to his companion. "Let's go upstairs." Both of them climbed the stairs to the second floor and inspected the three bedrooms. Again, none of the bedroom windows had a view to the North Star.

"I bet you, the spot we are looking for is in the secret room upstairs," Fotis said with conviction. Theo nodded his head to indicate his approval of the other man's assessment, and, one behind the other, they climbed the spiral case to the third floor. "Let's see what we can find here," Theo added, and unlocked the door with the squeaking hinges. He pushed it wide open, turned the lights on, and both of them entered in silence. The setting, the furniture, and the articles that lay on its floor were as enigmatic in nature as Nestor himself. Examining the circular walls of the room, one of the windows caught their attention. This window was facing north and was lined up nicely with the North Star.

"This is it!" Fotis exclaimed, and turned the lights off for Theo to have a better view at the North Star through that window. Theo walked around the floor with his sight fixed on the upper, left corner of that window. He finally stood on a spot of the floor from which his sight projected directly to the North Star, through the upper left corner of the window. Fotis turned the lights on, tore a piece of tape, and. stuck it next to Theo's feet. He turned the lights off and Theo inched backwards until he found the point on the floor from where he could see the star through the lower left corner of the window. Fotis turned the light switch on again and marked that spot with another piece of tape. Following the same procedure, Theo and Fotis located the points on the floor from where they could see the star from the lower and upper right-hand corners of the window and, again, marked these spots with tape. Finally, they turned the lights on and connected the four points with a continuous piece of tape. The marked area circumvented a perfect rectangle which was directly proportional of the north window itself. Regardless where they stood within this rectangle, they could see the North Star. The star was not in view, if one stood outside the taped area. Was this rectangular part of the floor the key to Nestor's secret? Cursory inspection of that part of the floor did not seem to hold encouragement to either Theo or Fotis at this late hour and under the dim light in the room.

It was getting late by now, and both of them were spent of energy to do anything else. They wanted to inspect all the things that stood in front of them, but they were fatigued from all the activity of the day. Instead, they walked out of the room and on their way out, they turned the lights off. Theo locked the door and the two men walked out of the building in deep thought. On their way out, Theo secured the place by locking the main entrance and the outside gate. Finally, Theo and Fotis, exhausted from all the things they had done during the day and part of the evening, entered the Fiat and drove home in total silence. They only stole glances at one another as if they had something to say, but that "something" never came out of either man's mouth. At last, they arrived at the village, said goodnight to each other in front of Fotis's house, and Theo continued his driving until he reached the home of his parents. He parked the car, entered the house, took a shower, put his night attire on, slipped under his bed covers, closed his itching eyes, and immediately fell asleep. The bells from the church toll twelve times and disturbed his sleep. He opened his eyes and noticed that it was only midnight. He tried to go back to sleep, but he was not able to convince himself to do so. He reached over to his night table, turned the light on, picked up his *A Brief History of Time*, and read, one more time, the chapter about Black Holes in the sky. "…Although we would not be able to see them because the light from them would not reach us, we would still feel their gravitational attraction. Such objects are what we now call Black Holes…," Stephen Hawking wrote in his book, and the brilliant astrophysicist went on to say that these regions in the sky absorb everything that comes close to them, even light; thus, they become invisible.

Theo saw a similarity in the existence of black holes and Nestor's existence. Both were enigmatic and mysterious, and little was known about their origin and the secrets they held inside them. Someday, Theo said to himself, scientists will learn more about the black holes, and if I am lucky, I will learn more about Nestor's secret life during the coming week. He put the book aside, turned the light off again, closed his eyes, and this time he went to sleep until nine o'clock in the morning. Nothing disturbed him until a thunderous knocking at the door woke him up. There was Fotis asking Theo to stop at his home and have breakfast with him on his way to the mountain.

"Go back and start the coffee. I will join you in ten minutes," Theo said, and hurried to get ready. He decided not to drive the short distance to his cousin's home today. Instead, he walked the short distance. The morning was perfect for an inclined stroll. Besides, he needed the exercise to loosen up his aching muscles and take a look at the surroundings in the light of that bright morning hour. He wanted to step on the same stones that stubbed his bare feet when he was a boy, to see the houses that lined the street, and to reminisce about the good times he had playing with the children who lived in these modest dwellings. He hoped to experience the gayety of human life once again, hear the barking of the dogs, amuse himself with the crocking of the roosters, and ponder the meaning of the horse's whining. But there was nothing to be seen on the streets or to be heard from the confines of the stone, little houses with their wooden verandas protruding toward the street. Everything was quiet.

The inside of his cousin's house did not look anything like the place he remembered, playing with Fotis as a child. Fotis had remodeled it and had created an environment of modern, living atmosphere. The old fire place was gone and the wood burning stove was not anywhere to be seen. Fotis had divided the living space into two bedrooms, a kitchen, a dining room, and two bathrooms equipped with toilets, showers, and marble covered vanities with both hot and cold, running water. There was a refrigerator in the kitchen, and a propane cooking stove had replaced the old fireplace and the wood burning stove. All the floors were covered with warm-colored, ceramic tiles, and the windows were enlarged, to allow natural light to come in through their large, glass panels. The ceilings were covered with elegant acoustic tiles, and electric lighting had replaced the oil lamps that used to hang from the ledge of the fireplace.

"Hey, cousin," Theo exclaimed. "You did a good job fixing up the old house. I like it very much."

"Thank you cousin," Fotis said with an air of pleasure and satisfaction. "It cost me a 'pretty penny' like you used to say, but I enjoy living in it. As you well know, I existed in poverty all my life, and now that God decided to make me a lonesome old man, I want to be comfortable," he continued with a noticeable suspire. "My kids have been good to me now that I cannot work the land anymore. Well, let's not talk about the house and let us drink our coffee before crickets jump in it," he said, with a faint laugh. Theo detected Fotis's sadness in having lost his wife so early in his life, and he welcomed the opportunity to change the subject. They walked toward the dining room table and took their seats in front of a spread that consisted of fresh coffee, thick yogurt, orange-blossom honey, home-made marmalade, wholesome toast, and an assortment of fresh fruit in a reed basket. Fotis did not believe in serving eggs with ham or bacon for breakfast. He believed that the best breakfast is fresh fruit, whole grain bread, aromatic coffee, and yogurt with honey.

"I make the yogurt from the milk I get from my goat, and the honey is my own production, from my own beehives. The marmalade is from the berries I gathered from my mulberry trees. Adding petals from fresh roses to the pot when I stew the berries with my honey, makes the marmalade aromatic. The fruit you see in front of you is my production too," Fotis said, and he took his place at the table.

Theo enjoyed eating home-made yogurt with honey, whole wheat toast with marmalade, and a flavorful, Greek coffee. When he finished, he acknowledged to Fotis that he enjoyed the breakfast immensely, and that he looked forward to doing it again some other day. The basket with the fresh fruit was tempting. Theo helped himself at the juicy grapes first, then, he peeled several, succulent, black figs and ate them. Fotis felt satisfied that he pleased his guest in his own home with his hospitality and with the things he had made with pride and personal care.

"I will go up there again today, and I will do my best to see if anything on those floors, or on the walls of the rooms, makes any sense," Theo told his cousin. "I will comb the place for any obvious clues, and when I get tired, I will return to have dinner with you and Zacharias. Let's have him make something for us tonight. I promised him that I would stop at his caffenio one of these days, and I want to keep my commitment. Let's give him a few Euros, don't you think so Fotis?" he said. The other man did not raise any objections having dinner at the caffenio tonight, and that pleased Theo.

Theo thanked Fotis again for the wonderful breakfast and on the way out, he said. "I will stop at Zacharias's place, and I'll ask him to prepare dinner for the three of us," and he took the downhill, short walk to his parental house. There, he entered the Fiat and on his way to the mountain, he stopped at the caffenio and asked Zacharias to have dinner for the three of them, at six o'clock. Without additional delay, he took the road back to the summit. His plan was to spend all day there and search for clues to learn as much as possible about the past of his deceased mentor and friend.

He did not bother stopping at any of the rooms on the first or the second floor. Instead, he ascended directly to the third floor where the secret room was, opened its door, and entered. He was amazed with all the things he did not notice the night before. Every piece of furniture was made with high grade mahogany wood. A full-size desk with three comfortable chairs was in the center of the room. Two smaller desks were positioned by two of the three windows, and a single chair was between the desk and the window. Nothing, but nothing at all, occupied the space by the northerly window. Everything in this room was orderly arranged. The books on the book cases against the walls, were stacked one next to the other in alphabetical order. Decorative, brass statuettes of animals and birds separated one group of books from the group next to it. The floor was tiled with chips of marble of various colors and sizes, and the walls were freshly painted a creamy, white color. The ceiling was plastered and painted the same color as the walls. Writing paper, pens, pencils, and mail envelopes that someone had opened, were neatly placed on trays, or were stacked perpendicularly in a wire holder. Nestor's old guitar was resting against the side of the main table. There are so many things I have to inspect today, Theo murmured to himself. I have to start somewhere soon, for otherwise, I will never finish my searching.

He first examined the floor area that he and Fotis had taped the night before, but he did not notice anything unusual. Nothing stood out to catch his fancy, and that disappointed and disheartened him. Next, he turned his attention to the objects that were meticulously placed on the center table and on the book cabinets around the walls. There were old and new books, some of them written in foreign languages and others in Greek.

Theo spent several hours thumbing through each one of the books, but nothing attracted his attention at the time. Apparently, Nestor read them all at one time or another, for there were sentences and paragraphs meticulously underlined in colored pencil. Unfortunately, none of this marked material seemed to be related to Nestor's secret life. The underscored material stated the author's personal convictions on the subject that he presented in the book, or contained original ideas quoted from some other book. Before he picked up the next book from the shelf, Theo made sure that he had placed the first book in the spot where he had found it. He did not want to disturb anything that might be important for future re-examination of the book cases. When he was through thumbing through the books, he turned his attention to the objects that lay on the main desk.

There were several writing pads on the table with Nestor's handwriting on some of their pages. A pile of neatly arranged mail envelopes was on the far left of the main table, and a holder with several pens and pencils was at the other end. The writing pads contained notes Nestor had made researching some name in some far away place. Theo did not dwell on the notes because he could not see at that moment any connection of the notes to the past of the writer. He finally took the stack of the letters in his hands and briefly read through each one of them. Nestor had written on the face of two of the envelopes the name *Chrisoglu,* which Theo never heard, or had seen anywhere before. Apparently, Nestor was researching the name Chrisoglu in his communications with some of the most prestigious schools and libraries in Eastern Europe. All the letters were his recent correspondence with librarians of several schools. Unfortunately, the responses were brief, saying that the sender regrets to inform the recipient that he was unable to assist him in his search. The response from a university in Turkey was a bit more interesting and informative to Theo. The writer apologized that no records were kept on the number of Armenian people who were expelled to the desert of Syria in 1915, to find death from thirst and starvation. He also claimed that no estimated number of casualties or the names of people who were massacred during World War I, by either the Turks or the Armenians, were available. Finally, the letter concluded with the following sentences:

"...Those were turbulent moments in the history of the Turkish nation. In moments like this, the primary concern of the authorities was to prevail and establish order. ... Keeping records of victims was unimportant to the men in the field of action. Atrocities were inevitable and were perpetrated by both the Turkish army and the Armenian resistors. We regret to inform you that we cannot shed any light to your subject of interest," the writer of the letter had concluded.

Who was that Chrisoglu person, Nestor was so interested to know about, Theo wondered. To the best of Theo's knowledge, Chrisoglu was not a famous Armenian fighter or a Turkish hero. Was Chrisoglu a link to Nestor's past? As he pondered the question of who Chrisoglu was, he remembered what Nestor said when he was explaining to him the principles of evolution, at the time Theo was a high school boy. Nestor told him then, that the ancient Greeks believed in ridiculous Gods who supposedly dwelled on the summits of Mt. Olympus.

"My dear young man, your ancestors believed that there was a bunch of gods living on the top of Olympus...." Nestor did not say "our" ancestors. Was it a figure of speech, a careless mistake in using proper diction, or was it a slip of the tongue to reveal that he was not Greek-born after all!

Was Nestor trying to locate an Armenian relative who had perished at the hands of the Turkish army, or was he looking for a Turkish relative who died at the hands of the fierce fighters of the Armenian resistors at that time? Theo was inclined to believe that the name Chrisoglu was Armenian, and not Turkish. If there was a family connection between Nestor and

Chrisoglu, and if Chrisoglu was in fact an Armenian, then Nestor was of Armenian descent. This assumption would explain Nestor's use of the word "your" instead of saying "our".

Theo returned to the letters and read each one of them sentence-by-sentence, to be sure that he did not overlook anything important, but to his disappointment, he came up with no substantial clues to shed light to his quest of who Nestor was. At last he read again a letter that was sent to Nestor from a university in the Ukraine. This letter contained only one sentence: "We are sorry to inform you that we have no records available for casualties in Armenia during World War I", the letter said. Theo was ecstatic and thrilled to read that single sentence. In his estimation, this letter confirmed that Nestor was looking for a person he suspected was missing, in Armenia during World War I. He apparently had addressed his letter to the university in the Ukraine, because he knew that the Russians supported the Armenians in their struggle to free themselves from the Ottoman yoke. Consequently, Nestor surmised that the Russians would have information about Armenian casualties of the war between the Turks and the Armenians during that time. Theo knew now that the person Nestor was looking for, lived in Armenia during World War I and his/her name was Chrisoglu.

The old guitar, the guitar that Nestor had when he appeared in the area years ago, was still in the same case and was resting against the table in the center of the room. Theo decided to meticulously examine the object because he knew that the old guitar was valuable to Nestor. It might contain something of value to Theo's search on Nestor's life. He was hoping to find a name of some person who had given Nestor the guitar for his birthday, perhaps, or for some other occasion that could shed light to Theo's question. He picked up the wooden case with the guitar inside, laid it on the table and opened it. There was the old, worn-out guitar with all its strings intact. Several picks were lined up in holders on the inside cover of the case, some used, others new.

Theo did not know how to play a string, musical instrument. He only knew how to blow notes through his home-made flute. He took the guitar out of its case, placed it on his lap, and gently twanged the strings with his fingers. Awful notes filled the air and he realized that Nestor had loosened the strings to relieve the tension they exerted on the wood. Theo knew that loosening the strings in a stringed instrument is a common practice all musicians follow to avoid warping of the wood during storage. He carefully examined the bridge, its six strings, the fret and the peg box with its six screws, and noticed nothing unusual. He went as far as loosening the strings to the point that he could insert his hand through the sound hole to examine the inside walls of the instrument. He pressed one of his hands inside the cavity and found nothing there. At last, he turned the instrument over and examined its reverse side, and although it appeared to be of good quality and craftsmanship, the manufacturer's name was nowhere to be found. Theo's hopes to discover something interesting on Nestor's dearest possession faded away. He returned the musical instrument to its case, placed it where he found it, and returned to the rows of books on the long, wooden cabinets that lined the walls. He was not sure about what he was looking for and therefore did not know where to start his searching again. He only followed his intuition that something must be hidden in the books that lined the book cases on the walls. He was only hoping that serendipity would prevail, and something would jump out from one of the books to help him learn Nestor's identity. He took several of them out of their places and piled them on the table in front of him. He opened one at a time, and thumbed through their pages again. When he had inspected the first stack of books on the table, he returned them to their places and brought back a new stack for inspection. The hours clicked away one after the other, and Theo realized that thumbing through the books was also fruitless.

Going through Nestor's collection of books was a fascinating and rewarding experience for Theo. Some of the books were original prints, while others were copies or translations to Greek from some other language. One of them was written in an alphabet that was not Latin, Cyrillic, or Greek. It looked like it was written in Arabic or Hebrew characters, and Theo could not read it. All the books were hard covered, some leather bound and others cloth bound, but none of them was autographed by its author. When Theo finished inspecting the books, he felt his head spinning and walked out of the room to take a break and clear his mind. He walked out on the veranda, stretched his arms apart, and twisted his upper torso left and right to relax his aching back. It was late afternoon now and the shadow of the mansion was getting longer and longer against the slope of the mountain on which it was projecting. He paced the floor of the veranda a few times, marveled at the beautiful valley, with its little villages clustered among the green olive-tree orchards, and admired the mountains in the far distance. These were the same mountains that the goat-legged god, Pan, where he presumably introduced the reed pipe to the goatherds and taught them to play melodies as sweet as the nightingale's song, dancing with Bacchus and the nymphs. After a while, Theo felt the urgency to walk the cobbled sidewalks in the garden. He wanted to admire the rows of vegetables from a close distance, lazily wonder under the fruit trees, and smell the beautiful roses that were in full bloom at this time of the year. On his way downstairs, he heard the sound of an approaching vehicle, and he hurried to the gate to greet the visitor. The car pulled in front of the gate and a young man came out and approached Theo with an envelope in his hands.

"Are you Theo?" the young man said.

"Yes, I am Theo," Theo responded.

"I am sorry, I am late bringing the death certificate," he said, and handed Theo the envelope containing a single page of a printed stationary. "The coroner's secretary is on her honeymoon in the islands this week, and we could not prepare the document in time," he apologized. Theo realized that he was dealing with a bureaucratic screw up, stuffed the envelope in his pocket, and acted as if he appreciated the young man's sincere effort to bring the death certificate to him. "I got to get back," the young man said, and without any undo delay, he returned to his vehicle and sped away as fast as he had come up minutes ago, leaving Theo standing at the gate with the envelope in his hands.

Theo paced the garden back and forth several times, read the death certificate again and again, and thought about the things he learned today about Nestor. Most likely, he was an Armenian, and some relatives of his had perished during the upheaval of World War I, Theo muttered to himself. On the other hand, there is a hole in my logic in this assumption. There is no connection with him being an Armenian, and the clue to look at the "North Star". Still, Nestor being an Armenian and the North Star clue are not mutually exclusive either, he thought further. Other things, in addition to being Armenian, might become obvious when I unravel the "North Star" riddle, he counter-argued with himself.

For no particular reason, he stopped under one of the pear trees in the garden and noticed that the color of the pears was mostly golden yellow with a splash of red on the side of the fruits that faced the sun during the day. They also discharged a delicious aroma that saturated the air around the tree, and this fragrance of natural ripeness made Theo to pick a few of them. He reached up, collected a handful of them, washed them with cold water, and bit into one of them. A burst of fresh-fruit aroma mixed with a honey-sweet juice, filled his mouth. He walked over to the grape vine canopy, sat on one of the benches and enjoyed eating the rest of them. Finally, he washed them down with fresh, cold water from the cistern, and felt satisfied and content.

The grapes that hung over his head in big clusters had a deep purple color, but they were not ripe yet.

It was late afternoon, and he had enough researching for the day. He returned to the mansion, locked the door to the secret room, walked out of the place, locked the entrance and the outside gates, and went to his car with the intention to drive back to the village. He was hungry, and he remembered that he had a dinner engagement with Fotis and Zacharias at six o'clock.

Nature around him was serene, and all things appeared as if they were in harmony with one another. The sun was playing hide and seek behind big puffs of black clouds that hung over the mountains on the western horizon, and the afternoon, northerly breeze felt good on his face. The long stem, violet flowers of the wild onions that grew in abundance between rocks, swayed back and forth in harmony with the waves of the breeze, and honey collecting insects swarmed around them. Grasshoppers were dancing on the ground, and mountain lizards soaked the last rays of the sun before crawling into their burrows to spend the night in safety. A chucker on one of the lower slopes was calling his mate with his repetitious chucking call, and a red eagle flew overhead toward the forested portion of the lowland to spend its night there. Foxes and rabbits were not out of their burrows yet. They were waiting for night to set in before venturing from their hiding places. The smell of wild sage mixed with those of amaranth and melilot was discernible in the air, and reminded Theo of the days he was a goatherd in this part of the world.

Before entering the Fiat to return to the village, Theo felt the urge to walk along the ridge that he had traversed many times, when he was a goatherd in his youth. He carefully picked his way through the stones and the shrubbery, and after a while, he found the exact spot he was looking for.

He found the chair-shaped rock where he used to sit and eat bread with olives, that he carried in his knapsack, and where he sat to play the flute he had made from a foot long, bamboo stick. He climbed the precipice and sat at the exact location as he did in his youth. Far away, the valley, doted with tiny villages, olive and citrus tree orchards, was spread wide in all directions. But not everything he remembered was there. His goats were missing. Their bells were silenced, and their bleating was nowhere to be heard.

Unconsciously, he ran his right hand over the side of the rock he was sitting on, and as he was moving his hand up-and-down, he felt several deep grooves on the smooth, stone surface. Then, it dawned on him. Theo had forgotten that these were the grooves he made with a pick he had fabricated from the antenna of a discarded umbrella. He went fifty years back in his life, recollecting the many hours he spent gouging his initials an eighth-of-an-inch deep, on the face of this rock. They were still noticeable under the lichen growth that covered the limestone. He dismounted his seat and examined the grooves closely. He was now convinced, beyond doubt, that the markings were, indeed, those he carved years ago.

He ran his fingers over the grooves several times, and a melancholy deluged his heart. Those cuttings reminded him of the grouted spaces that separated the marble tiles in the floors of the mansion, and this chain of thought brought to his attention a casual observation he made when he looked at the area he and Fotis marked the night before. There was a section of that part of the floor where the mortar between the tiles looked slightly different from that of the surrounding tiles. Apparently, this part of the floor was recently disturbed. Overwhelmed with so many other things at the time he made this observation, Theo paid no attention to that detail. Now that this casual observation came back in focus, he could not stop wondering if there was a connection between the writing on the ring and the seemingly repaired floor. Was that part of the floor opened for a reason? Was something hidden underneath that spot? Was it the spot that Nestor was talking about when he said to start the quest at the North Star window? Theo stood in his favorite spot a little longer and pondered these thoughts. The more he thought about it, the more it made sense for him to pursue this thinking further. He had no other leads, except the blank piece of paper he found in Nestor's charm.

The sun was setting, and he was spent of energy. He was very tired to return to the mansion and resume his searching for new clues. He would rather return to the village for his dinner engagement. Tomorrow is another day, he mumbled, and walked back to his car. Sunk in deep thinking, trying to figure out what the freshly repaired floor meant, he entered the vehicle and drove toward the village. I'll sleep on it tonight, and I'll decide my course of action tomorrow morning, he whispered again and kept rolling the car on the downhill, winding road toward his village.

It was almost 6:00 p.m. when he passed by the caffenio. His nose detected something delicious coming from the little kiosk, but he resisted the temptation to stop. Instead, he kept driving until he reached his cousin's house. Fotis had just milked his nanny goat and was washing his hands in the kitchen sink when he heard Theo calling his name from the street. Fotis stuck his head out of his kitchen window and responded to Theo's call.

"I'll be there in a flash," he shouted, drying his hands with a towel he kept handy, when he was working in the kitchen. Fotis was a wipe "nut". He was in the habit of wiping and drying his kitchen's counter and the dinner table over and over again, after he had cleaned them with soap and water. He put his cap on his hairless head and met Theo on the street where he was waiting.

"What took you so long cousin?" Theo asked. "It took you more than ten 'flashes' to come down, not one," he commented, with a broad smile and a giggle in his voice.

"Oh, our 'flashes' here in the village are longer than the 'flashes' you know in America," Fotis retorted with a thundering laugh.

Both Theo and Fotis drove to Zacharias's caffenio, parked the Fiat outside, and one behind the other entered the place without knocking at the door. Zacharias was putting his final touches on the cooking, when the two cousins walked in.

"Friends, you are in for a real treat tonight. I managed to bring in a five-kilo hare, and my wife took the time to bake it in the oven using her secret garlic sauce. A mixture of string beans, okra, eggplant, fresh tomatoes, potatoes, and parsley will be your side dish. For dessert, you can choose either yogurt with honey, or an assortment of fresh fruit. Now, if you are generous and leave a portion of the hare for me, I will consider offering you both the yogurt and the fruit for dessert." he said, with his eyes wide open, covering his mouth with his hands, pretending he was wiping his mustache. In reality, he was covering his mouth to conceal his snigger on his own humor. His guests understood the true meaning of his statement and broke into a silly laughter too.

All three of them sat at the wooden bench that served as a dinner table, and Zacharias's wife walked in with a big baking pan loaded with something covered with aluminum foil. She placed the steaming pan on the table and returned to the kitchen to fetch the stewed vegetables which she had meticulously arranged on a flat platter. Zacharias placed the dishes, the silverware, and the empty glasses in front of each one of them and said, "What will it be, red or retsina. Both wines are aged to perfection."

"Let's drink retsina tonight," Theo said, and his companions nodded their approval by moving their heads down and up quickly. Without any delay, Zacharias walked into the cellar where he kept the barrels with the wine and returned with a glass pitcher filled to the brim with the gold-colored wine. With finesse, he carefully poured some of it in all three glasses and said to his companions, "Let's dig in fellows," and removed the aluminum foil that kept the contents of the pan concealed from their view. Under that cover were hunks of cooked hare meat in a thick garlic sauce that made their mouths salivate. The three men filled their plates and before they started eating, they crossed themselves and raised their wine glasses to wish health and happiness to one another.

The food was outstanding; the wine was mellow with a distinct taste and a light aroma, and the company was pleasant. After Zacharias had cleared the table, both Theo and Fotis acknowledged to the lady of the house that she was a master cook and thanked her for preparing such a wonderful dinner for them. Before they dispersed their company to retire, Zacharias casually said to Theo,

"You said in your eulogy yesterday, that the hermit was your special friend during your high school years, and that you will miss him now that he is gone. I myself had the good fortune to meet him once when I climbed the mountain. I had a good feeling about him. He had a magnetic personality that commanded your attention. Do you know anything about him? It seems that nobody else knows his real name, or the place of his birth."

"Yes, he was my friend and as I said yesterday, he taught me a lot about life in general. Too bad, he is not with us any longer," Theo responded, with an obvious sadness in his voice. "I went through some of his belongings today, and I came up empty handed. I only have a hunch that the man was not Greek-born, after all. I am determined, however, to find out as much as I can about him in the days to come," he added, and asked Zacharias for the bill.

"Give me 200 Euros," Zacharias said, with modesty and reservation, fearing that he was asking too much for the dinner. Theo paid the bill without protesting the price, and thanked both Zacharias and his wife one more time for the hospitality. At last, the two cousins entered the Fiat, and with a stomach full of good food and wine, they sped away to go home and retire for the day.

"It's time for a cup of coffee at my house," Fotis said to his cousin. "Don't you think so? Besides, I would like to hear about the new things you discovered at the hermit's mansion today."

Theo was not in the mood to talk about this subject any more today, but he felt obliged to give Fotis an explanation; so, he kept driving without saying much until they arrived at his cousin's house. There, they exited the car, and Theo followed Fotis to the kitchen where the host made fresh coffee. Finally, Theo broke the silence and said in a bewildered voice.

"Going through some old notes and correspondence he had in one of his desks, I am convinced that Nestor was not of Greek descent," he said to Fotis, who had glued his eyes and his total attention on him. "A couple of old letters revealed that he was researching the name Chrisoglu in Armenia during World War I. I believe Nestor is more of a mystery than I thought he would be. The real truth about his identity and his finances will be difficult to know in its entirety. The things I know so far don't logically connect one with the other. For example, his instruction to look at the

North Star through his window does not have any logical link with my supposition that he was an Armenian."

"I also have this little piece of paper that he kept close to his chest in a little leather pouch," Theo continued with perplexity. "It seems to be blank. If it is blank indeed, why did he value it so much to the point that he kept it safe in the leather pouch, with the key to the secret room? What secret does it hold?" he said, and handed the aged paper to Fotis.

Fotis carefully unfolded the paper, looked at it, slightly rubbed his fingers over the paper's smooth surface, and without thinking, he laid it on the table that he had just wiped with his wet towel.

"Look, look," Fotis exclaimed, and he pointed his finger at the slightly moistened paper on the table. Theo bent over the paper and to his amazement he could clearly read six words: "*I was Chrisoglu, now David Koch,*" was written on the paper in Nestor's own handwriting.

"Of course", Theo exclaimed. "He wrote his message using as ink, a secret mixture of a drop of olive oil in lemon juice. This secretive writing was common during the middle ages. It was used by military men and kings to send clandestine messages to one another. The writing becomes imperceptible when the paper dries, and the message becomes discernible again, when the paper becomes moistened," Theo declared with delight.

"We now know that he changed his name three times in his life," Fotis said. "His last name was Chrisoglu. Sometime ago, he changed it to David Koch for some reason and finally, he became Nestor for us," he added.

"Hum," Theo said. "I bet you, his parents or his siblings disappeared during the struggle of the Armenians with the Turks", he exclaimed. "Now we have a lot of work ahead of us. Oh, one more thing," Theo added. "Returning to the village earlier this afternoon, I could not get away from thinking about an observation I made, on the part of the floor we marked with tape last night. I noticed that the color of the grout between some of the tiles was slightly different from the rest of the surrounding grout. At first glance, I thought nothing of it, but as this observation started to sink in later on, I became convinced that the floor was redone at this spot.

Do you think that the hermit hid something under the tiles?" Theo said, hoping that Fotis would agree with his assessment.

"Quite possible," Fotis added. "Your assumption dovetails with his instruction to look at the North Star through the window. If I were you, I would take another look at this spot, and if it looks like something might be hidden there, remove a tile or two, look underneath, and place the tiles back where they were. All you need is something like an ice pick or a small screw driver to scrape the grout away and pry the tiles off the floor."

"We will have a problem removing the tiles," Theo said in deep thought. "The floor in this room is made with chips of marble, not with regular tiles, and it will be hard to lift each and every one of these chips without breaking them," he continued and looked at Fotis for his help. Fotis said nothing as if he did not understand Theo's statement. "Anyway, I'll look at this spot tomorrow, and I will estimate the complexity of getting into the area below. There is also the possibility that the marble chips on the floor outline some figure, an arrow perhaps, that points to something, somewhere else in the room. Right now," he added, "we should retire and go to bed. I don't know about you, but I am very tired and in a desperate need for a cool shower and a restful night."

On his way out, Theo received from Fotis a bag with tools he might need to remove the tiles from the floor tomorrow. The two cousins said good night to each other, and Theo returned to his parental home to retire for the night. He showered and called his wife to tell her that he was fine. Their conversation was the routine, "I love you dear" and "How is the weather there," etc. Anastasia detected Theo's unusual way of expressing himself, but she said nothing. She assumed that he was extremely tired and let him go to bed with an audible kiss at the end of their brief telephone chat. Theo's mind was stuck on that part of the floor with the fresh grout like iron sticks on a powerful magnet. No matter what he was saying or doing, his attention was fixed on the assumption that the key to Nestor's true identity was to be found within that spot on the floor. His imagination was running wild. He envisioned finding a compartment, in the concrete below the tiles, containing an untold wealth of treasure. Nestor might have hidden there an ancient scroll bearing information about Noah's Ark that presumably rested on the peak of Ararat in his native land of Armenia, after the Great Flood. Or, he might simply find the manuscript of Nestor's autobiography in his own handwriting, together with volumes of classic books that were not known up to this moment. The possibilities were unlimited. Nestor was an enigmatic person, and one could expect surprises when he explored his untold past. Well, whatever will be, will be, Theo muttered to himself, and after taking his much needed shower, he went to bed. He had grown accustomed to sleeping without Anastasia, eating late at night, and drinking local retsina. Tonight, he fell asleep as fast as he crawled under his soft blanket and heard nothing until six o'clock the next morning, when Zacharias woke him up with his loud voice from the street, commanding his donkey to go forward.

Theo got out of his bed and opened his bedroom window.
The sun was several feet above the eastern horizon, and the
azure sky was as clear as ever. He shaved, brushed his teeth,
put on his clothes, and thought that it would be best if he
had his coffee with his cousin again, this morning. He felt
the urgency and the need to be in someone's company,
before returning to the gruesome task of researching a dead
man's belongings in a ghostly mansion. He entered the car
and drove the short distance to his cousin's home where he
found Fotis seated on a low chair, milking his nanny goat
in the front yard of his house.

"Good morning cousin," Theo said cheerfully, "I see we
will have fresh milk with our coffee this morning."

"Hey cousin, I was not expecting to see you here this
morning," Fotis said, "Please come in. I will be with you in
a minute." Theo walked into the house and having nothing
else to do, he gazed at the pictures of Fotis' family that were
neatly arranged on one of the wall panels in the dining
room. The picture of his son and his family were to the left
and that of his daughter and her family was to the right.
The portrait of his departed wife was above the other two
pictures. A few minutes later, Fotis appeared, holding in his
hands a glass pitcher with fresh milk he had just collected
from his nanny goat.

"I am pleased to have coffee with you in my house
again," Fotis said, to Theo as he entered the kitchen. "I was
thinking about you last night and strangely enough, I was
not thinking about the things you said about the hermit.
My mind was wandering on the things we did together as
boys here in the village. Do you remember the fun we had
hunting hare on the slopes of the mountain when the ground
was covered with snow? I remember we followed their tracks
to their den like hounds, flushed them out, and fired our
guns at them. I remember one time you killed two and I

bagged one in an hour before the sun melted the top layer of the snow and obliterated the tracks of the animals."

"Those were the good old days Fotis," Theo reflected melancholically. "I vividly recollect the good time we had dancing with the girls and the boys from our village. Sometimes, I wonder where we found all that energy to dance continuously all night and work the land the next day."

The two cousins sat facing each other at the dinner table and reminisced the time they spent together as children and young adolescents, until Theo left the village and Fotis stayed behind to become a husband and a father. Now, in the sunset of their lives, they both wished to go back in time and re-live the times when their lives were uncomplicated. Fotis, in particular, voiced his unhappiness of being a lonesome old man.

"Since I lost my wife, my life is like a fake diamond," he said with a deep suspire. "It shines on the surface but it is not real. I live from day-to-day without anyone to talk to and nothing to look forward to. I am terrified, Theo, thinking that the only thing I have left in life is death. My children live far away, and they are preoccupied with their own lives. Granted, they are good to me. They send me a good allowance every month to meet my daily expenses. The only thing that keeps me from going mad is my nanny goat. She talks to me and I talk to her when she comes and asks me for the outside leaves of a cabbage, or for the core of my apple. She loves the clippings from the end of the string beans, and she enjoys eating potato peels," he said, with a deeper moan this time that shook Theo emotionally and rendered him speechless. The only thing that Theo was able to do under the circumstances was to fix his eyes on his cousin and grasp his hands with a brotherly passion.

"I perfectly understand the predicament you are in, Fotis," Theo managed to say. "Unfortunately, all of us are destined to die as soon as we are born. Look at your life from the positive point of view. You are blessed to have good children, a long life, a comfortable house, and good health. Consider yourself blessed. You manage your own affairs without becoming a burden to others. You are fortunate to be what you are at this point in your life, cousin," he said, hoping that he had uplifted the other man's sunken spirits.

"I guess you are right," Fotis said, and he changed the subject of their conversation. "Do you need my help today?" he asked, and he fixed his attention on Theo for his answer.

"I don't think so," Theo responded. "I will take another look at the floor in the private room, and I will decide if I have to remove the tiles or do something else. There is nothing else left to investigate, unless something new pops up in front of me today. In any case, I plan to be back early tonight. Honestly, I am tired doing the things I have been doing so far. Anastasia might think I am nuts running around trying to answer a moot question. I want to wrap this thing up and go home, as soon as possible." He paused for a second, and he added. "Yet, if I give up at this point, I will look languid, and that I have no determination to bring the search to an end. If I quit now, the question of who Nestor was will only have a speculative answer. Don't you think so, Fotis?"

"If that's how you feel about the whole thing," Fotis said, "go up there today and turn the damn place up-side-down until you are convinced that there is nothing else of interest hidden somewhere."

"By God, I will do just that," Theo replied with alacrity. He finished his coffee, lifted himself off the chair, said goodbye to Fotis, entered the Fiat, and drove toward the summit one more time. On his way, he summed up in his mind the things he knew about Nestor, and the information he needed to solve the rest of the mystery.

Ok, I know that Nestor was Armenian, Theo said to himself. His real name was David Koch and before that, he was a Chrisoglu of unknown first name, he continued, as he was winding his way up the road to the summit. Let's assume for a moment that he was a war orphan, someone adopted him, and changed his name from Chrisoglu to Koch. The war orphan scenario is supported by the fact that he went out of his way to find something about a Chrisoglu during World War I. So far so good, he added, satisfied with his reasoning. The thing I know nothing about is his finances. One has to assume that he was wealthy; otherwise, he could not build this lavish mansion. Keeping inconspicuous from the rest of the world up here, makes me suspect that he was concealing his wealth, or he was hiding the manner by which he acquired it. If he had inherited the money, he did not have to go out of his way to be unnoticed.

Theo drove the rest of the way without talking to himself, for the beauty of the landscape stole his attention. At last, he reached the outer gate of the mansion, parked the car in front of the gate, opened it, and entered the garden area. Walking under the canopy of the grape vines toward the entrance to the mansion itself, he noticed that the grapes were not ripe yet, and that the flowers on both sides of the walking path were in desperate need for water. He stopped in front of Bougainvillea that lined both sides of the pathway and said to the wilting flowers in a sympathetic voice. "Beautiful red flowers, pray for a good rain. There is no Magdalene any more to water you," and he kept walking until he reached the main entrance with the solid brass knocker depicting a double-headed falcon. He opened the door and went directly to the secret room.

He turned the lights on, and he found the part of the floor that he and Fotis had marked with the tape two days ago. Walking around the rectangle that was enclosed by the tape that was still stuck firmly on the floor, he meticulously examined the enclosed area from near and from far away. He still saw the same thing he observed the day before. Indeed, the color of the grout that outlined a particular spot within the rectangle was lighter than the rest of it. Theo could still see a discernable difference in color. After a closer examination, he identified a small rectangular portion in the floor structure that stood out from the rest. Four triangular marble pieces of approximately the same color and size were positioned in such a way that their outside periphery formed a small, perfectly shaped rectangle of only six by ten inches, and that observation discouraged him. If this was the secret place where Nestor has hidden the things Theo was hoping to find, it was not big enough to fit "immense treasure," "scrolls," or "ancient books". A small bush hides a big hare he whispered, and he kneeled down, holding in his hand a small screw driver Fotis gave him the night before. He placed the sharp edge of the instrument in the grout and forcefully pulled it along the line of the peripheral grout. He occasionally hammered the screw driver with a small mallard Fotis gave him the previous night, just like he did when he engraved his initials on the lime stone years ago.

Every time he dragged the point of the screw driver along the line, a portion of the grout gave way and turned to dust. He continued the gouging and hammering until he cleared away the grout from all four sides of the rectangle. Using a little spatula Fotis had given him; he pried the rectangle away from its place. It came up all in one piece, and Theo noticed to his amazement that the four triangular marble chips were firmly glued atop an iron plate. He put the plate on the side and inspected the hole with great anticipation.

To his disappointment, he discovered that there was only a single, aluminum box in the 6X10X4 inch cavity. He reached inside, picked up the precious box, and without attempting to open it, he carefully examined its outside appearance for a few seconds.

The box was enfolded in several layers of plastic film then, wrapped over with several turns of clear adhesive tape. He felt the initial rush to tear away the plastic cover and find out what was hidden inside, but his better judgment told him to be more cautious. There might be something of value hidden between the layers of the plastic film or under the tape, he said to himself. I must open it like a brain surgeon opens his patient's skull. He put the cover plate back in its place, filled the gap around it with the pulverized grout he had removed with his screw driver, wiped the floor clean with a wet towel, removed the masking tape off the floor, and with the box in his hands, he went to the kitchen to perform the delicate operation of opening it. As soon as he sat at the table, with a sharp knife in his hands, he heard the roaring sound of a vehicle coming toward the mansion. Quickly, he hid the package away and walked to the gate to greet his visitor. Unexpectedly, there was Magdalene with a man of her age, who came out of the car and greeted Theo with flabbergasted expressions on their faces.

"Greetings Mr. Theo," Magdalene managed to say. "My neighbor and I took a ride up here to water the garden and collect some fruit and vegetables for dinner. We hope you don't mind us picking some," she continued with a blush on her face.

"Magdalene," Theo retorted. "This place and these gardens are not mine. They belonged to the late Mr. Nestor. I am sure he does not object you helping yourself to the fruit and vegetables, provided you take care of them the way you use to, when Nestor was still alive. We all have a responsibility to keep the property intact until the legal owner comes along to claim it."

"Mr. Theo, I am Nicolas. I live next door to Magdalene," Magdalene's companion said to Theo, and he extended his hand to shake hands with Theo. Theo grasped the other man's hand and said with a warm expression in his face,

"Nicolas, I am so glad that I met you. Please go ahead, water the garden and the trees. I would like to spend a few minutes with Magdalene, if you don't mind! I want to ask her a few questions about Mr. Nestor."

Nicolas went to do the watering, and Theo and Magdalene walked to the kitchen and sat at the table facing each other.

"Magdalene," Theo said, in a friendly voice. "Tell me, how often Mr. Nestor went away and for how long he was gone? Tell me everything you remember about his disappearances from here."

Magdalene nervously rubbed the palms of her hands and began to narrate Nestor's trips.

"Most of the time, he was planning his trips weeks in advance," she said. "On a number of occasions however, he told me at dinner time, that he was going away the next morning. He always took with him a small suitcase with an extra pair of slacks, shirts, socks, and underwear. He never took with him suits, ties, or an extra pair of shoes. He had the same taxi picking him up early in the morning, and the same taxi brought him back when he decided to come home. Sometimes, he was gone for two to three days. Other times, he made me worry about his safety because he was away for almost a week."

At this point, Theo interrupted her and said, "Do you remember anything about the taxi driver himself, or the city he was coming from?"

"I assume he came from Turkohori," she said. "He had an unusual name that stuck in my mind. He also had a gypsy face, I remember. He was a tall man in his fifties, had curly black hair, a hook-like nose, and a healthy mustache. Mr. Nestor told me one time to have *Bash* come in and wait for him, and that's how I learned the taxi driver's name." Theo listened to her attentively, hoping to learn something revealing about Nestor's occasional trips and his affiliates.

If I can find Bash, he thought while Magdalene tried to organize her next statement, I may be able to learn from him, where he dropped Nestor off, and where he picked him up to bring him back to the mansion. If time permits it, I should stop at the taxi terminal in Turkohori, and look for the dark haired Bash, Theo premeditated.

"Can you tell me anything about the way Mr. Nestor spent his idle time while he was here?" Theo continued his inquiry.

"Oh, he was reading and writing a lot," she responded. "There were all kinds of people visiting him, you know! They used to sit in the meeting room and spend hours talking and having coffee. They were people from the city, people from the villages around here, and complete strangers from other places. After dinner, provided he had nothing else to do, Mr. Nestor used to retire in his private room upstairs, and stayed there until he was ready to go to bed. Quite often, I could hear the passionate notes of his guitar and his rustic songs that I never heard before. The songs sounded strange to me. I could not understand the words he was saying."

"Do you remember him having the same visitor coming up here more than once?" Theo inquired.

"No, not that I remember, but, of course, I never paid attention to whom was coming to see him," she replied in a laconic way, and she added. "Mr. Nestor was a kind and generous man, Mr. Theo. He helped any person who came up here asking him for his counseling. For example, he gave wise advice to my children, and on a number of occasions, he gave them money to buy their books for school," she said with a deep sigh. At this point, Theo noticed that she was crying and interrupted her narration to allow her to recover from her sadness.

"Magdalene," he said, "We all owe a big thanks to the man we know little about and his personal life. We know that he was a kind and a wise man, but that's all we know about him. He helped me too to build confidence in myself, and in my abilities to accomplish things. He taught me that I could be whatever I wanted to be in life. I am glad I was in the position to be by his bed during the last hours of his life. I still do not know where he came from and what his real name was. I would like to find his family, bring them the sad news of his death, and deliver to them some of his personal possessions I found in his private room. Did he ever talk to you about his family? Can you help me find them?"

"Mr. Nestor never talked to me about his family," she replied. "Only one time, when he was talking to my children about the value of family and education, he said that they should respect their mother. 'I wish I had my mother to be kind to,' he told them, and from that statement, I understood that his mother was either dead, or that he never knew her."

Magdalene's last statement hit Theo like a bomb shell. Was his mother dead, or did he become orphan early in his childhood and therefore, he did not remember her? Was he an abandoned child who was taken in by the Koch family and raised as such? Theo wondered aloud.

"Is there anything else you can tell me about him, or about the unusual way he conducted his life up here?" Theo added, hoping that Magdalene would say something revealing.

"If anything else comes to my mind, I'll let you know," Magdalene responded, and got off her chair to join Nicolas in the garden.

"Oh, by the way," Theo said to her. "Come up here as often as you can to water the trees, the flowers, and the garden. Mr. Nestor would have liked to see his place as orderly, and as beautiful as it was when he was still alive. Naturally, the fruits and the vegetables will belong to you if you take time to care for this place. As for myself, I will be gone away on business for a few days." Theo was thinking that he may be able to learn something knew from someone at the university, if he delivered the brown envelope in person. "Then, I will briefly return, before I leave to go back home," he added.

Magdalene joined Nicolas who was watering the garden, and Theo returned to the secret room with the box in his hands. He locked the door behind him, sat in Nestor's chair at the main desk, placed in front of him the box and the envelope Magdalene pulled out from under Nestor's pillow, and took another look at them. The brown envelope had nothing else written on it and its seals were still intact. He placed it against the light, and he could see that it contained only two or three sheets of paper, folded together. He felt the urge to tear it open and examine its contents, but his better judgment commanded his hands to do otherwise. Oh, I don't have any right to open the mail that belongs to another person. I will soon take a trip to Thessaloniki, and I will deliver it to the school in person, he muttered, and returned it to his pocket. Then, he picked up the box and inspected it carefully one more time. The plastic adhesive tape that was wrapped around it looked fresh. It was not brittle at all, and that indicated that the wrapping was done recently. The tape held firmly on the underneath plastic that protected its enwrapped aluminum box. Theo found the outside end of the tape and pried it out with his fingernails. Holding this end with one hand, he unwound the tape away from the plastic over-wrapping. Now he could see that the box under the plastic over-wrapping film was tan aluminum, not brown as he thought at the beginning. He stretched the tape on the desk and meticulously examined both sides for any visible markings that might be clues to something else, but he noticed nothing unusual. Unconsciously, he crumbled the tape to a ball with his hands and placed it in front of him. He vigilantly removed each layer of the plastic film and examined it as he was pulling it away. Here again, he noticed nothing unusual. He wrapped the plastic film around the ball of the tape and put it aside on the tabletop. Finally, he held in his hands the closed, tan, aluminum box with something inside. Instinctively, he pulled out the top drawer of the desk, and retrieved Nestor's envelope opener with the letters "D. K." engraved on its handle. With utmost care, he slipped the pointed blade under the lid of the box and delicately pried it open. A chill ran up his spine, and he felt the rush of his blood pounding in his ears. He was holding in one of his hands a metal box that presumably contained valuable information about who Nestor was, and in the other hand, he held Nestor's personal letter opener with his initials engraved on its ivory handle. His heart was pumping faster now, and he realized that his hands were shaking. He took several deep breaths to calm down, and to gain mental strength to look inside the box. With tender care and with a sympathetic sense of gentleness, he reached inside the tan box and retrieved two sealed, smaller envelopes, a hand written note, and two keys.

On the broad face of one of the sealed envelopes, Nestor had written in bold letters: "***To be opened in your presence by the president of The National Bank of Greece.***"

On the other sealed envelope he had also written in bold letters: *"To be opened in your presence by an officer of the Swiss Bank."*

The hand written note was brief and gave instructions to the possessor of these items what to do with them. Nestor had written two laconic paragraphs:

"You are trusted to disperse my wealth as directed in the contents of the two sealed envelopes you have in your hands. Both the Swiss Bank and The National Bank Of Greece have my written authorization for you to open the security deposit boxes with the two keys you found in the metal box you took out of the hall in the floor.

The contents of the boxes in the two banks are for you to use as you wish, but the trusts are to be dispersed by the banks as I direct in the sealed envelopes. You are to travel to Zurich and to Athens and deliver the envelopes in person. Have my death certificate and this letter with you when you visit them".

David Koch.

One of the keys was an ordinary flat key with several unevenly cut notches on one of its edges. A number was clearly stamped on one of its flat sides. The number was preceded by one of the letters from the Greek alphabet, and Theo concluded that this key should open a box in the Greek bank. The other key was bigger and ornate. Its identification number appeared to be engraved by a jeweler and the handle itself was gold plated. Its overall appearance indicated that it should fit to a security box, most likely, in the Swiss Bank. Theo placed the two envelopes and the hand written note in the pocket he had the other envelope in and zipped it close. He retrieved his wallet from the back pocket of his trousers and secured the two keys in the same compartment he kept the spare key, to his home. He rose off his chair, paced the floor several times to calm down and to take hold of his excitement, and readied himself to go back to the kitchen. He locked the door to the secret room and walked downstairs to where Magdalene and Nicolas were getting ready to leave. They had finished watering the garden and the flowers, and had collected three baskets of fruits and vegetables to take home.

"Mr. Theo," Magdalene said, "You mentioned earlier that you will be going away soon. May I ask when you are leaving and when you will return?"

"I will leave tomorrow morning, and I hope to be back in about a week. This place is going to be locked up for safety reasons, but I will leave the outside gate unlocked, in case you want to come back to water the garden and help yourself to the vegetables and the fruits."

Magdalene thanked Theo for allowing them to pick fruits and vegetables from the garden, and Nicolas expressed his pleasure in meeting him. With a warm feeling in their hearts, Nicolas and Magdalene entered the run down, Nissan pick up and drove away.

Theo returned to the secret room, opened the door, picked up the wrapping material and the empty, metal box he had forgotten on Nestor's table, locked the door again, and walked out of the building. He was holding in one hand, the bag with Fotis's digging tools and in the other, the metal box and the wrapping plastic. He locked the main entrance behind him and returned to his car that stood idle by the gate. He placed the items he held in his hands inside the trunk and retrieved the ignition key from his pocket to drive the Fiat back home. A strange desire to pace the walkways in the garden overcame his intention to drive away. He put the keys back in his pocket, returned to the garden, and spent a few peaceful moments in tranquility, among the fruit trees and the flowering shrubs. He sensed the need to put his thoughts in order and to get hold of his emotions before driving back to the village. So many things had happened since he left home. Just days ago, he was talking to a man whom he had admired all his life for his wisdom and his kindness. Nestor, in the course of a few days, became David Koch and Chrisoglu. In the span of that short time, Theo learned that Nestor was born in Armenia, at the beginning of the twentieth century. Above all, Theo was entrusted with the dispersion of Nestor's fortune, and that he was the only owner of the contents in Nestor's safety deposit boxes. Still in mystery were the circumstances of Nestor becoming Koch from Chrisoglu, and the way he acquired his wealth. Other questions kept coming up in Theo's mind as he was thinking about his hermit friend. Was he a child whose parents perished in the war, and brought up as David Koch? Was he an illegitimate child of some woman that in retrospect, she did not want or could not afford to be a parent? In any case, where had he received such a splendid education, and most importantly, why did he become a hermit?

Theo walked back and forth several times along the garden paths and felt much better. Suddenly, he decided to pay Nestor a visit at his resting place. He collected a bouquet of roses from the garden, and with a heavy heart, he walked to where Nestor was buried. He kneeled over the newly dug soil, and said with a deferential tone in his voice:

"Friend, I hope you hear me, and that you understand the emotional state of my mind. I am your truest friend, and I am saddened that I cannot talk to you person-to-person, anymore. I want you to know that I never forgot you in the past, and I will never forget you in the future. You did so much for me, and I did not have the opportunity to do something for you in return, until now. Rest assured that I will do exactly as you asked in your hand written note I found in the tan, metal box which I retrieved from under the tiles in your private room. I consider it a great honor to be of service to you, my best friend and teacher. I will fly to Switzerland tomorrow to deliver the envelope to the Swiss Bank and on my way back, I'll stop at the university in Thessaloniki to give them the envelope you kept under your mattress. Before I return home to join my wife, I will stop in Athens to see the president of the Greek National Bank, and I will deliver the other envelope, per your instructions." At the end of his brief talk with his dead friend and mentor, Theo deposited the bouquet of roses on the burial grounds, wiped his wet eyes, and slowly walked to where he kept the Fiat. He retrieved the cell phone out of his pocket and, before he started the car to return to the village, he made arrangements with a travel agency in Athens to fly to Switzerland early the next morning.

It was early afternoon and the sun had just tipped toward the western horizon where heavy clouds were accumulating. He saw streaks of lightning crossing the western sky and heard the rumble of thunder in the distance. We are going to have another stormy afternoon, he said to himself, and started driving toward his village. By the time he was at the foot of the mountain, the sky burst open with lightning and thunder, and rain came down with ferocity and converted the road to a muddy stream of rushing water. He pulled the car to the side of the road and waited for the rain to subside before he resumed driving. Minutes later, the heavy clouds broke apart, the lightning and the thunder stopped, the rain went away, and the sun showed his face anew from behind the clouds. A colorful rainbow arched from behind the mountain to the distant valley and the muddy water drained away from the road. Theo started the car again and resumed his driving toward the village. He stopped at Fotis's house, handed over the bag with the tools and told him that he was going away for a few days.

"Come in for a minute," Fotis said to his cousin. "I made fresh yogurt last night and it is just right for eating." Theo accepted the invitation and took his place at the kitchen table. Fotis brought a bowl of yogurt, placed it next to the pitcher with honey on the table, and sat down across from Theo.

"Did you accomplish anything today?" Fotis said, and pushed the bowl with the yogurt toward Theo.

"Quite a bit," Theo said, and dipped his spoon in the contents of the bowl. "I dug out from underneath the tiles some very important documents," he reported, and went on to describe the contents of the metal box he found, in the hole under the tiles, in the secret room by the north window.

"I am going to Switzerland tomorrow and on my way back, I will stop in Thessaloniki and Athens," he said, and filled his plate with yogurt.

"Was there anything for you?" Fotis bluntly asked.

"Your question has to wait for its answer until I visit the Swiss Bank and the First National Bank of Greece," Theo responded, and smothered his yogurt with some of the honey, from the pitcher that stood in front of them.

"Do you know anything new about Nestor himself?" Fotis asked, and started to eat the yogurt he had piled into his own bowl.

"I now know that he was an Armenian orphan during World War I, and that he was raised under the name David Koch. I hope that my visits to Switzerland, Thessaloniki, and Athens will provide additional information to know the man's true identity and past history. I have a plan of action in mind, but its implementation depends upon what

I will learn on my trip, that will start tonight," he said. He, then, dipped his spoon in his yogurt again. "I am leaving tonight for Turkohori to catch the train to Athens. I must be at the international airport tomorrow morning to make my connection for Switzerland; otherwise, I lose a whole day." Fotis was looking at Theo as if Theo was possessed by evil spirits, but he said nothing more. They finished their yogurt, and Theo got off his chair, thanked his cousin for the delicious yogurt and with a brief adieu, entered the Fiat and drove to his parental house. Minutes later, Fotis heard the roaring of the Fiat's engine and saw Theo at his doorsteps again.

"Here are the keys to the house," he said to Fotis. "I will see you in about a week," he continued, and hurryingly drove away in the Fiat.

This man is going out of his mind, Fotis muttered, and crossed himself three times! He stuffed the key in his pocket and walked inside his house holding his head between his hands.

Chapter Seven: "Zurich"

Theo drove to Turkohori and turned the rental car in. There were many places in this town he would like to visit, but time was not permitting it. The evening train to Athens was leaving in fifty five minutes, and he had to be at the station in advance, to procure his boarding ticket. He flagged down a taxi that happened to go by and asked the driver to take him to the train station. Like most taxi drivers, this man was talkative and jovial, and Theo took the opportunity to ask him about the taxi driver that Magdalene described early this morning.

"Do I know Bash?" the taxi driver replied with a dry laugh. "Who does not know the Armenian gypsy," he added with a sneer in his voice. "Why are you so interested knowing about him? Did he swindle someone you know and took his money? He is good at it."

"Nothing of that," Theo replied. "I'm trying to locate a childhood friend, and people tell me that he was Mr. Bash's frequent customer. I simply would like to ask Mr. Bash where I should look for my friend's family."

"Friend, in the taxi business, especially in a small town like this, every driver knows what the other driver does. I can tell you how many ladies 'lay' with each one of our drivers, if you get the drift of my comment," he said with a questionable look in his eyes. "I can sit here and tell you names of 'fat cats' that cheat on their wives and how many 'devoted wives' have fun with other guys at the parks of the city in the moonlight. We all knew that Bash used to pick up a strange man in a remote castle somewhere east from here, and he would drop him at the train station. Days later, this same person used to call in and asked for Bash to pick him up at the coffee shop by the station. No other driver was good enough for him, except Bash. Bash claims that his father and the strange man were born in Armenia, and both ended up in Greece after the Turks took over their country. According to Bash, the strange man never told him the circumstances of his arrival in Greece, nor his true first name. Bash kept calling him 'Mr. Chrisoglu'."

By now, the taxi had arrived at the train station. Theo paid the driver, took his belongings in his hands, thanked him for his interesting conversation, and walked toward the ticket window. Theo never told the taxi driver that the "strange man" Bush was picking up was the same man he was interested in. The taxi sped away toward the center of the town, and Theo walked up to the ticket window. He purchased his ticket and strolled over to the coffee shop for a cup of coffee, before boarding the train to Athens. The coffee shop was not very busy at this hour and his coffee with a glass of cold water arrived at his table on time. He leisurely sipped the coffee, drank the water, paid his bill, and walked to the train that had just arrived at the station on route to Athens. He boarded, found an empty seat, placed his suitcase on the rack above his head, and made himself comfortable for the three hour trip.

It was still daylight when the conductor closed the doors and signaled the train's departure with his whistle. The train moved at a snail's pace at first, puffing black smoke from the chimney of its locomotive, and finally accelerated forward through the olive tree orchards with an occasional whistling to warn animals and pedestrians. The air inside Theo's train compartment was uncomfortably hot. He lowered his window and stuck his head outside to cool his face, with the draft that was created by the speeding train. He gazed toward the mountains in the far distance and felt for a moment that the olive trees were moving, not the train. He had the impression that the trees were running in the opposite direction from a train seemingly standing still.

A robust country fellow in his late-eighties with a weathered face was sitting next to him. His white mustache was tinted yellow, directly in front of his nostrils from where the smoke came out when he puffed his cigarette, and his uncombed, white hair covered part of his forehead. The country fellow decided to display his Greek hospitality to the man next to him. He tapped Theo on the shoulder to get his attention, and extending toward Theo his hand holding the open pack of cigarettes, he said in a deep voice, with a mannerism that expressed the man's obvious friendship,

"Would you like to join me for a smoke?" Before Theo had the chance to respond, the old man forcibly silenced and re-positioned himself in his chair. He drew a deep drag from the burning cigarette he held between his lips, puffed his chest outward, and exhaled a cloud of smoke from both his mouth and his nostrils, with an extended, dry cough.

"No thanks," Theo politely told the stranger. "I gave up smoking thirty eight years ago, and I promised myself not to touch the stuff again. Do you know how much harm you do to your health by smoking?" he asked the stranger. The smoking man removed the cigarette from his lips, squeezed and knocked away the burning part from the rest of the cigarette with his thumb and index finger, dropped the cinder on the wood floor, and stepped on it. He put the remaining butt of the cigarette back in his pocket, re-positioned himself on his seat again, and defended his smoking habit.

"People tell me that smoking will ruin my lungs. I am smoking all my life, and here I am. I am eighty eight years old, and I am on my way to see my grandson graduating from a big school to become a lawyer. There is nothing wrong with my lungs friend," he said, and broke into a dry coughing once more. "This damn cold lingers with me all year round," he added to justify the cause of his coughing.

"If I were you," Theo said, "I would go and see a doctor about this coughing. It can be something serious and you can prevent it from becoming a major health problem."

"Nonsense son, this cough is the result of a bullet wound I received in my chest, from a German rifle when I was a resistor with *Zervas* in 1943. Have you ever heard of Zervas?" the old man cleverly said, to change the subject of their conversation.

"Yes, I heard of him, and about all the good things he did for Greece," Theo said in a complementary tone of voice. "However, what one reads in books and newspapers is often distorted, for they are second hand information. Do you mind telling me your adventures during those years? I heard so much about all those brave men who joined Zervas, and about the risks you took to interrupt the German plans to destroy the free spirit of the Greeks."

"I have narrated this part of my life story many times before, and every time I go through it, I remember things I have forgotten," the old man said with pride. "All of us were good patriots," he said, and coughed again. "Many of us were ex-policemen, some were military officers like our commander, and a few of us were just dedicated patriots, willing to risk our lives to make Greece a free nation again. We also had with us a few Greek Jews from Thessaloniki. They joined our group by necessity, not necessarily by choice, for they were prosecuted by the Germans in the city. They found safety and brotherhood with us in the mountains. All of them hated the Germans with a passion and became brave and valiant comrades.

"Our mode of operation was hit-and-run, not facing the enemy in the open plains. The Germans had an organized war machine with tanks and airplanes, and we only had rusty riffles with a limited supply of bullets in our hands and a few hand grenades hanging from our belts. We were successful in ambushing German dispatches going from one place to another, for we knew the terrain and could choose the field of action. Many of our men were locals, and they knew every ravine and every 'blind spot' in the area, that was ideal to hide and wait for the enemy.

"I clearly remember the time when four of us blew up a bridge on the border of Serbia and Greece and sent a small train into the chasm below with a good number of German soldiers in it. That was the time when a bullet entered the right part of my chest and came out from my back, just inches away from my spine. My other three comrades did not make it. We found the bodies of the two ex-policemen two days later, but the body of our Jewish friend from Thessaloniki vanished, probably, in the muddy waters of the river below.

"They say that the train carried money that was collected by the Gestapo, as ransom from the Jewish population of Thessaloniki. There must be some truth to this rumor because later on, one of our search parties found two small, gold ingots among the wreckage, where the cars crashed on initial impact, just before they rolled into the bottom of the gorge. There were no enemy survivors, but several of them were finished execution-style. Bullets were fired at them from close range by someone, probably by a posse of local liberation fighters. Our searching men found me semi-unconscious, and brought me back on a stretcher, made from a blanket tied on two long posts. The doctor, who examined me at that time, said that my chances for recovery were nil, but the Man upstairs thought otherwise. Here I am flapping my mouth to a stranger," he said with a roaring laugh and a dry cough.

"I am sorry," Theo said apologetically. "My name is Theovulos", and shook the old man's hand that felt like a sledge hammer in Theo's hand.

"Call me *barba Costa*, my son," he replied, and re-positioned himself in his seat one more time. "I have to move quite often, otherwise my bones become stiff and I cannot get up to go to the men's room," he said, and he denoted with this comment that he had surrendered to the perils of old age.

"You know something about me, and I only know your name. Tell me something about yourself son," barba Costa said and started to cough again.

"I was born in Peloponnesus, went to school there, served the army like all other able young men, and finally, I went to America where I have my home," he told the old man. "Personal business called me back last week, and as soon as I am through, I am going back."

"Oh, you are an American!" Costas exclaimed with awe in his voice. "Tell me, do you consider yourself an American or a Greek?" he said, and fixed his gaze at Theo to see and gage the intensity of Theo's reaction.

"Barba Costa, I am an American of Greek descent, and I am proud of it," Theo emphasized.

"America is the most powerful nation in the world," Costas said, in deep thought. "Your president takes advantage of it, though. He runs the affairs of the world like the Emperor Constantine did two thousand years ago. That's wrong, son! I am afraid that the day will come when you will not have any friends to stand on your side, and your country will become another Russia. More than two thirds of the people on earth are Chinese, Vietnamese, Laotians, Cambodians, North Koreans, etc., and none of them is your friend. Furthermore, you will be hard pressed to find a Muslim nation that is willing to be on your side in case of war. Turkey, Egypt, Pakistan and Saudi Arabia, for example, are not your friends at all. They play the double game. Your neighbors in Central and South America hate your guts too," he added. He stopped talking, and cough again to clear his lungs. After a brief silence, he spoke about the perils that loom on the global horizon.

"Every one knows that China, Russia, North Korea, Pakistan, India, Iran, Israel, England, France, and probably Germany, possess the same weapons of mass destruction that you have in your arsenals. The only difference, between most of them and you, is the sophistication needed to deliver such weapons to designated targets from a long distance. Tell me son, how long will it take for them to acquire that technology too? Don't you think that your president should be less bullish and more conciliatory in his disputes with the rest of the world?" At this moment, the ticket inspector appeared in the aisle and interrupted their conversation.

"Gentlemen, may I see your tickets?" he said, with an authoritative look on his face. Barba Costa and Theo handed their tickets to the inspector who examined them carefully, made a hole in each one of them with a puncher, returned them to Costa and Theo, and moved on.

Their conversation resumed when the inspector was gone, but their subject was different this time. They talked about their children, their wives, and Costa's grand children until the train arrived in Athens. A well-dressed man picked up barba Costa at the train station, and Theo flagged a taxi, to take him to the travel agency, where he was to pick up his plane ticket to Zurich.

Theo procured his plane ticket, and when he returned to the taxi that was waiting in front of the travel agency, he asked the driver to take him to a hotel near Constitution Square. On his way to the hotel, he thought that it would offend his sister and his brother-in-law, if he spent the night in a hotel. He decided there and then to pay them a visit unexpectedly. He took the cell phone out of his pocket and dialed their number.

"Hello," he heard his sister's voice say, at the end of the other line.

"Hello sister! This is Theo," he said, with a detectable giggle in his voice. "Make fresh coffee and I'll be there in fifteen minutes."

"Jesus and Virgin Mary," his sister screamed at the top of her voice. "Where are you my dear brother? Are you calling from America or are you indeed here?"

"Make the coffee and I'll be there in fifteen minutes, I tell you!" he repeated, and instructed the taxi driver to take him to Plato Boulevard, instead of Constitution Square. Fifteen minutes later, the taxi rolled into Plato Boulevard. Theo did not remember the number of his sister's house, but he remembered that it was the only house in the block with a veranda facing the street. He asked the taxi driver to go slow, so that he would have time to take a good look at each house as they went by.

"Stop here," Theo said and pointed his finger to a modest house in the middle of the block. The taxi pulled to the curb, the driver received his fare, and Theo with his suitcase in his hands, climbed the three steps to the entrance of the house. At the door, he met the smiling face of his sister and the bewildered expression on the face of his brother-in-law. After the initial emotional outburst of a sister meeting her brother, after a long absence, they walked into the house and settled down around the dining room table. His brother-in-law asked Theo about Anastasia and their children, but his sister kept looking at him with an inquisitive expression on her face, as if she had something important to say to her brother.

"What is on your mind sister?" Theo finally asked her, "You look at me as if you have never seen me before."

"I cannot get over it brother," she finally said, "I don't believe that you changed so much since the last time I saw you. I see a few wrinkles on your face! You are a bit overweight, and you look different with that cropped gray hair on your head," she said, and broke into an uncontrollable giggle that was punctuated with a sisterly love in her face.

"Ok, enough of this silly talking," her husband interrupted her. "The man is probably tired and hungry. He is, most likely, thirsty for a glass of wine or something better," he continued, and turned his eyes toward Theo to receive his affirmation for his speculation. Theo denoted with a motion of his hands and a nodding of his head that the brother-in-law's assessment was correct. When the wine and some cold cuts of sausage, black olives, and feta cheese came to the table, Theo told them that he had to be at the airport early the next morning, to fly to Switzerland on important business.

"Don't worry about that," the brother-in-law said. "I will drive you there tomorrow morning. The airport is only ten minutes from here." But his sister insisted that he should delay his trip for another day to spend time with them. Theo took the time to explain to her that it was imperative for him to be in Zurich early the next day.

"No," Theo said emphatically, "I have to be in Zurich tomorrow morning. This trip cannot be postponed for another day."

The rest of the evening went by amidst brotherly talk, until the time came to retire for the night. Theo's sister escorted him to the guest room, familiarized him with the surroundings, and said to him, "You are terribly pre-occupied with something, brother. Is everything ok with you and your family? You are not the laughing brother I used to know. Is there something we can do to eliminate the things that bother your mind?"

"Everything is fine sister! You imagine things that are not there," he said, with a broad smile, and with a goodnight hug. "There are only business matters that need careful attention." His sister took a long look at him one more time and exited the room without saying anything else. Theo closed the door, took a quick shower, called his wife, and went to sleep.

The next morning, he got up at 6:00am, shaved, dressed, and had his breakfast with them in the kitchen, before they drove him to the airport. At the airport, he kissed his sister goodbye, gave a bear hug to his brother-in-law, and said to them, "I'll see you before I leave for America." He picked up his suitcase and disappeared into the crowd of other passengers who cluttered the inspection gate. An hour later, he was sitting in an airplane that was about to take him to

Zurich, to deliver the sealed envelope in accordance with the instructions from his late friend and teacher. Why does Nestor want me to be present when they open the envelope, he wondered aloud. What is the purpose of my witnessing the opening, and seeing what is inside? The "why" and the "what" have to wait a few more hours to be answered, he said to himself, just as the plane taxied in line for departure.

The small jet glided westward over the Peloponnesus, Theo's birth place, crossed the small stretch of sea that separates the west cost of southern Greece from the east cost of Sicily, and finally traversed over Italy from south to north. It followed a flight path over Sicily, Naples, Rome itself, Florence, and finally over Milan, before entering the sky over Switzerland. At the time the jet was flying over Rome, the Greek-speaking crew served breakfast. The scrambled eggs tasted like aged leather, and the coffee was bitter and tart, as if it was left over from the day before. Theo drank only the orange juice and ate the peanuts and his toasted bread, smothered with plenty of orange marmalade. At last, the plane flew over the snow covered peaks of the Alps and approached the international airport of Zurich, flying over picturesque Lake Zurich. At last, the plain made a smooth descent and landed without incident in Zurich's International Airport. Customs inspection was uneventful, and Theo found himself outside the airport with his suitcase in his hands. He stopped a taxi and asked the driver to take him to the main branch of the Swiss Bank.

"Yes sir", the driver said in an extremely polite manner and stepped on his taxi's accelerator. It was not long before the taxi arrived in front of a guarded gate that led into a well-maintained estate. The estate was surrounded by a high, wrought iron fence with a large entrance, and Theo could see in the distance, a massive building with only a few small windows. He compensated the taxi driver, approached the guard at the gate, and explained the purpose of his visit. The guard asked his name, and motioned him to sit in the reception room. On his way into the reception room, Theo heard the guard saying something in French, into a communication microphone he hung on his lapel. He sat there not more than a minute, when he saw a golf cart approaching the gate from the massive building in the distance. The vehicle stopped at the gate, and Theo almost passed out when he laid eyes on the driver. She dismounted the golf cart, and Theo stood in front of a perfectly feminine figure with a radiant personality and a long smile that captivated his imagination.

"Good morning Mr. Theo," she said in French and took his hand in a gentle hand shake. "What brings you to our bank today?" she continued in English this time with a French accent. "Oh, by the way sir, you may leave your suitcase here. You will re-claim it on your way out."

Theo recovered quickly from his initial shock, surrendered his suitcase to the guard, and handed Nestor's note to the lady. This note instructed Theo to deliver the sealed envelope to the bank in person. He also gave her the envelope itself and began to explain how he came to be in possession of these items.

"Please save your explanations until we meet the vice president, who handles these matters," she said. She handed the envelope and the letter back to Theo and motioned him with her hand to board the golf cart. He climbed the vehicle and sat on the passenger's seat next to a perfect woman, who smelled like a mountain Lilly in May. The golf cart rolled slowly toward the big building ahead, and he noticed that surveillance cameras were installed on each of the light posts along the way. The shrubs that lined both sides of their way were trimmed with care, and all kinds of flowers were planted in the spaces between them. Finally, they arrived at the entrance, and another guard opened the door for them to enter into the hallway area. The lady inserted her security card into the slot next to the door, that led into one of the reception rooms, and she placed her face against a small camera which identified the retina of her eyes. At last, the door opened and they entered one of the reception rooms. There, the lady told Theo that the vice president would be with him shortly, and she disappeared behind an ornate, glass door that closed behind her automatically. Her delicate perfume lingered in the air for a while after she was gone, but the picture of her waving body in that business suit, stayed with him for a long time.

Theo sat on a plush chair and retrieved from his pocket the three items he needed to talk to the vice president about. He placed on the table next to him, the envelope to be opened by an officer of the bank, and next to it, he laid Nestor's hand written letter of instruction and the death certificate. He kept the vault key in his pocket for the time being.

A green light flickered on the wall, and a panel rotated to allow the vice president to enter the room.

"Welcome to Switzerland Mr. Theo! I am Mr. Felix, the vice president of the bank," he said, and shook Theo's hand. "Please sit here," said Mr. Felix and pointed at a chair located in front of the desk at which Mr. Felix took his place. Theo sat in the designated chair holding in his hands the papers he needed for the meeting.

"Let's see how we can help you today," the vice president said, and extended his hand across his desk to receive the letter, the sealed envelope, and the death certificate. "David was not only a good customer; he was my good friend too," he said with a seeming melancholy in his voice. "Our legal department was instrumental in recovering most of Koch's lost property during the war, and David was appreciative for that," he said, as he was reading the letter of instructions.

Theo sat there speechless looking at Mr. Felix reading Nestor's two paragraph letter and the death certificate.

After the vice president read the letter, he picked up the phone and asked, "May I please have file #121532? Oh yes, have one of our lawyers join me as soon as possible," he said, and turning to Theo, he added, "This case is a bit more complicated than I thought at the beginning. We need legal advice to handle it properly. The death certificate verifies that a Nestor is the deceased person, not a David Koch." Theo re-positioned himself in his chair and said nothing to Mr. Felix.

Minutes later, a secretary escorted by a lawyer entered the room from a side door, greeted Theo politely, and handed a file over to the vice president. Mr. Felix thumbed through several pages until he found the page he was looking for.

"You can go now," Mr. Felix said to the secretary and motioned the lawyer to sit next to him. He handed the lawyer the single page he had retrieved from file #121532 and asked him to render his legal interpretation on its contents. The lawyer re-adjusted his spectacles on his nose and fixed his attention on the contents of the page he was holding in his hands.

"Mr. vice president, your question is answered in this sentence," he said, and read aloud the following:

...*"I was born Armenian. My last name was Chrisoglu but I know nothing about my first name. My parents were killed when the Turks enforced genocide to all non-Moslems in the land. The Koch, a Jewish, childless couple, took me to Thessaloniki where they raised me as David Koch. For reasons that I do not care to explain here, I adopted the name Nestor later on and lived alone in southern Greece for the rest of my life...."*

"Clearly sir, the Chrisoglu lost child in Armenia is the same person under the name David Koch in Thessaloniki and the same man known as Nestor in Peloponnesus, Greece. Legally sir, this death certificate verifies that the person mentioned in file #121532 is dead."

"Very well then, let's open the sealed envelope in the presence of Mr. Theo, as our dear friend instructed us to do," and he motioned Theo and the lawyer to stand by his side to witness the opening of the letter. He reached into his desk, retrieved his letter opener, slit the envelope open, and took out its paper contents. He unfolded the papers and showed to Theo and the lawyer, two trusts and the last testament of David Koch. The trustee for both trusts was the Swiss Bank, and the earnings were to benefit two Jewish entities. The earnings from one of them were to be funneled to the "Jewish/Greek Friends" at a university in Israel, and the earnings from the other were to benefit "The Jewish Brotherhood of Thessaloniki."

"Mr. Theo," the vice president said, "We will initiate legal proceedings to comply with Mr. Koch's wish as soon as possible. From this point forward, the earnings from the trusts will go into separate escrow accounts until channels of communication are established with both the Jewish/Greek Friends in Israel and The Jewish Brotherhood of Thessaloniki."

Theo had not said a word until now; he sat there listening to Mr. Felix who stopped talking, reclined in his chair, and took a look at his wrist watch. At this moment, Theo reached in his pocket, took out his wallet, retrieved the key to the vault from the little pocket in his wallet, and holding it between the first two fingers of his left hand, he said to Mr. Felix, "Now that we took care of the important business, let's open the safety deposit box. I am sure Mr. Koch has his written authorization in your file to permit the holder of this key to open the box," he added and placed the gold plated key in front of Mr. Felix.

"Indeed he has," the vice president said and turning to the lawyer, he dismissed him from their company. "Let us go and see what other surprises our late, mutual friend has for you," he continued with a smile on his face. He picked up the key and motioned Theo to follow him. Walking side-by-side the two men stopped in front of an elevator. Mr. Felix entered his code number to the elevator's electronic panel and the door opened to receive its passengers. The doors closed again and the vice president touched a button by the doors. The elevator moved downward until it reached the basement of the bank where the doors opened again, and the two men walked out. They approached a counter, Felix said something in Italian to the clerk behind, and turning to Theo he said, "You are through with me Mr. Theo. The clerk will escort you to the box momentarily. You can either keep the box for one more year or you can remove its contents and turn the key over to the clerk. It is all up to you. If you need a briefcase to carry things with you on your way out, the clerk will be delighted to give you one." He handed the key back to Theo, shook his hand, and walked away to take a phone call that was announced through the paging system. Theo sat in a waiting room for a minute, until the clerk summoned him over to sign a card.

"This card will be kept as the record that you visited the box today, the clerk said, and added,

"Do you care to have one of our briefcases?" He asked politely.

"I would appreciate having one of them," Theo responded.

"Do you have any preference of color? I have Black, Maroon, and Russet," he added.

"Black will be fine," Theo responded with an uncomfortable feeling that they were making a fuss over the color of an ordinary, leather briefcase. The clerk reached under his counter, retrieved a black, leather briefcase with the emblem of the bank imprinted in gold on both sides and handed it to Theo with a smile. Another well dressed guard came out from behind the counter and escorted Theo to another room, with rows of security boxes mounted on all four walls. Private rooms were erected in the center of the floor with a big number printed on the face of each door. As soon as they entered this area, the guard asked Theo for his key and walked with him directly to the box whose number matched the number of the key Theo handed to him. The guard inserted Theo's key in one keyhole, his master key in the other, and turned one key to his left and the other in the opposite direction. A green light flickered above one of the keyholes and the guard pulled the little door open. He removed the two keys from the keyholes, returned Theo's key back to him, and secured his master key in a leather pouch that was hanging from his belt under his jacket. With outmost care, the guard pulled out of the wall, a stainless steel metal box and handed it to Theo. The box felt substantially heavy in Theo's hands, but he did not make any comments to the guard about it.

"Sir," the guard said. "Enter this room here and conduct your business in total privacy. Remember that you have to use your key to open the box and please, take all the time you need. When you are through, press the button on the wall above the desk, and someone will be there to assist you."

Theo followed the guard's instructions and entered the room to open the mystery box that he was holding in his hands. The door closed automatically behind him, and a "clicking" sound indicated that an automatic electric lock secured the door shut behind him. Now that Theo was away from the security cameras and the eyes of everyone in the bank, he felt comfortable inside the well-ventilated cubicle. He placed the box on the padded desktop and sat in one of the two lavish chairs in front of the desk. He rested the briefcase on the other chair and took several deep breaths to relax and regain his composure before unlocking the box. His anticipation for the great event made his heart race faster, and he felt perspiration moisten his hands and face. He took the key out of his pocket and inserted it in the key slot, but he realized that he was hyperventilating. He moved away from the box for a moment, took off his jacket, wiped his forehead and his hands with his handkerchief, and paced the floor in the tiny room several times to calm down. The mystery of the box's contents overwhelmed him. Finally, he returned to the box and turned the key to the "open" position. With unsteady hands, he lifted the top panel of the box and took a peep inside. Nestor had placed a piece of red velvet cloth over the contents in the box, and that cloth obstructed Theo's view. He could not wait any longer to find out what was under the velvet cloth, and he decided to remove it and expose the box's contents. He felt the rush to know what was there for his labor, and for the time he spent to fulfill Nestor's wishes. He grabbed the velvet cloth, slowly dragged it away from the box, and placed it over the black briefcase on the empty chair next to him.

The inside of the box was divided into two compartments, a large one and a small one, next to it. Several rolls of coins were neatly stacked inside the small compartment and a number of meticulously folded pages of cream-white paper occupied the larger section. Theo automatically responded to his initial instinct. He picked up one of the rolls, and with outmost anticipation, he tore off the paper that held the coins together. A handful of gold English pounds, with the face of the Queen imprinted on one side and their face value on the other, spilled on the padded tabletop. They were spectacular to behold, for they shined like the morning sun. He was looking at twenty four karat gold and plenty of it! He retrieved the velvet cloth from the chair, spread it on the table and placed both the loose coins and the rest of the roles on it. Next, he turned his attention to the folded paper.

His eyes popped wide open when he unfolded the heap of papers. There were several legal size pages of good quality parchment paper, with the legal stamp of the Swiss Bank across the top of the page. Below that, the statement "Negotiable Note" was printed in large black letters. A six finger number was embossed across the face of each parchment page and the same number was worded at the bottom of the page, just above the five signatures that authenticated the documents. Theo was ecstatic with joy and awe when he counted the pages, especially when he mentally calculated their total value in dollars. He could not believe that his fortune brought him so much wealth in such a short span of time. He put the notes on the padded table and looked again in the box. There was nothing else in it. Yet, human insatiability overrode his best judgment. He lifted the empty box off the table and examined it again until he was convinced that it contained nothing more that belonged to him. He placed the box back on the table with its key still in the keyhole and whispered to himself with disgust, aware that he had disgraced himself with his gluttonous action. Pathetic Theo, you are as insatiable as any other man. Don't be so covetous! You have enough money in front of you to make your life comfortable as long as you live. What else are you looking for?

He sat there for a few minutes longer to absorb the box's revelation and to return to himself. Finally, he placed the notes in the briefcase and pulled its zipper closed. He wrapped the pounds in the velvet cloth and tied its four ends in a knot to keep the coins together. He examined the desktop once more, looked in the box again, and after he was convinced that he had not left anything behind, he placed his finger on the button over the desk, and pressed it once. Seconds later, another guard appeared, unlocked the door of the cubicle, and said politely, "Are you through, sir?"

"Yes I am," Theo responded in an equally polite manner. "Would you mind directing me to the cashier? I still have unfinished business with the bank," he said, and lifting his briefcase in one hand and the velvet cloth package in the other, he followed the guard. They walked through two long corridors, entered the elevator that took them to the main lobby, and finally he found himself in a large room where a number of cashiers stood behind bullet proof windows. Theo thanked the guard, approached one of the windows, and said to the lady behind the glass,

"I have here several English pounds, and I would like to cash them. Furthermore, I would like to convert them to American dollars and transfer them to my checking account in Chicago. Is this possible?" Theo said, and placed the velvet package on the cashier's window.

"This matter needs the attention of one of our coin specialists, sir. He has to determine their true value," the cashier said from behind her window, and she motioned one of the coin specialists in the back office to come to her assistance.

A middle aged man appeared behind the cashier, took a look at the package, opened the side door, and invited Theo inside the restricted area. He motioned Theo to follow him to a small office with several chairs around a roomy desk, and he asked him to sit in one of the chairs by the desk. The coin expert walked behind the desk, re-adjusted his tie, rubbed his palms one against the other, and sat down in his chair.

"Let's see what you have there," he said, and pointed at the heavy and cumbersome red velvet package that Theo had placed at the desk between them. Theo reached over, untied the knots he made earlier with the four corners of the velvet cloth, and said, "There are several English pounds here, and I wish to transfer their monetary value to my checking account in Chicago."

"We do these kinds of transactions quite often, especially with customers from your country," the coin expert replied with a broad smile. We only have to determine their actual value in order to be fair to you and to our institution," he said, and took his jeweler's loop, a pencil, and a yellow pad out of his drawer. In the meantime, Theo began stocking the rolls of coins in groups of tens on the desktop between them.

"You have quite a bundle there," the coin specialist said with another smile.

Theo decided not to answer the coin expert's last statement, for he did not know the actual value of his possession. He did not know either the number of coins he had in the velvet bundle or the actual value of each coin. He picked up the loose coins that came out of the roll he opened earlier and handed them to the coin specialist who kept making notes on the yellow pad. The specialist placed the loop on one of his eyes and went to work, while Theo kept opening the rolls. As the inspection process went on, the specialist made two piles of coins in front of them.

"The coins in this pile are rather old," the coin specialist said when he finished examining the whole lot. "Because of their age and excellent condition, they have collectors value. The others are new and their value has not changed. The bank will pay you the collector's value for those," he said, and pointed at the small pile, "and will pay the intrinsic value for the rest."

"It sounds fair to me," Theo said, feeling helpless. What other choice did he have, other than accepting this man's proposition? He was in a country that he had never been in before, knew nothing about auctioning collector's coins, and flight restrictions did not allow him to carry all this gold elsewhere. He felt comfortable, however. He was dealing with the most trustworthy bank in the world and therefore, he had no reason to question the bank's reputation and the man's integrity.

The coin specialist drew the keyboard of his computer close to him, punched a few keys, and made notes on his yellow pad. He took an official bank form, wrote numbers in the empty spaces, and highlighted the number he wrote in the space next to "Grand Total." At last, he put down his signature, handed the form to Theo, shook his hand, and said, "Take this paper to the cashier. She will do the transaction immediately and please, keep the deposit receipt in a safe place. You may need it for tax purposes in the future. I suggest you find a lawyer with experience in handling cases like yours," he said, and prepared himself to show Theo the way out of the office. Theo took the velvet cloth in his hands, folded it neatly, and stuffed it in his briefcase where he kept the notes. He rose from his chair, thanked the coin specialist for his courteous service, and walked to the cashier's window again. He handed her the form that the coin expert gave him and smiled broadly. The cashier handed Theo a little card and asked him to fill the empty spaces. Theo printed, on the card, his full name, his Social Security number, his mailing address, his phone number, his bank's name and address, his checking account number, and returned it to the cashier. She, in turn, pressed several keys on her computer and the printer spat out the deposit receipt.

"You are all done sir", she said with a smile and handed him the receipt.

"Thank you very much," Theo said, and opening his briefcase, he secured the deposit receipt with the negotiable notes he had placed there earlier. With the briefcase under his arm and with his mind cluttered with a thousand thoughts, he walked into the main lobby of the bank. There, he was greeted by another lady who drove him to the main entrance on a golf cart.

"Do you need a limousine or have you already made your arrangement sir?" the cart driver asked politely.

"I would appreciate it, if you make this arrangement for me," Theo responded with equal politeness. She said something in German into her lapel microphone, dropped him at the entrance where he claimed his suitcase, and a few seconds later, a shining limousine stood there with its engine running. Theo came up to the limousine from the side, where its driver was holding the door open for him and handed the driver his suitcase.

"Where are we going today, sir", the driver asked.

"To the airport, my dear fellow," Theo said, with a charm resembling English upbringing. The idea of spending the rest of the afternoon and evening in Switzerland, passed through his mind several times, but it did not make sense for him to dwell alone among people with whom he couldn't speak their language. Instead, he hoped to fly to Athens and visit the National Bank of Greece, early the next day. He wanted to make his Odyssey as short as he possibly could and return home to his wife with the pleasant news of being a wealthy man.

The driver secured Theo's suitcase in the trunk of the limo, moved to the driver's seat and started driving toward the airport when Theo said to him, "Drop me off at the international terminal, please. I hope I can make my connection to fly to Greece this evening."

The limousine driver responded with "yes, sir," and fixed his attention on driving amidst the heavy traffic on the main boulevard that connected the bank to the airport. Cars sped by at more than eighty miles per hour, but Theo did not notice any of that commotion or the picturesque scenery along the way. His mind was fixed on the things that happened this morning at the bank. He could not believe his good fortune. At this moment, he had no idea what to do with all the money he had in his briefcase and in his checking account back home. Still, the dilemma of finding ways to properly use the money was not as perplexing as the question that kept coming back to his mind to torment him. Why did Nestor turn the bulk of his fortune over to the two Jewish entities? Was he an Armenian Jew? Grant it, he was saved and raised by a Jewish couple, but not by the Jewish race. Was he indebted that much to the inheritance of his adopted parents that he left most of his wealth to The Jewish/ Greek Friends in Israel and to The Jewish Brotherhood of Thesssaloniki? This question kept his attention pre-occupied and his thoughts fixed on it. He saw nothing of the sprawling beauty around him, and he heard nothing else until the limousine stopped in front of the entrance to the international terminal.

"We are here, sir," the limousine driver said, and interrupted Theo's deep thoughts. Theo paid him, took his suitcase in one hand and his briefcase in the other, and followed the line to the security inspection station. The inspector at the station looked at Theo's passport, then at him, and back at the passport, and said, "What brings you to our country Mr. Theovulos?"

"I always try to combine business with a little pleasure," Theo responded with a smile. The inspector looked at him one more time, stamped Theo's passport with his rubber stamp, and allowed him to enter the area where the ticket counters were located. Without delay, he walked to the counter of the Greek airline and asked the attendant for a ticket to Greece.

"The only seat I have is in a coach flight to Thessaloniki," the attendant said.

"I'll take it," Theo snapped back and pulled out his American Express credit card and his passport. A minute later, he handed the attendant his suitcase, received and placed his boarding pass in his shirt pocket, secured his briefcase under his arm, and leisurely walked toward the gate where he was to spend the next hour, waiting for the plane to take him to Thessaloniki, Greece.

He had not eaten anything today, and the smell of hotdogs sizzling on the grill in the stand by the corridor was tempting. Instead of walking toward the gate, he stopped at the food stand, took his place at a tiny table, and asked the waitress for a jumbo hotdog with everything on it and a tall glass of beer. The busty and somewhat overweight waitress brought him his hotdog and the beer, placed them on the little table in front of him, and without saying much to him, she walked away to attend to other customers. Theo devoured the hotdog like a hungry wolf and downed the beer between mouthfuls of food. His thirst was not satisfied with one beer, however. He motioned the waitress back and asked her for another glass of beer. This one went down slower followed by intermittent belching that relieved the gas pressure in his stomach. Content with his accomplishments in Switzerland and with the perfect mix of hotdog with beer in his belly, he paid his bill and walked to the end of the corridor where his gate was located for his departure to Thesssaloniki.

Chapter Eight: "Thessaloniki"

The waiting room was only half-full, and Theo threw himself in the first empty chair he found close to the ticket counter. He secured his briefcase between his body and the armrest of the chair and closed his eyes to relax and digest. Instead of just relaxing, the traveler fell asleep, until someone poked him on his arm and woke him up. He did not even hear the call for boarding.

"Sir, wake up," he heard a feminine voice calling him. "The flight to Thessaloniki departs in ten minutes," the boarding gate attendant continued.

Theo jumped off his chair, retrieved his briefcase, presented his boarding ticket to the kind lady who had saved the day for him, walked into the plane, and took his seat for the short flight back to Greece. The plane took off on time and before he knew it, they were flying over Macedonia toward the northern part of Greece. The pilot announced that they would make their approach to the airport of Thessaloniki from the Mediterranean Sea to avoid military traffic in the area. Finally, the 727 glided smoothly toward the runway, made contact with the ground, and stopped at its arrival gate. Theo knew that there would be delays at the customs inspection line, and he decided to avoid the hassle and the bustle at the inspection counter. Instead of rushing to the exit, he sat in his seat until all the passengers were out of the plane, and with his briefcase under his arm, he followed the flight attendants out of the plane. He retrieved his suitcase at the baggage claim area and entered the line for the customs inspection. The customs officer looked at his passport, stamped one of its pages with his rubber stamp, and waved him to move on to the luggage inspection area. Another inspector took a cursory look at his belongings in the suitcase, closed it again, and allowed him to move out of the restricted area into the main lobby.

It was late at night now, and Theo felt the chilled breeze from the Mediterranean Sea penetrating his wind breaker. He flagged down a taxi and asked the driver to take him to the best hotel in town.

"That would be the Macedonian Palace," the taxi driver said and stepped at his accelerator.

The drive was only minutes to the hotel. The Macedonian Palace was located on grounds elevated above the city and had a commanding view of its surroundings. Theo checked into the hotel and took occupancy in a plush room facing southeast toward the Aegean Sea. The bell boy, who escorted Theo to his room, took time to familiarize him with the amenities the room offered. He did not neglect to check the thermostat by the entrance to be sure that it was set at the right temperature. Apparently, he noticed the briefcase in Theo's hands and made a point to show him where the security box was and how he could set his own combination on the lock. At the end, Theo handed the bellboy five Euros, thanked him for his assistance, and told him that he would call the front desk if he needed anything else. As soon as the bell boy left the room, Theo locked the door, placed the briefcase on the night table by the king size bed, and walked outside onto the balcony to enjoy the fresh air and to look at the sprawling city in front of him. Standing at the balcony with only summer clothes on, he felt the cold of the night breeze going through his attire, and he decided to return to the comfort of his air conditioned room. He took his shower, called his wife, put on the robe that the hotel provided for its guests, and sat at the desk to look again at the contents of his briefcase.

It was almost 11:00pm, and instead of inspecting the contents of his briefcase as he was planning to do, he secured the briefcase into the safe box and returned to his bed with *A Brief History of Time* in his hands. He slipped under the bed covers and read the eighth chapter that dealt with the origin and fate of the universe. "…God allows the universe to evolve according to a set of laws and does not intervene in the universe to break these laws. However, the laws do not tell us what the universe should have looked like when it started-it would still be up to God to wind up the clockwork and choose how to start it off. So long as the universe had a beginning, we could suppose it had a creator. But if the universe is really completely self-contained, having no boundary or edge, it would have neither beginning nor end: it would simply be. What place, then, for a creator?" Hawking said. Theo closed the book and tried to comprehend the true meaning of what the astrophysicist wrote. Things may be better understood, in terms of the Antropic Principle, which can be paraphrased as "We see the universe the way it is because we exist," Theo thought, and he added that it is possible that the universe is not neither endless nor finite.

It could exist in some other form that we are not aware of, and we perceive it the way we perceive it, not the way it is, in reality. Do we see it the way we see it, because we exist? After all, Nestor told me once that there is such a thing as anti-matter. "Don't label me a heretic young man, when I tell you that it is possible for anti-gravity, anti-magnetism and an anti-universe to exist," Nestor exclaimed once, and he added, "If anti-matter exists, it is safe to assume that an anti-universe exists, and that will explain the properties of the black holes in the sky." Theo put the book away, turned the lights off, and thought about his late friend again. I wish I could talk to Nestor, he said in a whisper. At last, he closed his tired eyes and went to sleep without having answers to his cosmic questions. The answers to those questions were beyond his knowledge like the answers he was seeking about Nestor's past.

The next morning, Theo woke up early, as he always did. He put his robe on, wrapped himself in one of the blankets from his bed, and daring the morning chill, he walked onto the balcony to watch the sun rising. The view in front of him was spectacular! The sun gradually rose above the water level of the Mediterranean Sea like a big firing ball and brought in view, the city. Among the massive office buildings and condominiums that dominated the modern city of Thessaloniki, there were churches and minarets side-by-side. The new Jewish synagogue was visible to his left, and the university dominated the hill to his right. Farther out in the distance, were the blue waters of the Aegean Sea, with sailing boats entering and exiting the harbor constantly.

Theo had not visited Thessaloniki before, but he knew a great deal about its history. He knew that the city had endured the ravages of war, earthquakes, and major fires during its long history, but it always bounced back and flourished to become the second largest city of modern Greece. He was aware that Thessaloniki is a major cosmopolitan city and a vital import-export center in the Balkan Peninsula today, for it links the Black Sea, Asian Minor, and Egypt with the rest of the Balkan nations and with the other countries of central Europe. He also knew that its population is mostly Orthodox Christians, with some Catholic Christians, a few Muslims, and several thousands of Jews who live in harmony with their Christian and Muslim neighbors. He sat on the balcony of his room a little longer and contemplated the history of the city.

Thessaloniki was founded about 315 B.C. on a site of old, prehistoric settlements going back to 2300 B.C. by *Cassander*, King of Macedonia. The king named the new city Thessaloniki after his wife's name Thessaloniki, who was the sister of Alexander the Great.

Thessaloniki was a Jewish center throughout its history until its occupation by the Germans from 1941 to1944, when some 96% of its Jewish population was exterminated by the Nazis. But, that was not the first time the city experienced mass extermination. In 1430, for example, Sultan *Murat II*, the city's conqueror, pledged his fighters: "I will give you whatever the city possesses, men, women, children, silver and gold. Only the city itself you will give it to me." As a result of this declaration, the entire population was either massacred in the city's streets, or driven like animals to slave markets. In May 1821, *Yusuf Bey*, a deputy Pasha with unchecked authority in the city, took harsh measures against the Greeks to dampen their spirits. He suspected that they were planning an uprising against their Ottoman despots like their fellow Greeks in Peloponnesus had done two months earlier. He ordered his men to kill any Christians they found in the streets. For days and nights thereafter, "the air was filled with shouts, wails, and screams. They had all gone mad, killing even children and pregnant women," *Ibn Sinasi Mehmed Agha*, a *mullah* in the city, recorded in his memoir at the time.

The time when the Jews first settled there is a question that has not yet been historically resolved. There are indications that Jews lived there during its founding but in reality, Jews came there from Alexandria in 140 B. C., adopted the Greek language and became known as the *Romaniotes*. According to the Acts of the Apostles, St. Paul visited the city in 50 A.D., and taught at the synagogue on three consecutive Saturdays. However, the majority of Jews arrived around 1492 from Spain during their persecution and became known as the *Sephardic* Jews.

I will visit the Jewish Brotherhood tomorrow, after I deliver Nestor's envelope to the Department of Philosophy at the university, Theo said to himself. It would be nice if I found credible records of the Koch family here in Thessaloniki. I may even be luckier and track down a relative of the Koch clan, who will tell me more about Nestor and his wealth or, I may find written records about money he inherited from his adopted parents. Still, any way you examine Nestor's life, the pieces do not fit the puzzle unless, one assumes that he acquired his money, at least some of it, in a fraudulent way. That is the only scenario that explains the reason of him becoming a hermit. Is seems that I have to spend time here in this town to search libraries, community records, and interview survivors of the Holocaust to answer my question, Theo continued with his reasoning. So far, he knew that Nestor was an Armenian war orphan, adopted by the childless Koch couple, brought to Thessaloniki, and raised as David Koch. He did not know where he was educated, if he was ever married, and why he became a hermit. The logical place to start searching is the records that the Jewish Brotherhood and the city of Thessaloniki should have kept, from 1900 to 1950, he thought. At present, he wanted to have an early breakfast before he began his search. He cleaned up, dressed, walked down to the lobby, and had his breakfast at one of the restaurants. Talking to his waiter, he learned that the office of the Jewish Brotherhood of Thessaloniki was within walking distance, and instead of calling a taxi, he decided to walk there.

To Theo's disappointment, the man at the Brotherhood did not know anything about David or his parents, and had no records of the holocaust victims either. "Our mission is to support the efforts of the present Jewish community to re-establish its roots here in Thessaloniki," he said to Theo. "The past belongs to the past, my friend," he added laconically.

Next, Theo visited the Jewish cemetery, but he came up empty handed again. The old cemetery was desecrated during the lawless years of the German occupation, and most of the head stones were removed and used as construction material by unscrupulous people in town.

His luck searching the city records was equally unproductive. The person in the library who was assisting him in his search told him that all the archives were destroyed by fires, kindled from bombings during the struggle to liberate the city from the Nazis. Theo had run all day from place-to-place and, at the end of the day, he came up empty handed and badly disappointed with the results of his searching. He did not know whether he was visiting the wrong places for the information he was seeking or, there were no information anywhere to be found about Nestor.

It was late afternoon when he returned to his room, thoroughly disgusted with himself and physically exhausted from standing in line or walking on the hot pavement of the streets all day. He sat in one of the chairs in his room and began thinking that he had reached the end of the road, looking for the answers to his life-long questions of who Nestor was.

Well, I will deliver the envelope to the university tomorrow morning, and I will take off. I think I had enough of this venture in this town, and as soon as I consummate my business with the bank in Athens, I am going home, he thought to himself. Presently, I should make arrangements for dinner.

Suddenly, he was struck with the idea to call his old friend Kosmas Tsaruhoprokas, whom he met in the plane from New York to Athens a few days ago, and hopefully, have dinner with him. He phoned the hotel operator and asked to locate the phone number of Kosmas Tsaruhoprokas in town. After a quick shower, he wrapped himself in his robe and walked toward the telephone on his night table. He noticed that the red light on the phone flickered on-and-off, which indicated that a message was waiting for him. He picked up the receiver and dialed the number that the hotel operator had left on her message, hoping that Kosmas would answer the phone.

"Hello, this is Kosmas. Who is there, please?" Kosmas said in a moderate voice.

"This is your old pal Theovulos," Theo responded with a faint chortle in his voice.

"Theo, for Christ's sake, where are you?" Kosmas said, expressing his pleasure hearing from his old friend again.

"I am here in Thessaloniki, and I thought to look you up and invite you to dinner tonight," Theo responded, trusting that the other man would not turn down his offer. He was tired of being alone or talking to his cousin with his pessimistic outlook on life. Further, he was disappointed and depressed with the results of his first day's research on Nestor's past. He was in need for lively company and hopefully, a cheerful atmosphere to change his mood.

"The pleasure will be mine," Kosmas responded, with detectable excitement in his voice. "I will pick you up, and after we have a drink in my apartment, we will decide where to dine. Tell me, where are you?"

"I am at the Macedonian Palace hotel," Theo responded quickly.

"Ok, you are not too far from me. I'll be there in twenty minutes," Kosmas replied. "Oh by the way, plain clothes like old times," he said laughingly, and hung up the phone. Theo secured his valuable briefcase in the safety box, freshened himself, took the elevator to the first floor and sat on one of the couches in the lobby.

The two old friends met in the lobby of the hotel. Kosmas drove to his apartment, which was on the twelve floor of a new building across the bay from the hotel. There, Kosmas and Theo sat for an hour, dredging up memories of their college life, sipping on ouzo, and nibbling hors d'oeuvres.

Kosmas bought the apartment several years previously and spent half of his time in New York and the other half in Thessaloniki, as freelance writer. He was never married and was not bound to live in any particular place. He was a free spirited individual and lived his life without responsibilities or commitments to a family, just the way he wanted to live. He was an avid hunter and a dreamer. He spent countless hours planning a hunting trip and believed that there was always a better way to do things, like raising goats for a lucrative profit, or raising shrimp under controlled conditions, for a better yield.

Their aimless conversation finally settled on the question of what had brought Theo to Greece and to Thessaloniki in particular.

"I had a mysterious friend who died alone in Peloponnesus and I came to bury him," Theo said to Kosmas. "Before he died, he asked me to deliver a sealed envelope to the university here in Thessaloniki, and that is why I am here."

"What is so mysterious about a man trusting his friend to do him a favor?" the astute Kosmas retorted.

"You don't know the entire story! This man lived a hermitic life on the top of a mountain," Theo added, and continued his description of Nestor's life. "No one knew anything about his past, or about his considerable wealth. Even I did not know his true name, or the place of his birth. I recently discovered that he was born in Armenia, was adopted by a Jewish family and grew up here in this town. While I am here, I wanted to research his name and learn as much as I could about him and his history."

"I may be able to help you research your friend's connection to the Jewish community," Kosmas said contemplatively. "I did a little research in this field a few years ago, and I still have my notes. At that time, I was writing an article about the exact amount of ransom money the Jews paid to the Nazis to free other Jews, who were held in prisons during their persecution from1941 to1944. You will find reliable information in my notes about the Jewish community in Thessaloniki during those days. You are welcome to read through them."

"Let's talk about all these things later on, Kosmas," Theo said, with relief of the tension he felt talking again about things that were associated with dead people. "You have to pick a good place to eat, preferably with some kind of entertainment. I need to vent the loneliness out of my system and uplift my spirit. I need to do something different than talking about dead people."

"There are many places in this town that will meet your desire Theo," Kosmas said, and scratched his head. "A place by the sea shore that plays Turkish music and features belly dancers would be my choice. I know you will enjoy the food and the show there."

The two friends finished the ouzo in their glasses, and Kosmas made reservations for two, at the Hubbub Restaurant. Before they left the apartment, Kosmas took the time to show Theo his collection of guns that he kept in a fireproof, steel case equipped with a built-in, combination lock. Theo took a look at the collection and noticed that Kosmas owned only shot guns and rifles, not handguns.

"You do not have any handguns, do you?" Theo said, to Kosmas.

"It's illegal to possess a handgun in this country," Kosmas said to his friend. "As you can see, all my firearms are registered with the police who seal them during the off season," he said, and pointed at a strip of thin metal wrapped around the trigger and the trigger guard. "You cannot fire the gun unless you destroy the seal," he continued. "When the hunting season opens, we bring the gun to the police station and they remove the seal. They also issue the hunting permit at that time."

The taxi brought them to the Hubbub on time, and a young man dressed in Turkish attire of the nineteenth century escorted them to their table. He was tall with dark skin and healthy, curly hair that protruded below the fez on his head. A well trimmed mustache covered his upper lip, his eyes were black, and he had a rather elongated nose and a pleasant personality. He wore a white, collarless shirt with oversized sleeves, and over the shirt, he wore a red, sleeveless vest decorated with ribbons, buttons, and shining beads, that were arranged in elliptical lines over the entire garment. His legs were covered with a silky, white pantaloon constricted at his ankles, and his red foot wares were light like house slippers ending in an upwardly pointed end at the toe. Most noticeable however, was his red fez with its black tassel hanging from the top down to one of his shoulders.

Theo and Kosmas sat at their table and noticed that many customers were sitting cross-legged on pillows that were placed on the floor, or they were sitting on low couches in front of tables with short legs.

Their waiter took their order and immediately brought them a big pot of tea and two small cups. Shortly thereafter, the flavorful food was placed in front of them, and the two friends enjoyed their appetizers, their main course, and picked from an assortment of sweet deserts that came in platters to their table.

Until now, the place was rather quiet. A group of musicians kept jingling their stringed instruments on stage, while a man sung rustic songs, in Turkish, that neither Theo nor Kosmas understood. The singer displayed a sad, melancholic expression on his face, and he sounded as if he were singing lullabies. Suddenly, the amplifiers were turned up, the music became deafening, and beautiful girls poured onto the stage and danced their traditional belly dances. Each one of them wiggled their slender bodies under their see-through, silky dresses in tune with the music, as if they were serpents moving in air. A shrilly flute and a loud drum overpowered the rest of the musical notes, including the sound of the tambourine and the little bells that the girls had fastened on their fingers. New waves of girls kept coming to the stage, to replace the ones who were exhausted from dancing, and the show went on for an hour between intermissions. After the second intermission, Kosmas and Theo had enough of the hand clapping and the cheering from the customers. Against Kosmas's insistence to have the honor of treating his friend in his town, Theo paid the bill, and the two friends walked out of the noisy restaurant. Under the star lit sky, they took a short walk by the seashore to clear their lungs from the cigarette and the water pipe smoke that saturated the air in the confines of the restaurant. They stopped in front of the White Tower of Thessaloniki by the waterfront, and admired the landmark for a while. They stood there for several minutes and watched the Greek flag flapping in the gentle breeze, from its tall, flag staff mounted at the very top of the tower.

Kosmas told Theo that the tower dated from the reign of the Ottoman *Sultan Suleiman* the Magnificent (1520-1566) and that it was used by the Ottomans successfully as a garrison and as prison. "At the order of the Sultan Mahmud II in 1826," Kosmas said, "a countless number of Greek prisoners were executed in the courtyard by Ottoman torturers and executioners, and the tower acquired the name 'Tower of Blood', which it kept until the end of the eighteenth century. The tower is a museum now," Kosmas noted. "It has been adopted as both the symbol of the city of Thessaloniki and as a sign of Greek sovereignty over Macedonia."

The breeze coming from the Aegean Sea was piercing through Theo's summer attire, and he realized that he was rubbing his arms and legs to keep them warm while Kosmas was absorbed in the narration of the Tower's history, and of its significance to Thessaloniki and to Greece in general. At one point, Kosmas turned his head toward Theo and noticing his friend's discomfort, suggested that they should get out of the wind and continue their conversation at his apartment or, at Theo's hotel room. The Macedonian Palace was very close to the tower, and the two men decided to walk there and continue their conversation in the comfort of Theo's room. They entered the hotel and took the elevator to the floor where Theo's room was located. Kosmas sat on the couch, while Theo sat in one of the chairs and called the front desk for two cups of Greek coffee. While waiting for the coffee to arrive, they returned to the conversation at the point they left earlier, when they were in Kosmas's apartment.

"As I was telling you earlier," Theo began again, "my friend was a World War I orphan who was abandoned or lost in some place in Armenia. Under unknown circumstances he was taken in by a Koch family, and he was raised as David Koch in the Jewish community. His true last name, before his adoption, was Chrisoglu, but he never knew his first name. During our civil unrest of the 40s, this man appeared in the area around my village as a musician. He became known as Nestor and all of a sudden, he decided to become a hermit. He built an extravagant castle with his own money, and there, away from the world, he lived for the rest of his life. The man was good-natured and his personality was amiable and genial," Theo said, and took a noisy sip from his coffee mug, that had just arrived in the room. "I recently learned that he had a lot of money. He left a bundle to the Jewish Brotherhood of Thessaloniki and another to the Jewish/Greek Friends, at one of the universities in Israel. In accordance with his last request before he died, I am to deliver tomorrow, a sealed envelope to the Department of Philosophy at the university here in Thessaloniki," he said, and paused to catch his breath. "I want to know something about the Chrisoglu child, where David Koch found all that money, where he was educated and what all of a sudden prompted him to become a hermit and hide his true identity."

Kosmas was dumbfounded listening to the bizarre story that unraveled in front of him. He was wondering whether he should believe the story, or he should question the mental stability of his old friend.

"There were several Koch families that went to the concentration camps, and none of them returned to Thessaloniki to re-claim whatever was left after the German occupation", Kosmas said. "To the best of my recollection, one of the Koch families was a very wealthy merchant with a thriving business here in town. You will find information about victims of the holocaust among the letters and memorabilia that are collected and are on display at the holocaust museum. There is also an extensive archive collection of written documents from actual survivors of the holocaust in the possession of the museum. I spent hours digging information from this source when I was doing my research. For example, I found out that the Germans collected 2.5 billion drachmas or $8.4million ransom, from the Jewish community of Thessaloniki, to obtain the release of relative prisoners that the Gestapo kept incarcerated for one reason or another. The $8.4million was big money at that time, you know. There are credible estimates that the Gestapo looted billions of additional drachmas in gold from the Jewish jewelers in town, converted it to small ingots, and shipped it to Berlin along with other Greek money that they converted to English pounds on the black market. Other valuable articles such as art collections and antiques from the classic Greek era were confiscated and sent to Germany at that time."

Theo's eyes popped wide open and his mind raced in all directions when he heard Kosmas telling him about the treasure that the Germans had shipped from Thessaloniki to Germany. He remembered the conversation he had with barba Costa on the train two days ago, in route to Athens from Turkohori. During his conversation with that old partisan of the Greek resistance against the Germans in the 1940s, Theo learned that there was money in the train that he and his comrades derailed and sent to the bottom of a gorge. He also remembered learning that mbarba Costa's Jewish co-resistor was never found after the brief clash with the German security that escorted the train. Theo's mind began to fabricate scenarios which tied together Nestor's disappearance, and changing his name from David Koch to Nestor. Was David Koch the missing Jewish resistor who survived the brush with German security before the derailment? Had he recovered the money and disappeared with it to the mountains of Peloponnesus, to avoid being discovered that he was still alive? Was Nestor the surviving Jew, who had the German loot that belonged to the victims of the holocaust? This line of questioning explained Nestor's social reclusion and financial picture. A new yearning was born in Theo's heart. He wanted to renew his research and to know the truth. He wanted to prove or refute the speculation he made about his dear late friend, whom he had respected and admired all his life. Kosmas noticed the bewildered expression on Theo's face and stopped his narration about the atrocities that were perpetrated by the Germans against both Jews and gentiles, during those days.

"What's the matter old pal? Did I say something that offended you, or did I say something that you find to be out of the realm of possibility? I can see your mind searches for an answer to some important question!"

"Oh no", Theo replied, "I was just thinking that someone ended up with the treasure and lives happily, spending money that belonged to brutally exterminated people."

"Theo," Kosmas said, with a philosophical expression and in a low tone of voice. "No war was fought for anything else but material gains and religious differences between combatants. Conquering armies invaded neighboring lands to take away what they needed, and to impose their will on the inhabitants of those lands. You must agree with me that the German conquerors of Thessaloniki in 1941 were as barbarous as the Turks were in 1430. The Turks conquered the city to extend the realms of their Ottoman Empire and to control the trade in the Balkans. In doing that, they destroyed human resources like the Axis Forces. Both the Turks and the Germans took what they wanted from the city and exterminated a segment of its inhabitants for reasons still hard to comprehend today. People were brutally exterminated because they were Christians in one instance or Jews in the other. Why they did such heinous crimes against innocent people is hard for us to understand."

The conversation seemed to have reached the end for the time being, and Kosmas suggested that they should go to bed.

"It's getting late," he said to Theo. "Let's go to bed and meet early tomorrow at my apartment, to go through my old notes. You'll be amazed to learn the truth about the money the Germans extorted from the Jews before they shipped them to Auschwitz and Birkenau for extermination," and saying good night to Theo, Kosmas went home.

It was past 10:30 p.m., and Theo called his wife to let her know that he was fine. They talked for a while, and after exhausting the customary expressions a couple-in-love uses to express their inner selves and their dedication to each other, Theo told Anastasia to check their checking account, as soon as possible and be sure that a new, rather sizable, deposit was recently posted in it.

"Take the entire amount of the new money and give it to our financial manager," he said to Anastasia. "Tell him to open an escrow account in our name and keep the money there until I return," he said, without elaborating any further on the source or the amount of the new money. He did not want to discuss the subject in details on the phone, for he did not know who could be listening to their conversation.

"What kind of money is it and may ask where you found it?" she insisted to know.

"The money is a gift to us from my late friend Nestor," he replied. "I will explain the details when I return in a few days. I still have things to do here and as soon as I finish them, I'll be on my way back home. You will see, sweetheart, that this venture was a trip worth its inconveniences," he added.

"My dear Theo," Anastasia said, with passion in her voice. "Please hurry up and come home! You have no idea how difficult my life has become without you!"

Theo sensed the pain Anastasia felt and responded with the same passion. Sweetheart, being away from you, I realized that my life is worthless without you! It will be only three to four more days, and we will be back in each other's arms, I missed you too!"

"Ok, then," Anastasia said, with a faint sobbing in her voice that pierced Theo's heart. "Call me just before you enter the plane. I don't care what time it will be, just call me!"

Theo assured Anastasia that he would call her before he departs, and with "I love you" and an "I love you too" exclamation, they terminated their conversation.

Theo took a shower and went to bed feeling good that he heard his wife's voice. Tomorrow, as soon as I am through with the notes that Kosmas has, I will visit the university to give them their envelope and if there is time left, I will visit the Holocaust Museum, he said to himself, and crept under his bed covers.

The much needed sleep came fast tonight. No dreams disturbed his deep slumber, and he heard nothing until the next morning when he woke up at 7:00. He shaved, dressed, brushed his teeth, and retrieved from his briefcase, the envelope addressed to the university. He had his breakfast in the restaurant at the main lobby of the hotel and phoned Kosmas.

"Hello, this is Kosmas", a man's voice answered the phone.

"Good morning Kosmas, this is Theo." "Are you awake or did I interrupt your sleep with my call?" Theo asked politely.

"Oh no, not at all," Kosmas replied, and added cheerfully. "My day starts at six. I am up early to tackle another day. Come on over."

Theo walked to the front of his hotel, waved a taxi, and gave the driver the address of his destination. The taxi sped away, and minutes later Theo was knocking at the door of his old friend. The door opened and a blond, blue-eyed lady in her thirties, not Kosmas, greeted him at the door with a distinctly foreign accent in her voice.

"Mr. Kosmas is having his coffee. Please do come in. He is expecting you," she said cheerfully, and walked toward the dinning room with an obvious swinging of her slender, well shaped hips that rested on two long, well-shaped legs. She was tall and well-dressed, but that did not arrest Theo's attention. As she was walking in front of him, he noticed that her waist was half the width of her hips, and the distance between her hips and the lower part of her ribcage, as well as the distance between her shoulders and the base of her head, were much longer than that of a typical Greek woman. She was not robust to be a servant and she spoke with an accent indicating that she was not one of his friend's relatives. Theo walked close, behind his charming hostess and could not help wondering who she was, and what she was doing here at this hour. Kosmas told him that he was not married.

Seated at the diner table, Kosmas was comfortably sipping his coffee and eating some Greek cookies piled on a platter to his left. To his right, he had piled several pages of notes in his own handwriting.

"Sofia," he said to the blond lady, "Make coffee for my friend and leave us alone until I call you." The lady obeyed the order she received from him without objection, and with her characteristic swinging of her hips, she walked toward the kitchen. At this moment, Theo mustered enough courage and asked his friend about the lady in his life.

Kosmas swallowed the cookie he was chewing, and interrupting his statement by taking a ship of coffee to dislodge the cookie crumbs that persisted to stick in his mouth, he said, "She is a Hungarian immigrant who comes to clean the place every so often and to keep me company at the same time," and cleverly he skipped additional explanations about the lady's presence in his apartment at this early hour. Instead, he pointed at the loose pages of paper in front of him and took another noisy sip from his steaming coffee.

"You may find valuable information here, or you may get directions where to start your searching," Kosmas said, in a voice that denoted modesty and humbleness. "Please take your time and go through them. Enjoy your coffee and don't forget to help yourself to the cookies! If you need anything else, do not hesitate to call Sofia. She is helpful in all respects," he said, and winked his left eye at Theo with a broad smile.

Theo thanked his host and took his place in front of the hand written notes. He picked up the first page and began reading, holding in his hand the pen that Kosmas handed him on his way out of the room. Before Kosmas left the room, he also placed a writing pad in front of Theo and said,

"Feel at home Theo. I will return shortly," and he walked out of the room to answer his telephone that was ringing persistently.

Theo had not finished the third page yet, when Sofia came in with his coffee and a glass of water on a silver tray. She placed the tray with its contents in front of Theo and with a broad smile and constricted eyelids over her blue eyes, she charmingly said, in her whispering voice.

"Is there anything else I can do for you Mr. Theo?" and with her hands, she pushed aside her blond hair that had fallen over part of her pinkish face at the time she bent over to place the tray in front of him.

"No, that will be all, thank you," Theo responded and returned to his reading. Sofia walked out of the room with an audible "click-click" of her heels and closed the door behind her.

As the thumbing through the pages was progressing, Theo was making notes of names, places, and dates he found to be relevant to his interest. He had read all the pages he had in front of him in one hour and made two pages of his own notes on the writing pad. He learned that the Germans had extorted money four consecutive times from the Jewish population, before they rounded them up and sent them to the concentration camps in Poland.

Theo made the following notes:

"On July 11, 1942, all male Jews between 18 and 45 years of age were ordered to present themselves at Eleftherias Square. After incredible humiliations, their names were recorded and they were led to labor camps. Later on, the community paid a 2.5 billion drachma ransom to free them."

"At the end of the same year, all Jewish businesses were confiscated…"

"On March 15, 1943, the first train left for the death camps of Auschwitz and Birkenau. Through August 1943, another eighteen convoys would follow…," read another brief note.

"It is well established that of the 50,000 Jews of pre-war Thessaloniki, less than 2,000 were saved by their Christian and Moslem friends and neighbors," he read, in another page of his friend's hand written notes.

A note in the margin of one of the pages said that most of the information regarding the extermination "was gathered from the archives kept in the Holocaust Museum of Thessaloniki."

Theo had finished reading through Kosmas's notes and got off his chair to view the city from the window that faced east, toward the Mediterranean Sea. He could hear Kosmas talking to Sofia next door in a stern voice, but he could not understand what he was saying to her. His voice was firm and direct, and Theo gathered that he was explaining to her the things he wanted to be done in his apartment. All of a sudden, their conversation became louder, and Theo heard the entrance door slam shut. Alarmed from the abrupt shouting of Kosmas and the whining of Sofia, Theo exited the dining room and found Kosmas fuming with anger in the hallway of his apartment and swearing like a "drunken sailor" at the same time. Theo felt very uncomfortable in this hostile environment. He debated to either excuse himself and leave, or give it a few minutes until his friend could return to his normal self. He felt that the former was a rude action to take and the latter was the prudent thing to do. He stood there for a few seconds until Kosmas, in a humble voice, apologized to Theo for his behavior, and said, still in anger.

"I know that this behavior is not characteristic of me Theo, but this woman pushed me over the edge. I had to defend my grounds, you know," Kosmas said, and took a deep breath, as if he had unloaded a heavy burden off his shoulders. "They come from a different culture, and it becomes difficult for them to adapt to our way of living. I only asked the "bitch" to clean the toilet and sanitize the floor. Now, you find her logic! She did not mind cleaning the toilet, but she refused to sanitize the floor," he said, and threw his hands up in the air with another outburst of anger and vulgar expressions. "She is like a tiger, you know! I must keep a whip in one hand and a three-pointed fork in the other, like the tiger trainer does. Otherwise, she will maul me like a rag doll and become my master," he said in a calmer voice, and he added. "I love and hate with the same passion, for I am a Greek, but I will not put up with this irrational thinking! No sir, I will not."

Theo decided that it would be best to say nothing and allow Kosmas to vent his anger and justify his behavior in his own way of thinking. He stood there looking straight at the other man's face with an inquisitive expression on his face until Kosmas, pacing the floor with his hands in his pockets, finally apologized again for his outburst and said in a normal voice, "Did you find anything useful in my notes?"

"I found a plethora of things about Thessaloniki and about the terrible things that happened to the Jews in the 1940s," Theo said, choosing his words cautiously, so as not to inflame the anger of his friend. "Your notes gave me plenty of information for places to visit and people to interview. I made two full pages of my own notes, from material I copied down from your papers. Thank you for the help," he said. The tone of his voice made Kosmas understand that it was time for his old friend to leave his company.

"What are you planning for dinner?" Kosmas said, thinking that it was his turn to buy dinner this time.

"Let's leave dinner open," Theo said in a friendly way, hoping that he did not offend Kosmas with his denial of dinner. "I have a great deal of grounds to cover today, and I don't know when I'll be through with the things I want to do and still have time for dinner." Thinking over what he had just said, he added, "May I call you when I finish? If time allows it, I would like to dine with you again tonight," and with that comment, Theo inched toward the door.

"As you wish friend," Kosmas said apathetically, and escorted Theo to the door. "I will probably be here all day," he added, and the two friends shook hands warmly and parted company.

Before he knew it, Theo found himself again on a busy street of Thessaloniki waving a taxi to take him to the university. As the taxi was riding in the congested streets, Theo's mind was elsewhere. He was not thinking anymore about the incident in his friend's apartment or about the outcome of his meeting with the representative of the university. He was not even thinking about any potential surprises hidden in the sealed envelope. Strange unexplainable feelings had occupied his heart and invaded his mind today. He was thinking about the noble feelings he had all his life about his late friend and mentor. He could not get away from the sensation that he was about to discover that Nestor was not as noble and ethical a man as Theo thought Nestor was, and that disturbed him today. He wanted to remember Nestor as an honest, wise and just man, but the feeling that he had acquired money that was brutally extracted from innocent people, bothered him! If Nestor, David Koch, was what Theo thought he was, he should have made an honest effort to return the money he found, to the victims, or to their families. Theo wanted to believe that David Koch was not the man who gathered the gold from the wreckage of the train. He wanted to think that his late friend's wealth was money inherited from his adopted parents, who were presumably wealthy according to Kosmas. However, this assumption did not explain David Koch's disappearance in the mountain of Peloponnesus and the concealment of his true identity. The core of this thought gnawed at Theo's troubled and distressed mind today.

The taxi pulled in front of the entrance to the impressive university that looked like the Parthenon itself. Theo paid the taxi and mounted the long marble steps toward the entrance of the educational institution. He was greeted there by a young man in an official uniform who explained to him that the school of philosophy was located in a separate building, and he politely handed Theo a ground diagram on which he circled the building Theo was seeking. He even walked Theo back to the staircase and pointed the building that housed the school of philosophy, located a few yards away.

Theo walked the short distance at a brisk pace and before too long, he found himself reading the directory in the lobby to locate the dean's office. "Dean's office, room 101", the board read, and Theo proceeded walking down the hallway. He found a door that was decorated with a brass plate on which the number "101" was engraved in large numbers, and the words "Dean's Office", were prominently engraved below the number. Theo knocked at the door and a man's voice invited him in.

The room was plainly furnished with modesty and simplicity. There was only one office desk with three chairs lined in front of it. A middle aged man occupied the chair behind the desk. An uncombed crop of hair covered the dean's head and fell over his forehead, his ears, and his neck, down to his shoulders. An untrimmed mustache and whiskers two to three inches long, covered the hairy part of the rest of his face. He wore spectacles, and his tie did not match the color of his checkered shirt. However, behind the prescription spectacles, was a pair of bright, dark eyes that pierced like needles. The dean behind the desk got off his chair, extended his hand toward Theo, and with a firm hand shake, he said politely. "I am the dean of the school. In what way I can possibly assist you my dear fellow? Please sit down," and he pointed at one of the empty chairs on the other side of his desk. Theo introduced himself as "Theovulos" and proceeded to explain his reason for his visit.

"I was the dear friend of a man who chose to live the life of a hermit, in a mansion he built at the top of a mountain, close to the village where I was born," Theo began. "This man was known to everyone in the area as 'Nestor'. He recently died in my presence, and we buried him next to his mansion. Searching his belongings, I found this envelope." Theo retrieved the sealed envelope from his pocket and placed it in front of the dean. "As you can see," Theo continued, "the envelope is addressed to your school, and I felt that it was necessary to bring it here in person, instead of mailing it."

The dean took the envelope in his hands, turned it over several times, took a look at Theo, and glanced at the envelope once more. He stopped looking at it for a moment, fixing his eyes at Theo, and asked the obvious question.

"What was the last name of this 'Nestor' person?" he said with an enigmatic look in his piercing eyes.

"I have reasons to believe that the true name of Nestor was David Koch who was a citizen of Thessaloniki," Theo replied and continued. "I am hoping that the school has some sort of records available to validate or refute my information." The dean leaned over the monitor of his computer and punched the key board several times with his fingers.

That's impossible, let's try again, the dean said to himself. He repeated the process on the key board and exclaimed with a questioning tone in his voice. "Impossible, David Koch died years ago," the dean said, and gaped at Theo's squinting eyes. "Yes, we had a David Koch who taught here for a while before Greece was invaded by Germany. They tell me that he was an outstanding professor who earned his advanced education in Germany. He came here when the Nazis took over Germany, and he became one of our visiting professors. After the Germans took over Greece, he left the city and joined the resistance with a few other students and faculty members. The last time we heard about David, was when he was declared missing during a clash with the German army, on the border of Greece and Yugoslavia. His parents, Solomon and Rebecca Koch were also lost during the upheaval of the German occupation. They were sent to the villainous concentration camps in Poland, and they never returned home."

"Is it possible that the missing David Koch was not dead and that he was just missing?" Theo asked the dean.

"Possible," the dean said, and pushing himself away from his desk; he stroked his hair backward with both hands, adjusted his spectacles on his long nose, and added. "But why didn't he return to claim his prestigious position, after the Germans left?"

"Well, that is the question that I am trying to answer. The answer to our question might be hidden inside the envelope that lies in front of you Mr. Dean," Theo declared and pointed at the envelope that lay in front of them.

"Let us see what we have here," the dean said. He slit open the envelope, reached inside, and took out three legal size pages that contained boldly typed words, from top to bottom. The name of a legal firm was printed at the top of each page, and several signatures concluded the document. The dean read through each page carefully and turning to Theo, he said,

"Yep, the missing David Koch was not dead after all." Here he grants custody of his mansion to the school and donates a generous sum of his money to the school of philosophy. Unfortunately, he does not explain his reasons for becoming a hermit after he left the university. He probably became a pessimist after having everything and losing the most important things in life, his parents," he observed with a sad note in his voice.

Theo was disappointed to hear that his question still remained a question, and that he would like to look elsewhere for his answer. He was convinced by now, that David Koch had found the ransom money in the wreckage of the derailed train, kept it, and changed his name to hide his identity. David most likely felt that he did not do anything illegal, in this case. He came upon a considerable amount of gold and money that did not belong to him, or to any other known living person, for that matter. Under these circumstances, he decided to be silent and live in obscurity to avoid legal harassment from the banks of Thessaloniki, or from people who might claim ownership of the money. A little parsimony may also have promoted his desire to keep the money for himself. He probably reasoned that since the legal owners of that money were dead and he was the fortunate one to find it, he should be the claimant of the treasure and say nothing to no one about it.

There was another probable reason for his disappearance as David Koch, Theo thought. After surviving the scrimmage with the Germans, he realized that being a partisan with Zervas was risky. He probably hid the money in some cave, disappeared in the forested mountains of northern Greece, decided to save his life by not returning to the resistance army, and went into hiding, among the people in isolated villages, until he finally drifted to Peloponnesus. There, he made up his mind to settle down and spend the rest of his life as a hermit, under his fictitious name of Nestor. Still, it is quite possible that he did not even know that the money he had found was the money that was extracted from the Jewish community of Thessaloniki.

The dean interrupted Theo's thoughts with a comment that came as no surprise.

"Other professors, who knew David in person, tell me that he had an impeccable character and a wealth of knowledge in philosophy. They tell me that he had a broad understanding of both the ancient and the continental thinkers from Plato to Hume. Unfortunately, the world is deprived of a great teacher," the dean concluded.

Theo acquiesced with the dean's statements, lifted himself off the chair, thanked him for making time to see him, shook his hand, and walked toward the door of the office in the dean's company.

"It was a great pleasure meeting you Mr. Theovule," the dean said and before the other man had a chance to respond, he added. "On behalf of the entire school, I want you to know that we appreciate your taking the time to deliver the envelope to us in person. Thank you sir, for being so considerate," and he shook Theo's hand again.

Theo walked the corridor back to the parking lot, then to the main street where he waved another taxi and asked the driver to take him to the Holocaust Museum.

It was noon now, and the streets were busy with buses, cars, motorcycles, bicycles, and pedestrians who were taking their traditional two hour break for lunch. The taxi pulled in front of the museum and Theo walked to the door without paying his fare. To his disappointment, he found a sign hanging from the door knob: "Closed for lunch. We will return at 2:00," the sign read. He returned to the street, and realized that he had forgotten to pay the taxi that was idling there, still waiting for him.

"That will be all," he said to the driver and paid him the money shown on the meter. The taxi sped away, and Theo decided to walk to the seashore to spend his time until the museum opened again. He walked all the way to the pier where the light house was and sat near an old man who was fishing.

The fisherman had two fishing rods. He was holding one of them in his hands and had wedged the handle of the other into a crevice between the boulders that formed the pier itself. At the moment, he was absorbedly concentrating on a slight movement that the tip of his rod was making and at the vibrations he felt on his fishing line, from a fish that was apparently nibbling at the bait. All of a sudden, he snapped the rod backward and exclaimed with satisfaction. "I got you good this time sucker," and began to reel in his fishing line. As he reeled, the fish made occasional desperate efforts to escape from the fisherman's hook. During those instances, the fishing line started to unwind again for a few seconds until the frantic fish became exhausted, and allowed the man to drag it toward the sea shore again. This tug-of-war between fish and fisherman continued for several minutes until the man finally managed to bring the fatigued fish within his reach. He scooped it out of the water with a big net that he kept next to him, grabbed it with his left hand from under its gills and with a rusted pliers he kept in his tackle box, he removed the dreadful hook from the fish's mouth. Finally, he threw the fish into a cooler, half full of ice, and wiped his hands with a raggedy, wet towel he kept next to him.

"Good dinner," Theo said to the fisherman hoping to start a conversation with him, while waiting for the museum to open.

The fisherman took a brief look at Theo and responded in a dry voice, "Yep, brown snapper is always a good eating fish," he responded and reached into his bucket where he kept the live shrimp he used for bait. He picked up one of them between the fingers of his left hand, ran his hook through its tiny body, and with a coordinated swing of his fishing rod, he sent the baited hook as far into the ocean as he could. The bait quickly sank into the bottom of the sea, and the man took his place in his folding chair holding his rod with both hands. Theo realized that the fisherman was not in the mood to talk and kept quiet.

Look how unfair life is, Theo said to himself. There are people like Nestor with a lot of money, and there are people like this fisherman, who hustle a miserable fish out of the sea for dinners. I would like to help this poor fellow, but I am afraid that he would misunderstand my intention. It would be best to leave him alone, for he is not talkative and I cannot judge his temper. I should stay away from him! Instead of making another attempt to talk to the fisherman, Theo walked to a nearby stand, purchased a gyros sandwich and a cold beer, and sat on a bench located in the shade, under an acacia tree. There, he enjoyed his lunch alone in peace and tranquility. When he finished his lunch, he disposed of his plastic cup and the wrapping paper into a nearby trash holder and returned to his bench. There were a few more minutes left until the museum would re-open, and he used the time to scan through the notes he made at Kosmas's apartment. Most of the things he had scribbled down were historical events associated with the Jewish Greeks in Thessaloniki, or were about events he was well aware of. Three sentences that he had written in the margin of his second page of notes caught his attention, nevertheless: "The determining factor for the decline of the Jewish vivacity in the 17th century was Sabetai Sevi who was a self-proclaimed Messiah. He appeared in Thessaloniki in 1655, and developed a considerable number of followers, but his popularity alarmed the Ottoman authorities. A year later, they arrested him and condemned him to death. In order to save his life, Sabetai Sevi denied his Jewish faith and converted to Islam, together with three hundred Jewish families who followed his example. This mass apostasy destroyed the spirit of the Jewish community, which did not recover until the latter part of the 1800s."

Who was that Sabetai Sevi anyway? Theo wondered aloud. Was he a rabbi, a hermit like Nestor, a truly divine person, a first class swindler, or a combination of all the above? He, certainly, was a gifted man, able to convince three hundred families to follow him on a mass apostasy, something unheard of among Jews, he thought.

A barefooted, raggedly dressed, young lady with a baby in her arms approached Theo on his bench and in her broken Greek, she interrupted his contemplation.

"If God has only one blessing to send on earth to his children, let it be delivered to you my dear fellow," she said in a sad voice. "I have nothing to give to my baby, who hasn't eaten anything since last night. Can you find it in your heart to help me?" she asked, and extended her unsanitary hand for help. Theo looked at her, then at the baby and saw that the baby was sleeping in her arms. He reasoned at once that the baby would be crying his lungs out if he hadn't eaten anything since the night before. Nevertheless, his immense love for children flooded his heart, and his thought was overshadowed with altruism. He knew that the woman was fibbing about her poverty. He reached toward the baby, touched the angelic head, and said to the mother.

"My dear girl, I know that you do not tell the truth. Your child is well fed and sleeps happily in your arms. It's you that needs the help, not the baby! Here, take this money and buy clothes to dress your angel and please, buy soap and wash your miserable body," he said to her in a caustic tone of voice. She shoved the money in her pocket and understood nothing of Theo's emotions. Instead, she walked away, to continue the begging that she had found to be an easy and convenient way to live. She was certainly young, and if she had taken a bath and dressed properly, she could have been a presentable young mother. Poverty and wealth live side-by-side, he whispered and took a look on his wrist watch. It was almost 2:00 P.M. He closed his notepad and leisurely started to walk back, toward the Holocaust Museum.

The sign was removed from the doorknob and Theo walked in without knocking at the door. A thin, middle aged lady, wearing bifocals that hung low on the bridge of her long nose, greeted him politely, as soon as he entered the museum. She wore a one-piece dress that loosely draped her thin body to her ankles, and her waving hair was tied in a pony tail. She had a dark complexion, deep black eyes, and did not wear any makeup on her face. Theo paid his entrance fee and was allowed to view the modest exhibition of relics and artifacts from the holocaust. There were an untold number of memorabilia in cases covered with thick plates of glass. There were pendants that belonged to the victims of the holocaust, their pictures, the clothes they wore while in captivity, and their memoirs, written in all sorts of writing media. A voluminous catalogue containing the names of those citizens who were lost in the concentration camps, was prominently displayed at the center of the room. Theo found it more convenient to search the name "Koch" in the computer monitor that was available to everyone. He found several entries of Koch, but only one Solomon and Rebecca Koch were listed as husband and wife. Since the place was not busy, Theo approached the lady who greeted him in, and asked for her help.

"I am interested to know as much as possible about Mr. and Mrs. Solomon and Rebecca Koch," he said to her in a friendly voice. "In what way can you possibly help me with my search?"

"There was quite a bit written about Solomon and Rebecca. Unfortunately," she said, "the records the Jewish community kept throughout the years were destroyed during the German occupation. People say that Mr. Koch was a successful import-export merchant, and Mrs. Rebecca Koch was a famous doctor in town, before the Nazis arrived here. Regrettably, they went to Auschwitz and never returned home. The only child they had, David, died, fighting the Germans with the rest of the Zervas resistors, and that event discontinued the line of that Koch family. They say that this particular Koch family had its origins in Alexandria. They came to Thessaloniki in the first century after Christ and became successful merchants selling indigo and silk to the Slavic kings of Kiev, throughout the generations that followed."

"What do you know about David in particular," Theo asked.

"Oh, David was a brilliant young man. At the age of 17, he went to Berlin and studied philosophy for a while, achieving all kinds of honors and receiving several diplomas there. He finally taught philosophy at some German university, until he was forced to return home. In addition to his teaching, David wrote articles for the university newspaper and critiqued manuscripts of upcoming writers. When the Nazis took over Germany, he 'read the writing on the wall'. He returned to Thessaloniki and became a visiting professor in our university until he ran out of luck."

"It seems to me that you are well informed about this particular Koch family," Theo said. "Are the Koch relatives of yours?"

"No, but I know something about them," she said.

Can you tell me everything you know about them, or where shall I find additional information?"

"The Koch family was living next door to my parents," she replied, "and my father and Solomon became close friends. Of course, I was not born yet, but according to my father, Mr. Koch was proud of his inheritance, and he enjoyed talking to my father about his family. Later on, my father helped me with my term paper on the holocaust, when I was in college, and that's how I learned about Solomon Koch and his family."

"Was David ever married," Theo asked bluntly.

"Not that I am aware of. That does not mean he was not married while he was in Germany," she said in deep thought. "Probably, we will never know that," she finally declared.

"People say that David was not the biological son of Solomon and Rebecca. Is there any truth to that?" Theo said.

She stopped fooling around with the keys to her computer, looked directly at him and surprised at her guest's statement, she said to Theo, "I haven't heard that before! Who told you that?"

"In order to answer your question, I have to consult notes I made during interviews with other people," Theo said, to avoid answering her inquiry.

"You seem to be very interested in David Koch, Mr...." she said, and Theo realized that she did not know her visitor's name.

"Theovulos," Theo added quickly to take her out of her predicament. "Yes, I want to learn as much as possible about David's past. David was alive and lived in total seclusion, until last week when he died in my presence. I was one of his trusted friends and I would like to find any of his descendants, to deliver the sad news to them.

"Are you absolutely convinced that we talk about the same David Koch, the only son of Solomon and Rebecca?" she re-emphasized to clarify any possible misunderstanding.

"My dear lady, I am talking about David Koch who was born in Armenia, came here as a refugee with his adopted parents Solomon and Rebecca Koch during World War I, and grew up in this town," Theo said with emphasis.

"Then, we are talking about the same person," she agreed. "There is only one person in town that might be able to tell you more about Solomon and Rebecca," she added. "*Mr. Paul Garidis* is a surviving holocaust victim who spent time with the Koch couple in Auschwitz, and he was with them until Mr. Solomon died. I don't think he can tell you what happened to Rebecca though. He has been a valuable source of information for the museum, and I am sure he would be glad to talk to you about his dreadful experience there," she continued. She took her personal telephone directory out of her desk and located Mr. Garidis's telephone number. "There it is," she said, and without hesitation, she picked up the phone and dialed Paul's number.

"Mr. Garidis," she said on the phone. "This is the Holocaust Museum, and I have an American with me, who wants to talk to you about Auschwitz and about Solomon Koch in particular. Can I send him over to see you?" She paused for a second, to hear Paul's response and continued, "Very well, he will be there shortly," she said and looked at Theo to verify that he was willing to visit Paul now. Theo moved his head up-and-down to confirm that he was ready to visit Mr. Paul, and she hung up the phone. She wrote Paul's address on a piece of paper, handed it to Theo, and turned her attention to a group of Asian people who had just walked into the place and were taking pictures of the displays. Theo thanked her warmly and quickly walked outside to get out of her way and to summon a taxi.

Mr. Paul Garidis was living in a modest, one bedroom apartment, on the first floor of a multi-unit condominium building. Theo pressed the button next to the name Paul Garidis, and he heard a buzzing sound indicating that the door was unlocked for him to enter. Once in the hallway, Theo looked to his left, then to his right and saw an elderly man with a walking cane in one of his hands, waving to him with the other, to come over to him. With brisk steps and great anticipation in his heart, Theo came up to the old man and extended his right hand to shake the old man's hand. Paul offered him his bonny hand and with a pleasant expression on his face said, "Come in son, I am Paul Garidis."

Theo released the old man's hand and said with affection. "My name is Theovulos Mr. Garidis, and I am a Greek American. Allow me first of all to express my gratitude for receiving me on such a short notice. I appreciate that sir."

"Quite all right son," the old man replied and balancing his weight on his two trembling legs and his cane, he invited Theo into his apartment. Theo shuffled his feet on the oval, multi-colored, rag rug that was spread on the entrance and followed the old gentleman in his living area. The old man sat down in his padded reclining chair, and Theo moved a chair in front of him and sat down too.

"So, I understand you are interested to know about my dear friend Solomon, aren't you?"

"Yes, I do," Theo responded. "The lady at the museum told me that you knew Mr. Solomon Koch well and that you two were in Auschwitz together. I am particularly interested not only in Solomon but in his son David, who is listed as missing during a skirmish with the Germans on the Yugoslavian border with Greece."

"I did not know Sol until we met in the concentration camp," Paul said, and that dampened Theo's high hopes to obtain specific information on David.

"I arrived at Auschwitz two days before Sol, and they put me in a large room with other prisoners. Two days later, Sol and his wife arrived, and he took the empty space next to me which was vacated three days earlier. Rebecca was taken to the women's building, and that was the last time Paul saw Sol's wife. Sol and I became good friends and talked a lot at night about our businesses, our families, and our futures. We wanted to believe that things would improve and that we would return home soon to resume normal living. Yes, he spoke often about his son David, for he was proud of him. He never knew that David died before him."

"Did he ever mention to you that David was not his biological son?

"Yes, he did. Toward the end of his life when all hopes for our survival had vanished, he sat against the wall the night before he died and wept bitterly. He cursed the moment he was born and we both regretted that we were born a Jew. In his desperate talk that night, he apologized to David for not telling him the real truth about his identity. Later that cold night, he told me that he was not feeling well, and turning to me, he said passionately. 'Paul, it looks like I will never come out of this hell alive. I want to trust you that if you return home, find my David, and tell him that he was not my real son,' he said and broke down in loud sobbing. When he regained his composure, he told me the rest of his story.

"'I don't know if you are aware of it or not,' Sol said to me, 'domination of Armenia was a continuous conflict between the Russians and the Turks as far back as the latter part of 1800. In 1914, the Turks drove the majority of the people of Armenia out into the Syrian Desert, in order to stop them from helping the Russian army who tried to stop the Turkish expansion into the territories around the Black Sea. Hundreds of thousands of Armenians died of starvation, exhaustion, and sunstroke in the desert. Experts estimate that more than a million additional Armenians perished during World War I when the Turks finally declared genocide against non-Muslims, in Armenia. With their scimitars, the Turkish cavalry beheaded Jews and Christians at will or shot them to death on sight like mad dogs. Like so many other Jewish merchants, I abandoned everything I had and ran for my life toward the Black Sea, where Greek fishermen were waiting to take us to safety. Running through a clearing, I caught up with a one-horse buggy loaded with a Chrisoglu family. My Rebecca was not a member of the Chrisoglu family. She was a medical student at the time, and she was just traveling with them. At the moment, she was walking several paces behind the buggy with the Chrisoglu baby in her arms. She wanted to give time to the baby's mother to re-adjust herself in her uncomfortable seat next to her husband, who was stirring the horse away from any unevenness on the dirt road. Before we reached the seashore, the Turkish cannons started to fire at us from the hills above. A shell exploded on top of the buggy, and the flesh from the baby's parents commingled with the carcass of the horse itself. The explosion threw me on the ground and, I believe, I lost consciousness for a while. I lay motionless and unhurt for a while listening to the desperate moaning of the dying horse. When the shelling stopped, I mustered enough courage to lift my head to see if there was anybody else alive besides me. A few feet away from where I was laying, I saw Rebecca in a state of shock holding a newborn baby in her arms. She was sitting against a huge oak tree and had buried the baby's face in her bosom to muffle his crying. She was in a state of shock but miraculously, she and the baby were not hurt, either. Intuitively, I leaped to her and held her in my arms, as if I had known her all my life. I cannot tell you how long we held each other with the baby between us, but when dusk covered creation, we resumed our walk toward the sea, and later, all three of us arrived safely at the shore. We hid among the trees, ate berries and drank brackish water, until the Greek fishermen picked us up and brought us to Thessaloniki. At Thessaloniki, we declared that we were husband and wife and that David was our only son. Soon thereafter, Rebecca and I got married. She finished her medical studies, and I started my new business,'" he said, and broke into loud sobbing again. "'I raised David in our Jewish tradition and educated him to be a worthy citizen of our town, but I never told him that Rebecca and I were not his true parents. I did not want to risk his devotion and love toward Rebecca or his respect for me until he would be old enough to accept the truth,'" he said, and looking directly at me, he said again."

"'If God grants you the good fortune to return home, find my dear son and tell him what I just told you, would you please Paul!.' After receiving an affirmative answer from me, he was silent for the rest of the night. The next morning, the guards came in and found Sol dead, wrapped in his rags, leaning against the cold wall of our tin-roofed barracks.

"I looked all over town for David upon my return to Thessaloniki," Paul continued, "but David was nowhere to be found. It was several years later that I learned of his tragic end. For your information, David died fighting the Nazis as a resistor somewhere northwest from here," Paul said and stared directly at Theo for his answer.

Theo's thoughts either to tell Paul everything or to conceal the truth about David, came and went through his mind like bees in a beehive. On the one hand, he did not want to inflate the kind old fellow and on the other, he did not want to disappoint him for not fulfilling the promise he made to his dying friend in Auschwitz. Theo sat there petrified, looking directly at Paul's wrinkled face and hairless forehead, pondering his predicament. Finally, he made up his mind to tell Paul the truth as he knew it, when the old man adjusted his spectacles that had slipped down toward the tip of his long nose. At that instant, the long sleeve of his shirt slipped backward on his bony arm, and Theo noticed an ugly black number on Paul's forearm. That was the I.D. number his captors tattooed on him, while he was a prisoner awaiting a gruesome end to his life. A piercing chill ran down Theo's spine and at this moment, he made up his mind to tell Paul all he knew about David.

"Would you believe me Mr. Garidis, if I tell you that David was living in obscurity until a week ago?" Theo said to Paul.

"Inasmuch as I find it rather impossible, I am nevertheless willing to have you convince me that David Koch, the adopted son of Sol and Rebecca Koch, was alive all these years," Paul said with incredulity.

Theo proceeded to explain to Paul the close friendship he had had with Nestor as a high school boy and the admiration he had for him all his life. He then went on to describe the way David spent his life as Nestor, alone in a mansion he had built on the summit of a mountain. Theo finally summarized the way David distributed all his wealth in a philanthropic way, and in a rather graphic way, he narrated the final days of David's life.

A two inch gap between the upper set of Paul's teeth and his lower set had formed, as he was listening to Theo's incredible story.

"But why did David hide himself away from the world until his death?" Paul managed to articulate.

"This is the only unanswered question I have about the mystery of David's life," Theo said and he added. "Do you have any clues to share with me?"

"I gave you all the information I have regarding Sol Koch's life. I know that he was a *Romaniotis*, not a *Sepharadim*, and he was proud of it. I also know that he was a very successful businessman, here in town, with money and real estate. Sol also told me that Rebecca was not born Jewish. She was an Armenian Christian who adopted Judaism later on, when they came to Thessaloniki with the baby. Paul also told me that Rebecca was a descendant of the famous apostate Sabetai Sevi, who escaped to Armenia to avoid prosecution by the Jewish community of Thesssaloniki."

Theo felt at this point that there was nothing else he could learn about David Koch from Paul Garidis. He also realized that the "old chap" was getting tired, and he suggested that it was time for him to go.

"Are you absolutely convinced that your friend Nestor was unquestionably David Koch, the adopted son of Solomon and Rebecca?" Paul said to Theo, who stood at his door ready to say goodbye.

"Mr. Garidis," Theo said with a convincing tone in his voice. "I never claimed that I was right all the time in my life, but this time, I can tell you without any uncertainty that Nestor was the David Koch we are talking about." Finally, Theo took Paul's bonny palm in both his hands and said goodbye to a page of history from the annals of World War II.

Theo felt that he had accomplished his mission in Thessaloniki and had learned a great deal about Nestor. He was convinced that it was of no value to do additional research on David Koch and about his life in Thessaloniki. He knew now that Nestor, or David Koch, was the adopted son of the businessman Solomon Koch who died in Auschwitz. Yes, Nestor was the biological child of some Chrisoglu couple who perished in route to the Black Sea, to escape the genocide at the hands of the Turks between

1914 and 1916. He also knew that David Koch was a resistor around 1943 and had disappeared without a trace during a brief battle with the Germans. The only two questions that remained unanswered to this point were the question of David having the loot from the derailed train, and the reason of him becoming a hermit.

Well, the answer to these two questions might never be known, Theo said to himself. But the very thought that he would not know Nestor's complete life story made him feel uneasy and defeated. He was not a person who gives up, or surrenders without a fight, and a thousand thoughts muddled his mind. I need to somehow find out if David Koch took the treasure from the train. Otherwise, I will never know why he hid himself away from the world for the rest of his life, he muttered under his breath, standing on the street waiting for a taxi. David was not a pessimist and his life before the incident with the train, proves that he was an optimist. For example, he worked with diligence to obtain a first class education, to escape the Nazis from Germany, and to return to Thessaloniki to continue his teaching ambition. This, in itself, proves that he was interested in living a normal life. Furthermore, he joined the resistance to save his person and to eventually return to his roots, not to waste the rest of his life alone, at the top of a mountain!

A taxi came along and Theo instructed the driver to take him back to his hotel. On his way back, he felt an unexplained urgency to leave for Athens, as soon as possible. There is nothing else here for me, he reasoned. I have gone far enough with this adventure. My dear wife will question my sanity. I am exhausted running around all day. I will leave for Athens this evening. Who knows, I might be luckier tomorrow, when I visit the bank in Athens and open the safe box there. With an indubitable determination, he approached the hotel's cashier and said,

"I am checking out shortly. Please have my bill ready as soon as possible. Oh yes, I would like to have a good rental car. I will drive it to Athens and turn it in at the International Airport in three or four days from now." The clerk responded with a "yes sir", and Theo took the elevator to his room to pack his belongings. It was late afternoon now and he knew that the drive from Thessaloniki to Athens was tiresome at its best. Part of the road went over mountains, while other parts traversed through inadequately, lit tunnels and narrow bridges. For these reasons, he wanted to leave at once. Besides, he wanted to see some of the historic sites on his way to Athens before it turned dark. He wanted to see Thermopylae, where King Leonidas with his three hundred Spartans challenged the advancement of King Xerxes with his Persian warriors. Theo also wanted to see the planes of Thessaly, from where the legendary Achilles of the *Iliad* and Jason who led the Argonauts in search of the Golden Fleece, came from. Before he left his room, he phoned Kosmas and told him that he was leaving for Athens.

"I regret that I am not able to have dinner with you this evening, Kosmas," Theo said. "When you come to New York, don't forget to come to Chicago for a visit."

Kosmas sounded disappointed for not having the opportunity to buy dinner for Theo, but he assured him that he would see him in Chicago, in the near future.

With his suitcase in one hand and his briefcase in the other, Theo approached the cashier's counter and paid his bill with his American Express credit card. He walked to another office down the corridor in the hotel, signed several forms and received the key to a convertible Mercedes that stood idle in front of the hotel. He placed his belongings in the trunk of the car, secured himself in the seat with the safety belt, and after a few minutes driving through the streets of the city, he entered the main expressway toward Athens.

Chapter Nine:
"Athens"

Thermopylae was less than an hour drive from Thessaloniki, and Theo planed to be there, far before sunset. When he entered the expressway that connected the two metropolitan cities of Greece, he glanced at the gauges on the dashboard and found that everything was normal. The gas gauge read "full" and the performance of the car was satisfactory. Speeding at 100 km/hour, he found himself crossing the marshes of Thermopylae in no time at all. He had imagined the narrow pass of Thermopylae to be the 50 foot narrow pass between the cliffs of Mount Oeta and the sea. He did not know that alluvial soil had converted the narrow pass to a wide, marshy plain through the centuries. As soon as he crossed the marshes, he exited the expressway at the designated exit, and found himself face-to-face with an impressive, marble monument. Modern Greeks erected that monument at the foot of the mount in memory of

Leonidas and his brave comrades, who stood fast against the waves of the Persian warriors on August 15, 16, and 17, 480 B.C. "Oh stranger who passes by, tell the citizens of Sparta that we lie here obeying the laws of the Spartan state," the epigram at the base of the monument read.

It was late in the afternoon and all the curious visitors had gone away. It was only the monument and Theo facing each other. Theo's imagination flew 2,500 years back, and he heard the thundering voice of Leonidas reminding his warriors that the state of Sparta sent them to this place, to win a battle in the name of Sparta, or to die like Spartans and be carried on their shields. *"E tan e epi tas,"* (either with it or on it) the mother said to her son, when she handed him the shield before he went to war. He saw with the eyes of his imagination, the wedge formation of the Spartan warriors holding their long pikes in one hand and the mighty, brass covered shield in the other. He heard the cries of the combatants charging at each other, and he visualized the long pikes of the Spartans piercing the gold decorated bodies of their foe. He thought that he heard the voice of Leonidas ordering the men in the front line to retreat, in order to be replaced with fresh troops on regular intervals. He was certain that he saw the narrow pass littered with the bodies of Xerxes's immortals, and he was sure he heard the cries of the wounded and dying at the end of the day. He finally saw the mountain pass of Kallidromos tramped by the immortals, who attacked three hundred Spartans from all sides. And he finally saw all the Spartans fall dead around their brave king. He saw with the eyes of his imagination the victorious Persian King marching toward Athens, where a bigger surprise was waiting for him on the straights of Salamis. Theo took another long look at the monument and with a heavy heart entered his car and headed south toward

Athens like the king of Persia, but not for the same reason the "Great King" did.

The key to open the safety box at the First National Bank of Greece was still tucked securely in Theo's wallet. Nestor's original introductory letter, the envelope that said "to be opened by the president of the First National Bank of Greece", the original copy of Nestor's death certificate, the negotiable notes, and the red, velvet cloth, which Theo kept as a souvenir, were still in his briefcase.

I hope that my visit to the bank tomorrow will conclude this odyssey, he said to himself and kept driving on the International Highway that traverses the planes of Thessaly from north to south. It was here that Philip II, King of Macedon, defeated the Thessalians in 344 B.C. and added these fertile plains to his kingdom. He also named his newborn daughter "Thessaloniki," meaning "victory in Thessaly", to immortalize the historic event of his accomplishment.

Minutes before, Theo passed by Mount Olympus that still stood grand and impressive. Nothing has changed. The summit of the mountain pierced above the clouds and hid the palaces of the Gods of Olympus from human view. Soon thereafter, the sun disappeared behind the western horizon, and darkness engulfed nature. He could only see the road ahead of him and the bright headlights from cars that occasionally came from the opposite direction. His radio was blasting Greek music that came from a local radio station. An announcer occasionally interrupted the music, updated the prediction for the weather and summed up the regional events of the day. As he cruised through the city of *Lamia* toward the city of *Thebes,* Theo realized that his driving attentiveness faded away at times. He was apparently exhausted from his activities of the day and from driving at 100 km/hour at night. The driving was tiresome and he wondered if he could make Athens tonight, or spend his night in a motel and resume his driving the next morning. At the outskirts of Thebes, he noticed in his rearview mirror a flashing, red light following him, and before too long, he realized that the vehicle was driven by a police officer in uniform. Theo pulled off the road, and the police vehicle parked a short distance behind him. The officer exited his squad car, re-positioned his hat on his head, stretched his thin jacket downward, adjusted his tie, and approached Theo.

"Would you turn the engine off and exit the vehicle sir?" the officer commanded. Theo complied and upon the officer's request, he handed him his Illinois driver's license and the ignition keys.

"Ah, you are an American," the policeman said, while examining Theo's driver's license. "I gather from your name that you are a Greek too, aren't you sir?" he added in English this time.

"Yes officer, I am," Theo responded in a polite manner. "May I ask what infraction I committed that prompted you to stop me at this hour?" he added. The officer did not answer Theo's question, instead, he said.

"Mr. Theovule, walk behind my vehicle and wait for me there. I'll be with you shortly," and he pointed in the direction where his police vehicle stood.

Theo did as the officer commanded, and from the corner of his eyes saw the officer watching his gaiety and the sturdiness of his steps. The policeman opened all four doors of the rental car, looked inside, examined the space under the seats, looked inside the glove compartment and finally, he opened the trunk. "Do I have your permission to open your suitcase sir?" he said to Theo.

"Be my guest officer," Theo responded without hesitation.

The officer unzipped one of the compartments of the suitcase, aimed his flash light at its contents, zipped it again, and slammed the lid of the trunk. He closed all four doors and briskly walked over to where Theo stood. He handed the key and the license back to him, and said in Greek this time.

"Mr. Theovule. Ten kilometers back, you passed me at the speed exceeding the speed limit. What prompted me to stop you, however, was not the speed in which you passed me; it was the manner in which you were driving. It seems that you cannot keep a straight line while driving; that indicates that you are either intoxicated, or you are sleepy. I tend to believe that you were not drinking tonight, am I wrong sir?" he emphasized and brought his face close to Theo's face, pretending that the noise of the oncoming vehicles interfered with him hearing Theo's answer. In reality, he wanted to take a good whiff on Theo's breath when he opened his mouth to reply.

"Honestly officer," Theo said in a clear and well articulated voice. "I did not have a drop of any alcohol today, or yesterday for that matter. Your second assumption regarding my erratic driving is probably more to the point. I have been running around like a demon for the last two weeks, and I am in a desperate need for a long rest. I was hoping to reach Athens tonight and have a long sleep at my sister's house," he continued speaking in Greek.

"The law allows me to either issue a fine for one hundred euros or a warning citation for exceeding the posted speed limit. However, my best judgment tells me that your infraction does not warrant either the issuance of a ticket or a warning," the officer said with a comical smile. "You may be interested to know that I lived in Chicago for five years before I realized that the way of living in the U.S.A. did not agree with my expectations from life, and I returned home. My knowledge of the English language qualified me to be an officer here on the International Highway. We have officers who speak French, others who speak German, and still others who speak English like me. All of us assist the tourists who visit our country," he said, with a tone in his voice that expressed his pride of being an officer on the international highway.

"Officer," Theo interrupted, "I appreciate you being generous with me regarding my careless driving. I don't think that it will be wise for me to continue driving tonight. Can you direct me to a nearby hotel or a motel? I really need to go to bed," he added, and a loud yawn escaped his mouth.

"I hear your message loud and clear Mr. Theovule," the officer said, with a broad grin on his face. "Five kilometers ahead, is an exit. Exit there, and look for the motel on your right. It is a quiet and clean place to spend your night in peace. Better off, I will follow you to the motel to be sure that they will not take advantage of you, and that they will provide a clean room to spend the night in comfort."

Theo sat behind the steering wheel, buckled himself up, and drove with the police car behind him. After a while, he pulled in the parking lot of the motel, while the officer parked his vehicle in front of the entrance to the motel. The officer entered the lobby before Theo was there, and seconds later, they met face-to-face at the door, at the time the officer was exiting and Theo was entering the place.

"You are all set for tonight," the officer said, and he patted Theo on the shoulder. As he turned his attention to his microphone that hung on his shirt, Theo noticed that the officer's last name was Zervas, and he wondered if the young man was a descendant of the commander under whom Nestor served in the 1940s. The officer said something to his command center, and quickly added, "I have an emergency call and I must hurry up. Have a good night sleep and a pleasant stay in our country," he hastily added, and entered his police vehicle. Theo ran after him, stuck his head in the police vehicle and asked.

"Are you related to captain Zervas?"

"He was my grand father," the officer retorted, and turning his siren and his red lights on, he sped away. Theo did not have the chance to say anything else. He only managed to deliver a hand wave at the officer, who quickly entered the expressway and disappeared in the darkness. Only mountains never come closer to each other, Theo said to himself. The last person I expected to meet tonight was a policeman who spent time in my town and who is the grandson of the celebrated hero of the resistance, during the German occupation. I wish I could talk to him about his grandfather, Theo thought. He might have inherited his grandfather's memoir, and one expects to find an entry in one of its pages about David Koch's disappearance.

Theo registered as a customer at the front desk and procured the key to the door. The receptionist was not busy at this hour, and he took the time to show Theo his room. Theo, in turn handed him a handful of loose change, he had in his pocket, closed his door, and took a shower. Refreshed from the shower, he spread himself on his bed and called his wife before he went to sleep. Husband and wife exchanged their customary expressions of devotion to each other, and at the end, Anastasia demanded to know where he had found all that money he had transferred to their checking account, earlier.

"It's all legitimate," Theo said. "The money is a gift dear. Before Nestor died, he gave me the key to his safety box in one of his banks with his authorization to open it and take everything that he had there. Among other things, I found some English pounds which I converted to dollars and wired them to our checking account. I will explain everything to you in three to four days when I'll be home. In the meantime, don't you worry about anything," and with that note in their conversation, they ended their dialogue.

Theo went to sleep with a thousand thoughts rolling in his head. Thoughts like, did I explain clearly to Anastasia the source of the money? I should have told her about the negotiable notes, kept rolling in his head after he said good night to her. I don't know who might be listening to my conversation, he muttered to himself, and tried to justify his action. Finally, he crawled under the covers, turned the lights off, closed his itching eyes, stretched his sore back on his bed, and went to sleep.

Back home, Anastasia spent most of her day with a girlfriend and with aunt Katerina, and when her day was over, she returned home and went to sleep, still wondering what other surprises Theo might have for her. Although she was convinced that she was the only woman in his life, the thought that there might be untold secrets in her husband's life occupied her mind and made her sleep, restless. The house was too quiet without his snoring. She could hear sounds that she never paid attention to, before. She thought that the air conditioner was making a deafening noise, and that the refrigerator sounded like it needed to be replaced. Even the dog at the end of the block sounded like a howling wolf. When the day broke, Anastasia woke up early and visited aunt Katerina again, to have breakfast and keep her company for a few hours.

Theo woke up early too. He had his continental breakfast in the lobby of the motel, packed his belongings in the trunk of the rental car, paid his motel bill, and entered the expressway toward Athens. He wanted to be in Athens early, and he was hoping to finish his business at the bank before noon. His plan was to leave Athens to go to his village as soon as he could, and make the village before dark. Today, he was not thinking about the meeting he had with the president of the bank, or about any legal complications that could pop up during the visit. The contents of the envelope he was carrying were mysterious like the man who sealed it, and Theo expected surprises when the president of the bank opens it. He anticipated some sort of a pleasant surprise when he opens the safe deposit box, but these pending revelations did not enter his mind, today. Instead, he was mulling in his head, words and phrases he wanted to use for the epitaph on the headstone he planed to place on Nestor's grave. Combinations of words to create a descriptive phrase about Nestor, constantly came and went through his head, but all the things he could come up with did not satisfy the demand of his soul. All the ideas he had, did not satisfy the cries he heard inside him. They either sounded untrue or they were not descriptive enough.

The phrase, "the best man to have as a friend and as a teacher" persistently returned to his mind.

No, that's incomplete, he said to himself. That doesn't describe Nestor himself. It only expresses what he meant to me, not the person himself.

I was born as Chrisoglu, raised as David Koch, and died as Nestor, was a better statement than the first one, Theo concluded; yet it said nothing about the man's inner qualities. Combining both statements in one was something worth considering, Theo continued with his train of thinking.

He exited the expressway at the first exit he found, filled his gas tank at a gas station he spotted down the road, and bought chocolate covered raisins and jelly beans to munch on while driving. Before he resumed driving, he retrieved his yellow pad from his briefcase and wrote down, "He was born as Chrisoglu, raised as David Koch and died as Nestor. He was generous with his friendship and with his advice." He read this statement again and said to himself. That says all I know about him. If I re-write it and arrange the words differently, it would probably look better on white marble, he muttered, and secured the pad in his briefcase. He entered the car again and continued driving until he reached the congested area of Athens. He knew from previous experiences that driving in a city where he was not familiar with its traffic rules, would only be a challenge to his fortitude. Furthermore, he had no idea where the bank was; so, finding the place would be another test to his patience. Assessing the complexity of getting to the bank by driving his rental car, he decided to have a taxi take him there. He exited the expressway and drove at one of the main streets looking for a place to park. Two blocks down the street, he spotted a public garage and entered the place. He parked the Mercedes in the first parking space he found open, locked his suitcase in the trunk, and with his briefcase in his hands, walked back to the main street. He flagged down a taxi that happened to pass by, and said to the driver, "To the First National Bank of Greece. Do you know where it is?"

"There is only one First National Bank of Greece in Athens, and anyone who claims to know Athens, should know where the King's Palace, Acropolis, and the First National Bank are located. The bank is one of the oldest and most impressive buildings by the Constitution Square, close to the King's Palace," the taxi driver said. "I will have you there in fifteen minutes," he added, and drove away whistling notes from the lyrics of the song, "Never on Sunday". Theo, sitting in the back seat of the taxi, was still pre-occupied with the epigram for Nestor's head stone. Regardless of how hard he tried to come up with a better phrase, he couldn't put together anything wittier than the one he had scribbled on his yellow pad earlier.

Well, let me think about it a bit longer. Perhaps, the people at the place where I will order the head stone will have suggestions, he thought, and tried to dismiss that consideration from his mind. He opened his briefcase and made sure that he still had in there, Nestor's introductory letter, his death certificate and the sealed envelope. He knew that the security deposit, box key was in his wallet that he kept in his pocket.

The heavy traffic that kept rolling on the street, in front of the bank, was momentarily stopped by the traffic light ahead, and Theo took that opportunity to get out of the taxi. He quickly paid the taxi and dodging between the standing cars, he walked to the other side of the street, where the bank was located. With the briefcase under his arm, he walked up the steps and greeted the doorman good morning. The doorman opened the heavy, glass door, and Theo entered the main lobby. Marble columns supported the high ceiling, and the floor was tiled with large, rectangular, marble tiles. Several cubical rooms were erected against the opposite wall where cashiers conducted business with the bank's customers. Spacious offices occupied the spaces to the left and to the right. Two receptionists behind a marble counter in the center of the floor, answered questions and assisted the customers. Several small, marble tables, surrounded by comfortable chairs, were placed throughout the rest of the floor area. Two armed guards in impressive attire, paced the floor area and assisted customers to find their way around the place. Theo glanced around and noticed that the two receptionists behind their counter were not busy. He walked directly up to one of them, interrupted his conversation with his co-worker, greeted him good morning, gave him his name, and stated the purpose of his visit.

"You can see our vice president, Mr. Theovule," the receptionist said to Theo. "The president will not be available until after 9:30. Please sit down at one of the tables, and I will call you as soon as the vice president is ready to see you."

Irritated, for having to sit and wait until the "fat cat" in the big office finished his coffee and thumbed through his newspaper, Theo took his place in front of one of the marble tables that faced the receptionists. He unzipped his briefcase, took out the papers that he planned to show to the president, and zipped the briefcase again. He read, one more time, Nestor's introductory letter, glanced at Nestor's death certificate, and tried to guess the contents of the envelope by running his fingers across the face where the statement "To be opened by the president of the First National Bank of Greece" was written.

Theo sat there for almost thirty minutes waiting for someone to call his name. Finally, he ran out of patience. He got off his chair, walked to where the two receptionists were sitting, and attempted to remind one of them that he was still waiting to see the vice president. The two receptionists were engaged in a heated conversation about local sports at this moment, and neither of them noticed Theo standing by the counter. Theo tried to get their attention by tapping his fingers on the top of the counter. Instead of offering Theo a response, one of the receptionists stretched his arm toward him with his palm open and gestured that he did not wish to be interrupted. At that moment, he was responding to some comment the other receptionist had made about the outcome of a soccer game, between the two rival teams in town. His gesture intimidated Theo, and Theo's good nature changed to a mild rage and anger. He grabbed the protruding fingers in his right hand, twisted them slightly and said in a low but firm voice that revealed his anger.

"Listen here, young man! I can see through the glass door that the vice president is filing his pinky behind his desk, and I am sitting here like a donkey that waits to be watered by the well. I want to see him now," he said louder, and released his grip. His voice attracted the attention of one of the guards who walked over and said, "What seems to be the problem here gentlemen?"

"Oh nothing at all," the receptionist responded. "Mr. Theovulos and I over-extended our handshaking," and rising off his chair, he escorted Theo to the office, with "Vice President" in gold letters written on the glass door. "I am sorry for the mishap," he said to Theo, as he opened the door and quickly returned to his station. Theo entered the vice president's office, shook hands with him, and introduced himself in a calm and collected manner.

"What can we do for you Mr. Theovule?" the oversized man behind the desk said, in a distracted manner, without even asking Theo to sit down.

"I have an envelope which must be opened by the president of the bank," Theo responded, still standing in front of the vice president's desk. "Your receptionist told me that the president will not be available for a while and suggested that I should see you instead." At this moment, Theo took the initiative and sat in one of the chairs without receiving the vice president's invitation to do so. He took the envelope out of his pocket and handed it to the big, intimidating man behind the desk. Theo felt uncomfortable in the company of this uncharacteristically, unfriendly man who apparently felt that he was a superior being, simply because he held a vice president's job with a prestigious bank.

"Unscheduled visitors to the president are cleared through me first," the vice president said in an authoritative voice and that statement, fortified Theo's conviction about the vice president's attitude. "Tell me where you found this envelope and why you are taking the time to bring it here in person," he added.

"In order to avoid repetition sir, I would like to save my explanation until we see the president," Theo firmly responded. "I believe you will be pleasantly surprised when we open it."

The eyes of the man behind the desk popped wide open, and his lower jaw dropped when he heard Theo's wish to explain the details of his visit, only to the president. Apparently, the vice president was not accustomed to people avoiding his questions. In this instance, he swallowed his anger, picked up the phone and said to the person on the other end of the line,

"Mr. President, I have a demanding customer in my office who insists on seeing you now! Do you have time to see him or shall I schedule him to come back another time?"

"Tell him that my visit pertains to Mr. Koch's estate," Theo ruddily interrupted with a voice loud, enough for the president to hear him on the phone. A "bring him in" answer, apparently came back to the vice president, and in silence, he slowly moved his bulky body from his chair and without articulating another word, he walked with Theo to the president's office.

The office of the president was located behind the cashier's station, away from the view of people in the main lobby. The inside of this spacious room was richly decorated and stylishly furnished with lavish chairs and couches. Several pictures of past presidents hung on the two side-walls, and an enormous world atlas covered the space behind the president's impressive desk. Three mahogany chairs stood in front of his desk and an oval shaped Persian carpet covered part of the floor, between the entrance and the president's desk.

The president himself was the opposite of the vice president in physical appearance and manners. He was a thin and clean shaven man with short hair and a radiant personality. His face was that of a person who cares about his health, and his shirt and tie were modest in color and shape. He had a broad forehead and a friendly disposition. His eyes, behind his spectacles, were bright like stars, and a perpetual smile radiated from his facial expressions.

As soon as Theo and the vice president entered his office, the President sprang off his chair and met them in the middle of the room. He extended his hand toward Theo for a hand shake and introduced himself with humility as *Nicolas Marinacos,* not as president. "I am pleased to have the opportunity to meet you Mr. Theovule. Please sit here," he said and pointed at a roomy couch. "Let us be acquainted first before you tell me why you are here."

"Mr. President," Theo said, "The pleasure is mine, having the opportunity meeting you."

"I would rather have you call me Nicolas, if you don't mind," the president responded and sat at the chair, that was located on the other side of the cocktail table which separated Theo from him. At this moment, the vice president excused himself and walked out of the president's office.

"I guess you live abroad, in England or in the USA Theovule," Nicolas said and paused to hear Theo's answer.

"I am an American citizen. I was born in the Peloponnesus, and after I finished my military duties here in Greece, I immigrated to the USA where I established myself, and became an American citizen. I recently learned that my mentor and childhood friend, David Koch, was breathing his last breaths and wanted to see me before he died. He trusted me to see that the distribution of his wealth would be carried out according to his wishes, and that's the reason for my visit today. I spent the last two days of his life with him, and among other things, he gave me this envelope with his strict instructions to have the president of the First National Bank of Greece open it, in my presence," Theo said. He handed the envelope over to Nicolas. "He also gave me this letter in which he mentioned, that you have his written authorization for me to fulfill his wishes as expressed in the contents of the envelope you have in your hands. Here is his death certificate too."

"Oh, I am so very sorry to hear that our mutual friend passed away," Nicolas exclaimed with obvious sorrow and sadness. "Mr. Koch and I spent many hours talking about the distribution of his wealth. I personally had a great deal to do with his final decisions to leave his money to trusted organizations with worthy causes. I also remember him mentioning your name several times during our conversations," Nicolas said, and snapped his fingers to emphasize his statement. "David trusted my sincerity and honesty to the point that he revealed to me a big part of his true identity. Tell me, who told you that his real name was not Nestor?" Nicolas added.

"After his burial, I thumbed through some of his belongings, and I came upon some of his writings where he revealed that he was an orphan of World War I, that he was adopted by a Koch couple, and that he was raised as David Koch in Thessaloniki," Theo responded. He did not mention to Nicolas that David was an Armenian orphan, nor did he reveal any details about his adoption by the Koch couple. He wanted to see how much Nicolas knew about Nestor's untold, life story.

"David told me that he was the child of an Armenian couple who perished at the hands of the Turks during World War I," Nicolas said. "Unfortunately, death followed David in Thessaloniki after the tragic death of his biological parents in Armenia. His adopted parents were lost in the concentration camps during World War II. Did you know that his adopted father was a Jewish merchant in Armenia before he came to Thessaloniki? The poor man escaped the Turkish genocide there, only to face the German genocide against the Jews in Thessaloniki. David also knew that his adopted mother was not born Jewish. She was a Christian who converted to Judaism later. I assume you also know that she died in Auschwitz with her husband and some 48,000 other Greek Jews from Thessaloniki. During one of our conversations, David confessed that Solomon and Rebecca, his adopted parents, found him abandoned somewhere in Armenia. According to David, his biological parents died, trying to escape the genocide against non-Muslims in Armenia, at the time. The only thing he knew about his true parents was their last name, a piece of information that came from his adopted mother."

"I am curious; what was his name before he became David Koch," Theo asked Nicolas.

"David was reluctant talking about the circumstances that led him learning the truth about his biological parents," Nicolas continued. "'My adopted mother came to Germany to be present during my graduation,'" "David said," "'and after the ceremony, she spoke to me heart-to-heart, during our dinner. She told me, at that time, that my true, last name was Chrisoglu, not Koch, and she narrated the circumstances of my adoption. She also made me swear that I should play ignorant to that detail for as long as my adopted father was alive.'"

"Did he ever mention anything about having been married?" Theo said. "I wonder if he left any descendants. David left a rich collection of rare books and an impressive mansion on a mountain where he lived, until his death. It would be nice to find any of his descendants, deliver the sad news, and tell them that a small fortune waits for them on the mountain."

"Ah! I specifically asked him about it several times during our conversations. 'All my love relations ended up in disaster,' he responded and changed the subject," Nicolas said.

"I wonder what prompted him to isolate himself and hide his identity," Theo asked emphatically, and he fixed his total attention on hearing the answer from Nicolas.

"Unfortunately, I do not know the answer to that question, either. When I asked him about that, he responded; 'It seems that it will rain today.' It appears to me that David had something hidden deep in his soul that made him uncomfortable to face it, or to accept it. I don't think he isolated himself to hide away from some authority. He was a brave man. I believe he isolated himself to accomplish something else, perhaps, he did not want to stand face-to-face with the world in order to justify some act for which he never spoke to anyone about," Nicolas concluded.

The president picked up the introductory letter and read it aloud. "That's David alright," he said with a smile. He also read the death certificate and smiling again, he added. "Dr. Gliadis was my classmate in college. I see him often." Finally, he picked up the envelope and using a tiny pocket knife he produced from his pocket, he opened it. He removed its contents, placed them on the table in front of them, and said to Theo, "I will read each page aloud and I will pass it on to you to read it also. It's only two pages!"

Nicolas picked up the first page and read slowly in a soft and clear voice. Moments later, he passed that page to Theo, and began to read the second page. Finally, he handed Theo the second page, and re-positioned himself on his comfortable chair. Theo had just scanned through the first page when the last page arrived in his hands. He superficially read through the second page and said to Nicolas, "It seems that he authorizes your bank to make money available to the university, here in town, for archeological excavation in a specified area close to Olympia."

"Yes. David was convinced that the grounds around Olympia have not been fully excavated yet. He believed that the marshy area between the river and the old theater that was brought to light years ago, hid significant archeological remains that can be brought to light," Nicolas said. "I assume that he gave you the key to his safety deposit box, did he?"

"Yes he did," Theo said, and took the key out of his wallet and handed it over to Nicolas. Nicolas examined it carefully, returned it to Theo, walked behind his desk, and called his secretary to escort Theo, to the room where the safe deposit box was located. "Tell the guard that Mr. Theovulos is authorized to access the box," he said to his secretary. As a final point, Nicolas turned to Theo and said, "Theovule, it was a pleasure meeting you. Have a nice trip home," he added, and extended his hand toward Theo for a hand shake.

"May I assure you that I had a pleasant experience in your company, Nicolas," Theo responded, and he firmly squeezed the president's hand in a friendly and affectionate handshake.

The secretary entered the room and Nicolas asked her to photocopy the introductory letter and the death certificate, and return the originals to Theo. She did as Nicolas instructed her to do, and motioned Theo to follow her down the long corridor to the safety box room. She introduced Theo to a guard who opened the door, and walked away, leaving Theo to the care of this man. Theo and the guard introduced themselves to each other, and they walked over to one of the walls where the safety box was located. The guard unlocked the safe box on the wall, drew out a long metallic box, handed it to Theo, and said, pointing at one of the private rooms. "Enter this room and take all the time you need. When you are through, bring the box to my desk."

Theo entered the tiny room, placed the box on the counter in front of him, and closed the door behind him. He opened the box and saw that it contained a fat wad of Euros, a small cloth bag that appeared to contain jewels, and a stack of pages with Nestor's handwriting on them. The pages were held together with an oversized metal clip, and the word "*Memoir*" was calligraphically printed on the first page of the stack. Theo opened his Swiss Bank briefcase and transferred everything from the box to the briefcase without counting the money or examining the contents in the cloth bag. He only took a few moments to quickly thumb through Nestor's manuscript. He noticed that the memoir was revised several times. He also noticed that it was an incomplete document. It only covered Nestor's experience as a resistor under the command of Zervas in Northern Greece. It said nothing about the rest of his life story.

I will take my time reading this material, inspecting the contents of the pouch, and counting the money later on, he said to himself. Let's get out of here and hit the road toward the village. He closed the briefcase, placed it under his arm, and returned the empty box to the guard that stood in front of his desk. "I don't need this anymore," he said to the guard, handing the empty box over to him. "Let someone else use it," and with his briefcase under his arm, Theo walked the corridor toward the exit. Passing by the president's office, he waved his hand to Nicolas in a gesture of goodbye. The president was not apathetic to Theo's gesture. Instead, he jumped off his chair, walked to his door, and met Theo in the corridor.

"I hope our services were satisfactory, Theovule," he said with a smile.

"Yes, Nicolas. Everything was fine, thank you!" Theo responded with a smile of his own.

"Are you leaving town or are you spending time in Athens," the president asked.

"I am heading to the village of my birth. I want to spend time with my relatives there, before I return home to my wife," he responded.

"You meant to say, return to USA from home," the president said, with a cunning smile.

"No, I meant to say return home from Greece," Theo responded, in his own cunning smile.

"Then, have a wonderful stay in Greece and a safe return home," the president said and shook hands with Theo again. Theo hastened past the vice president's office and by the station, where the two receptionists were still arguing about something. At last, he found himself at the exit of the bank where the guard opened the door for him. He said goodbye to the polite guard and exited with his briefcase secured under his arm.

It was past twelve o'clock now and the traffic on the street had eased somewhat. Theo walked to the curb on the boulevard in front of the bank, and he flagged down another taxi. He handed the driver a piece of paper in which he had written the address to the public garage, where he parked the rent car in the morning. He asked the taxi driver to take him there. The taxi took the short cut and Theo saw the garage down the street. He had no time to closely examine the new things in his briefcase. Inasmuch he was anxious to take a closer look at them, the time did not permit him to do so. He was in the garage already. He zipped his briefcase again, paid the taxi, walked to the spot where he had parked the Mercedes, secured the briefcase in the trunk, and drove away from the congested city. Minutes later, he entered the expressway, and drove south toward his birthplace, in the Peloponnesus.

The road was wide and newly paved, and Theo cruised at the posted speed limit without much effort. He was cognizant of the way he drove, for he did not want to run out of luck and meet an unfriendly officer. He drove through mountains and through several, fertile valleys on his way to his village. The mountain sights were grand, but the view of the valleys with their olive trees and citrus orchards were more captivating and inspiring, to behold!

Before I get to my final destination, Theo grumbled to himself, I owe it to myself to stop at the village of *Lathocambos* (Olive Valley) and taste the goat meat that this man roasts in an earth pit. They tell me that it's a unique experience, tasting this unusual cooking. Besides, I am in need for an early dinner. I don't think Fotis would have anything to eat, and I hate to burden him with cooking tonight. Furthermore, I don't feel like listening to his pessimism about old age. I want to be alone and read Nestor's memoir in privacy.

After driving an hour, he saw the sign "Lathocambos", on the side of the road. He veered to his right, slowed his car down to twenty five miles per hour, exited the expressway, and followed the signs to the eating place. The outdoor restaurant was located on the slope of a hill that was planted with fig trees. He drove the dirt road that was lined with fig trees on both sides, parked his car in front of the place, and joined the company of several, Swedish, college students who were there for the same reason he was.

The man, who made the village known for roasting a whole goat in a pit in the ground, was presently bent over an outside, wood fire, in front of the restaurant. He was in his 80s. He looked robust and in good health and had a cigarette in his mouth at the time. His cheeks were red like an orange, and his white mustache, which was yellowed in the center from cigarette smoke, covered his upper lip. A village cap, soaked in perspiration and cocked to one side of his head, covered the top of his bald head. He wore a white apron that was stained with blood and red wine, and the long sleeves of his checkered shirt were rolled above his elbows. His trousers looked home-made, and his bare feet were stuffed in a worn pair of hikers with hob nails. When he finished re-arranging the fire over the underground pit, where the goat was cooking, he wiped the perspiration off his face with the end of his apron, straightened up his back, and approached his customers to explain his novel technique in cooking goat meat.

"The goat that we are about to eat today", he began, "was a male yearling, that I butchered early this morning. I carefully skinned the animal, saved its insides to make tripe soup some other day, and I cut off the head and the lower part of its legs. I seasoned the meat with my special combination of salt, oregano, pepper, garlic, mountain sage, mountain tea, and sun-dried figs, and I re-inserted it back in its hide. Using strong wire, I tied and closed all, except one, of the skin's openings, poured in a liter of good wine though the last opening, and closed it tight with wire. In this way, the meat with the spices and the wine were enclosed air-tight, inside the animal's skin. In the meantime, I had pre-heated the earth pit for several hours, until the earth was nice and hot. Lastly, I placed the skin with the meat into the hot pit, covered it with fig leaves, placed a layer of gravel over the leaves, sprinkled soil over the gravel, and started the fire on top of it. The "thing" is in the pit four hours now, and when the meat is cooked, we will take it out and have a wonderful meal together."

"Hey mister," one of the young ladies said to the old man, "How do you know when the meat is cooked? It's still covered in the ground, isn't it?"

"Smelling the vapors that escape from the pit, I get an unexplained urge to dig it out. It is something like the urge you have to make love," he said, with a roaring laugh that made everyone break into applause with jovial cheering for the witty old man!

"Seriously, how long do we have to wait for the food," a young man asked. "The aroma that comes out of the ground makes me salivate like Pavlov's dog," he added.

"Patience son," the old man responded. "I will have it on the table shortly. 'He who had patience to wait, saw Jesus' the good book says," he added with his characteristic, witty giggle.

While waiting for the food, Theo sat on a stone under one of the fig trees in the yard and had an interesting conversation in English, with one of the students. The student was from Copenhagen and was collecting information to write his thesis on Byzantine mosaics, found in southern Greece. The student told Theo that he was on his way to see mosaics in several monasteries of the Byzantine era, located around historic Sparta. Theo in turn, told the student that he was an American and gave him a condensed version of his visit to Greece.

"The food is ready," the old man declared, and he began to push away the embers with a metal shovel he kept by the pit. Next, he carefully pushed away the hot gravel and removed the charred fig leaves from the goat skin, with a wooden scoop. Using outmost care and dexterity, he placed the steaming skin with its contents on a wide board and carried it to a wooden bench he kept under the fig tree, in front of his store.

"It will be delicious. I can tell before we open it," he declared, and asked for a volunteer to do the incision, on the steaming skin. "You look wise and brave enough to do us the honor," the old man said, and pointed at Theo with the hand, in which he held a sharp butcher knife. "Come on over and cut it open if you want to eat," he added, with a mild sarcasm in his voice.

Theo walked over to him, took the knife in his hands, and pondered where and how to make the first cut. He had opened butchered goats before, but the sight of the steaming skin in front of him was different. At last, the old man pointed to the spot where he wanted Theo to insert the knife and pointed with his finger to the direction in which he wanted him to cut. A whishing steam escaped from the hole that Theo made with the knife, and a delicious roast meat aroma filled the air. Following the old man's instructions, Theo removed the cooked meat away from the skin, placed it on two large copper platters that the old man brought out from his store, and discarded the skin in a plastic bucket, under the bench. Finally, Theo handed the knife over to the old man and said in Greek, "Now, you do the rest barba."

"Hey devil," the old man exclaimed. "Are you Greek, and you said nothing all this time you sat under the fig tree? Fill your plate with meat and don't forget to help yourself to the tomato salad." Turning toward the rest of his customers, he added. "Boys and girls, it's all yours. Come and get it!"

The meat was unforgettably delicious, succulent, and tender. The tomato salad with wedges of cucumber and thinly-sliced onions was slightly tangy with home made vinegar, but the generous amount of olive oil, goat cheese, cured olives, salty anchovies, and mountain oregano gave it a distinctive character. The hungry northerners ate their fill, thanked the old man for the service and his personal entertainment, and hurried away to their destinations.

"Now that the young strangers are gone, let us have a glass of wine in peace," the old man said, and poured two glasses of red wine for them. Theo lifted his glass, and wished the other man good health, sending half of the liquid into his stomach to keep company with the goat meat and the salad. He rested his glass on the table and said, "Let me pay my share for the food, and I will get out of your way. I have a long way to travel and drinking wine is not a good idea."

"The students already paid for the food yesterday," the old man said. "You own nothing son! Go to God's blessing and have a safe trip."

Theo felt uncomfortable, thinking that he had mooched for his food, but it was too late to do anything about it. Against the protests from the old man, Theo took several Euros out of his pocket, laid them under his half empty glass, and said goodbye, with a sincere "thank you" to the kind, cheerful, and simple tavern operator of Lathocambos. An hour later, Theo reached Turkohori, and the first thing he did was to stop at a cleaner in town. He emptied his suitcase on the counter in front of the lady, who answered his call, and asked her to have his clothes cleaned and ready for him the next day. When he received an affirmative answer from her, he entered his car and drove the short distance to his village. He stopped by Fotis's house to let him know that he was back and to get the key to his parental house. Fotis was watering his garden at the time and did not notice Theo approaching from behind. Nevertheless, he was thrilled to see the traveler back safe and sound. He asked Theo to join him for a cup of coffee, but Theo declined the offer. He explained that he was in a desperate need for a shower and would like to have the key to his father's house. He also said that he would like to be alone for the rest of the day, to rest and relieve the tensions from the long trip. Fotis walked into his house and seconds later, he returned, with the key in one hand and two glasses filled halfway with retsina in the other. Theo took the glass in his hand, wished "to your health" to Fotis, downed the gold colored liquid in one gulp, received the key from Fotis, and said, "Thank you cousin, I needed that. I'll see you tonight for dinner, or did you make other plans already?"

"No cousin. I haven't," Fotis responded. "Let's forget about cooking dinner tonight. When you are ready to eat, let's drive to a near-by place where they make excellent *souvlakia*."

"It's a deal," Theo said, and re-entered the Mercedes to go home for his shower and for a much needed rest. He was also eager to take an inventory on the things he retrieved from Nestor's safe deposit box in Athens, early in the morning.

He parked the car by the main entrance to his parent's house, picked up his briefcase from the trunk, walked to the door, opened it with the key Fotis gave him, and entered. He rested the briefcase on his bed, took his badly needed shower, and dressed in his evening attire. With the briefcase in his hands, he walked out onto the veranda, stretched his arms apart to relieve the tension in his muscles, took several deep breaths to relax his mind, sat on the lounge chair next to the little wooden table, and opened the briefcase. He first counted the wad of the money, mentally calculated their value in U.S. dollars, and placed them back in the briefcase. Next, he opened the little cloth bag and emptied its contents on the table next to his chair. There were two platinum rings with a large diamond mounted on each one of them and several strange objects that he did not recognize at first glance. One of the rings looked like a lady's engagement ring, and the other was definitely a man's cocktail ring. The diamond stones on both rings were huge and shone brilliantly. Was the lady's ring an engagement ring that David Koch had probably bought for a sweetheart? Or did it belong to his adopted mother? And what's about the man's cocktail ring? Theo could not locate any initials or any other signs which would help him identify the owners, or the intended owners for either of the rings. So, he put them aside and turned his attention at the strange objects that came out of the cloth bag. These strange objects looked like round, shining pebbles. They were yellowish-brown in color, hard to touch, geometrically amorphous, and all of them were different in size and appearance. He picked up one in his hands at random and examined it carefully. It looked like a big drop of dark honey that had turned to stone. As he was turning it over and over in his hands, he noticed that this translucent, stone-like object contained within itself, the remains of tinny flying insects that were frozen in time. He picked and examined the rest of them, one at a time, and noticed that all of them had a small insect trapped inside. The only difference between them, was their size and the kind of insect they contained. Rolling one of them in his hands, he remembered that he had read an article in some scientific magazine that dealt with these unusual objects. He couldn't recollect verbatim the contents of the article, but he remembered the general explanation of the stone's formation and its scientific value. He remembered reading that petrified, pre-historic rosin, secreted from ancient pine trees, was discovered in several parts of the globe. Those drops were priceless to Paleontologists, for they contained information about life on earth during the time they were formed. Entomologists, in particular, valued them highly, for they allowed them to study the insects that lived on earth during that era. Biologists had extracted grains of pollen from such objects and had collected valuable information about the plants that flourished on earth, at that epoch.

Theo put the rings and the petrified rosin back in the bag and secured them in the briefcase with the money. Hum, I was not aware that Nestor was interested in pre-history and that he collected these petrified objects, he said to himself!

Theo finally picked up Nestor's hand-written memoir. He turned to the first page and began to read. The document looked like a part of an original manuscript, for it did not have an introduction, and contained a number of afterthoughts scribbled in the margins of several pages. The manuscript began by telling Nestor's life story at the time he realized that his life was in danger, while he was a professor in Berlin. "It became apparent to me that Hitler planned to drive all the Jews out of Germany, and he was prepared to do it by any means available to him..." Nestor opened his first paragraph. He then continued, by saying that living in Germany had come to an abrupt end for him. On his second page, he wrote about his decision to abandon his bright future as a professor in Germany and his reason for returning to Thessaloniki. He admitted that he did not know anything about extermination camps at that time. He went on to explain that Nazi propaganda perpetuated a rumor that those Jews who were arrested, had disobeyed laws of the land and were incarcerated in prisons located in the newly acquired Poland. He went on to describe his new teaching position at the university in Thessaloniki and about his new ambitions for a new start there. "I finally accepted my parental reasoning to find a 'nice Jewish girl' and get married..." he wrote. Two striking sentences written in the margin of one of the pages caught Theo's interest. "...and at this stage of my life," the insert in one of his paragraphs read, "I knew that I was not born in Greece, or born to Solomon and Rebecca Koch. My Jewish inheritance was questionable at its best." Theo put the memoir on the table next to him and tried to understand what Nestor had in mind, when he made this afterthought insertion to the text. Why was he concerned about not being born in Greece, or that his true parents were not Jewish. Furthermore, what did he mean by saying that his Jewish inheritance was uncertain? Was he reacting to the fact that he did not know much about his biological parents, or was there some other deeply rooted psychological complex that bothered him? Did this uncertainty of who he really was have anything to do with his final decision to stay single for the rest of his life, or was he rebelling against parental pressure to find a "nice Jewish girl", marry her, and raise a family?

The sun was about to disappear behind the western horizon, and the slopes of the mountain to the east had taken a different look at this hour. The green color of the forest had taken a deeper, green shade, and the cliffs protruding above the tree tops looked like heads of great giants, who woke up to resume some mysterious nocturnal activity. The branches of the olive trees in front of the house were moving in concert with the gentle breeze that blew from the west, to cool off God's creation. Bats, mice, scorpions, rabbits, foxes, hedge hogs, and the rest of the night dwellers of the land, were about to come out of their hiding places in search of food and water.

Theo felt the chill of the late afternoon penetrating his bed attire and decided to seek shelter inside the house. He picked up the briefcase and Nestor's memoir, walked inside his bedroom, placed everything on the night table next to his bed, and walked into the kitchen for a glass of water. The spicy, roast goat meat he ate earlier was a bit too much for his digestion. Once in the kitchen, he changed his mind to have just a glass of water. Instead, he made Greek coffee. He paced the kitchen floor and sipped the coffee in the cup he held in his hands and thought about the contents of Nestor's memoir. When he finished his coffee, he returned to the sink and washed the coffee cup. As his eyes were aimlessly exploring the things in the kitchen, his attention was drawn upon a bottle with ouzo, that was starring at his face from one of the kitchen's shelves. He walked over, picked it up, and read its label. "Metaxas authentic Greek ouzo," the label read. What the heck, Theo said to himself. Let's have a shot of this good stuff, and picking up the glass that stood next to the bottle, he poured in it several gulps of the clear liquid. He drowned three cubes of ice in the glass and returned to his bedroom with the glass of ouzo in his hands. He sat on the edge of his bed and tried to occupy his mind with something cheerful and pleasant, not necessarily interesting or informative. The epitaph for Nestor's head stone and the contents of his memoir were spinning around in his mind like the spars of a windmill that chase each other during a gale. He brought the glass to his mouth and took a healthy sip of ouzo, followed by a deep breath of cold air which alleviated the burning sensation on his tongue. Seconds later, he repeated the nipping several times until his glass was half empty.

The sipping of ouzo, brought some of the care-free moments of his military life to his mind. He remembered the fun he had as a soldier with that overweight seamstress on the border of Greece with Bulgaria. The seamstress was a young widow who was making her living altering uniforms, at a reasonable price for the soldiers of the garrison post, there. She also used to secure favors, in the privacy of the fitting room, from soldiers she found to be of her choice. In return, a glass of ouzo, olives, cheese and pieces of smoked chub that she re-heated over the flame of a burning piece of newspaper, was the expression of her gratitude. A peculiar smile flourished on Theo's face thinking about these embarrassing moments in his life, and as he was staring at the opposite wall of his room, he noticed the nameless icon that was believed to be the icon of Saint Kassiani. The icon was resting on a wooden ledge under an oil lamp, that hung from the ceiling and which had not been lit for years.

"We all have secret pockets deep in our hearts where we hide our most intimate experiences in life," he confessed looking at the icon, hoping that the pretty Byzantine face of the saint would understand what he said, nod her head with a smile, and agree with him. However, the icon stood there as if she did not hear his comment; she did not even blush a little. "Crafty young lady," Theo said to the icon with a grin on his face. "The entire Christian world knows about the fun you had with the married Emperor in Constantinople, at the time your fiancé was away fighting barbarian tribes in North Africa," he added. Bringing his glass to his mouth for the last time, he drank the rest of his ouzo. He sprawled out on the bed and dozed for a few minutes, until the darkness had crept in.

Fotis would be waiting for me, Theo thought, and put his clothes and his shoes on. He walked to the car and drove to Fotis's home, where he found him ready for dinner. He had fed his nanny goat and the chickens, and was in the door waiting for Theo.

"I thought you fell asleep," Fotis said.

"I almost did," Theo responded, "Now, where are we going pal? Tonight, you are the navigator and I am the skipper. Tell me, where are we going?"

"Let's drive east across the canyon to the foot of the mountain," Fotis said. "An entrepreneur has an outdoor taverna there and serves excellent souvlakia."

They entered the Mercedes, and Theo drove east on a dirt road until they arrived at the foot of the mountain, at a clearing where water was gushing out from an opening under a cliff. The water ran through the man-made clearing and descended into the canyon below. A big plane tree shaded part of the clearing, and a barbeque pit was built under a tin-roof canopy on the far end. Several wooden tables with outdoor chairs around them were placed on the clearing; some of them were under the shade of the tree, while others were under umbrellas in the clearing. Sizzling souvlakia were on the barbeque grill at the time the two cousins arrived. Three tables were already occupied by some noisy tourists, and Theo and Fotis sat on one of the tables on the opposite end of the clearing. The proprietor brought home-made suflakia and cold, local beer to their table. They did not want to drink wine tonight. The mountain air that blew from the east, together with the rustling sound of the running water, had altered their mood and taste for retsina. The owner of the enterprise kept bringing souflakia and beer to their table, while the two cousins talked about old times and about Theo's travel to Switzerland, Thessaloniki, and Athens. Before too long, Theo noticed that they had consumed a dozen souflakia and drank ten bottles of beer in the course of two hours, while enjoying each other's company next to nature.

"Hey Fotis," Theo said in amazement, "Do you realize that we ate and drank too much for guys our age? I think we should quit eating and drinking, and return home."

"I was thinking to remind you about it, but I did not want to interrupt your pleasure nibbling on the food and sipping on the beer, while telling me about your last week's traveling experience," Fotis said. They got off their chairs, Theo paid the bill, entered the Mercedes, and cautiously Theo drove back home. He dropped Fotis in front of his house, said good night to him, and continued driving until he reached his paternal house. He parked the car in front of the house and went directly to his bedroom. He put his night attire on again, and sat at the edge of the bed, to relax before he went to sleep. Minutes later, he felt the need for fresh air.

He walked to the veranda, sat on the old wooden chair, and fixed his gaze at the cloudless and moonless sky above his head. The moon had not risen yet and not even one cloud was anywhere to be seen. A countless number of glittering stars in the dome above his head, starred at him. He also noticed for the first time, that the constellation Cassiopeia, was in the up-side-down position, and he wondered why she was in the inverted position at this time.

The chill of the night breeze forced him to abandon his celestial contemplations and return to the shelter of his bedroom. He retrieved Stephen Hawking's book from his briefcase and located the passage that answered his question about the position of Cassiopeia. "…Again, the fact that space is curved means that light no longer appears to travel in straight lines in space," Stephen Hawking declared. "That means that light from a distant star that happened to pass near the sun would be deflected through a small angle, causing the star to appear in a different position to an observer on earth…" There is the answer to your question of why Cassiopeia is in the inverted position, Theo said to himself. The stars that make the constellation of Cassiopeia, are many light years away, and the fact that they are in vastly, different distances from us and from each other, the light they emit deflects along different angles to make Cassiopeia look inverted, Theo continued his reasoning. Thinking again about his complex interpretation of his observation, he remembered that Stephen Hawking had a simpler explanation. "…whenever you look, distant galaxies are moving rapidly away from us," the brilliant man said. Cassiopeia probably rotates around some axis as she travels in space and therefore, she assumes different positions at different times, Theo finally concluded. He put the book away, and crawled under his covers light-headed and happy. The beer had diffused throughout his body, and he felt content and sleepy. He turned the light off, and without even calling his wife, he closed his eyes and went to sleep.

It was light outside when he opened his eyes the next morning. He got out of bed, performed a few stretching exercises to soothe his sore muscles, brushed his teeth, shaved, dressed and combed his hair. At last, he made a cup of fresh coffee and with a new vigor, he took Nestor's memoir in his hands and started to read where he left off the night before.

Nestor had written several pages describing his teaching job at the university in Thessaloniki and about his ambitious plans for his future there. "…Thessaloniki surrendered to the Axis Forces on April 9, 1941 and my parents were shipped to Auschwitz on March 15, 1943, never to return home again…" he had written. "After my parents were gone, I met with several students and faculty who belonged to a secret underground organization, and the idea of joining them, came to me. A few days later, I joined them, and I became one of their most important and trusted members, for I knew both the Greek and the German languages…" he continued. "… dressed in a German officer's uniform, I walked up to the guard, greeted him in perfect German and entered the office of the Gestapo officer, holding my pistol in my hands. Before he had time to react to my presence and to my pistol aiming at him, I pumped several rounds into his miserable body. I stood there for a second and, strangely enough, I enjoyed seeing his red blood oozing profusely through the holes on his uniform. Without thinking about anything else, I jumped out of a window facing the street, and I disappeared into the darkness of the night…" he wrote, on the following sentence. He went on to say that some of his close friends advised him, the next day, to leave town, because the Gestapo suspected him of killing their officer. On another page Nestor explained that the only safe haven available to him now, was to enlist himself as a volunteer in the liberation forces of Zervas. One of his descriptions was about a scrimmage he had with the Germans, and that part was particularly interesting to Theo.

"...We arrived there before the day broke and set our explosives at the base of two of the columns that supported the bridge. The four of us hid behind some rocks, at a distance we thought was safe from the explosives and waited for the train to show up, holding the two wicks that were connected to the explosive charges. As soon as we heard the train coming around the corner, we pressed the button and the charges exploded. The bridge bent downward into the river. All four of us, huddled together, behind the rocks again. The train reduced its speed, and all of a sudden, hand grenades and bullets came flying our way, from the armored car with the German soldiers, who escorted the train. The train failed to stop on time and seconds later, it derailed and plunged to the bottom of the deep ravine. I laid there for a moment longer and heard the moaning of one of my comrades calling for help. The other two were blown to pieces by a hand grenade that landed between them. Miraculously, I was not hurt. I had crouched behind a big rock that protected me from the firing. When everything was rather quiet, I stood up and looked at my wounded friend for a few seconds. He was lying face down, bleeding profusely from a hole in his back. The sight was horrifying, and I assumed that he had no chance of surviving. I felt the pistol in my hands, and the urge came to me to take Costa out of his misery. However, something inside me told me that I should save my bullets for Germans who might have survived the crash.

Picking my way through the rocks, I reached the site where the train cars had landed and went through the wreckage looking for survivors. I only found six wounded

Germans, and I made certain that they would never walk
the earth again. I emptied a whole clip of bullets into one
of them who attempted to draw his pistol on me. Roaming
through the wreckage looking for more living enemies, I
came upon a strong, wooden box that caught my fancy.
One of its planks was broken and I could see through the
opening, that the box contained gold ingots and gold coins.
The sight of the treasure, the close call I had with death,
and the destruction of human life overshadowed my best
judgment. I, there and then, made up my mind to abandon
Zervas and take my chances of surviving as a deserter. I
dragged the box with the gold, a few meters away from
where I found it, lowered it into a gapping crevice between
rocks, covered it with several layers of smaller stones, and
disappeared down the river," Nestor had written. The rest of
his memoir dealt with his ventures hiding from both friends
and foes. "I was wanted by Zervas's men for my desertion
and by the Nazis for the killing of the Gestapo officer…"
he had added in red ink, on the margin of a page. "I drifted
from village to village using different names and earning my
living by offering my labor. I also earned a few drachmas
playing an old guitar I found, abandoned in the house of a
man who hired me to help harvest his olives," he continued
toward the end of his memoir.

Theo took a look at his wrist watch, and he realized
that he was late for the breakfast that he had promised
Fotis the night before. He quickly put the memoir in the
briefcase and walked to the car holding the briefcase in his
hands. He secured the briefcase in the trunk and drove to
Fotis's home. Fotis was pre-occupied with making fresh
coffee when Theo arrived there, and he did not notice him
entering his house.

"Good morning cousin," he said to Fotis. "I hope I did not make you wait for me. I am late this morning."

"Not at all," Fotis responded and turned his head toward Theo to greet him good morning, also. The two cousins took their places at the table, had their coffee with toast, smothered with butter and marmalade and followed with home-made yogurt topped with honey. Fotis sat in his chair with his attention completely absorbed in Theo, who was talking about the epigram for Nestor's headstone. When Theo finished talking, Fotis said, "It never crossed my mind that the man was not a Greek."

"Well, what makes a man to be a Greek?" Theo asked. "Nestor was raised in Thessaloniki, spoke the Greek language and lived all his life in Greece. That makes him more of a Greek than I am," he added.

"But, I assume he was not a Christian like the rest of us, was he?" Fotis said, offended somewhat by the comments his cousin made.

"Be open minded cousin," Theo said to Fotis. "All the people who are Greek citizens are Greeks as far as the law is concerned. Look at our last name, for example. It does not sound anything like a typical, Greek last name. Is it possible that our forefathers came here from another country?" Suddenly, he changed the subject of the conversation, for he had sensed that Fotis was irritated and offended by his reasoning, in defining the identity of a Greek.

"I am going to Turkohori this morning to order a head stone for Nestor," Theo said. "Would you like to come along to keep me company and have lunch with me?"

"No, I cannot. I have my nanny goat and my chickens to attend to. They are part of my life, and my neighbor who takes care of them, when I am not at home, is not feeling well today," he said, with a melancholic voice. "Go on and do the things you have to do. We will have a glass of wine together when you return."

"Fair enough, I'll see you tonight," Theo said, and walked toward his car. Halfway there, he stopped, turned to Fotis and said, "Then, I'll bring something for dinner. Don't bother with cooking."

As soon as Theo arrived in Turkohori, he first stopped at the cleaner and picked up his laundry. Next, he drove to the stone cutter's place to select Nestor's headstone. The man who greeted him at the stone yard was sensitive to the trauma people experience when they lose a member of their family. He took time to explain to Theo the various types of monuments his artisans could create and showed him samples and pictures of their work. After a lengthy deliberation on which design would be suited for Nestor, Theo finally picked a simple head stone that reflected Nestor's religious belief and his simplistic way of living. The marble stone was shaped into a half-moon and had two angels engraved toward its top, one on each side. During their discussion about Nestor's epitaph, the stone cutter quoted Pericles, the Athenian statesman, to emphasize the value of the person, not the writing on his headstone. "What you leave behind is not what is engraved in stone monuments, but what is woven into the lives of others." With that quotation in mind, Theo finally selected a modified version of the phrase he originally wrote on his yellow pad.

FROM ...CHRISOGLU TO DAVID KOCH, THEN, HE BECAME NESTOR HE WAS A WISE ADVISER AND A FRIEND TO ALL.

"That sounds good," the stone cutter said, and wrote it on his standard form. He carefully checked the spelling of each word and handed the paper to Theo for his final review and approval. Theo read the statement, and before he wrote his signature, he inserted the completion date in the space provided. Finally, he signed the form and handed it back to the stone cutter. At last, they agreed that the price included the placement of the headstone on Nestor's burial grounds, and that he (the stone cutter) would receive the balance of his payment from Fotis upon completion of the job. Theo gave the stone cutter deposit money, obtained a receipt for it, and both men walked to Theo's car. There, the stone cutter thanked Theo for his patronage and Theo in turn, thanked the stone cutter for his help to re-write the epitaph. At last, they shook hands, and Theo drove away with the satisfaction in his heart that he had done all he could do to immortalize the memory of his late mentor and friend.

On the way back to the village, Theo decided to pay Nestor a visit, for the last time before returning home. He took the road up to the mountain again, and when he arrived there, he felt good and comfortable that the head stone and epitaph he selected for the man that meant so much to him were appropriate. It was late afternoon when he arrived in front of the mansion's big gate. He parked the car and with an unexplained feeling of sadness and satisfaction, he walked directly to where Nestor was interred. The sun was blazing on Theo's head, and his thoughts were occupied by mixed emotions. When he arrived at the burial grounds, he noticed that a smartly arranged bouquet of flowers was wilting on the stones over the grave, and he wondered who placed it there. Did Magdalene come back for more fruits and vegetables, or was there someone else who harbored deep feelings for the departed Nestor? Theo stood there for a few seconds to understand his mixed feelings of sadness and pleasure and to figure out who would be the person who placed the roses on Nestor's grave. He was inclined to believe that the flowers were not placed there by Magdalene, for the soil in the garden and around the flowers was not moist. He finally knelt in front of the grave and said in a whisper.

"Friend, I am grateful for the many things you freely gave to me. You consoled me when I was in need for guidance, and I kneel in front of you to show you my gratitude for your guidance. You taught me to distinguish right from wrong, and I bow my head over your grave to show my appreciation for it. You recently changed my financial picture, and I genuflect in front of you to tell you that my wife and I are grateful for your generosity. Rest assured that I executed your wishes at the Swiss Bank, the First National Bank of Greece, and the University in Thessaloniki in strict accordance with your instructions and wishes. Now, the time has come for us to part company for ever. You were my teacher, my friend and my benefactor, and I will never forget you. *Gia su gia panda*" (good buy for ever), he exclaimed, in a voice that was barely heard, and slowly lifted himself from his kneeled posture. He wiped his wet eyes and stood there a little longer wondering if Nestor had heard him. Finally, he dusted off the soil from the knees of his slacks and with his head hanging low over his chest, walked back to his car. Taking another look at the ghostly mansion in front of him, he noticed for the first time, that a heavy chain connected to a padlock, secured the gate close. He also noticed a small sign posted under the chain. "Keep out. Private Property, The University Of Thessaloniki."

Theo took a last look at the mansion, entered the Mercedes and drove to the place where he had dinner with Fotis the night before. He purchased a dozen fresh souflakia, and at long last, he returned to the village and had a quiet dinner with his cousin Fotis. The two cousins spoke heart-to-heart one more time, and Theo gave Fotis the rest of the money he owed to the stone cutter, for Nestor's headstone. As a token of gratitude, he handed Fotis an additional thousand Euros and thanked him for all his help. Finally, Theo went home and called the travel agency in Athens to arrange his flight back to the USA. The agent told him that the flights for the next five days were booked. "You have a good chance of finding a cancellation though, if you are at the airport early and register as a stand-by customer," the agent said; "otherwise, the next available seat I have for you is five days from now." Theo made up his mind to go to bed early and wake up before sunrise to drive the 200 kilometers back to Athens. I should spend time with my sister before I leave, he thought. It will not look nice, if I leave without saying good buy to her and her husband.

He took his shower, crawled under the bed cover, and called his wife to tell her about his return trip. He was not that sleepy yet, and decided to retrieve *A Brief History of Time* from the night table and read its conclusion. "We find ourselves in a bewildering world. We want to make sense of what we see around us and to ask: What is the nature of the universe? What is our place in it, and where did it and we come from? Why is it the way it is?" Stephen Hawking said, in the first paragraph of his conclusion.

Indeed! "The world is bewildering and we cannot make sense of what we see around us," Theo repeated word-for-word what the astronomer had written. I know a trifle of the mysterious Nestor, and I know nothing of where his spirit is now. Is his soul still hovering around his mansion, or has it been transported to some far away place like galaxy M104, which is 28 million light years from earth, has 8 million suns, and is 50,000 light years across? It became apparent to Theo that our knowledge of ourselves and our surroundings is limited in comparison to the total. Scientists and philosophers have not been able to provide us with the knowledge we need to satisfy our questions of what is our place in the universe, where we come from, and why things are the way they are, Theo whispered. The last sentence of Stephen Hawking's conclusion put Theo's mind at ease. "However," Hawking had written, "If we do discover a complete theory, it should in time be understandable in broad principle by everyone, not just a few scientists. Then we shall all, philosophers, scientists, and just ordinary people, be able to take part in the discussion of the question of why it is that we and the universe exist. If we find the answer to that, it would be the ultimate triumph of human reason- for then we would know the mind of God." Only then, Theo muttered to himself, I would know more about Nestor's secret life and what happened to him after he stopped breathing. He turned over in his bed, closed his eyes, and went to sleep with *A Brief History of Time,* still in his hands.

The next morning, he woke up early and made his coffee before leaving the village for Athens. While sipping his coffee, he took out Nestor's memoir one more time and began thumbing through its pages again. He did not know what he was looking for, but he was slowly turning over the pages, reading a little more attentively this time. He was sure that Nestor had written only on one side of each sheet of paper. The other side was blank. When he read the last page and turned the manuscript over, he noticed that Nestor had added an afterthought in red ink, on the back of the last sheet. This entry had escaped Theo's attention until now.

"When I arrived in the Peloponnesus," Nestor wrote, "I was planning to stay there for a while and return to Thessaloniki to resume my normal life. It was at that time, that I learned from a communist resistor that my adopted parents and the rest of the Greek Jews from Thessaloniki were

probably dead. The same man told me that a certain David
Koch was wanted by both Zervas and the Gestapo. That was
the moment that I decided to abandon the professorship, in
order to fulfill my life- long dream of becoming a writer. I
was accepted as one of the folks in the area, and living at the
summit of the mountain appealed to me. So, I went ahead
and built my mansion on the grounds of St Elias, using
some of the gold I had hidden in the ravine where the train
crushed. Later on, I retrieved the rest of the gold, converted
it to Greek currency in the black market, and deposited it
in The First National Bank of Greece. Only at this time, I
learned through the newspapers that the gold was probably
the ransom money that the Germans had extracted from
the population of Thessaloniki." Further down toward the
bottom of the page Nestor had written, "I find it just that
I should give the money I have in the Greek bank, to the
university, for the sole purpose of archeological excavations
at Olympia. The money I have in the Swiss bank is money
that came directly from the estate of my adopted Jewish
parents, and for this reason, I deem it equally just to give
it to Jewish-Greek organizations, with the hope that they
will promote friendship between the two nations… I have
already arranged that the royalty earnings from the sale of
my books be funneled to a certain clandestine organization,
which is dedicated to finding war criminals and bringing
them to justice. The same organization watches that the
world will not experience holocausts against people like the
Armenians and the Jews in the future," Nestor had finally
concluded.

Now I know all I want to know about Nestor, Theo
murmured. I know he was an Armenian orphan who never
knew his first name or his biological parents, was raised as
a Jew by the Koch couple and had adopted their last name.
He was educated in Germany, was that Zervas's resistor who

recovered the ransom gold, and therefore, I know his real reason of becoming a hermit. Unfortunately, I don't know his pen name to locate and buy his books.

Theo got off his chair, sipped the last drops of his already cold coffee and folded the memoir, placing it in his briefcase with the other valuable items. He gathered the rest of his belongings, packed them in his suitcase, set his bed, locked the door and walked away with the suitcase in one hand and the briefcase in the other. With a light footing and a heavy heart, he walked to the car, secured the suitcase and the briefcase in the trunk and drove to Fotis's home. When he arrived there, he saw Fotis standing by his kitchen window. Theo made a brief stop in front of Fotis's home and met his cousin at the threshold of the entrance to the house. The two cousins hugged each other, and Theo handed over to Fotis the key to his paternal house. Finally, the two cousins said goodbye to each other with tears in their eyes and with their hearts inundated with emotions. Theo left Fotis sobbing in the threshold of his house, entered the rental car, wiped his wet eyes and drove away toward Athens. In his rearview mirror, he saw Fotis standing at his door, waving a white handkerchief at the Mercedes that sped away.

The ride to Athens was smooth, and four hours later, he was riding on his sister's street. His brother-in-law met him at the door while his sister was in the kitchen preparing supper. Theo brought in his suitcase with the briefcase packed inside it, and followed his brother-in-law who escorted him to one of the bedrooms. "Put your stuff here," the brother-in-law said to Theo, "and let's see what your sister is cooking for us." One behind the other, the two men walked into the kitchen and found the lady with a long fork, in one hand, holding an insulated glove in the other. She interrupted her cooking task momentarily, and Theo hugged and kissed her with brotherly love and affection.

"I am cooking your favorite dish," she said to Theo, "I am making braised lam with spaghetti." The two men left the lady to her cooking task, walked in the garden, and sat under the shade of a big pine tree that grew at the end of the property. In that quiet environment and under the cool shade of the tree, the two brothers-in-law sipped ouzo and talked for a while about their families and their futures, occasionally interrupted by his sister, who was coming in-and-out from the kitchen to participate in their aimless conversation. At the dinner table, Theo told them a few things about his unexpected trip to Greece, and he gave his sister a generous portion of Nestor's money which he had found in the safe deposit box at the Greek bank in Athens. He spent the rest of the night with them. The next morning, they said good bye to one another with tears in their eyes! Finally, Theo drove to the airport, turned the rented Mercedes in, and placed his name on the list of the standby customers for a flight back to the U.S.A.

It was late morning, and the crowd at the airport was not heavy at this hour. Theo sat in the waiting area and having nothing else to do, he recounted last week's events.

Lord, ten days ago, I was enjoying breakfast in the company of my dear Anastasia, planning our modest vacation to Minnesota where Anastasia's brother has his bait shop, Theo recounted. In the span of this time, I visited New York, Athens, the village, Nestor's mansion at the mountain's summit, saw Nestor again before he died, buried him with dignity, stopped at the bank in Zurich, paid a visit to the university in Thessaloniki, and finally visited the First National Bank of Greece in Athens. Most importantly, I learned that Nestor was born in Armenia, grew up as a Jew, received his education in Germany, taught philosophy in

Germany and Greece, became a fierce resistor for a while, never got married, and ultimately, he became the possessor of at least some of the ransom money that the Germans extracted from the Greek Jews in Thessaloniki. Finally, he had retired to the mountain to write books. Unfortunately, I do not know the books he published in the past, but unraveling this secret might be another venture into Nestor's past. At this point of his last week's recounting of events, Theo felt his eyes overflowing with tears and sensed a big lump in his throat. He inconspicuously wiped his eyes with the palm of his hand, and, as silently as he could, he cleared his throat. He remembered Nestor's degenerated body spread on his death bed and heard Nestor's voice asking him to stay by his bed a little longer. He re-lived the moment that Nestor drew his last breath and felt a dagger piercing his heart. He re-positioned himself on his chair and realized that he was sobbing and that his hands were shaking. He retrieved his handkerchief from his pocket, wiped his eyes, blew his nose, and fixed his gaze at the briefcase that was resting on his lap.

Ten days ago, I was a man of modest, fixed income, he thought. Now, I have enough money to live in luxury for the rest of my life. God, I have enough money to do all the things my wife and I wanted to do, all our lives! I even have enough to help my children and my grand children. Again, he felt tears saturating his eyes. He pulled the handkerchief out of his pocket one more time and brought it to his eyes. He pressed the white cloth against his wet eyes and realized that most of his thoughts and all his emotional outbursts were associated with events that took place in the past few days. The past is history and the future is mystery, he whispered to himself. The present is a gift, he continued, and he placed the handkerchief back in his pocket. An audible sigh and a deep breath followed. While pre-occupied with his thoughts and overwhelmed with his emotions, he did not notice that all the passengers had entered the plane, and that he was the only person in the waiting area. One of the flight attendants walked over to him and told him that there was a first-class seat available.

"I'll take it," Theo snapped without hesitation and presented his American Express card to pay for his boarding pass. While he was waiting for the issuance of his boarding pass, he called his wife to let her know that he was on his way home. The phone rang several times, then, it switched to the message mode. Apparently, Anastasia was not home to receive his call, and he wondered if something was wrong with Katerina or with one of their children. At the tone, Theo said, "Sweetheart, I am on American Airline's flight number 325, and I will be home tonight. No, it will be early afternoon your time," correcting himself and turning off his cell phone. He put the phone away, picked up his briefcase in one hand and his suitcase in the other, and he hurried to board the plane that was scheduled to fly non-stop to New York, then, on to Chicago.